Rex Dancer

Simon & Schuster
New York London Toronto Sydney Tokyo Singapore

SIMON & SCHUSTER
Rockefeller Center
1230 Avenue of the Americas
New York, New York 10020

This book is a work of fiction. Although reference is made to several noted figures of the past and present, all of the characters in this novel are fictional and are not based in any way on any actual person, living or dead, nor does this story involve any actual motion picture project, political campaign, or any other actual event, whether in New Orleans, Houston, or anywhere else.

Designed by Deirdre C. Amthor
Manufactured in the United States of America

10 9 8 7 6 5 4 3 2 1

Library of Congress Cataloging-in-Publication Data
Dancer, Rex.
Bad girl blues/Rex Dancer
p. cm.
1. Photographers—Louisiana—New Orleans—Fiction.
2. New Orleans (La.)—Fiction. I. Title.
PS3554.A514B3 1994
813'.54—dc20
93-47452 CIP

ISBN 0-671-88007-1

For Roma Downey

le gra

Acknowledgments

The author would especially like to thank stage and film actresses Roma Downey and Kelly McGillis for their help and advice on the movie-making aspects of this novel, as well as Washington photographer Ernie Cox for his expertise. Newsman Christopher Drew of New Orleans and Washington was also extremely helpful, as were Dallas socialite Brooke Stollenwerck, Dallas model and fashion consultant Jan Strimplc, and Houston-born fashion lcgcnd Diannc deWitt.

Many thanks to Jeff Neuman and Stuart Gottesman of Simon & Schuster, to Susanne Jaffe, and to that most admirable of literary agents, Dominick Abel. The author is grateful to his wife and two sons as only they can know.

1

Candice shook André Derain awake and told him she heard a scream.

"In New Orleans? Impossible." He rolled over and looked at her in the dim light floating in from the balcony. Her long hair was in disarray, as was the expression on her beautiful model's face.

"No joke, Andy. It was a scream."

"You never worried about screams when we were in New York."

"In New York you didn't have a second floor bedroom and sleep with the doors open."

"Don't worry about it. This is the French Quarter. Here we live and let live."

He closed his eyes. It was dawn, and they had not been asleep for all that long. The air was still and hot, remarkable at this hour even for New Orleans in July. He and Candice Browley lay naked on his rumpled bed without a top sheet, their sweaty bodies not touching, though they had gone to sleep in each other's arms.

The sound came again, and it was sure enough a scream. Andy lifted his head. Candy's blue eyes were wide open.

"You heard that, right?" she said.

"I have a lot of strange neighbors. Maybe it's just someone at Bleusette's enjoying himself."

Bleusette was a hooker who also happened to be his landlady, owning both his house and the big one across the courtyard that fronted Burgundy Street. But she'd been working the hotels that night, and when she did that, she usually didn't return home until breakfast. Unless, of course, she'd had a slow night. It happened, even with business girls as good-looking as Bleusette. She was probably the best-looking hooker in the city—certainly the highest-priced.

His pillow was soaked with perspiration. He'd forgotten all about the summer heat when he'd moved back to New Orleans the previous September, even though he'd grown up in the city. You put it out of your mind, the way Chicagoans did January.

Andy lived on the shabbier side of the Quarter up near Rampart Street. Before the Civil War, his little frame house with apartment above and photographic studio beneath had been slave quarters, serving the more substantial dwelling across the courtyard that was now the residence of Bleusette Lescaut. Later, near the end of the last century, when the neighborhood had been acrawl with sporting ladies with names like Kidney-Foot Jenny, Gallus Lu, Bricktop Jackson, One-Legged Duffy, Fightin' Mary, and Sister Sal—who had become One-Eyed-Sal after a brawl with Fightin' Mary—the section became known as Smoky Row. Back then, blood-stained empty wallets and the occasional dead body routinely turned up in the gutter litter out front. Derain's house had been part of one of the more thriving, notorious, and dangerous establishments in the area.

But the Quarter had changed enormously in the many decades since. If still raffishly uninhibited, it was now perfectly respectable—attracting every class of society and as many T-shirted tourists in a year as Disneyland, which its Mississippi riverfront blocks were coming to resemble. Even Bleusette was considered respectable. She conducted herself like a lady of the Garden District, and, when working, dressed like one. She'd never once been arrested in a hotel.

Another scream, this time quite loud and clear, and near.

"Someone's in trouble," he said.

"Imagine."

He wondered if it meant some violent form of robbery. Because of the tourist invasion, the police worked hard to keep the Quarter one of the safest neighborhoods in an otherwise rough and seriously impoverished city, but muggers did their work when and where they could. Perhaps it might only be one of the drunks and assorted street people who inhabited the alleys, gangways, and doorways at night—some poor wretch awakening from a bad dream to delirium tremens, or simply voicing a sudden rage at the world. During the nearly ten years he'd lived in New York, Andy had often felt like doing that.

He sat up, hearing nothing more. He looked over at Candy's long, white body, turned slightly away from him now. In many ways, they might have been siblings. She was five-foot eleven, just an inch shy of his own height. Though she was much thinner, both had the same slender build and long hands. Their eyes were close to the same amber shade of brown. Even their hair was the same light brown, though his tended to turn blond from the sun, and hers did not. His was now also beginning to turn gray. But Andy was almost thirty-seven. Candy was five years younger.

Thirty-seven. Close to forty, and back where he'd started from. But that was the idea.

"I think it's all right," he said.

He started to sink back against his pillow when there came yet another, even louder scream. He realized it was coming from the courtyard just below his balcony.

"Andy! Do something!"

He responded by patting Candy's shoulder in false reassurance, then leapt to his feet and moved in a rush through the open doors to the balcony railing.

There was a struggle going on in the gloom below—two men, one desperately pulling away, the other clutching the first, raising his hand and jabbing downward at the man's back. When he brought the hand back up again, Andy could see the dull glint of a knife.

Perhaps it was anger at having his courtyard invaded and his sleep disturbed. Perhaps it was an urge to play hero for Candice. But, foolishly—still as naked as the woman whose side he'd left—Andy hurled himself over the railing, landing bare feet–first on top of the two intruders, sending them both sprawling. Andy fell sideways, rolling painfully over his shoulder and onto his back. The man with the knife got to his feet before Andy could catch his breath. He raised his arm in a forlorn attempt to ward off the expected slash of blade, but the assailant, after a quick, furtive glance, proved more interested in escape. He fled through the courtyard gate and out the passageway to the street. Andy struggled up and ran after him. This was truly glorious stupidity, but it seemed the thing to do. He couldn't just crawl back into bed with Candice.

Derain was tall and long-legged. The attacker was older, short, and if more muscular, probably had more bad habits. Bounding along barefoot, Andy easily caught up with him just past Bienville Street heading toward Canal. He grabbed the back of the man's sweaty shirt, slowing him, then struck at the fellow's head with the side of his fist.

He might as well have swatted at the bastard with a handkerchief. The man whirled around, pulling free, and lunged at Derain with the bloody knife. Andy leapt back, but lost his balance. Once again he found himself flat on the pavement, counting seconds until death. A fortune-teller in Jackson Square had once told him he'd meet his end at the hands of a woman. You never could believe those people.

There was shouting. He sensed people on the street. The man hesitated, gave Andy a quick, lightning bolt of a kick in the groin, then hurried away. Doubling up, Andy fought his agony with clenched teeth. When he looked up again, the attacker had vanished.

He tried to stand, and finally succeeded. He was far from alone, though he didn't recognize any of the scruffy bystanders who had materialized from nowhere and now stood abjectly around him on the sidewalk. Drunks and street people mostly. None came forward to help, though he habitually gave these characters money.

A siren's wail pierced the odd quiet, increasing rapidly. As Andy turned and began to hobble back toward his house, a patrol car, lights flashing, rounded Conti and skidded to a stop. The uniformed officer behind the wheel jumped out, weapon in hand, then relaxed, holstering the revolver as he walked over. He and Derain knew each other. The odd photography jobs Andy took to support himself included stringing for the local newspaper and the AP. He'd been to a number of crime scenes since he'd been back in New Orleans, and he also knew several policemen from when he'd lived here as a boy and young man.

"You out for an early morning run there, Mr. Derain," said the officer, whose name was Hernandez, "or just sleepwalking?"

Andy winced. There was no point in trying to cover himself.

"There's a wounded man in my courtyard. I tried to stop the guy who stabbed him, but he got away. Heading toward Canal Street."

Hernandez quickly returned to his car and rattled off some coded police jargon into his radio microphone. He glanced over Derain's nakedness as he strolled back, looking vastly amused.

"Aren't you going after him?" Andy asked.

"Got some cars and scooters on the way to do that. And an ambulance coming. Let's go see if it's going to be in time. And maybe you might get dressed, Andy. It ain't Mardi Gras."

The ambulance wouldn't be in time. The stabbed man had thoroughly died, his face the color of the gray early morning sky. He lay on his side, his body contorted, one arm twisted back grotesquely. Squatting carefully to avoid soiling himself from the spreading pool of blood, Hernandez gently turned the body face up. The victim was thin but muscular, with a youngish face, slim moustache, and shaven head. He wore an earring, tie-dyed T-shirt, tight jeans, and tennis shoes. There was an expensive-looking watch on one wrist and a heavy bracelet on the other. His dark eyes stared helplessly up at the gray sky, as though imploring God for succor, without response.

"He got stuck pretty good," Hernandez said. "I count five or six wounds here."

"I never saw so much blood. Bleusette's going to have one of her fits."

"He's got some stuff in his pockets, but I think I'll wait on that."

"Andy!"

He looked up to see Candy standing on the balcony, wearing one of his shirts and nothing else. She looked angry enough to throw a brick at him.

This sort of thing didn't fit in her lifestyle. She had never been a superstar like her fellow Texas models Dianne deWitt, Jerry Hall, and Jan Strimple, but Candice Browley had earned as much as $400,000-a-year in New York when Andy had been at his peak as one of that city's top fashion and celebrity magazine photographers. Theirs had been one of the more celebrated love affairs in the business—handsome Andy, knock-out Candy, the "beautiful couple."

He was never as good-looking as she, but time was favoring him now. The lines that formed around his mouth and eyes when he smiled or frowned seemed to suggest substance and character—in keeping with his thin, patrician lips and strong jaw—and lent him as well an air of worldliness. He supposed he was far more entitled to the worldliness than to the character. His soft brown eyes were deceiving, too. They always somehow looked friendly and cheerful, even when he was angry or in deep despond.

At her peak, Candy's beauty had come near to the fashion world's exacting notion of perfection. But now, past thirty in a business in which a single wrinkle was considered a career challenge, her incomparable loveliness was beginning to fade and crumble at the edges. She was still an extraordinarily striking woman, but time had begun tapping out its message to her.

It was really no wonder that Candy had taken a model's form of semiretirement, marrying one of the wealthiest men in Texas, a man who had been trying to acquire her as he might some company in a takeover. Living now in Houston, she still worked the runways and fashion shoots, taking jobs in cities around the country where her beauty and modeling skills remained at a premium. If the Seventh Avenue fashion czars no longer considered her a star, department stores in Los Angeles, Miami, and Chicago did.

It had taken Andy less than a year to burn out in New York after she had left him for the Texas moneyman—something she may have sensed coming. Bent on forgetting her, he'd returned to his native New Orleans as a shipwrecked man might swim to a lifeboat. To his surprise, Candy had seized upon his nearness to Houston to resume the affair, arranging rendezvous on her way to or from out-of-town modeling assignments. She'd come into New Orleans the previous afternoon, on her way home from Miami. This was the first time they'd been together in two months.

She was looking at him now as though she wished she had taken a direct flight to Houston. Andy hurried back into his house.

"Did he see me?" she said, when Andy rejoined her in the bedroom.

"Who?" Derain began putting on a pair of khaki shorts, adjusting them carefully. The man's kick was going to be no boon to his sex life for a while.

"That cop."

"Probably. You were kind of noticeable out there on the balcony."

"Not as goddamn noticeable as you. Is he dead, the man down there?"

"Extremely. Someone stabbed him, back and front. Must have followed him into the courtyard."

"And you went after him? Stark naked?"

"All part of Neighborhood Watch."

"Doesn't any of this bother you?"

"Of course it bothers me."

"For God's sake, Andy. I really do think you've lost your mind."

He stuck his feet into a worn old pair of boating moccasins, then pulled on a shirt.

"I didn't exactly invite them in," he said.

"Shit."

"Nothing to do with us, Candy."

She took off the shirt she'd put on, then stood uncertainly, putting a hand to her narrow hip. In that odd, early morning light, it would have made a wonderful photograph. Andy had taken many pictures of her in the nude. She was one of his favorite subjects. He wondered how soon he'd be able to make love to her again.

She looked to the bathroom door, then said "shit" once more and went to her small suitcase, heaving it onto the bed and quickly pulling out some clothes. She doubtless desperately wanted and needed a shower. But she was in too much of a hurry.

"You're leaving? Now?"

"I've got to get out of here, Andy. For God's sake, it's a murder. Cops. Reporters. I can't get mixed up in this. Have my name in the papers. You want Ben to find out I was here? You want two more murders?"

She was exaggerating, but he wasn't sure how much. Ben Browley, her very rich Texas oilman, banker, real estate developer, and radio station–owner husband, must have some suspicions about a wife this beautiful and so frequently away from home, yet she said he never confronted her with them, and never interfered with her travels. He understood, she said, that she had to be willing to take whatever work came her way, no matter how distant, to keep her career alive. Andy supposed that if she weren't a model, her value to Browley as a trophy wife would be much diminished, and Browley was a man fond of his possessions.

"The alley outside the kitchen door will take you to Rampart Street," he said. "You should be able to get a cab."

She looked at him, shaking her head in frustration. "I should never have come, goddamn it."

"We've never had a problem before."

"We've been imbeciles, Andy, parading around town together. My God, we had dinner at Brennan's last night. Brennan's! Anyone could have seen us. His company's got an office here, remember? I don't know why I ever agreed to this."

"One, it was your idea. Two, you said something about still being in love with me."

Candice didn't respond, concentrating on getting dressed. She didn't bother to put on underwear. A blouse, matching skirt, sandals, a few drenching splashes of perfume, and she was done. She turned to zip up her bag. "What will you tell them? About me?"

"I'll tell them I was with a prostitute. Someone I never laid eyes on before."

"Thanks."

"I can't think of anything else to say."

"Will they believe you?"

"One of my friends is a police lieutenant. He likes to believe me."

"Do you ever do that? Bring prostitutes here? Like that Bleusette?"

"Downstairs, to take their pictures. Occasionally. I don't sleep with them. Only you, Candy."

"Bullshit. You're like that Bellocq you talk about all the time."

The now long-dead Ernest Bellocq was the photographer famous in New Orleans as the portraitist of the legendary pre–World War I red-light district called Storyville. His antique glass plates of whores taking their leisure, prints of which had been affectionately preserved at the Historic New Orleans Collection Museum over on Royale Street, had fascinated Derain for much of his life.

"I don't think he slept with very many of them," Andy said. "He was mostly just their friend."

She didn't want to pursue that. "I've got to go."

He followed her to the door, pausing only to snatch up one of his cameras.

"What in the hell are you going to do with that?"

"There's a dead man on my doorstep. I photograph things like that."

"For the newspapers or for those damned picture books you've been working on forever?"

"Sometimes just because they're there."

She made a face, then hurried on, clattering down the stairs. At the kitchen door, she turned to him one last time.

"There's a dead cockroach on the table. Are you going to take a picture of that, too?"

"I don't do cockroaches."

"Look how you live, Andy. Look at what's happened to you."

The room was a messy shambles. The remains of a long decaying dinner moldered on the kitchen table. Dishes and glasses were everywhere. Derain's black cat, Beatrice, had scattered kitty litter over the unvarnished floor, probably in protest of his neglect of the box. The furniture was cheap, the wallpaper decrepit. He'd told her it was typical New Orleans decadence, but she hated it.

"You were the top of the heap in New York," she said. "There wasn't a finer fashion photographer in the business. For God's sake, Andy, you've had pictures in *Vanity Fair!* You had one of the nicest apartments on the Upper East Side. But look at you now. Squalor. Filth. Hookers. Dead bodies. You live a dirty life now, Andy. I can't stand it."

"Candy . . ."

She opened the door, taking the suitcase from him. "Candy and Andy, the perfect team. You keep asking me to leave Ben and come back to you. To this? I love you like crazy, Andy. But this, this isn't crazy. This is goddamned nuts!" She stepped outside. "God, this heat."

The door slammed behind her as final rebuke.

Just a few hours before he had thought himself one of the happiest men on the planet—or at least New Orleans, which was all that counted. Candy had just hurt him a lot worse than the man who had kicked him.

• • •

In short time, there was a small mob of policemen in the courtyard, including a couple of detectives obviously from the midnight shift, wearing rumpled, sweat-stained summer suits. Prominent in the group was a rotund cop in much crisper uniform, bars gleaming on the shoulders—Lieutenant Paul Maljeux. He was a bluff, cheery, paunchy fellow with a face like a cherub and bright blue eyes magnified by a pair of aviator glasses. He took off his hat to run a handkerchief over his thinning blond hair. He and Andy had known each other in high school, but Maljeux's lack of hair and his bulkiness made him appear much older. He noticed Andy, who nodded to him, then moved forward to go to work with his camera. Estimating the exposure, Andy set the f-stop, then leaned over the back of one of the detectives to snap off a quick succession of shots. The close-ups he got of the dead man reminded him of some of the faces in the war paintings of Goya, and Germany's Otto Dix.

When he stood up, Lieutenant Maljeux was at his side. He took Andy's arm and led him over to the far corner of the courtyard, where they could speak more discreetly.

"Understand you were guilty of a little public nudity here, Andy."

"I didn't know what else to do. I thought I should try to stop the man."

"Well, this is the Quarter. *Laissez-faire, laissez-faire*. Sure isn't the first time we've had such a salacious display. You get a good look at the fellow you ran after?"

"A look. I don't know how good. Wasn't a lot of light. Still isn't." He grimaced. The pain in his groin hadn't diminished much. "His knife was a little distracting. So was his foot. Caught me in the crotch."

"Next time you go running around like that you ought to at least wear an athletic protector." Maljeux looked back toward the dead man. "We know this dead fancy boy here. Albert Ferrier, though he ain't lived here long. Been a guest of the city a couple of times on male prostitution. Suspected drug peddler, thief, knife artist. I heard he had himself a well-to-do lady friend, over in Faubourg Marigny, no less. Went both ways, Albert. Don't know what he was doing back on the street. Guess they had a falling out." He looked up at the big house opposite Andy's. "You don't suppose this has something to do with Bleusette? Ferrier's not exactly her class of folks."

"I don't think she's even home."

"You wash these bricks down good, hear? After we're done. I wonder why he came in here."

"Just trying to get away from the other one, I guess."

Maljeux gave him a curious look. "Hernandez says you've got a woman up there."

"Did. She got spooked by this and ran off. I can't say I blame her."

"Anyone I know? Someone workin' for Bleusette?"

"Bleusette's not hiring anymore. But, yes, the lady was a working girl. I paid her to pose for some pictures. For my book of nudes. She asked to stay the night. Had no place else to go."

Maljeux gave him another look. "You're real good to a lot of bad women, Andy. Gonna be sorry about that one day. Took off, you say. Pity. We're a little short on witnesses here."

"I'm not enough?"

"Hernandez said she was quite a beauty. Not many good-lookin' hookers working this end of the Quarter, except for Bleusette."

"I made her acquaintance over by Jackson Square."

"That's even worse. You get her name?"

Derain paused. "Simone, I think."

"No last name?"

"None that she was willing to share."

"Maybe we could take a look at those pictures you got of her when you develop them. Maybe one of our vice detectives might recognize her."

Andy paused again. "I think she swiped the camera I used. It happens, if you're not careful."

A smile Andy didn't appreciate crept onto Maljeux's face. "Then we can pick her up on burglary charges."

"Is it all that important, Paul? She didn't see anything I didn't see. Probably not as much."

The smile became a grin. Maljeux patted Andy's arm.

"Why don't you get yourself a little sleep? You probably didn't get much, taking pictures all night. We'll be out of here pretty soon. Then maybe you can drop by the station later this morning. Give me a statement, and help us work up an artist's sketch."

"I have to work today. I've got a job taking production stills for that movie company that's in town. They're doing a street shoot over in the Garden District today."

"I'll call them for you—tell them you're a witness in a homicide. They won't object to your being a little late. They have to clear everything they do with us, you know."

"All right."

"Come by around noon, Andy. You can buy me lunch at Mr. B's."

It was one of Derain's favorite restaurants, but far too expensive for his present state of finances.

"Am I in that much trouble, Paul?"

"You're not in trouble at all. But a little chat after you've freshened up your mind some would be helpful. We'll have sandwiches then. Some muffuletta. In my office."

"I'll be there. Presuming the man with the knife doesn't come back for seconds."

"And keep your clothes on. Let's not scare the tourists."

Once back inside, Andy went to his studio. The first thing to attend to was the framed enlargement of Candice in the nude he had hanging among many others on the wall. Hernandez would recognize her in an instant. He took it down, looked around the room, then slid it behind a file cabinet.

Candice might have to wait at the airport for hours for the next plane to Houston. He wished her gone and well clear of New Orleans, back safe in her house in time to clean up and look her normal highly presentable self before any encounter with her husband.

But he missed her already, almost as much as when she'd left him in New York.

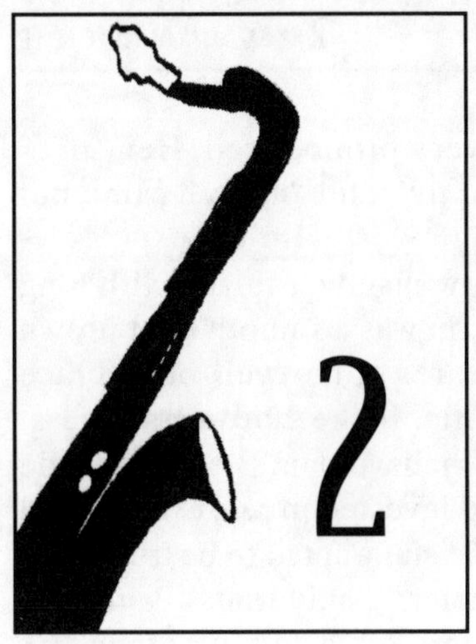

After the police had gone, taking the dead man with them, Andy set about cleaning up the courtyard. Pouring an entire bottle of disinfectant into a bucket of hot water, he took it outside and sloshed it over the drying bloody pool, then hosed down the entire courtyard, wondering how many times the old bricks had received that treatment in the abattoir days of Smoky Row.

Behind him, a screen door slammed with a bang.

"What the goddamn hell's been going on here, Andy?"

It was Bleusette, sounding cranky. If she'd just come home, she'd gotten out of her street clothes in a hurry. She was barefoot, and wearing only a slip. Off-duty, Bleusette's taste in clothing was fairly simple. When in her house, she usually didn't wear anything at all.

"We had a murder here," Andy said, quietly.

"That's what the cop out on the street tell me. But he don't know why this happens in my courtyard."

"I don't know either, darlin'."

"This does not make me happy, Andy."

Bleusette was both Cajun and Creole in ancestry, with some very visible Irish in her as well. There was also a touch *de couleur,* as New Orleanians sometimes referred to things African, which she didn't like to talk about, though it made no difference to Andy or anyone else in the Quarter. She'd been born out in the bayous and had grown up in New Orleans and, later, on one of the French islands in the Caribbean, returning to the city at age seventeen to take up her mother's profession. Her accent was still very pronounced. Her "th's" were spoken with a Cajun "de." "Happy" and "Andy" came out French: "Happee" and "Andee."

She was a small, slender woman, now just over thirty, with long dark hair and eyes almost black. Her skin was a smooth light brown that looked a permanent tan. The features of her well-boned face were extremely fine, indeed, aristocratic. If she'd been an actress, she would have been cast for parts as a rich woman. Bleusette made a lot of money at her trade, which she'd invested in real estate. He'd wondered why she hadn't retired. Maybe she wanted to be truly rich.

"The dead man's name is Albert Ferrier," Andy said. "Paul Maljeux says he's a street hustler with all kinds of nasty ways of making his living. Someone chased him in here. Stabbed him to death under my balcony."

"Maybe we should keep the gate locked up, yes? Like I always tell you?"

"Maybe we should."

"This has nothing to do with you, Andy?"

"I sure hope not."

"Well, it has nothing to do with me, *bien sûr.* I do not want trouble at my place. I have it very good here now. I do not want things fucked up, *compris?"*

"Entendu, Bleusette."

"I do not like to be unhappy. I've had enough of that shit."

"Me too."

"You still have that girlfriend here?"

"She left."

"Went back to Texas?"

Bleusette knew all about Candy, though Andy couldn't recall telling her much.

"Yes."

"She's gonna be big trouble for you, Andy. You should find yourself a nice New Orleans lady. Maybe one without a husband."

"It's working out."

"I hope so," Bleusette said, "but I don't think so." She looked where Andy had been cleaning, then made a face. "I am going to bed now. It will be quiet, yes? No more police?"

"Probably not."

"I am very tired. It is very hard work, what I do."

"I guess it is."

"Not like taking goddamn pictures. You clean this up good, Andy. I will talk to you later."

He watched her walk back to her door. She should have been an actress. Moviemakers would pay a lot for that walk.

• • •

He finished up, listening to the rhythm-and-blues recording Bleusette put on her machine at high volume, a sign of her lingering displeasure, then glanced about the courtyard, his eyes finally settling on the passageway through which the victim and his predator had come. It was dark and narrow. The dead man could not have known the courtyard gate was unlocked. Why did he come in here? There had been people on the street and there was an all-night grocery on the corner—a much likelier haven. If Andy had been running with a knife artist at his heels, the last place he would have chosen was a dead-end courtyard at the end of a narrow passage.

After washing his hands with more disinfectant, he took a very thorough shower, dressing afterward in khakis, his boating moccasins, and a frayed old khaki shirt—his standard working uniform in the summer. He paused in his kitchen only long enough to feed Beatrice, deciding to ignore the dishes, since Candy was no longer around to complain. He loaded his camera bag with a Nikon, his small Canon, and a telephoto lens, plus exposure meter and a dozen boxes of high-speed black-and-white film—supplies to last him the day.

There was time for a stop at the Razzy Dazzy Café on Dauphine Street, where he often began his day, or ended his nights.

The dingy old bar took its name from a celebrated group of turn-of-the-century Storyville street urchins—Emile "Stalebread" Lacoume and his Razzy Dazzy Spasm Band—whom Al Rose and other noted New Orleans historians had credited with being the city's first jazz musicians, though they were white. There was a copy of an old 1897 photograph of the ensemble hanging framed behind the bar, showing them as little more than boys, barefoot and in ragtag clothes, posing somberly with their instruments, which included

Stalebread's cigar box violin and a piano-crate bass fiddle. They went by their street names—Whiskey, Cajun, Monk, Warm Gravy. Like so many musicians in the Quarter, they had gained fame serenading customers in the sporting houses. One member of the group had gone on to become a police captain.

Paul Maljeux was something of a trumpet player himself. The police chief in the Quarter, Captain George Bourgeois, was a highly regarded amateur photographer. Stephen Hand, the director of the Vieux Carré Commission, was also a landscape architect. Instead of producing the torpor one invariably found in Biloxi or Houston, New Orleans heat seemed to set the artistic juices flowing. Andy's, too. Much more than New York ever had. He had nearly enough photographs amassed now to complete both of the picture books he was working on—one of New Orleans street life, another of female nudes.

The Razzy Dazzy was licensed to serve liquor around the clock seven days a week, and received its patrons in recurring shifts. A few of the night people were still in evidence when Derain entered, a couple of them sleeping face down at their tables. Andy took his usual stool at the near end of the bar. His mind was fixed on death, and the anger of two women. He needed some mood-altering substance in a hurry.

"Virgin Mary?" asked Freddy Roybal, the leather-skinned bartender.

Roybal was an artist, too. He'd spent thirty-six years of his life in various jails and prisons in Texas and Louisiana, including a long stay for manslaughter and another for armed robbery. There he'd learned the "handkerchief" art originated by Mexican-American convicts in New Mexico. It was extraordinary stuff. Using ballpoint pen, these inmates produced often exquisite drawings—mostly of naked women—on sheets, pillowcases, handkerchiefs, whatever came to hand in prison. Some they kept for masturbatory pleasure. Other pieces they traded for cigarettes and shaving cream, if they had no money. Roybal had converted several of his sketches to designs for tattoos, which now covered his back, chest, and upper arms. He was wearing a sleeveless undershirt, and a woman lowering her panties was visible on one arm, a rose on the other. When he flexed his muscle, he could make the disrobing lady's behind jiggle.

"Real one this time, Freddy. Tabasco on the side. It's that kind of morning."

"Heard you got a dead man over at your place," Roybal said, reaching for a reasonably clean glass. He spoke slowly in the New Orleans manner, but with a Tex-Mex accent. New Orleans had no accent—certainly no southern one. Andy had grown up with a touch of his mother's native upriver softness in his speech, though it now had something of a New York clip to it.

"He was alive when he came into my courtyard."

"Fancy boy? That's what they're saying."

"Paul Maljeux says he was. How'd you hear about this so fast, Freddy?"

"You know the Quarter. Man can't take a piss in the river without someone over on Rampart complaining about it. Hear you took off running down the street buck naked. That's what they say."

"I was after the bad guy."

Roybal set down the freshly made drink. Andy shook in several generous drops of Tabasco, gave the mixture a few stirs, and then took a healthy swallow. It kicked like an electric jolt, searing his throat, clearing his nasal passages, and bringing tears to his eyes.

"Did he cut him or stick him?"

"I guess the word is stuck," Andy said.

"Colored man?"

Derain shook his head. "Both white. The bad guy got away. I got some pictures of the dead one."

"Always taking pictures, Andy. Don't know why. Ain't nobody paying for that kind of thing. Dead bodies. Street creeps."

"I'm paying for them."

The bartender didn't quite understand, but nodded sagely.

"Is Long Tom around?" Andy asked.

"In back. A little breakfast meeting. He'll be out."

One of the reasons Derain hung out in the Razzy Dazzy was the music. For years, Thomas "Long Tom" Calhoun, the owner of the place, had kept a phonograph behind the bar. He'd since replaced it with a tape machine, which played more or less continuously, when there weren't live musicians in for an evening. At the moment, it was quietly giving forth a recording of a tune Andy recognized from repeated listenings as "Cake-Walking Babies from Home," by the Red

Onion Jazz Babies. Never once had Andy heard such music in the city of New York.

He also came into the Razzy Dazzy for the local politics, which were as tasty and zesty as New Orleans food—indeed, to New York and Washington politics what Tabasco was to mayonnaise.

Long Tom was a former city councilman and state legislator who had left office, but not politics, probably wielding more power and enjoying more fruits of corruption now as a full-time backroom deal-maker and influence broker than he ever had when obliged to be accountable to voters. Claiming illegitimate—and ironic—descent from the legendary pre–Civil War champion of "slavocracy," John C. Calhoun, Long Tom had a droll wit, an easy, amiable manner of speaking, and a wisdom learned in hard and unsavory ways. He was quick to do favors, and long in remembering for whom he'd done them. He'd done one for Andy in helping persuade the Vieux Carré Commission to approve a permit for him to open his photography studio in his little run-down house, which, like all the buildings in the Quarter, was designated a historical landmark. Andy's father, who had also been a state legislator, had done his share of favors for Long Tom when Tom had first come to Baton Rouge, and they'd become political friends. His father's fellow white patricians had looked upon this eccentricity with some disfavor, but accepted it. His father was known to have a randy side.

Andy counted Long Tom among his best friends in the Quarter. He was a crook, but a true gentleman and to Andy's mind an honest man. He kept his word, and never pretended to be anything other than what he was.

The walls of the Razzy Dazzy were decorated with pictures and memorabilia of things they both liked—all manner of photographs of early jazz musicians and old streetcar-era New Orleans street scenes, as well as a few cheap and faded photos and sketches of the town's more famous painted ladies, most of them—like the "followers of Venus" who had given Smoky Row its name—black women. One wall was covered with political souvenirs, with a glass-protected Huey Long campaign poster prominently displayed as well as several from Long Tom's early career.

Andy was startled to see a brand-new one there, a huge, multi-colored graphic that advertised the political and civic virtues of none other than U.S. Senator Henry Boone. Above a slick, glamorized photo of the man—an artful triumph of cosmetics and blow-dried hairdo over lean and hungry, pockmarked raw-boned reality—were the block-letter words: "HANK BOONE: He Stands for You."

What the slick former furniture salesman and lay preacher stood for was some of the most insidious bigotry and hate-mongering to have seeped to the surface of the South in recent decades. To Andy's mind, Boone was every bit as loathesome as the ex-Klansman David Duke who had enjoyed a brief celebrity in Louisiana and national politics, and far more dangerous, because he'd proved eminently electable. Unlike the feckless Duke, Boone was a lifelong Democrat, and one of the most skilled campaigners in the state. The religious fundamentalists of the back country considered him entirely respectable. Boone sometimes styled himself as "Reverend."

Becoming a minor millionaire after opening and expanding a chain of cheap, easy-credit furniture stores, Boone had taken to politics with the same zeal and relish as he had to the lay pulpit. He really didn't need all the clever code words he used to become a symbol of white voter backlash. He had established his base early in his political career with a single, controversial, but highly consequential act. Three black youths had attempted to snatch a woman's purse outside one of his stores. Boone had rushed outside and shot two of them dead. It hadn't mattered to the jury that tried and acquitted him or to the electorate at large that none of the boys had been armed with more than a knife. He had stood up against crime, against blacks, against "the threat." The prosecutor who had had the courage to bring charges against him had lasted one term.

Long Tom Calhoun was very light-skinned and had two white great-grandfathers, but by all southern standards he was every inch a black man. Yet here in the sanctity of his saloon, where black, white, and brown mingled every day and night in vice and abandon—and usually friendship—Tom had put up a Boone poster.

"What the hell's that damn thing doing there, Freddy?" Andy asked. "Tom having himself a little joke? Or is it for target practice?"

"It's part of my get-out-the-vote drive."

Long Tom was standing in the rear doorway, wearing a pale gray double-breasted suit, white shirt, purple print tie, and a crisp new Panama hat pushed back on his head. He strolled over to the bar and leaned on it. He was taller even than Andy. Had he grown up in New York or Philadelphia, he might have played basketball for a living.

"That man ain't never going to get to the White House, much as he may think he is," Tom said. "But when he runs in Louisiana, the black vote turnout jumps up to better than ninety percent. That time when I lost, Boone wasn't on the ballot, and we didn't get fifty percent of our people out. I'm thinking of running for my old legislative seat next time, 'specially if Boone goes for the presidency. Nice town, Baton Rouge."

Andy wanted to change the subject.

"I had a problem at my place this morning, Tom."

"You had a dead man. One Albert Ferrier."

"You know him?"

Calhoun shook his head. "No friend of mine. Just another hustler. Kinda new in town."

"Can you find out something about him?"

"You want to send flowers to his family?"

"No, I just want to know who he was, how he came to get carved up like that in my courtyard."

"Isn't that what the police are doing?"

"If the police knew how to find things out the way you do, Tom, there'd be a lot more people in jail."

"I'll ask around." He watched Andy drain his glass. "Can I buy you another drink?"

"No thanks. I'm on my way to the police station. To tell Paul Maljeux what I don't know."

• • •

As Andy approached the Vieux Carré police station on Chartres Street, the tourists became more numerous, crowding the sidewalk. He supposed that without them the Quarter might lapse back into the dead-poor, violence-prone hellhole it had been at various times in its long history, but he hated their inexorably increasing numbers. The Quarter had been settled by the French and Spanish, been home to waves of Irish, German, and Italian immigrants, to island people from all over the Caribbean, and to artists, writers, and an urban gentry. None of these people had ever worn T-shirts that said "Gumbo" or "Jazz."

Stepping around a young couple taking pictures of each other in front of an old carriage, he turned into the police station. There were three horses tied up beneath the trees on the lawn, a row of motorscooters drawn up along the walk, and, to the side of the entrance, tables and chairs set up in the manner of a sidewalk café. Inside, in the big central room where the desk sergeant sat, the high white walls were decorated with historical southern paintings and frescoes of famous early nineteenth-century Americans. Andy nodded to a policewoman leaning against the desk—a beauty, like several assigned to this station. Her name was Desirée.

Maljeux had a reporter with him in his little office, a young man in glasses named Carl Bashaw whom Derain had worked with occasionally at crime scenes. He seemed happily surprised to see Andy there.

"If you've got a minute, I'd like to talk to you," he said, "about the stabbing this morning."

"Why don't you just run along back to your paper instead, Carl?" Maljeux said. "Mr. Derain and I are going to be busy for quite a little while here. You can catch up with him some other time."

"I've just got a few questions."

"Andy don't have any answers I haven't already told you," Maljeux said. "If you want to find out more about that dead boy, go chase up some of those people who might have known him. Andy sure as hell ain't one of those."

Looking not a little abashed, the young reporter thanked Maljeux for his time and left. When he was gone, the lieutenant lifted up a basket containing the muffuletta sandwiches—big, thick buns filled with mounds of Italian sausage, ham, and assorted garnishes and seasonings.

"You drinking today, Andy? I got a couple of frosty bottles of good Jax beer."

"I'm drinking, but I had my morning's worth at the Razzy Dazzy. Coke'll do."

"Always got that."

Eating muffuletta was a messy business not conducive to serious conversation. Maljeux waited until they were finished before bringing up what was most on his mind.

"As you damn well know, Andy, *laissez-faire* ain't the only operative philosophy we've got working down here. There's *le tout ensemble,* the good of the whole. We're not exactly sticklers on every point of the law. Can't deny that. We'll wink and we'll bend and we'll let a few light-fingered lads and languorous ladies like Bleusette walk when we need to, but that's because we try to keep in mind what's best for the whole community. The Quarter takes care of its own. As regards you and this business this morning, I don't want to see the case pursued and prosecuted in a manner that's going to cause any undue trouble and embarrassment for you. As far as I'm concerned, you got involved in this just trying to be a good citizen."

Derain shrugged. "That's the truth."

"It's not the truth I'm worried about. It's the talk. That dead boy wasn't just one of the local AC-DC hustlers, he was into some real nasty business—drugs, pimping underage runaways, anything to turn a dollar. He's from Mississippi. Ain't been here all that long. But he'd already got himself a reputation worse than some of the local boys. We checked out his former domicile over in Faubourg Marigny. The residence belongs to a lady of color—what in the old days they used to call a quadroon—the prettiest I ever saw. She says Ferrier—the deceased—was only an occasional visitor, but the neighbors say he was there all the time, until he cleared out a couple of weeks ago. The pretty colored lady pays her rent in cash. We can only guess where that comes from."

"What does all this have to do with me?"

"Shouldn't have anything to do with you, but with that *au naturel* appearance of yours on the street right after, well, there are people here who can put one and one together and come up with eleven. Now, we've got about every kind of sexual preference there is here in the Quarter. *Laissez-faire*. Live and let live. That's fine with me. But over in the Garden District where you come from? Up among the swell folk along Lake Pontchartrain? Well, it won't do you a lot of good to get mixed up with any such association. You won't get a lot of business taking pictures at society weddings."

"I only do that when I'm really broke. And I don't give much of a damn about what those people think about anything. But why would they think that about me?"

"Andy, Mr. Ferrier had your name and address in his pocket—on a matchbook. You have any idea why that is?"

"Your name means 'bad joke' Maljeux. Is this one?"

"I'm dead serious, Andy. They've got the matchbook down in the evidence and property section, if you want to look at it."

The thought gave Derain as many creeps as looking at the dead man's body had done. "No thanks."

"It was in his handwriting. We checked it out. It was kinda scrawled, like he was writing down what someone gave him over the phone or something. He wrote down 'in rear,' so we don't think this had anything to do with Bleusette. No sir, it was your name. Any idea why that is?"

"None whatsoever."

"You're sure?"

"Absolutely."

"Well, he sure was where he was trying to be, and the other fellow sure was hellbent on stopping him. Maybe you should be kinda glad he did. We found a straight razor in Ferrier's pocket. Real shiny and sharp."

"A lot of people carry those things." The words masked his fear, which had crept into his brain. Albert Ferrier was dead, but whoever had given him Andy's address was still out there.

"Don't I know it. Took one off a hooker last night they could have used on Marie Antoinette." Maljeux drank some of his beer, wiped his mouth, burped, and then sighed. "All right, Andy. I put it in the report what you said about entertaining a business lady upstairs name of Simone. But, friend that you are, I know that's a whole lot of plain bullshit. Hernandez described the woman to me. My guess is she's the same lady I've seen you with more than once before—that out-of-town fashion model."

Andy frowned. Maljeux leaned forward.

"We're gonna have to be real serious about this case, my friend. A crime like this in the Quarter is going to make the papers and the TV news tonight. We mean to catch that son of a bitch with the knife, if only to make it clear to one and all that this was some private matter between unsavory elements who might have strayed into the Quarter, and not the kind of rampant street crime that scares away tourists."

"Are you working for the Chamber of Commerce now?"

"*Le tout ensemble,* Andy, *le tout ensemble.*" Maljeux leaned even closer now. "Now, that fine-lookin' lady of yours is the only other witness we have in this case. I know, you say she didn't see a whole lot, but we didn't have a chance to talk to her and establish that as fact. She might have seen more than you know about. She might have heard that dead boy's last words on earth."

"She's married, Paul. Her husband's the kind of man who can make life very unhappy for her—and me."

"This a serious thing with you and that babe?"

"For a long time now. At least it was."

"Well, I don't want to mess that up for you. I sure don't. Don't want to mess up her happy little marriage, either." Maljeux leaned back in his chair, which gave out a loud creak. "When you leave here, I want you to sit down with Detective Sergeant Pettigrew and give him a statement. He'll also want you to look at some pictures, in case that fellow with the knife is in our little photo gallery of local colorful characters. If he isn't, I want you to help our artist work up a portrait."

He scratched his belly. He was in need of larger-sized shirts. "Now, it's all right with me if you tell Pettigrew that nonsense about a Simone, and how you never saw the woman before and don't expect to again." Maljeux came forward in his chair again. "But we need your help, Andy. I want you to get hold of that lady friend of yours and have her tell you everything she saw and heard. Everything. Then you tell me."

"Whatever she has to say, it'll be just between us?"

"*Entre nous.* Just like always."

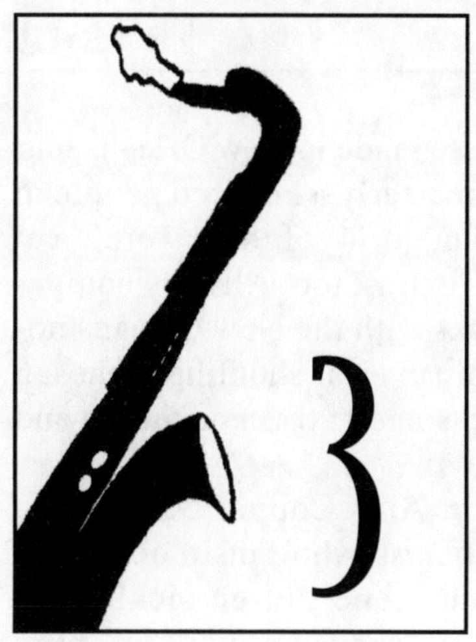

3

Pettigrew took Derain's statement without asking any questions beyond the facts of what Derain had seen and done. Andy dutifully went through the books of mug shots, looking at a lot of terrible faces and worse photographs, but finding no one who much resembled his assailant. Consuming more time, he helped a police artist with a sketch of the man, though the result looked scarcely human. Andy doubted the man could make a living doing caricatures of tourists in Jackson Square.

After leaving the police station, camera bag on his shoulder, he walked over to Canal Street to catch the St. Charles streetcar out to the Garden District and the movie shoot, not wanting to spend money on a cab.

Derain had a car—though some might consider that an exaggeration. It was an ailing 1977 white and rust-colored Cadillac convertible with a leaky roof and lethargic battery. But, even if he was able to start it, he was reluctant to give up his parking place, which was directly in front of his house. He enjoyed the streetcar rides anyway. The St. Charles Avenue line was the last left in the city. Its old olive-drab cars had huge, wooden-framed windows kept open for the breeze, and motormen who could clang the bells with as much esprit as King Oliver playing "Dippermouth Blues."

Maljeux had given him excuse enough for being late to work, not that Derain thought it would matter much. Even with the best director, movies got made the way grass grew. Because of the cheap labor and local color, a lot of pictures were made in New Orleans, but New Orleans had the slows. There were nearly a hundred people in the cast and crew of this one, and the majority of them were local hires—drivers, grips, electricians, and extras, too. All very competent, but inclined to go about their tasks with the New Orleans notion of deliberate speed. When the company was shooting scenes in the French Quarter, it was hard to keep some of them on the set and out of the bars.

Compounding matters, the director, Alan Cooper, was a temperamental, insecure, would-be perfectionist, who'd insist on dozens of takes of even the most unimportant scenes, often picking the worst of the lot for his final cut. Andy had seen him spend an entire day setting up a ten second shot of a car driving past the Superdome.

Thanks to good scripts and strong casts, Cooper had had three big hits early on in his career, but his luck had run out thereafter. Now he was making what must have been his fifth or sixth attempt at a comeback, and this one seemed unusually cursed. Andy wondered how he'd managed to scrape up the money for this picture, which had been budgeted for $15 million and was showing every sign of running over.

It was a formula action cop drama, and a salt-and-pepper buddy picture rip-off of the Mel Gibson–Danny Glover *Lethal Weapon* films to boot—without the comedy. The storyline had a troubled, hard-drinking, violence-prone white detective teamed with an older, wiser black partner in a two-man crusade against drug smugglers using New Orleans as a port of entry, with the detectives' corrupt lieutenant in cahoots with the bad guys. The cliché-laden script called for lots of car chases, some of which had yet to be shot, and a foot chase through the French Quarter. The climax, the most expensive part of the film, was to come on a riverboat. The details of that scene had yet to be worked out, depending as they did on how much money they'd have left for it, but plans now called for a riverboat—an old hulk retired from tourist service that Cooper had bought cheap—to be blown up in the middle of the Mississippi.

The title of the movie, more or less stolen from New Orleans' own Tennessee Williams, was *Street of Desire*. The hard-drinking detective was being played by James Ball, an aging if athletic pretty boy who hadn't had a sober breath since his last good picture, which was several years before. His black partner was former National Football League running-back-turned-actor Hub Cleveland. Veteran character actor Anthony Montaigne was the drug smuggler, and Oscar-winner Paris Moran was the smuggler's beautiful if hard-edged blond girlfriend, a worldly, mysterious woman who, according to the script, had come to regret her sordid life and was supposed to fall for the detective and help him bring down the drug ring. A young ingenue Andy knew little about, Emily Shaw, played the detective's pretty, estranged wife.

The location street shoot they had scheduled for that day was simple enough: the detective, after spending the night with his wife in an apparently successful attempt at reconciliation, was to make the mistake of having the mysterious underworld lady pick him up in the morning to take him to a rendezvous with a local lowlife who had a tip on a big drug deal going down. The sweet young wife was to run out of the house after him and hysterically present him with an ultimatum: Come back inside and live happily ever after or go off with the underworld lady and kiss good-bye to marital bliss forever. No more second chances. Given a choice between personal happiness and his pursuit of justice, the detective was to opt for the latter, speeding away with Paris Moran in her Mercedes convertible while the young Emily Shaw ran after them, taking a painful fall in the street. Women were always getting hurt in Cooper's films.

As Andy had guessed, they'd been working on the scene since early morning, without coming anywhere near Cooper's notion of success. According to the assistant director Derain stopped to talk to, Cooper didn't like the awkward way Miss Shaw came out of the house. He didn't like the squeak he heard in her voice when she called out the detective's name. He didn't like the rolling manner in which the stuntwoman doubling for the ingenue performed her running fall in the street.

They'd already shot seven takes. The stuntwoman was having her knees treated with antiseptic, and Emily Shaw, sitting off by herself on a folding chair, was on the brink of hysterics of a very genuine sort.

Worse, the once sunny sky was going gloomy with lowering clouds, with an accompanying increase in the already awful humidity and a change in the light. The street had been blocked off with barricades and the film company's trucks and trailers, but bystanders and gawkers from the neighborhood had filtered through and were standing here and there on the sidewalk. If one of them got in a film sequence, Cooper would probably start shrieking himself.

Andy had two old friends working on the movie. One was D. J. Cosette, the chief makeup man, a genius at his calling and a man Andy had known when Cosette had been practicing his trade in the fashion business in New York. The other was Paris Moran. Andy had shot the cover picture and inside spread for the story *Vanity Fair* had done on her the year she had won her Oscar. Her career had declined almost as badly as James Ball's and Cooper's in the years since—dragged down by several dreadful films, plus a very a good one that had failed at the box office. She didn't deserve to be in this wretched picture of Cooper's, but the first job of every actor was to have a job, and Paris hadn't had many lately.

It was Paris, bless her, who had persuaded Cooper to hire Andy for *Street of Desire*'s publicity still production shots.

It was easy enough work. Out of every scene, he was to produce usable close-ups of each actor, a medium shot of every dialogue exchange, and all-embracing wide shots of the action sequences. To Andy's surprise, Cooper hadn't bothered him much so far. The director was aware of his former status as a big-time celebrity and fashion photographer. According to Paris, he was even a little flattered to have him working on the project. But publicity stills were a minor component of this enterprise, unworthy of the great man's creative attention. All he asked of Derain was that he keep out of the way. Andy had been using a telephoto lens for nearly every shot, positioning himself well back behind the director and camera crew.

Paris noticed Andy unpacking some of his equipment and strolled over, as usual, smoking a cigarette. She was a tall, big-boned natural blonde—her hair dyed a shimmering platinum for this role. She had a tendency to weight that had at least kept her memorable face free of the lines some women experienced at her age, which was thirty-six. Her looks, ethereally regal in her early films, had taken on a harder edge in recent years, but that was fine for this part, and to Andy's mind, made her an even more striking woman.

"Hello, Andy. Welcome back to the shipwreck."

She exhaled a slowly drifting cloud of smoke, turning her head to watch Cooper berate a technician over by the sound equipment. Paris was wearing a flashy pink sundress with a low neckline suitable to the steamy climate, and to her bad girl role in the film.

"Did anyone tell him why I'm late?"

"I'm sure he didn't even notice, honey bunch. Anyway, some cop called the production manager to say they'd kept you. Are you in trouble or something?"

"I'm a witness to a murder. It happened right outside my place. Not the way I usually like to start my day."

"Fun town, New Orleans. You can tell me all about it, when we stop for a drink after we wind up today's endless succession of fuck-ups."

She took another drag and then dropped the cigarette to the sidewalk, crushing it out with her high-heeled shoe. Weight problem or no, she had marvelous legs.

"See you later, sweetheart. Now that he's chewed out everybody on the set, it looks to be 'places everybody' time again."

Keeping his distance from Cooper, Andy got to work, snapping several shots of Emily Shaw emerging from the house and a half dozen usable ones of Ball moving along the sidewalk. He changed to a wider angle lens while they set up the argument on the sidewalk scene, clicking off the rest of the roll as the two went through it. Both performers were tired, frustrated, and angry, which gave their play-acting a remarkable versimilitude. To everyone's amazement, Cooper called it a print. If Andy had arrived a few minutes later than he did, he might have missed it all.

While the crew prepared for the drive-away sequence, Andy reloaded and shot off another roll, taking candids of people moving and sitting about the set, including one of Cooper in which the director looked a little like Napoleon surveying the battlefield at Waterloo. Andy took some of the local spectators, as well. Two teenage girls from the neighborhood posed for him, hiking up their skirts a little and cocking their heads to one side. He decided to save them a couple of prints. The girls had been around the set every day.

Andy had learned a lot about moviemaking in his time, and wondered why Cooper was insisting on shooting the whole doorway-to-drive-away segment in sequence on the same day. The drive-off could just as easily be done another time. The assistant director made just that observation to Cooper, and regretted it.

"Do you see that sky, imbecile?" Cooper said, for all to hear. "If we have that sky for the sidewalk I want it for the entire scene. I match my shots! I do not do cheap bullshit pictures!" He turned to address the entire crew. "Let's get moving, you lazy bastards! Paris, get ready! Somebody get the car!"

The Mercedes convertible was still up the street, where Paris had left it after the last take. A crew member ran to fetch it, slamming the car into reverse and roaring backward toward them, steering nimbly past the closely parked trailers.

Andy was standing near enough to Paris to hear her say, "Slow down!" The Mercedes kept coming. The man behind the wheel looked down frantically at the floorboard, then back to the rear. Whatever he was doing, it wasn't slowing the car.

"Stop, damn you!" bellowed Cooper.

The Mercedes was heading right for Emily, who was standing next to her stunt double. Both women turned and ran, but not in time. The car bumped over the curb and struck a heavy light stand, causing it to topple over like a felled tree. A flange on the big fixture caught the stunt woman on the back of the head.

"You dumb son of a bitch!" cried Cooper. "What the fuck is wrong with you?"

Andy and several others ran to the injured stunt woman, the assistant director kneeling beside her. She was lying face down and appeared to be unconscious. The convertible had come to a stop against a tree. The driver stumbled out.

"The brakes don't work!" he screamed. "The fucking brakes don't work!"

Cooper was nearly crimson with rage and the heat. Someone with a medical kit got to the fallen woman's side, and slowly turned her over. She seemed to be alive. Andy moved back out of the way. Emily stood up, looking tearfully and helplessly about as Ball headed for his trailer, and, doubtless, a stiff drink. Paris came over and lighted a cigarette.

"Do you believe this, Andy?" she said. "I think there are movie shoots in Albania that go better than this."

"It was an accident," Andy said. "They happen."

"Every goddamned day on this set, honey bunch. I sure as hell hope she's all right."

The injured woman was now sitting up, blood streaming down the side of her face. Another man ran over to say he had called an ambulance.

With a thump and roll of thunder, it began to rain, a first-class New Orleans tropical downpour, soaking everyone and everything within seconds.

"That fucking well does it," Paris said.

Cooper was trudging off toward a trailer. "Okay, everybody," his assistant said. "That's it for today. Pack up."

"I've got a car and driver," Paris said to Andy. She nodded toward Emily. "Go get little Miss Muffett there and we'll head on back to the hotel."

• • •

The cast and crew were staying at the fancy high-rise Westin Hotel, which overlooked both the Quarter and the riverfront. Movie companies frequently used it to house cast and crews when working in New Orleans. Emily went to her room while Paris and Derain went to the upstairs cocktail lounge, which had a sweeping view of a long curve of the Mississippi, the docks and warehouses of the tough town of Algiers visible opposite. Their clothes were still damp, and Paris's hair was a stringy mess, but she didn't want to take time to change before she had a drink.

She smoked. A boat was pushing a long raft of coal barges downriver, making the turn with the bow of the rig just missing a tourist riverboat.

"I don't know about this picture," Paris said. "I didn't think it could get any worse, but it does every day. If there was a way to get out of my contract, I'd probably take it, even if it meant having to do dinner theaters the rest of my life."

"Do you mean that?"

"Some days I do. This is one of them."

"It doesn't seem all that bad a picture."

"Honey bunch, I've made some good ones and some bad ones, but this bow wow is headed straight for the back shelves of the video stores. If they're lucky, they may get a shot at cable TV. I think our backers have caught the scent of major stinker, which is why our beloved producer, Mr. Sommer, is out west today. Hold their hands a little and remind them they've got two Oscar winners in the credits. This is their first time putting big money into movies. They don't want to start out looking like fools. But fools they are anyway, the fucking chumps, buying into another Alan Cooper career death wish."

"How much do you need the work, Paris?"

She shrugged. Her tough-lady talk belied the fact that she had attended Berkeley for two years before dropping out to go to Juilliard. She was very bright and could have been anything she wanted to be. Andy had always wondered why she had become an actress. She couldn't have known in the beginning she'd make it as a star.

"I'm not quite as bad off as you, sport," she said, amiably. "But, who knows? My next step down, I guess, would be making movies in Italy like Brooke Shields. Remember her? Then soap operas. Maybe I'll just get married again. Some rich Joe who wants to buy a movie star." The smile returned. "Only kidding. It's just that I'm beginning to think this whole shoot is jinxed. It was all right when we were doing some of the early soundstage stuff in L.A., but ever since we hit this sinful little city of yours, it's been a virtual *Nightmare on Elm Street*. Fifteen million and climbing, all headed for the toilet. With my name on it."

She lighted another cigarette and looked out the window again. "Life is so fucking long. They made a film in this town with that line in it. Frances Faye, playing a madam, in Louis Malle's *Pretty Baby*. 'Life is so long.' "

Her large blue-green eyes became troubled.

"That Mercedes," she said. "We were going to use it in some chase scenes in the next shoot. I'm supposed to do some of the driving. If we hadn't done so many takes today, those brakes might have gone out with me at the wheel. Brakes don't go out like that, do they? Not on a Mercedes."

"Somebody ought to take a look at them."

"We'll have a new car by morning. More money into the toilet." She pushed back her chair. "I've got to go over my script, sweetums, which is a bullshit way of saying I think I'm going to go up to my room and try to get as drunk as Jim Ball manages to be by breakfast."

"Would you like some company?"

He said that only partly in jest. When he had shot the spread of

Paris for *Vanity Fair,* he'd taken a few pictures of her in the nude. One of them was hanging on his studio wall.

Being unfaithful to a married woman wasn't usually considered something worthy of the confessional—especially when Candice had just told him they were quits. He seemed to have largely recovered from the indelicate kick of the man he'd chased out of his courtyard. In any event, some things were worth a little pain.

"No thanks, honey bunch. I've trouble enough without getting mixed up in quickie amour with a rakehell New Orleans gent like you."

She stood up. "This town. I swear, if I was born here I'd be dead by now." She paused. "I don't mean to suggest anything strange, sweetheart, but if you find yourself with some time on your hands tomorrow, you might try to provide little Miss Muffett with aid and comfort. That young lady's so shook she can barely say her name, and Cooper's treating her the way Henry VIII did his wives. If we're ever going to finish this dog, we need everybody sane."

• • •

After leaving Paris at the elevators, Derain went to a public phone in the lobby, wondering if his telephone company credit card was still good. He was two months behind with the bill.

The phone company was being generous, or at least forgetful. After five rings, a maid with a Mexican accent answered the phone at Candice's house in Houston, saying Mrs. Browley wasn't home. He left his name and number, stressing the call was about a fashion shoot. He wasn't sure how much Browley knew about him.

The rain had stopped, but the water lay heavily in the streets, splashing into his old boating shoes as he walked across the Quarter to his house. The departing, lowering sun peeped out pink between layers of gray. There was music coming from seemingly every other doorway.

He went on to his studio and tried calling Candice again, with the same unhappy result. It had been a good ten hours since she'd left his place. He had to talk to her, if only because of his promise to Maljeux. The policeman had done him a lot of favors. They were not to be taken lightly, not from him.

Andy set about putting his raw film from the day through his developer. He always did his own darkroom work whenever possible, having once had an entire day's shoot with a $500 an hour, top-of-the-line model ruined by an incompetent at a commercial processor's in New York.

After hanging up his negatives to dry, he called Candy yet again. This time, Browley himself answered. Andy immediately hung up. He hated himself for being that frightened by the man. Candice should have left her husband long ago.

He glanced around the studio. The room was getting to look as bad as the kitchen.

There was a can of ravioli in a cupboard. It was a heinous crime to eat something like that when you lived in a neighborhood of wonderful restaurants, but he didn't want to be away from his phone.

It took only about five minutes to consume the almost tasteless meal. He washed the accumulation of dishes, then returned to his studio, picking up the clutter. There was an old leather couch against one wall, its many rents and tears covered with gaffer's tape. He sat down on it, staring at the telephone, and then at some of the photographs he'd hung on the wall opposite, his eyes lingering most on the one of Paris Moran.

The phone rang, startling him. It was Candice, sounding in a worse state than when she'd left.

"Goddamn you, Andy! Why did you call me at home? Why did you do that?"

"I've called you there before."

"Not when I've just gotten back from out of town. Not when I walk through the door looking like I'd slept in a bus station. Why did you hang up on him? Now he's sure something's going on. He's really spooky this time, Andy."

"Where are you?"

"At a gas station near the Galleria. I can't talk long."

"He's never been like this before."

"I know! That's why I'm so nervous. With his money, he can find out anything in the world he wants to know. It's a miracle he hasn't found out about us already. How could we be so stupid? My God, dinner at Brennan's? We might just as well have had sex on my front lawn."

"Candy, at the worst, this means he might ask for a divorce."

"You don't know Ben Browley."

"You said you might be willing to leave him."

"If I did, Andy, would you come back with me to New York? Would you be willing to do that, for me? Right now?"

He said nothing.

"I've got to go," she said. "I want you to get rid of those nude pictures of me. All of them. Don't throw them away. Burn them."

"Candice."

"I've got to go."

"There's something else, Candy. When that man was killed outside my place this morning. You went out on the balcony. Did you see anything?"

"I saw you run out on the street without any clothes on."

"Did you see the man I was after? Did you see his face?"

"I just saw his back. He was wearing a yellow shirt. And I think brown pants."

"What about the other one? Did you hear him say anything?"

"He was crying. Crying and swearing."

"No words? He didn't speak any words?"

"I'm not sure, but he may have called out something like 'doom.' "

"Doom?"

"He was dying, wasn't he?"

"Could it have been something else? A name?"

"I don't know. Blood was coming out of his mouth. It was horrible."

"Think, Candy. I've managed to keep your name out of this, thanks to my police lieutenant friend. But I need to help him."

"Oh my God! There's Ben's car! I've got to go. Andy, don't call me!"

The line went dead. He stood a moment, holding the phone uselessly in his hand, then slowly hung it up.

He looked at his watch. He could stay there and wait for her to call again, or he could go over to the Razzy Dazzy.

It could be hours before he heard from her.

For the first time since he had come back home to New Orleans, he felt terribly lonely.

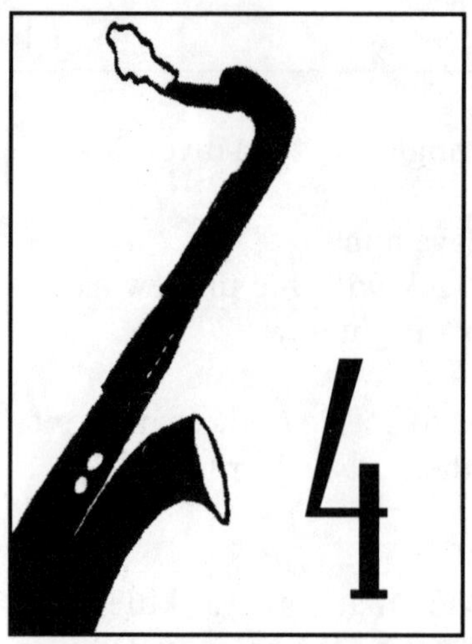

The saloon was crowded. A dark-haired woman was sitting on his usual stool, so Andy went to an empty one further down the bar, between a black man wearing a brown suit and a Chicago Bulls T-shirt, and a heavy white woman so voluptuous she had cleavage just about everywhere. Long Tom was busy with some serious-looking men at a big table in the rear. He waved, but continued with his conversation.

"Virgin Mary?" said Freddy Roybal.

"Whiskey. Double Jack Black."

"You must be having a hell of a day, Andy."

"I could do with tomorrow."

Roybal smiled, looking over at Long Tom, then moved down the bar.

The tape system was playing a sad, slow jazz tune—saxophone dominating piano and bass. Its late composer had been a saxophone player who had hung out more or less happily in the Razzy Dazzy for years, but who then made the mistake of falling in love with Bleusette. He was a good-looking man and a talented musician and she'd liked him. She'd even taken a vacation from the trade and moved in with him for a few weeks.

But he'd essentially been a loser, especially at love. Bleusette had tired of his boozing and drugs and self-pity and lack of cash. When he'd gotten busted on a marijuana buy, she'd moved out in a hurry.

After he'd served his ninety days, she'd kept away from him. He'd then taken to spending his every waking hour in the Razzy Dazzy in the almost religious hope she'd return to him there, because it was her favorite bar. This had only vexed her the more, and she'd asked Long Tom to eighty-six him so her life could return to normal.

The musician had gone home to his gin and dope and empty life and written this song. He'd recorded it on tape with some friends, and gave a copy to Long Tom to give to Bleusette as a last forlorn gesture. She'd told Tom to keep it for his collection. It was the final blow. The saxophone player drank himself to death in a week of determined effort.

This had made Bleusette very unhappy. Afterward, she'd sometimes come in and ask Tom or Freddy to play the tape, sitting by herself at an empty table, sipping a Pernod—her only drink—until it was done. Sometimes she asked to hear it again.

It was a truly beautiful piece, as was so much music inspired by misery. The saxophone player had named it "Bleusette's Blues," but in the Razzy Dazzy, everyone had taken to calling it "Bad Girl Blues." That's how the musician had talked about her, in his last days. "Bad girl." That's how some of the patrons felt about Bleusette because of this.

Andy looked around the saloon. Bleusette wasn't there.

The tape ended. Freddy put another on that began with an old jazz number, which Andy took to be "Carolina Shout"—Sidney Bechet. The next song was a non sequitur—vocal, the voice unmistakably Randy Newman's. Andy recognized the cut from Newman's album *Good Ol' Boys*. He had a copy of it himself.

He swore, loudly. The song was "Beware the Naked Man"—a weird, surreal ballad about a mysterious naked phantom on the run through the South, snatching old women's purses. Andy realized it was being played for his benefit.

Long Tom's mellow laughter rolled across the room. Freddy and a number of others joined in it. Many eyes were on Derain, including those of the dark-haired woman sitting on his stool. There was something odd about her, but she was quite pretty.

After his burst of humor had subsided, Long Tom motioned Andy over. The men at his table rose quickly and moved away. Most were black but there was also a white man—called "Ratty" because of his nose and teeth and narrow face—a political friend of Tom's from City Hall.

Andy pulled up a chair as bidden. The tape machine went back to its pleasant regular business of jazz and blues.

"I found out a little something," Tom said.

His low, rumbly voice had a rhythm like a freight train moving through the night.

He paused as Freddy brought over two whiskeys.

"Well?" said Andy. He didn't like Tom's somber look.

"This is just street talk, mind. I can't say I necessarily vouch for it, but the word is that Ferrier might have been fixing to kill someone."

"Anyone I know? Like me?"

"Ain't a lot being said about who he had in mind, but he was bragging about doing it. Some say he also might have been shaking somebody down, which could account for his own demise. He's been kinda flush lately. Usually he just scratched around for the odd dollar. One guess is he might have been leaning on his girlfriend in Faubourg Marigny. Or maybe the girlfriend's new boyfriend—someone who wouldn't want his association with the girlfriend gettin' talked about." Tom sipped his drink. "He killed a man before, you know. Ferrier did. Man in Pascagoula. The cops never got to him."

Andy drank. His nerves were a little jangly.

"He couldn't have been after me. I never even heard of him before."

"Anyway, that's what I heard. I'll keep asking around. You probably ought to tell Maljeux, but don't let on where you caught on to this. I don't think the lieutenant approves of me."

He looked over his shoulder. A young, attractive black woman in a bright blue dress was standing in the doorway, waiting.

"You got a piece, Andy?"

"As a matter of fact, I do. My father's old .32 Savage."

"Does it work?"

"It used to."

"Well, I don't know what the hell's goin' on here, but just to be on the safe side, I'd keep it handy when you go nighty-night. Now, how you doin' otherwise? I hear you and money been strangers lately."

"I've got some work. The movie project helps. The IRS takes a healthy share of what they pay me, though. I still owe a bunch of back taxes, from when the good times were rolling up in New York."

"I can't help you much with the IRS., but there's all kinds of ways to make some money."

"I'm fine, Tom. But it's appreciated."

"Old friends is the best friends." He drained his glass and rose. "I've got a little social engagement to attend to just now, but you come by tomorrow. I always enjoy our conversations, Andy. Some more than others."

• • •

The place at the bar where Andy had been sitting was now taken, but a couple of stools near his regular spot had opened up. He took one not far from the dark-haired woman, asking Freddy for another whiskey.

"Buy me a drink, sailor?"

Andy looked at the woman and smiled. That line had fallen into disuse years before she was born. He tried to remember the last time he'd even heard it in an old movie.

"I'm afraid I don't know you, ma'am. Have we met?" She didn't appear to be a hooker. Her long-sleeved black dress was too expensive; its skirt much too long—coming nearly to mid-calf. There was a been-around cast to her face; a few lines visible around her large, gray eyes and her mouth. Unlike the business girls of the Quarter, she wore very little makeup. Whatever her age, she was still very much a beauty—thin, her well-boned face almost gaunt, but in no way haggard. Candice would probably look something like this if she didn't take such obsessive care of herself, smearing creams and oils into her face every morning and night. He wondered if this woman at the bar had ever been a model. She was almost tall enough.

She moved one stool closer to him, sliding along her nearly empty glass, then lighted a cigarette. He could not recall a woman so worldly, not even in New York. When her eyes lifted to his again, he was struck by their haunted look—haunted, and haunting.

"I know all about you," she said. "The bartender's been telling me."

Freddy grinned, giving Andy another whiskey.

"You're the famous naked man of Burgundy Street," she said.

"The naked man of Smoky Row," said Freddy.

"You were on television tonight," the woman said, exhaling smoke through her nose. "On the news. You had your clothes on, though."

Derain was dead certain he'd never ever seen her before. "Did you come in here looking for me?"

"No. I was just trying to find a place where I could get away from the tourists. I moved into the Quarter a couple of months ago. I live over by the river, on Ursulines Street. Tourists everywhere down there."

Her accent was flat, middle-American—not quite northern, but not Mississippi River South, either.

"You're not from New Orleans."

She smiled. She had surprisingly good teeth. "I'm from St. Louis—and around." She reached out a long, narrow hand. "Katie Kollwitz. It's really Kathe Kollwitz, but I settle for Katie."

He shook her hand. The ring she wore had a sharp edge.

"Wasn't there an artist named Kathe Kollwitz?" he said. "German or Swedish or something?"

"Oh yeah? I'm no relation. And no artist." She withdrew her hand.

"I'm . . ."

"You're André Derain, the magazine photographer, though I think you'll go down in history as the naked man of Burgundy Street."

"It was an ugly thing, this morning."

"You take pictures of ugly things—prostitutes, street people, freaks, dead bodies, right?"

"How do you know that?"

"Bartender told me. We were talking about you before you came in, about the stabbing."

Roybal had moved down to the other end of the bar.

"I'm interested in pictures like that," she said. "I like them. Garry Winogrand, WeeGee, Diane Arbus. Robert Mapplethorpe. Photographers like you."

"Mapplethorpe was nothing like me. He was a fraud. He took ugliness and used romantic lighting to make it seem beautiful. Cecil Beaton, at least, never pretended to be anything but a high-priced cosmetician. Mapplethorpe prettied up depravity and made it chic, even pictures of nude men trailing vacuum cleaner hoses out of their rectums, all rendered as pretty as a vase of flowers. All tricks. Disgusting tricks. I don't do tricks."

"Mapplethorpe's dead."

"His pictures aren't."

"You never glamorized things with your pictures?

"Fashion models. A few celebrities. No one with vacuum cleaner hoses. Anyway, I don't shoot that stuff anymore."

"What do you shoot?"

"Whatever's real. Whatever's around."

"I'd like to see your pictures. What you're doing now."

"I'm working on a book—a couple of books."

She leaned near, her chin on her hand. Her ring had a small, raised silver gargoyle on its crown. Her long earrings bore similar images. This was a bit much. It had been months since Mardi Gras.

"Books about what?"

"Picture books. One's to be of what I see on the street. Here in the Quarter. People, situations, moods, *le tout ensemble*. But everything real. Exactly as I find it. The other's about women—pictures of women."

"Nudes?"

He shrugged. "It's not a girlie book. They're women in the nude, but in repose. Relaxed. Themselves. Not like Helmut Newton nudes. No edge like that. More like Ernest Bellocq."

"I know about him, too. He took pictures of the whores in Storyville, a long time ago. There are some up there on the wall. Is that what you're trying to do, same thing as Bellocq? Using modern day women?"

"Not really. He was obsessed with the life of the cribs and sporting houses. I just shoot women as women. Some of them have been prostitutes, but I've used all kinds: fashion models, actresses, even society ladies. You can't tell any of that about them. In the nude, you can't tell the prostitutes from the socialites. They're all just women. Of course, a lot of Bellocq's whores could have passed for socialites, too. A few of them married really wealthy men."

"I'd really like to see those pictures."

Her gray eyes had been full on his, but now strayed. A man had come into the bar, and many in the room were looking at him.

He was dressed mostly in black—black suit, black tie, black shoes, black band on his Panama hat. He might have been an old-time southern preacher—except for the hat, and the dark glasses, and the incredible sheen of his highly polished shoes. He reminded Derain of a line from Auden's poem, "Richard Cory": "He glittered when he walked."

The man went to the other end of the bar, content to stand, keeping on his hat. Andy watched as Freddy poured him a double shot.

He looked back to the woman, and her long black dress.

"You two didn't just come from a funeral?"

"I never met that man, but I do go to funerals. I like them. They're good theater."

"Not much in the way of happy endings."

"People who go to funerals get to walk away alive. That's happy, isn't it?"

"I suppose."

"You haven't bought me a drink, sailor."

He looked to Freddy, trying to remember how high he'd run up his tab. "What will you have?"

"Actually, Mr. Derain, as I think about it, maybe I'd better call it a night." She picked up her purse, putting her cigarettes and lighter into it. He was startled by her change of mind.

"Sure?"

"Why don't you walk me home?"

She scared him a little. She intrigued him a lot. He was still very worried about Candice. This wouldn't help.

"Everyone will think I've picked you up."

"You never do that?"

"I have a girlfriend. We come here sometimes, when she's in town."

"You can tell her I wanted to sit for some of your pictures. Nothing more."

"I've already used that line today. I'm afraid I still have some work to do tonight. Print up some negatives."

"I'm not asking to go to your studio. I'm asking you to walk me home. I know it's supposed to be safe around here, but the streets are kinda dark, aren't they? I'd feel a lot better if I had someone with me. I haven't been in this part of the Quarter before, not this late at night. I'd appreciate a gentleman's company."

The word "gentleman" proved the hook. Conducting himself as that was all his now-dead mother had ever asked of him. He'd resented her obsession with this, but after her death, he tried, though he wasn't sure he always succeeded.

"All right."

As they went out the door, Andy glanced back. As he had sensed, the man in the black suit was watching them.

But so was nearly everyone else in the bar.

• • •

The night heat made the darkness soft and enveloping. There was lamplight in some of the windows they passed. Laughter from others that were in shadow, or had shades drawn. Life flowed in and out of all the buildings in the Quarter throughout the day and night. It wasn't like New York, where people fearfully walled themselves away from life on the street.

She took his arm, but didn't pull close. She walked with a slow, graceful step, though with a slight limp.

For the most part, she was silent, letting him talk on about the Quarter—how different it was from any other neighborhood in America, how he had spent so much of his youth in its streets and hangouts, despite the disapproval of his mother. His father's were "Old New Orleans" people who had lived for several generations in the aristocratic Garden District and viewed the Quarter as a kind of sewer. He'd moved to New York to get away from them, in the process succeeding as a photographer beyond his most extravagant ambitions, but always wishing he was back in these streets.

"What was wrong with New York?" she asked. "Too big? Too cold?"

"Mostly it was the people I had to work with. I don't mean the models. There are a lot of lovely people inside those lovely bodies, beneath all that beauty and hauteur. And, anyway, it was their job to be artificial. There's a certain honesty to that. But the others. Those goddamned rich people—women who'd squander two million dollars on a daughter's wedding or a husband's birthday, and then hold a charity ball to show how concerned they were about the 'less fortunate.' I began to rot away, slowly, from the inside out. After a while, there was nothing there. Nothing inside of me. I'd look in the mirror, and I wouldn't know who was there."

"And you're happy here?"

"Mademoiselle, I am Br'er Rabbit in the briar patch."

"This is where I live."

It was a shabby but not disreputable building a half block from the French Market.

"Do you want to come up?" she said. "I'll show you my pictures."

"Are you a photographer? You said you weren't an artist."

"I collect prints. Not photographs. Art."

Derain looked at his watch, realizing it was a rude thing to do.

"All right. Sure." He was still intrigued. He half wondered if her apartment was full of Nazi insignia, and whips and chains.

"I don't have any whiskey. Just vodka."

"I don't need anything."

The building had once been a commercial structure, but had since been converted into apartments. As they climbed up, he could smell Cajun cooking, and hear faint violin music—a bayou country song. Her apartment was on the top floor, at the front, and quite small, only two rooms. The smaller, though intended as a bedroom, she apparently used as a sort of office. He could see a desk and a computer and stacks of newspapers. The larger chamber, with a small kitchenette at one end, contained most of her furniture—a small wooden dining table, a couple of straight-backed chairs, a large, worn upholstered chair, a crowded bookcase, a coffee table covered with more newspapers. Dominating everything was her enormous bed, which she had pushed up against the two front windows. The bedcover was crimson, with black tassels, and black cushions were piled up in a jumble at the center. She'd left the windows open.

The switch she snapped on as they entered brought forth only the feeble light from a small lamp in the corner, and he could barely make out the clutter of objects scattered about the room, or the details of the framed prints that were hung close together on every wall.

Some were reproductions of famous works. He recognized one as Edvard Munch's chilling, primal *The Scream*. There was another of

Seurat's dark drawing of his elderly aunt sewing, as well as some macabre Francis Bacon and Dubuffet skull-like faces. Another, hanging deep in the room's shadows, was a print apparently made from an engraving—a large, muscular, naked, middle-aged woman, cradling a small naked boy who appeared to be dead. He vaguely recalled the work from somewhere, but the artist's name eluded him, though he was sure he knew it.

The rest of the apartment was slovenly, carelessly arranged, but these pictures were organized as thoughtfully as a museum curator might organize an exhibition.

Andy stood awkwardly, waiting for her to turn on more lights. Instead, she just sat on the edge of the bed, motioning him to the upholstered chair a few feet away.

She waited until he had settled into it.

"I have trouble having sex," she said. Her odd, plain voice was very matter-of-fact, as though she were talking about bus schedules. "I mean, there's not much in it for me. I was very sick for a while. I had a big operation. It saved my life, but it cost me. I used to like sex. I liked it a lot."

"I'm sorry."

She shrugged, her hands moving to the back of her neck. He heard a zipper.

"I still like to take off my clothes, in front of men. I like to be with men without my clothes, though I don't usually do anything. Do you mind?"

"I won't be shocked."

"I guess you won't."

"I'm a little curious."

"Guess you'd be that, too."

The front of her dress came forward, falling to her waist, revealing low, well-formed breasts and a white flat belly with a large mole. She slipped off her shoes, then reached behind her waist. He heard the zipper again. She pulled the dress out from beneath her. Once it was clear of her legs, she set it gently on the floor, then lay back, leaning on one elbow. Bellocq had taken a photograph much like the image she now offered.

"You don't mind?" she said, more slowly.

"I'm flattered. You're very beautiful without clothing."

She had bandages around both her arms at the elbows. She caught him staring at them.

"I only have one kidney," she said. "Sometimes I have trouble with it, and have to have dialysis."

"It sounds serious."

She ignored this. "Would you like to take my picture?"

"Yes."

"I have a camera."

"Not now. I can't stay long. I really do have work to do."

"You ever been married?"

"No. Almost. I had a girlfriend for a very long time, but she married someone else."

"No one ever marries the one they should."

"Sometimes they do."

"I didn't."

"I'm sorry. Are you still married?"

"He's dead."

"I'm sorry."

"You just said that. Would you take my picture some other time? I'd like that. Very much."

"All right."

"Promise?"

"Yes."

"In your studio?"

"Maybe. Sure."

A dark, bounding blur moving across the floor caught Andy's attention. By the time he turned his head, it had vanished through the doorway into the smaller room. Whatever it was, it had come from the kitchenette.

"Do you have a cat?"

"It's not a cat."

"A little dog?" The creature was so quiet.

"It's a pet. It won't bother you. It won't come out again until you're gone."

The light from the little lamp caught her lower legs where they dangled over the edge of the bed. There was a long, ragged scar on her left thigh, and something on her right ankle—a dark design, probably a tattoo. He leaned a little closer, squinting slightly.

It was a gargoyle, almost identical to the one on her ring. She noticed him looking at it and lifted her leg slightly, as though to give him a better view.

"You like that?" she asked.

"Most women who have tattoos have them on their thighs or arms or . . ."

"You know women with tattoos, Mr. Derain? Aside from me?"

"Probably a dozen right here in the Quarter, including one who has great big eyes tattooed on both her cheeks."

"You mean on her ass?"

"No. On her face."

"I don't like to have marks, things, on my face."

"Your ankle is very pretty. It's as pretty an ankle as your face is a beautiful face."

She lifted her leg, studying the tattoo—in innocent fashion, exposing herself as she did so.

"On my ankle, I can always look down and see it."

"You have a thing for gargoyles?"

"I also like bones. I have a necklace, made of human bones. There's a store in L.A. that sells them. On Melrose. Do you know it?"

He shook his head. "Why all this interest in death?"

"I have to live with death. I learned to like it."

"Live with death?"

"I told you. I was sick."

She turned slightly toward the light and he saw more scars. One was neat, surgical, running from her navel to her pubic hair. There was another, smaller one, also neat, extending horizontally to either side of the first. Near their intersection were a few small circular scars—very faint.

"It gives you a kind of power," she said.

"What does?"

"When you're no longer afraid of death. When you learn to live with it."

She lay back, putting her hands beneath her head, spreading her legs slightly but crossing her ankles—Goya's *The Naked Maja*. Her gray eyes were so luminous in that pale light they distracted from the soft beauty of her body, from the sexual allure of her pose.

"Did you ever work as a model?" he asked.

"Yes. Thought you'd figure that out. Photographer's model. Print. Store catalogues mostly. Cheap stuff. I didn't like it much. I didn't make a lot of money, but it got me out of Missouri."

"To where?"

"To Chicago, Atlanta, L.A., Texas. Around. I was in television for a while, too. In L.A. Did some local commercials. Even worked for a while as a TV news reporter. It's not hard."

"And now?"

"I'm in public relations. For now. Someday—maybe someday soon—I want to go to Charleston. I don't know what I'll do there. What do you do in Charleston?"

"Worship ancestors. Sell antiques. Guide tours. Why do you want to go to Charleston?"

"I was there once. I liked it. It kinda excited me."

"If you like excitement, why leave here? I never thought of Charleston as exciting. Savannah's better. It's Charleston with sin."

"I'm getting tired of sin, and I didn't come here planning to stay forever. I want to end up in Charleston. It has those old houses, all those ghosts. You feel like you're traveling through the centuries, walking around those streets at night. I like that. I told you. It excites me."

He felt uncomfortable, almost creepy. He changed the subject.

"Not a healthy industry in this recession. Public relations."

"I do political work. That's always a healthy industry."

"Is that why you were in Long Tom's? It's kind of a political hangout."

"No. I went there off-duty."

"You work for one of the state legislators? Someone on the City Council?"

"Mr. Derain. I work for Senator Henry Boone, here in his New Orleans office."

He sat up straight in his chair. The gargoyles, the macabre prints, suddenly seemed to make more sense—though he wished they didn't.

He looked at his watch again. "I really have to go. A lot of darkroom work to do yet."

"Do you want to sleep with me, Mr. Derain? It's all right. It won't cause me any discomfort. It's been bothering me a little, you just sitting there, talking, like we were having tea or something."

She spread her legs more widely apart, arching her back slightly. He didn't stir.

"What do you do when you make love to a man?" he asked.

"What do I do? You mean, what little tricks do I know?"

She smiled. He didn't.

"No," he said. "What do you do for yourself?"

"If I'm feeling bad, or if I like the man a lot and want to make it better for him, I get a little drunk, and maybe I'll do some coke. I find my jolt. I find something."

Her eyes never moved from him. They were like a cat's in the darkness.

"You don't want to," she said.

"That doesn't adequately describe the complicated way I feel at the moment," he said.

"You've known a lot of beautiful women. Do you think I'm beautiful?"

"Yes."

"How beautiful?"

"Purely beautiful. Beautiful without embellishment."

"It doesn't last very long, you know. You have it, and then you don't, and you wonder why God bothered."

"It's lasted a long time with you."

She smiled. "I'm glad you feel complicated. I want to see you again."

He stood up. "Sure. Sometime."

"I mean it."

"I'm in the Razzy Dazzy a lot."

"Tomorrow night?"

He shrugged. "Probably. Does Tom Calhoun know you work for Boone?"

"I don't know, does he? What fucking difference does it make? He's got one of Hank's posters on his wall."

"Boone's a dangerous man."

"You're all dangerous."

She got up from the bed and came to him, moving with the same eerie quietness as had whatever creature it was that had bounded into her other room. Her eyes remained fixed on his, still expressing only curiosity.

Then suddenly her arms were tightly around him, her long nails digging into his jacket, her body close against him from chest to legs. Her lips came up to his, parting. He was enveloped in dizzying warmth.

In another instant, she broke away. Walking slowly, she went to the center of the room, and stood turned away from him, waiting, for him to go.

"Good night, Mr. Derain."

She was still looking away as he closed the door.

He descended the stairs slowly, stepping softly and listening ahead, as he had long ago learned always to do in the Quarter at this hour. Nothing. No one.

Outside, he looked up to her windows. They were opaque with darkness, the lamp light almost indiscernible, but he could imagine her face, her cat's eyes, hovering there, just within.

His feelings weren't complicated now. He wanted to go back up there, to feel that woman's warm body against his own naked flesh, to test the truth of her story, to find out if a kiss that passionate could come from a woman who could no longer know pleasure.

This was what she wanted him to do. He wasn't sure why. He realized he didn't want to know why. Not this troublesome night.

Walking quickly now, his rubber-soled boat shoes making little noise, he headed across the Quarter. Nearing Dauphine Street, he passed a man sitting cross-legged in a doorway, a man in dark clothes with a half-gallon jug of wine in his lap, well fixed for the night.

"I know you," the man said. "I know you, man."

"Evening," Derain said, and kept on.

"Satan's coming. Coming soon. To a theater near you."

Andy stopped. What was the man, a failed movie critic?

"I thought he lived here."

"He's coming for you, man."

The wretched fellow lifted his wine jug. His sleeves were torn at the elbows. Derain had never seen him before, or at least, had never noticed him.

Andy moved on quickly. At the corner, he suddenly stopped and spun around. While he'd been talking to the vagrant with the jug, he'd had a sense of movement down the street. He looked back down the sidewalk now.

The man he'd seen was nearly a block distant, but was unmistakable—Panama hat, black suit—the same strange fellow he'd seen in the Razzy Dazzy.

Andy moved faster now, heading along Dauphine toward Canal, then quickly darting into a narrow passageway, easing back behind a wooden gallery post as he waited for the man in the black suit to pass.

He never did. When Derain came quietly out to the street again, it was empty. A beaten-up old cab drove by, its roof light illuminated. A hooker leaning against a post looked at him and yawned. Nothing else. No one else.

When he finally reached his house, he realized he'd once again forgotten to lock the gate to the courtyard, as Bleusette had requested. She worried too much. Even if Ferrier did have his address in his pocket, the creep couldn't do anything about it now.

Once inside his own place, Andy set to work in his darkroom. He'd used up only four rolls of film that day, three at the movie shoot and one at the murder scene in his courtyard. He got out his print paper, set up his chemical trays, and turned on his enlarger projector. He was tired, almost groggy, but the work went smoothly enough, the images appearing quickly as the exposed print papers settled into the chemical baths. He'd not bothered with contact prints, and was making an eight by ten of every frame. He'd present Cooper with a large stack of stills—the quantity of work to compensate for his tardiness that day.

His close-ups of the dead man interested him. He examined each as he hung it up to dry, promising himself to take time to study the prints more thoughtfully in the morning; already sure he'd find at least one worthy of his book.

The movie shots he checked only for focus and possible imperfections. As he lifted one to the drying line, a detail in the background caught his eye. The picture was one of those he'd snapped of the local spectators peeping out among the parked trailers, this one of the two teenage girls in short skirts and halter tops who had posed as provocatively as their youthful awkwardness would permit. Delighted with the girls, he hadn't paid much attention to the rest of the shot, including the three or four people on the sidewalk in the background.

But by some tall bushes, only partially visible, was a male figure. Derain snatched up a magnifying glass and peered more closely. There he was again—black suit, black tie, sunglasses, and Panama hat.

Derain backed away from the print, all the way to his old leather couch. He sat down slowly, elbows on knees, head hanging wearily.

He felt numb, stupefied by the inexplicability of his discovery. If all the fiends of Hell wanted to visit the Quarter, they were perfectly welcome as far as he was concerned. But he didn't want them in his favorite bar, or on his heels on the late-night streets. He didn't want them uninvited in his pictures. Satan, indeed. Who was that guy?

Gently, he rubbed his eyes. All he wanted to do now was go to sleep. He moved over to the small lamp table where he kept his phone and turned on the playback of his answering machine. It gave him back nothing, only a hum.

Where was Candice? What the hell had happened to her? He was angry at himself for not waiting for her to call.

She had implored him to get rid of the nudes. He could at least do that for her before going to bed. Andy had no intention of destroying them, but he could find a safer place to keep them. Paul Maljeux often locked things up for him, no questions asked, in the fireproof file cabinet in his office.

The big picture of Candice would have to be taken out of its frame and rolled up. With great effort, Andy pushed himself to his feet and went to where he had left it.

Nothing touched his fingers. He got down on one knee and looked. The space behind the cabinet was empty.

Perhaps he'd misremembered, or moved it without thinking. He looked behind all his cabinets.

Nothing.

With some apprehension, he went to the big trunk where he kept the negatives and prints of his favorite work, a collection that included a lot of his most intimate and discreet pictures, among them the ones he'd taken, using a shutter delay, of himself and Candice, entwined and joyously naked on this very couch.

The trunk was locked, as he always kept it. The file was there, as always. But the folder was empty.

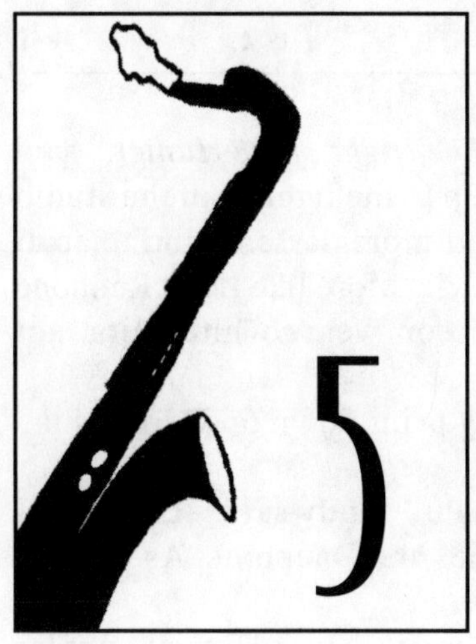

Andy awoke to someone shaking his shoulder. He'd been having an erotic dream, a dream about Katie Kollwitz. But when he opened his eyes, he found himself looking up into Bleusette's face, her hair falling slightly over her jewel-like dark eyes.

"I am sorry, Andy. You didn't answer the bell. Maybe it is broken. Maljeux is here. I let him in."

Andy sat up. Bleusette was in some of her working clothes—short black skirt and low-cut white designer blouse.

He yawned. "Thanks, I guess."

He was naked. She looked down at his body. He grinned, embarrassed, and got up, reaching for his shorts.

"You forgot to lock the gate last night," she said.

"Sorry. I don't think it's anything to worry about."

It was a silly thing to say. He'd gone to sleep thinking unhappily about the man in the black suit—and his missing pictures. He decided not to tell Bleusette about that.

"Tell Paul I'll be right down."

The lieutenant was waiting in the studio, looking at the prints of the stills Andy had shot at the movie location the previous day. Andy handed him the one with the man in the black suit visible behind the two teenage girls, then set about making coffee—double-strength, New Orleans style.

"I want you to look at that," Andy said of the print. "That guy's been following me."

"He looks like Robert Mitchum in *The Night of the Hunter,*" said Maljeux, holding Andy's photograph up to the light from the studio window, "only this fellow has a little more style. I don't recall Mitchum wearing sunglasses in that movie. More like Leon Redbone maybe, except no moustache. And Leon wears white suits, not black."

The police lieutenant set the glossy print down on Derain's lab table.

"He was in the Razzy Dazzy last night," Andy said. "Later on, I caught him following me, near Ursulines and Dauphine. As you can see, he was at the movie set, too."

"The Quarter's a small place, Andy, and the Razzy Dazzy's not far from Dauphine and Ursulines. He may be living around here, or staying near here. Sometimes I bump into the same people a dozen times a day. Like you, for instance."

"The movie shoot yesterday was way over in the Garden District."

"You say you never saw him before? He bears no resemblance to that guy with a knife?"

Derain shook his head. "I wouldn't think all that much about it, Paul, except that someone broke in here last night. Took some things."

"When did this happen?"

"After midnight. While I was out."

"What did they take? Cameras? Lab equipment?"

"No. Only some pictures."

Maljeux looked around at some of the prints on the wall, settling on Derain's big framed nude of Paris Moran.

"Which pictures?"

"I'm not entirely sure. I've got hundreds of prints and a couple thousand negatives in here. But some of the nudes are missing."

"Seems to me that if someone in the Quarter had a yen for pictures of naked ladies, he sure as hell wouldn't need to commit felony burglary to get a hold of some. There are ladies on these streets who'll show a man anything he wants to see for two dollars. If I was to steal something from here, I'd probably go for this real sexy picture of the movie star. Was the picture of someone this pretty, Andy? Maybe prettier, like your model friend from Texas?"

"Yes. A couple of the shots were of both of us. Delayed shutter."

"*Au naturel?*"

"Yes."

"And you say she's got a rich husband?"

"Yes."

"Well, sounds like you got a shit pot full of trouble on your hands, Andy."

"That's why I'm worried about the man in the black suit."

"Like he could be a PI, doing a little research on a pending divorce suit?"

Andy shrugged.

Maljeux paused to think a moment. "I've got no real grounds to pick up that fellow, but we can check him out. My big concern right now though is still the late Albert."

"I asked around about him last night. A friend of mine said he heard that Ferrier was shaking down someone, and that he had been boasting that he was going to kill somebody."

"Well, he sure done the job ass-backward. Which friend of yours was this?"

"Doesn't matter. Someone who picks up talk from the street."

"Ought to get yourself a better class of friends, Andy. Did you get to talk to that Texas gal of yours?"

"Briefly."

"She say anything helpful?"

"She said she heard Ferrier say something before he died. The word 'Doom.' Or something that sounded like that. Maybe a name."

"Like 'Doone'?"

"Maybe Boone."

"Boone?"

"There's a Henry Boone."

"The senator?"

Derain shrugged again.

"Andy, if you're suggesting Albert used his last breath to tell you how to vote, maybe you ought to go on the wagon for a while. Anyway, Boone thinks about as highly of homosexuals as he does of black people. He wouldn't have any truck with someone like the late Albert."

"Paul, what should I do? That guy in black is spooking me."

"Well, common sense might suggest cuttin' loose from that Texas gal, and maybe moving out of town for a while."

"I don't want to do either of those things."

"Suit yourself, friend. Meantime, I've got to keep on after this homicide. I'm on my way over to Faubourg Marigny to have another chat with the late Albert's lady friend. I'd like you to come with me. Won't take long. You're a photographer. You might notice something."

"Like what?"

"Who knows? Maybe she'll be wearing a Henry Boone campaign button."

• • •

There was another photographer besides Bellocq famed in New Orleans and admired in the greater world beyond—Clarence John Laughlin. What Bellocq had been to the city's whores, Laughlin had been to its grand old decaying houses. Bellocq's pictures were of naked and near-nude prostitutes at winsome leisure. Laughlin's lens pondered shattered panes and tattered, fluttering curtains, cracked tile and crumbling marble, weathered columns and peeling walls and debris-strewn mansion halls. Sometimes he peopled his black-and-white pictures with silent, mysterious figures, but even without them, one sensed a haunting presence in every image. If not something like a soul, at least spirits. One published collection of his pictures was entitled *Ghosts Along the Mississippi*.

The house in Faubourg Marigny that Derain and Maljeux drove to in the lieutenant's police cruiser could have been in that Laughlin collection. Though wedged tightly between its sagging neighbors, the house was wide and fronted with an ornate French gallery. Set back from the street far enough to accommodate a cypress tree and a patch of grass, it rose three stories. The once-white paint was peeling and green with mold. The flagstones of the walk were broken and the wrought-iron gate hung rusting on its hinges. It was the very picture of the fallen but still expensive grandeur for which Laughlin was so celebrated. It struck both Maljeux and Derain as extremely curious that a hustling fancy girl could afford it.

Her name, Maljeux had been told, was Danielle Jones. She was in her late twenties, lighter-skinned even than Long Tom Calhoun, with long, straight hair and very large brown eyes she heavily embellished with mascara. She answered the door wearing a dressing gown and spoke to them in a low but softly feminine voice.

"Remember me, Miss Jones? Lieutenant Maljeux."

"I've nothing more to say to you gentlemen. I answered all your questions yesterday." She gave Derain an odd look.

"Well, I've got some new ones," Maljeux said, pushing past her. She reluctantly stepped back. With equal reluctance, Andy followed Maljeux inside. The lieutenant said nothing about a warrant.

They were in a richly furnished and well-draped foyer that led to a large hall and a wide, curving staircase. In a sunny room beyond, Andy could see a large painting above a white fireplace—nymphs around a sylvan pool.

She invited them no further.

"All this stuff yours, Miss Jones?" Maljeux asked.

The young woman held her hands together at her waist. She lowered her eyelids slightly as she spoke.

"The house came furnished. I added some pieces of my own."

"The rent's a little dear, isn't it? Three thousand a month, right? We checked. How do you afford that, Miss Jones?"

"I earn my money."

"How?"

"I model."

"Model? In fashion shows?"

"I model privately. For private customers."

"For pictures?"

"Sometimes. On other occasions, I participate in *tableaux vivants*."

"What's that?"

"Recreations of famous paintings. Historical scenes. Sketches of our own devise. We pose."

"Like actors, then."

"No. Models."

Andy was looking at an antique chair upholstered with gold thread.

"Is that French?" he asked.

"I don't know," said the woman, irritated at the digression. "I suppose it is."

"Was Albert Ferrier a model, too?" Maljeux asked.

"Certainly not. Albert was a street criminal."

"How did you come to make his acquaintance?"

"I'm from Mississippi. So was he."

"Pascagoula?"

"Yes."

"You were friends there?"

"Yes."

"A very nice place you have here, Miss Jones. A handsome house, indeed."

"Thank you."

"Now, you told us yesterday that Albert Ferrier was an occasional visitor. Your neighbors say he used to come over here all the time."

"My neighbors, whoever they are, don't know what they're talking about. A lot of people in New Orleans look like Albert."

"Well, that's a fact, sure enough. Are you telling me you have a lot of people, who look like Albert Ferrier, over here a lot of the time?"

"I entertain."

The woman's eyes were flitting back and forth between Maljeux and Derain.

"Was Ferrier here night before last?"

"Surely not."

"You have any idea why he got killed?"

"He was a criminal. Criminals get killed."

"He sold cocaine. And little boys. Sometimes girls."

Miss Jones shrugged. "He used to be my friend. He did me some favors, looked out for me. When he was hard up, he'd come around and I'd help him out. Loan him money. Give him something to eat. I am loyal to a fault, Lieutenant Maljeux." She was staring at Derain. "Who is this man?"

"Why, this is André Derain, the famous photographer. He's a witness in this case. Mr. Ferrier expired in his courtyard. Now, you sure Albert wasn't living here with you, up until a couple of months ago?"

"No."

"Who pays the rent on this place, Miss Jones?"

"I pay the rent."

"In cash."

"Yes, in cash. Which I earn. As a model." She retreated a step. "I sleep during the day, lieutenant. It's not yet noon and I'm very tired. Do you have any more questions?"

Maljeux studied her a moment. "Albert Ferrier may have called out Henry Boone's name just before he kicked. Does that surprise you?

It certainly startled her. "Henry Boone, the senator? That racist?"

"Yes."

"Don't know anything about that."

"Okay, Miss Jones. Thanks for your time. We'll probably be back. Soon as I think up some more questions."

She stepped back further. "I've nothing more to tell you, but suit yourself."

• • •

Faubourg Marigny lay just across Esplanade Street from the French Quarter. Heading back toward the station, Maljeux drove the big police cruiser slowly along North Peters Street beside the river, past Elysian Fields Avenue, Esplanade, and then the French Market. Andy turned to look for Katie Kollwitz's building, catching just a glimpse of its dark brown facade. He wondered if she was still asleep. He checked his watch. She might be at work, at Henry Boone's office.

"So what do you think, Andy?"

"I met a lot of people like Danielle Jones in New York—kept women. Including the married ones. Especially the married women. The worst whores I ever met in my life were those New York women who'd married for money. Danielle is just weirder."

"I'd like to know who the sugar daddy is."

"What?"

"Danielle Jones's patron. Whoever is paying for that *maison elegante*. It strikes me that young Danielle may have been stepping out on the side with her old pal Albert, and sugar daddy found out. Had Albert done. Wouldn't be the first time."

"Shouldn't be that hard to find out, should it—who's paying the bills? It's got to be someone with a few dollars. That was an eighteenth-century chair. French, not colonial. She didn't know it from Sears Roebuck."

"The neighbors say there were other visitors, but the only one they remember well is the late Albert, because he used to come around during the day. The others were night folk. Very secretive. You suppose Bleusette knows something about this lady?"

"Bleusette knows something about everyone. I'll ask. Why don't you have the house put under surveillance?"

"Already decided to do just that."

"How old do you suppose she is, this Miss Jones?"

Maljeux shrugged. "Late twenties. Hard to tell with all that make-up."

They had turned up Dumaine Street. There was a house with a green door on the right. The door had latticed panels, and one of them was missing. Through the opening, Derain could see a woman's leg, a black woman's leg.

"Stop, Paul."

"What?"

"Stop! There's a picture."

Maljeux hit the brakes. Andy pulled a camera from his bag and leapt out. "Be right back."

He set his exposure on the run, crouched behind a parked car, adjusting the focus as he slowly rose. It was a quick shot. A moment later, the woman moved and the leg disappeared. He'd been just in time for what he knew would be a fantastic photograph. Once again, he felt very right about coming back to New Orleans.

"Thanks, Paul. All the years I've been here and I never had such a shot."

"We're here to serve," Maljeux said, putting the car in motion. "What did you get, a doorway?"

"More than that. A woman's leg."

"Just the leg? You usually go for *le tout ensemble*."

"It was a winner. You can come to my next one-man show."

"You can come over to One-Legged Duffy's tonight, speaking of legs. I'm playing. Loomis asked me to sit in for a couple of sets."

"A pleasure. I'm feeling happy again. That's probably dangerous."

Maljeux pulled up at the corner by Andy's place. "I make you late for work?"

"Not much. I'll take my car today, if I can get it to start. Find out about the man in black for me."

"Sure."

"It's a bit much, isn't it? Wearing all black. Like a costume." He wasn't thinking so much about the man in the Panama as he was about Katie Kollwitz, lady of the gargoyles.

"Most everybody wears whatever they want here, Andy. Hell, there you were on the street wearing nothing."

"You're never going to let me forget that, are you?"

"Come on, Andy. You're a local legend now. You want to fill out a report on your burglary? I can send some evidence technicians over to look for fingerprints."

"Somehow I don't think they'd find any."

"Well, you may hear about those missing pictures. And not from us."

"I'm afraid you're right."

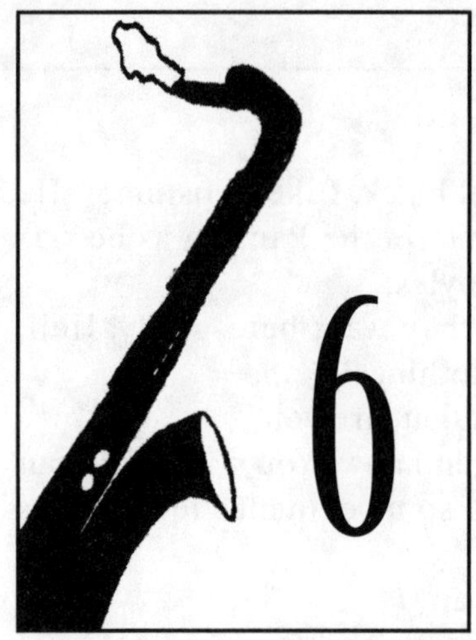

Andy stopped at his house long enough to change into more suitable clothing than the shorts and decrepit shirt he'd thrown on upon rising, and also to check his answering machine. There was no call from Candice. The only message was from the production manager at the movie shoot. They were doing the drive away sequence at the Garden District location all over again. Where the hell was he?

In a few minutes, he was in his old Cadillac. To his amazement, it started after only four weak turns of the engine, sending forth a billow of oily smoke from the exhaust. Andy waited until he was sure all eight cylinders were firing, then put down the top and lurched out into the traffic.

• • •

The movie crew had acquired a new Mercedes. The color was a slightly lighter shade of gray than the one they had damaged, and, instead of overcast, they had bright sunlight, so much of the sequence had to be reshot. James Ball was suffering from a terrible hangover, and the ingenue Emily Shaw had a case of nerves that made her previous day's behavior seem placid. Director Cooper was speaking quietly, in a low monotone, but it was obvious that wouldn't last. You could sense the early rumblings of the volcano.

Paris Moran was wearing dark glasses against the sunshine, but otherwise showed little sign of her solitary toot, if she'd actually gone through with it. Lighting a cigarette, she came over to Andy, putting her arm around his waist, then removing it to look through the stills he'd brought with him.

"I look old," she said, studying one, "even in your pictures."

"Not at all."

"Old, Andy. It's horror movies for me next."

"Your beauty is in full blossom, Paris. You could play Juliet."

"Not Juliet, Lady Macbeth, maybe. Or one of the witches. That's how I feel today, anyway. You know what was wrong with the car yesterday? A fitting on the brake line was loose. Almost completely off. Every time one of us hit the brakes, fluid shot out. By the time they got the car to a garage, the brake system was bone dry. Remember what I said about the chase scene? I could have gone into the river."

"Do they think someone tampered with it?"

"Maybe it was some well-meaning person who just wants to spare us the fate that awaits us from the film critics."

"Places everyone!"

Ball's detective character was supposed to look troubled, faced with a life-altering decision he didn't want to make. Ball's hangover helped, but Emily's nervousness didn't. She stumbled coming out the door of the house, almost taking a fall down the porch stairs.

"Cut! Goddamn you, Emily! Can't you even open a fucking door?"

Andy got off several close-ups of the girl as she cringed before Cooper's bellowing assault. She had a fresh, lovely, delicate face; shampoo-ad, burnished copper–colored hair, green eyes, wide cheek bones, perfect English features. Distraught, she had the look of a medieval martyr condemned to the flames.

Paris went up to Cooper, whispered something, then took Emily by the arm and led her over to her trailer. They remained inside perhaps five minutes. When they emerged, Emily's face was a little flushed. Andy suspected Paris had administered a calming dose of gin or vodka. Maybe two doses.

With the help of this tonic, Emily got through the scene rather handily, delivering her lines with far more spirit than Ball, who seemed to want to lie down on the lawn and go to sleep. Because of Ball now, Cooper kept reshooting the scene. After four takes, he finally went up to the actor, looked him carefully in the eye, and then kicked him hard in the shin. The actor's yelp was so loud it startled some of the spectators. Ball, at least, was now sufficiently alert for the next take.

Andy wouldn't be needed until they set up the drive-off shot. He drifted away. Remembering the two teenaged girls, he took the two copies he'd made of their sexy little pose from his camera bag, and then went out among the spectators in search of them.

It may have been too early in the day for them, or perhaps they'd become disenchanted with the laboriously slow process of moviemaking. Perhaps they'd just left in disgust after witnessing the wimpy way screen idol James Ball took the kick in his shin. But they weren't in evidence.

The company's trailers were taking up both sides of the street. Derain went along the near sidewalk looking for the girls, then crossed to the other side and worked his way back. He halted just short of the house with the high bushes.

There the bastard was again—black suit, black tie, dark glasses, same spotless Panama hat with the wide black band. His shoes looked as though he'd spent the night polishing them. The man was smoking a small, thin cigar. He paid no attention to Andy until he came and stood directly in front of him.

"Good morning," Andy said.

"Morning." The man had a voice as deep as Leon Redbone's, which was remarkable. Paris referred to Redbone as "that guy with four balls."

Andy held up one of his photos. "You haven't by any chance seen these young ladies this morning?" He intended it as an idle question.

The man glanced at the picture, without moving his head. He took a deep drag of his little cigar, afterward enveloping them both in its pungent smoke.

"Jail bait," he said.

Andy tried to assess his accent. It was broad and southern, certainly not New Orleans.

"What are you doing here?" Andy asked, stepping a little closer.

The man didn't budge. "Watching."

"This is a closed set."

"Hell it is."

"Do you want something from me? Or did you already take it?"

The head still didn't move. The eyes remained hidden behind the dark lenses. "Don't know you, friend."

"You weren't in my place last night? Browsing among my pictures?"

No response. The hand brought the cigar to thin lips. Another hanging cloud of smoke.

"Are you working for Ben Browley?"

Again no words. Andy felt like he was jabbering to some statue. He was so frustrated and angry he had an impulse to punch the man, right in those dark glasses. But fear restrained him. There was more than a touch of menace in the man's voice. He might have a gun. Or a knife. He might be one of those fabled people who could kill with a few quick blows of his hands.

An idea struck Andy. He stepped back, swung up his camera, and began shooting. Extreme close-ups. One after another. The rewind motor whining and grinding.

It worked. The man abruptly turned and began walking away, toward St. Charles Avenue.

"Andy! Get over here! We're ready for the shoot!"

Andy hurried back across the street in response to the assistant director's summons. Paris was in the Mercedes, smoking a cigarette. Cooper must have liked the touch. In 1950s movies, even Grace Kelly smoked. In modern-day films, smoking implied toughness, an inclination to sin.

Cooper had approved the cameraman's setup of the shot. His assistant was motioning the actors to their marks. The injured stuntwoman was still in the hospital, and they'd not replaced her. Cooper was insisting that Emily do her own fall. No wonder she was so nervous.

The director was doing everything in exact sequence. They did a medium shot of Paris waiting impatiently behind the wheel, then a cutaway to Ball walking toward the car, then a cutaway to a close-up of Emily watching him go. She shouted the detective character's name.

"Cut! One more time."

Andy moved off to the side to shoot the reprise. The first take had seemed perfect. After the next attempt, Cooper had Paris pull the car back a foot or two to eliminate some sun glare on the windshield. Then another take. Then another.

"Alan!" Paris said. "One more minute out here and this dress is going to be soaked through with sweat!"

Cooper threw up his hands. "All right, goddamn it, let's do the drive off!"

Cosette went to work repairing Paris's makeup while they shifted the camera to line up with the rear of the Mercedes. As Paris and Ball drove off, Emily was to run into the frame and then follow after the car, stumbling and falling. She practiced it twice on the lawn, without flinching. Paris must have given her a couple of really stiff belts.

"Places everyone!"

With the cue for action, Paris accelerated the Mercedes slowly but smoothly, watching the rearview mirror to keep the convertible in the shot. Emily ran out as directed, shouting the cop character's name. She followed her marks perfectly, and, at exactly the right spot, deliberately caught her right foot behind the heel of the left and took her tumble.

It was magnificent, and violent. She hit the ground on her knees and rolled, her robe flying open, exposing beautiful long legs and panties. She began crying. She pulled herself up to a sitting position, still sobbing.

"Cut!"

"It was beautiful, Alan," said the assistant director. Paris had stopped the Mercedes. Very slowly, she backed up, fully expecting another go.

Emily's shoulders were shaking. As no one else was moving, Andy went up to her and helped her to her feet. Both her knees were bloody.

He glared at Cooper, putting his arm around the girl. She turned to him, pressing her head against his shoulder. He could feel the wetness of her tears.

"It's a wrap!" said Cooper, amazing everyone. He motioned his assistants over to join him by his chair.

"Are you all right?" Andy said to Emily. A stupid question.

"No."

The first aid man came up, pulling Emily aside. He parted her robe, peering at her knees, then opened his kit.

"Not so bad," he said. "You'll be fine by tomorrow."

"It hurts like hell," she said.

"You're a game girl," the first-aid man said. He began daubing antiseptic on her abrasions, which were extensive. Andy was surprised that she didn't cry out.

The assistant director joined them, beaming. "Alan's very happy," he said. He looked to Andy. "Did you get that?"

"Yes. Every disgusting bit."

"Lighten up, Derain. We're making a movie. Emily, honey, you have the rest of the day off." He consulted his clipboard. "In fact, your next call's not till Friday morning. Five-thirty A.M. We're going to do chase stuff and shoot-'em-ups next two days."

"What about me?" Andy asked.

"Alan wants to work on the script this afternoon. Don't need you until tomorrow."

"That suits me fine."

• • •

Paris had script-change approval in her contract, and so elected to remain behind with Cooper to prevent him from attempting what she might consider outrageous rewrites. With Paris's encouragement, Andy asked Emily if he should take her home. To his surprise, she suggested lunch.

She went to her trailer to change, emerging in matching beige skirt and sleeveless blouse and sandals, both knees now bandaged. Her eyes were still a little frantic, but otherwise she was fairly calm—as though she had crossed a threshold, and the worst was over.

She eyed Andy's rusty old Cadillac suspiciously, but got in, wincing as she settled onto the cracked leather seat.

"Paris says you're a nice guy," she said.

"Try to be. Never steal candy from little children."

"I hope so. You'll be the first nice guy I've met in this town."

"New Orleans is full of nice people. Just not too many of them working for Alan Cooper."

"Aren't you?"

"Only because I need the money."

She smiled, the first he had seen from her. "Where are you taking me?"

"You feel like a noisy, crowded tourist joint?"

"Not particularly."

"Good. I've got a better idea. We'll have lunch with a lovely lady."

"Your wife?"

"No wife. My Auntie Claire."

"Where does she live?"

"Not far. In my house."

"You live with your aunt?"

"No. I don't live there anymore."

• • •

Andy had been well established in New York when his parents had died, one shortly after the other. Returning for the last funeral, he'd turned the big Garden District house where he'd grown up over to his father's elder sister, not giving the place another thought. It was in the same state of genteel decay as the Faubourg Marigny house Danielle Jones inhabited, though far from as richly furnished. It suited his Auntie Claire perfectly, however. Nearing seventy, she was a southern lady in the old New Orleans tradition, very feminine, very old-fashioned, extremely mannered, and slightly daft. She had more than a dozen cats, though she never seemed to pay them any attention.

She was delighted to see them, though Andy had pulled up in the narrow little driveway without giving her any notice of their coming. He tried to visit Claire regularly, usually on Sundays, but hadn't been by in nearly a month.

"André! I was wondering when I'd see you again. What a pretty young lady. She looks like a flower."

Claire gave him kisses on both cheeks. She was dressed in a very girlish floral print dress, along with a flowered picture hat and white gloves—as though she was about to leave for a garden party. She almost always wore such clothes.

Emily received a kiss on the cheek also.

"Is this your fiancée? Candice?"

"No, Auntie. Candice is not my fiancée, and this is not Candice. This is Miss Emily Shaw, a friend."

"Shaw? Are you one of the Mississippi Shaws? From Jackson?"

"I'm from California."

"Are there Shaws in California?"

"Miss Shaw is an actress. She's with the movie company I'm working for."

"That's very nice. I have to go out now, but you take Miss Shaw out onto the north gallery. It's cool and shady there. I'll have Zinny bring some lemonade and sandwiches."

Zinnia was Aunt Claire's housekeeper. She had come with the house, having worked for Andy's parents since he was a boy.

"Have her bring your medicine chest, too, Auntie. Miss Shaw's had a fall. Her knees need attending to."

He led Emily through a musty drawing room out onto a long, screened-in porch. It overlooked the house's rather unkempt garden, and caught what breeze there was. Setting the girl in a wicker chair, Andy drew up another, and invited her to prop her legs upon it.

"Zinny took care of just about every cut and bruise I ever came home with in childhood," he said. "You'll be in good hands."

Emily smiled. As he expected, she was calming down in these quiet, friendly, relaxed surroundings.

He knelt in front of her, and gently lifted her skirt. "Do you mind?"

"I trust you, I guess."

"Don't guess. You can." He took hold of the bandage the first-aid man had stuck slipshod on her right knee, and yanked. She yelped.

"You said I could trust you."

"Sorry." He got the other off less painfully.

"They look worse than I thought," he said. "I should get you to a doctor."

"No, I'm fine, really."

"If we had a doctor look at you, you could sue Cooper. You ought to. There was no reason for this to happen to you. The guy is a lunatic."

"It's my own fault. I don't want to get him any madder at me."

"Why not? Personally, I'd punch him out."

Zinnia, an elderly black woman with enormous hips, came through the doorway with a pitcher, two glasses, and a plate of small sandwiches. She set them down on a glass-top table, then bent over to look at Emily's injuries.

"What you done to this girl, Andy?"

"Wasn't me."

"I had an accident," Emily said. She picked up one of the sandwiches and nibbled it.

"Well, whoever tended to you ought to be run out of the parish. There's dirt in those cuts, honey. Don't you move now. I'll be right back."

"Did you grow up in this house?" Emily asked.

"Yes. Left after I quit college." He took a sandwich, noted it was made of white bread, cucumbers, and mayonnaise, then set it back.

"With your aunt?"

"With my parents. They're dead."

"I'm sorry."

"They enjoyed their lives. They lived pretty long."

"It's nice here. I feel at home."

"I hoped you would."

"Why don't you live here?"

"Not my kind of people, the Garden District. All my friends live in the Quarter. If you're going to be in New Orleans, there isn't any other place."

"You strike me as the kind of man who belongs here."

"Truth to tell, I've never been sure where I belong. I hope it's here."

Where did a photographer belong? Not in his own pictures. Andy had come back to New Orleans to take pictures—real pictures, of real life. That's what he had told himself. Now, a man had died in his courtyard carrying his name and address in his pocket. Andy was getting the terrible feeling he was on the wrong side of the camera in this one. He'd photographed dozens and dozens of murder victims, without their ever meaning very much to him, just as he'd photographed many beautiful women, all the while loving only Candy. They were just pretty faces, like this girl's.

Only Emily Shaw was beginning to seem more than a pretty face. He wondered if he was losing control, if he was allowing himself to be drawn into his own pictures of the movie shoot. A good photographer couldn't afford that. He had to keep on the other side of the lens.

"You certainly belong on this veranda," he said. "All you need is a picture hat and a long white summer dress, maybe with a sash."

"Like a Tennessee Williams character."

"Let's hope happier than that."

Zinnia returned, somehow managing to balance the medicine chest, a basin of water, a wash cloth and towel, and a bottle of gin.

"I don't need that, Zinny," Derain said.

"You ain't tellin' me nothin' I don't know, boy. This is for her. I'm afraid this is gonna hurt a little."

She poured the lemonade, adding a healthy amount of gin to Emily's, waiting for the girl to take a couple of swallows.

"I'm really not much of a drinker," Emily said. "But today's been . . ."

"Don't you worry about it none, honey. You just get yourself feelin' good while I take care of these pretty knees." Zinnia glared at Andy, as though his presence was inappropriate, and he was to blame for everything.

"I've seen women's legs before, Zinny."

"Don't I know, boy. Don't I know." She squatted down, with some effort, and began her work. Blood came away on the towel when she dried the girl's knees. She quickly applied some antiseptic, causing Emily to wince, then pressed pads of gauze over the wounds, wrapping adhesive tape around each.

"You change that dressing every day, now, hear? You'll be good as new by the end of the week."

"Thank you, Zinny," Andy said. "You're the closest thing to an angel there's ever been in this town."

"Glad to help, Andy. It's about time you brought a real lady around here, instead of those French Quarter girls."

When she had gone, Andy settled back into the chair next to Emily, taking a sip of his drink. She looked down at her bandaged limbs.

"It's a good thing I don't have any scenes left where I have to show my legs."

"What scenes do you have left?"

"Just one big one, actually. I come to the door when Jim, having vanquished the drug lord and seen the error of his ways, turns up on the porch and promises to start a new life. We kiss. Fade out to an overhead shot of the house. Pull back to an aerial view of New Orleans. Up music. Roll credits."

"They could have shot most of that today."

"I wish they had. I'll be glad to get away from here. Finish this wretched picture. Although, I must say, coming here today is an unexpected treat. I haven't seen much of the real New Orleans."

"Let me show you then."

She smiled. "You *are* a nice guy."

• • •

The old Cadillac was still behaving itself. He took Emily along St. Charles to Lee Circle, then on past the high-rise office buildings of Poydras to Canal Street, turning uptown. At Rampart, he turned right, then took a left onto what remained of Basin Street, passing along some battered old buildings and the Iberville Housing Project, and then a grassy park.

Emily seemed relaxed now, even content. "It's nice getting away from that bastard for a while, from all those bastards."

"Why are you making this film with Cooper?"

She sat forward. "I've hated every minute of this shoot, but I'm damned grateful to have the part. You know what my career has been like before this?"

"You have a fair number of credits."

"Most of those are TV, and most of the parts were walk-ons or one liners. And most of them I got because my mother's a casting director for one of the network series factories. I'm afraid I'm not much of an actress. Nothing at all as good as Paris. I mean she's just fantastic. You should ask her what she's doing in *Street of Desire*."

"Trying to keep working."

"Isn't this business the pits? My brother's not much of an actor, either. He mumbles. He can't remember his lines. He can't even do a love scene—at least not on camera. But he's one of the biggest stars there is."

"Your brother?"

"Richard Porter. He of the bare chest and the motorcycles. Our family's name is Preyszeski. He got Porter out of that. I just chose Shaw. I am a real Emily, though."

Porter was a long-haired muscleman of the beach- and biker-movie sort, a Patrick Swayze without talent, though he had a likable screen presence. His last picture had grossed more than fifty million dollars.

"I got this part all on my own. I did three auditions—three call-backs. I . . . I did it on my own. I really want this picture to succeed. I've done everything Cooper asked. Everything."

She was lolling back against the seat, her arm resting atop the door, her legs stretched out straight, her skirt pulled up slightly to keep it off her knees.

"This used to be Storyville," Andy said, gesturing at a decrepit building they were passing. "When they cleaned up the Quarter a century ago, they moved the red-light district to this area and legalized it—named it after the alderman responsible. It was about as tough a neighborhood as you could find—altogether tawdry but still rather elegant in its way. It was run by women—the madams, 'Daughters of Venus'—women with powerful friends. Some of the greatest musicians ever started here.

"There were a lot of murders, but no one much worried about them, unless a victim was someone important. A U.S. Senator was shot and killed here, by his girlfriend. One of the madams. The Navy closed it all down in 1917. Much of the wildlife moved back into the Quarter. Prostitution wasn't legal there, but they let it run wide open. It became a place of two-dollar whores. There were bars where girls danced naked except for stockings, to stick money in. They called them 'Baby Dolls.' There's still some of that around."

"You like it here?"

"I'm fascinated by it. Life in the raw, unvarnished and unadulterated. I've come to appreciate that."

She was studying him. He sensed a wariness.

"You should take pictures of beautiful things."

"I do. I did today. I took some of you."

His reward was another smile. She relaxed again.

"Let's go to the French Quarter," she said. "Show me where you live."

His parking place was gone, but he found another across the street.

"This section used to be called Smoky Row. I live in a little house behind that big one."

"That's where the murder was."

"Yes."

"Can we go in? I'd like to see some of your photographs."

"Isn't that supposed to be my line? Show you my etchings?"

"I didn't mean it as a line."

"Sorry."

Paris's body was full and womanly. Candice's was thin, elongated, the torso subordinate to her extraordinary legs. Except for the scars, Katie Kollwitz's reminded him of an artist's model's—of the bodies of women in a hundred or more paintings he'd admired.

What might this fresh young flower of a girl's body look like? Her waist was narrow above full hips; her breasts high and round, substantial enough to curve the fall of her blouse.

Andy felt warm and flush. He tried to forget Candice.

"Don't you want me to come in?"

"Yes, of course," he said, turning off the car's engine. "Sorry."

He took her directly into his studio. She stood in the center, hands folded, looking about. The windows were shuttered, and it was cool and dark. He turned on a lamp.

"Very artistic," she said. "Bohemian."

"Certainly that."

"And southern. Something else, too. Sensual, I guess."

"Sensual?"

"I don't know. Decadent."

"I'm glad someone appreciates that." He opened one set of shutters.

She was studying the pictures. "That's Paris Moran."

"In all her splendor. If not her clothes."

"You must be very good friends."

"It was all very professional. I was doing a magazine shoot."

"I wondered what she might look like. She has a fantastic figure."

"Makes me wish I was a sculptor."

"Why don't you become one?"

He laughed. "Since we're here, I might as well develop today's film. Would you like something to drink?"

She shook her head.

While he busied himself in his lab, he heard her puttering about, picking up things.

"You have a banjo. Do you play?"

"No," he said through the doorway. "A friend gave me that. I meant to learn someday."

"I know how."

Over his shoulder, he saw her take the instrument to his couch. In a moment, she was strumming a quiet little song, one he'd never heard before.

"That's beautiful."

"A musician is what I really am. I play the guitar. Classical, pop tunes, Mexican songs. I used to play at a little club in Venice Beach. It's what I thought I'd end up doing, if I didn't make it in movies."

He stepped into the doorway. "Why did you go into movies? Because of your brother?"

"My mother pushed both of us into it. But what else would I do in L.A.? Keep on playing guitar for tips in dinky little clubs? Work in an office? Model in car commercials? Marry some bastard like Cooper? If you can get work in the movies, you do it."

"Did you go to college?"

"Three years. Fine arts and music. It began to seem a waste of time."

Derain joined her. "The negatives are drying."

She set the banjo aside and started to get to her feet, showing her pain. He helped her up, his hands lingering a moment beneath her arms.

She took a step forward, coming close against him. She lifted her face to his, a flower yielding to the warmth of sunlight.

"I think that we should do this. Just this," she said.

Her kiss was very soft and gentle and sweet, and lingering.

"That's all," she said, stepping back.

"That's more than I'd hoped of today. You're my *lagniappe*."

"*Lagniappe*?" Her French accent was poor.

"A local word. It means a little serendipitous something extra. Something unexpected. A warm day in the midst of winter. Running into an old friend who buys you a drink. Meeting a pretty girl at a party you didn't want to go to. Or meeting one on a movie set."

She smiled. She had such lovely teeth. "Why don't you take me to dinner tonight? That will be my *lagniappe*."

"All right." The telephone rang.

It was Candice.

"Where have you been?" she said. "I've been calling you all day."

"I have a job, remember? Doing those movie stills."

"You could check your goddamn answering machine. I left a number. I waited there for more than an hour. A friend's house."

"I'm sorry. I just walked in."

"You don't sound very glad to hear me."

"I'm real glad. I've been worried. The way you hung up, I was afraid your husband was about to shoot you or something."

"He was mad enough. He asked about you, Andy. He knows something about you. I don't know how much. I've told him that you're just an old friend, that we've worked together. I showed him some of the magazine shots you did of me. He doesn't buy it. He's so goddamned relentless. He just keeps at it."

"Where are you?"

"In Fort Worth, at the moment. At a fashion show. Jan Strimple's the star. I'm second banana. I'm calling from a hotel women's room."

"You're all right?"

"Yes. But I'm sure he's going to have you checked out, if he hasn't already. You may get visitors."

"I think I have one. Someone's been following me."

"Did you get rid of the pictures, Andy?"

He paused. "They're gone."

"Thank God."

Why was he lying to her?

"Candy, someone took them."

"Shit! Are you serious?"

"I'm sorry. Someone broke in. I had them locked up. Whoever it was must have picked the lock."

There was silence. He could hear her breathing. Women were chattering in the background.

"You've completely fucked up my life," she said finally.

"It may not have been this guy who's been following me. Could have been anyone. You know the Quarter. Some light-fingered people around. I was on the news, because of the murder. It may have attracted someone's attention."

"You mean burglars?"

"Possibly," he said, though he knew it was nonsense.

"Did they take anything else?"

"No."

"Nothing else? Just my pictures?"

"I'm afraid so."

"Oh God. What am I going to do, Andy?"

He had an urge to tell her again that he loved her, but he knew that would accomplish nothing, and he didn't want to say it in front of Emily.

"Is there some place you can go?" he asked. "Some far-away friend? Your parents in San Antonio?"

"He'd explode if I did that. If he wanted to find me, he'd find me. I can't walk out on him now. I don't dare do that."

"I'll go talk to him. Have it out. Say it was all my fault. Tell him to take it out on me, not you."

"He'd kill you."

"Candy, this is America. Not Argentina."

"I'm in Texas. Do you know what can happen in Texas? Murder plots over cheerleaders? They killed the president of the United States here and got away with it!"

"My police lieutenant friend knows the situation. He hasn't told anyone, and he won't. But I can have him call Ben. Tell him to leave us alone."

"A police lieutenant? Andy, the man owns Congressmen."

He sighed. What was left to say? To do? His sense of obligation, of duty, was overpowering. So was his sense of helplessness.

He took a deep breath. "I'll go back to New York with you, anything you want. Everything."

"It's too late."

His frustration was turning to anger again.

"Don't you want to divorce him? Is that it? Are you afraid you'll lose everything?"

"You son of a bitch." She hung up.

He set his receiver down gently.

"I'm sorry," Emily said. "I didn't mean to stand here and listen to you. I didn't know where to go."

"It's all right."

"Are you in trouble?"

"Kind of. A friend of mine . . ."

"A girlfriend?"

He sighed again. "Yes."

"Oh."

"Past tense. I'm afraid I'm . . . I think that's all over. As of this very moment."

"Maybe we should skip dinner. I should leave you to deal with your problem."

"I'm unhappy enough as it is."

She frowned, uncertain.

"You think I can cheer you up?"

"Haven't a doubt."

"You did that for me today."

"Dinner with you would be a truly marvelous *lagniappe*."

"All right. We'll see what happens."

• • •

He dressed up for her, complete to tan poplin suit and tie, then drove her over to the Westin so she could change. While she was in her room, he waited in the lobby, over by the big picture windows that looked down upon the river.

Paris Moran found him there. He hadn't seen her enter. She announced her presence with a big puff of smoke.

"What are you doing here, honey bunch?" she asked. "They don't need you till tomorrow."

"I'm waiting for someone."

"Little Miss Muffett?" There was too much wisdom in Paris's eyes.

"Yes."

"I asked you to take her under your wing, Andy. Not into your nest."

"Already been there. Nothing happened. Perfect gentleman."

Paris nodded, as she might if he was telling her about the Easter Bunny.

"She's a good kid," she said. "You be real nice to her."

"That's precisely what I intend."

Paris stubbed her cigarette out in an ashtray. "We've got a chase scene tomorrow. Early call. I wish I had more guts."

"You have a stuntman driving for you, don't you? Wearing a wig?"

"For some of it. I've got to do some driving behind the camera truck. High-speed stuff. Down, what is it, Tchoupitoulas Street? How the hell do you pronounce it?"

"You got it right. Down by the waterfront. How did it go with the script?"

She made a face. "He wants a new ending. He thinks the happy one we have now is too pat, too trite. Now he's thinking *film noir,* some kind of shocker. He's been talking Oscar to our backers so much I think he's beginning to believe that bullshit himself."

"You going along with that?"

"Whatever gets it over with. Are you all right, Andy? You look a little pale."

"It's the heat."

"Hot town. Nighty-night, honey bunch. Don't get too many feathers in your nest."

• • •

He took Emily to Mr. B's. His friends there gave him a nice booth by the window, and came around to chat during their dinner. The maître d' asked her for her autograph. It was the first time that had happened to her, and she was delighted.

"How are your knees?" Andy asked, as he paid the check with a credit card, wondering if he had reached his credit limit.

"I've forgotten all about them."

"I haven't." He grinned. "Would you like to hear some music now?"

"I'd love it. Jazz?"

"Not the Bourbon Street tourist stuff. I know a place over in Faubourg Marigny. They have a good man sitting in on trumpet tonight."

• • •

Like Lulu White's Mahogany Hall, one of the most popular tourist night spots in the Quarter, One-Legged Duffy's was named for a whore. Lulu White had been a mulatto madam who had reigned as one of the queens of Storyville before its closure in 1917. Her saloon and adjoining pleasure palace had been among the most magnificent and famous establishments on Basin Street, and her legend such that Mae West had made a movie based on her life. The Mahogany Hall now located on Bourbon Street was a replica of her Storyville original.

One-Legged Duffy, born Mary Rich, was a far less grand personage and had never owned her own place. A femme fatale in New Orleans' outrageously lawless Civil War era, she had plied her trade on notorious Gallatin Street in hellholes like Archie Murphy's dance hall, famous among other things for the penchant of another prostitute named Lizzie Collins for stealing all the buttons off her customers' trousers.

Collins was run out of New Orleans for this vexsome habit. One-Legged Duffy fared worse. Her fancy man concluded one of their frequent quarrels by stabbing her repeatedly and then yanking off her wooden leg and caving in her skull with it.

Derain spared Emily this bit of historical color, telling her simply that the jazz club was not named for its present proprietor, a piano player and ex-bartender named Loomis Demarest, but for a lady long dead whose tragic story had struck Loomis's fancy.

It was a slow night, and there were a number of empty tables. Derain chose one near the band but to the side of the room, where he and Emily could sit side by side.

Maljeux was up on the bandstand as promised. He waved to them as they sat down. Dressed in a dark suit and an open-collared white shirt, he was playing trumpet with a combo that included Loomis Demarest on piano, plus a clarinet, saxophone, trombone, and bass player. The song was " 'Round Midnight," and Maljeux was using a mute, the ensemble bringing forth the sad old tune with a weary nonchalance. All the scene needed was someone like Paris Moran at the bar, smoking a cigarette and staring vaguely into her life.

"I was expecting Dixieland," Emily said.

"For Dixieland I'd take you to Preservation Hall—and one night I will. But you'd have to sit on the floor with a lot of sweaty tourists, and there's no liquor."

The set ended, and Maljeux strolled over, pulling up a chair and turning it backward before sitting down. Derain introduced Emily, who complimented him on his playing.

"That's an expert opinion," Derain said. "Emily's a musician herself. She's done club dates in L.A."

Maljeux eyed her appreciatively. "What do you play?"

"Guitar. Sometimes a banjo. In school, I studied the violin, but I didn't like it much. I like to sing. I usually sing when I play."

Maljeux looked over at Demarest, a dark-skinned man with glistening slicked-down black hair, who was wearing a white jacket and purple shirt. He was still at his piano, tinkering a little tune out of the keys and sipping a whiskey.

"Do you know any saloon music?" Maljeux asked.

"I know 'Skylark.' "

The police lieutenant nodded, then rose and went over to Demarest. The two spoke a moment, Demarest glancing over at their table. Maljeux patted the man's arm, and then returned.

"Loomis would be delighted if you'd do 'Skylark' with him," he said. "Then you can add One-Legged Duffy's here to your résumé."

She looked flattered, but uncomfortable. "I don't know how good I'd be."

"You'll be just fine, sweet thing. This is a real friendly place."

Persuaded, she got stiffly to her feet and went up onto the stage.

"It is a slow night," Maljeux said. "But she won't embarrass us, will she?"

"I don't think so. I expect not at all."

She was beautiful. It took Loomis a bar or two before he caught her tempo, but she sailed into the full high notes of the song like a professional torch singer.

"You get all the best ladies, Andy," Maljeux said. "Too bad you don't know what to do with them, except get into trouble."

Derain said nothing, his eyes fixed encouragingly on Emily's across the floor.

"I'll be real quick," Maljeux said. "We got a fix on your man in black."

"How did you do that so soon?"

"Simple enough. I had a plainclothesman follow you over to the Garden District. He picked up the black suit gent at the movie shoot, and tailed him back to his hotel, one of those traveling salesman hostelries over near Canal. He drives a Cadillac, just like you, only his is black and a hell of a lot newer." He paused for effect. "It's got Texas plates."

"I was afraid of that."

"He got clear of us after that, but it doesn't matter. Checked him out. He's registered as George Graves, from Houston. I called the Houston PD. They tell me he's a licensed PI—does mostly divorce work. I think what we've talked about is the genuine situation. I think you and that long, tall fashion model got yourselves in a truly large pile of shit—the kind that takes lawyers to shovel."

Derain smiled at Emily, but kept listening. Maljeux took a folded piece of paper from his pocket and slid it across the table. "I got it here for you, but that's all I can do. We might roust him for a firearm or something, but he's probably too smart to be carrying one. Our man took a quick look through his room, couldn't find anything but clothes and whiskey. I sure as hell can't have him picked up for the crime of walking the streets of New Orleans."

Derain put the paper in his wallet, looking unhappy. "What I don't understand, if he's one of those divorce sneaks, why is he so goddamn obvious about it?"

Maljeux shrugged. "Maybe he's already got everything he needs and he's just trying to make you feel bad."

"Well, he's succeeded, but I'm not going to let it ruin my night."

The policeman looked to Emily, then back. "I don't blame you." He leaned closer. "I'm gettin' nowhere on Danielle Jones and Ferrier. I've talked to Loomis. I've talked to all kinds of people in the community. I had Bobby work on his special friends. *Rien*."

By "community," Maljeux meant the gay community, especially the one flourishing lately in Faubourg Marigny. Bobby was a waiter at Duffy's and a friend of Maljeux—his chief source on untoward and unlawful activities in the "community."

"All anyone knows is that the late Albert was hanging out there for a while," Maljeux continued. "No one seems to know Jones, except as a friend of Albert's. No one has any idea who Jones's sugar daddy might be. Nobody from around here probably. Least not anyone who wants his taste in color known. Real discreet. Made his visits like a phantom in the night. These *tableaux vivant* she was talking about. No one in the community's ever been to one of them. Ferrier never talked about them."

"I can't help you on that score, Paul."

"I know. I'm just bringing you up to date on matters."

"My Texas lady doesn't want anything more to do with me."

"You're a dangerous man to be around."

Emily had finished. The people in the bar were applauding warmly. Andy quickly joined in.

• • •

They stayed at One-Legged Duffy's through the next set, slipping away just at the end. As Andy started the car, silently thanking it for being so reliable on this in many ways serendipitous day, he glanced at his watch.

"It's almost midnight," she said, looking at her own.

"Not late."

"I get to sleep in, but you have an early call."

"They'll be a while setting up that shoot, with the cars and all. I don't need much sleep. A choice between going to bed and being with you is an easy one."

He wished he'd phrased that differently.

"Where shall we go?"

"Back to the Quarter?"

"Are you asking me to go back to your place?"

"No." It wasn't a lie. If George Graves was still hanging around, Derain had an idea where he might be. "Do you mind another bar?"

"Does it have a band?"

"Sometimes. Probably not tonight. Music, though."

"All right. For a while. Is it nice?"

"I've never heard it called that. But I like it. It's kind of my second home."

They parked near his house, walking to the Razzy Dazzy. It was doing as little business as Duffy's, and all the customers were men, some of them drunk. Roybal was the only one working. After seating Emily at a table near the door, Andy went up to the bar to save Freddy a trip.

"Now that is a real nice-lookin' lady," the bartender said, after Andy had ordered their drinks. "Why you bring a girl like that into a joint like this?"

"Nothing illegal going on here tonight, is there?"

"No more 'an usual. Little game going on in the back room. Had a coupla hookers in, but they gave up on gettin' any business and left. Must be a slow night in the Quarter. That's what they say."

"Tom in?"

Roybal shook his head. "Got a meeting over Uptown. Politics." He set the drinks on the bar.

"Someone in here lookin' for you, though, Andy. Well, I don't know exactly she was lookin' for you, but after hangin' around here for an hour or so fending off some of the boys, she asked if you might be comin' in tonight. I said you probably would, because you always do, but I couldn't say when exactly. She left you a note."

Freddy plucked a folded-up cocktail napkin from a glass on the shelf behind him.

It read: "Call me." There was a phone number. Nothing else.

"Did she have dark hair? Funny earrings?"

"Yes sir. Same lady you left with last night." He nodded toward Emily. "Good thing you just missed her, I guess."

"You didn't tell her where I live?"

"No sir."

"How long ago did she leave?"

"I don't know. Half hour. She left with a guy. Couldn't figure it out. She gave the stiff to every man come near her, then this sportin' gent comes in and out she goes with him like he just offered her a million dollars."

"Maybe she knew him."

"Don't think so. He sat down on the other end and had himself a double shot, then he sends a drink down to her and, by the time I give him his change, he scores. He was in here last night, too. Guy in a Panama and black suit, and dark glasses."

Andy paid for his drinks, but left them on the bar. He didn't want to be in the Razzy Dazzy any longer.

"Thanks, Freddy. Tell Tom I'll be in tomorrow. I need to talk to him."

"Something wrong, Andy? You just got here."

"I decided you're right. A rum joint like this is no place for a sweet young thing."

He came up behind Emily and put his hands on her shoulders.

"I changed my mind," he said. "I think this is where I ask you to come back to my place. Unless you'd rather I take you home."

"No," she said, in a near whisper. "Your place."

• • •

Bleusette had locked the gate. Andy unlocked it, and left it that way, for when he would take Emily home. Her intentions—the same as his—were pretty clear, but he doubted she wanted to spend the night.

He turned on the lights in his studio. Nothing was amiss. If Candice's voice was waiting for him on his answering machine, he didn't want to find out. He switched it off.

"Do you want another drink?"

"No thanks. I think I've had enough of those."

It was hot, but he didn't want to unshutter the windows.

"I'll print up those negatives I shot of your big scene," he said. "It'll only take a few minutes."

He started toward the dark room, but she followed him, taking hold of his arm. He turned.

Her eyes seemed deeply green now. They were open very wide, full upon his.

"Let's stop fooling around, Andy."

Her kiss was warm and urgent. Her lips parted as she pressed herself tightly against him, her arms going tightly around him, her hands moving on his back. His own went to her shoulder and her waist, and then lower.

They kissed again, then parted, both breathing deeply. His hand moved to her blouse and quickly undid the buttons. She reached and unhooked her brassiere. He lifted it free of her breasts, then lowered himself to kiss them—the right, and then the left. She murmured, looking around her. There was only the couch.

"Let's go upstairs," he said. "It'll be cooler, if I open the doors to the balcony."

He led the way, shedding his jacket and removing his shirt. Stepping into his bedroom, she stopped just inside the door to slip out of her clothes. He went to the balcony doors and flung them open, admitting the sounds of the city night. When he turned back to her, she was lying on his bed, completely naked. He quickly got rid of the rest of his clothing, reached into his night table drawer for a small, foil-covered package, then lowered himself beside her, running his hands over her arms, her breasts, her stomach, reaching down to between her legs. She was very hot and moist.

Emily leaned over to kiss him, then took the package from him, opening it, and moving one hand to stroke him. It was hardly necessary.

"Your knees," he said.

"Some kinds of pain," she said, "I don't mind."

• • •

Afterward, he felt as heady as a drunk. Candice hadn't made him feel so dreamily, wondrously fulfilled in years. Emily was in no way artful, but she was so amazingly loving. His body hummed with what they had done.

There'd been a troubling moment, just before the end. Candice's face had glimmered into his mind's eye, as had Katie Kollwitz's. But that was gone. His thoughts now were fully about Emily—remarkably good thoughts.

They lay on their backs, sprawled in the heat of the bed, her head, her hair a little wet, on his arm.

He couldn't find any words. He didn't particularly want any.

"I don't do this," she said. "Make love on a first date."

"You just did."

"I wasn't sure it was going to happen, but now I'm glad I did." She lifted a hand to touch his cheek.

A horn honked outside, but they could hear the car drive on, accelerating. There was music playing somewhere, soft rock from a radio. He hadn't noticed it before. His senses now were alive to everything, every tiny sound, the heated scent of her perfume, the feel of her skin against his.

"The woman who called you," she said, "Is she . . . ?"

"She's married. That was our problem."

"And you and she . . . It's all over, as of today? Is that what you said?"

"I'm afraid so." He listened to himself. "I don't mean that. Not 'afraid.' It's a fact. It's over. Finis."

"Did you love her?"

"Yes. Very much. In the beginning. But she married someone else."

"But you didn't let go of her?"

"No. I should have."

"Do you love her now?"

"To be honest, I don't really know. Some kinds of love are habit."

"Am I . . . part of a rebound?"

"Not at all." He kissed his fingers and touched her nipple with them. "You're my *lagniappe*. And not just for the day. I hope."

"I have a boyfriend. Back in L.A. I'm not in love with him, but he's someone nice to go out with. A friend of my brother's. Very good-looking, but not terribly bright. He liked the idea of my being an actress. He pushed me into going for this picture more than anyone."

Derain said nothing. He imagined someone who probably looked a lot like Richard Porter.

"I think he'd leave me for a more famous actress if he could. He's real star-struck. He and my brother work out together, ride motorcycles, hang out together at the beach. All that 'guy' stuff. I sleep with him . . . slept with him. But I don't want to marry him."

"You don't have to tell me this." He wished she'd stop.

"Do you have anyone beside this Candice? Do you have a lot of girlfriends? I mean, all those pictures downstairs."

He didn't want to be discussing this, but she seemed intent on it—a desire to clear the air around them, to get things behind them, out of the way. He sensed there could be a future with this girl, if he wanted it, but the future seemed miles beyond his grasp.

"I don't play around," he said. "Not a lot. I mean, there's really only been Candice. She's from out of town, but we were together enough. Her husband doesn't sleep with her much. I'm mostly what she has. What she's had. Sex can be dangerous in the fashion business. Some of her model friends have stayed away from it for years."

"Is that what she is, a model?"

"Yes. I used to do a lot of fashion shoots."

"I know. You're quite famous, more famous than me."

He felt her tense.

"Andy, I lied to you. I said 'I don't do this.' It's mostly true. I don't sleep around, either. But I . . . I did something bad. I'm quite disgusted with myself. I really wanted this part, to be in this picture. Andy, I went to bed with Alan Cooper."

He kept his eyes from her.

"We all make mistakes," he said, finally.

"It was only once. In his office. On his damned desk. Degrading. I've never done that before, but he made it very clear that I had to."

"Why has he been such a swine with you?"

"Because after I signed the contract I wouldn't let him near me anymore."

"No wonder he liked your fall."

She rolled over on her side, her face very close to his. "Anyway, I won't have to do that anymore, will I?"

"No."

"Even if I never get to make another picture, I won't do that."

He put both his arms around her, stroking her back. "Just go to sleep, Emily."

"I should go back to my hotel."

"I'll get you there. I don't want to be without you just yet."

"I don't want to leave you either. You're the first good thing that's happened to me in a long time."

• • •

Emily slept, but Andy did so only fitfully, his troubles—his accumulating fears—chattering at the edge of his consciousness. He was thinking again of the man in the black suit when slumber finally came.

There was a soft thud, something fallen. He'd forgotten to feed his cat. Hungry Beatrice. Prowling for food. Showing her displeasure. He opened his eyes to see if she was in the room and saw a large dark shape at the balcony doors. It was moving.

Andy started to rise, but the figure was fast, bounding to the bed, arm extended. Just like the man in the courtyard the morning before.

Andy hurled himself forward, lifting his arm reflexively, but the blow didn't come to him. It fell on Emily. Her sudden scream inflamed his every nerve. Something then struck his head. He fell back but struggled forward, trying to thrust himself over her, to shield her. Another move of the arm. The sound Emily made was hideous. Andy lunged at the figure, hitting flesh and cloth. Something sharp cut across his forearm with stinging, burning pain. A worse pain then cleaved between his neck and shoulder. Emily's next scream ended with a sudden and horrible gurgle. Andy rolled and fell to the floor, rising to claw at the intruder, but there came another stab of pain. He went down, the attacker stumbling backward. Andy's head crashed against his night table. As he fought to remain conscious, he remembered his father's gun. He'd put it beneath the table and then forgotten all about it. The attacker came forward again. He desperately reached for the weapon. With his last strength, his groping hand went to the cold metal.

He fired a shot, aimlessly, hitting the floorboards. Rolling back painfully, he fired again, then again. He saw the dark figure at the doorway of the balcony. He pulled the trigger one more time. Then it was gone. Everything was gone. All went dark.

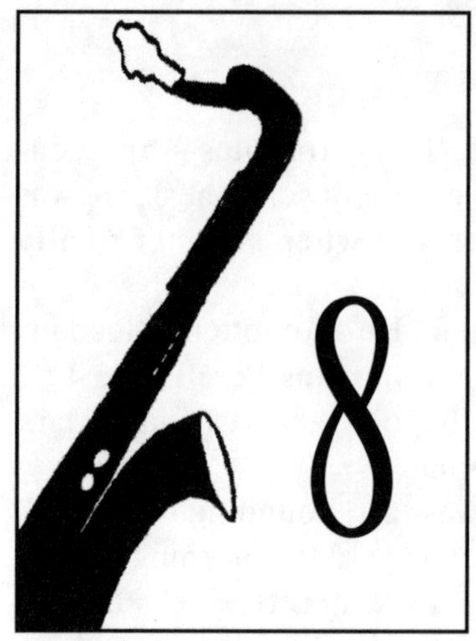

8

They took Emily away in the first ambulance that came, without telling Andy if she was alive or dead. He at first refused one for himself, then changed his mind when he realized it would be the fastest way to get to the hospital and learn her condition.

In the chaos of the emergency room, however, he could learn nothing, except that New Orleans was having a rough night. The brightly lit, hellish place seemed more abattoir than medical facility, with nurses, doctors, attendants, and policemen attending haphazardly to stabbing victims, gunshot victims, beating victims, and people who were violently or deathly ill. As he found a seat to wait for treatment, an old man who apparently suffered a heart attack died on a gurney just a few feet from him.

Andy looked over his own injuries. He'd managed to get on a pair of shorts and his boating shoes, nothing else. His chest and arm were coated with blood, but he didn't know how much was his and how much might be Emily's. His head was reeling. The pain in his arm and shoulder throbbed with every heartbeat.

A nurse came and began working on his wounds with disinfectant, ignoring his questions about Emily, even when he began shouting them at her. Finally, she grabbed his head with both hands, leaned into his face, and told him to shut up or she'd give him an injection to put him under. He fell silent.

Next, a young intern probed the edges of the cuts, talking as he worked.

"Sorry to take so long to get to you," he said, "but we do triage here and you're among the walking wounded. We've got a real bad night. You feel dizzy? You going to pass out?"

"No. I'm all right. What about Miss Shaw? Is she going to live?"

"Sorry. I don't know anything about your Miss Shaw. I don't even know the name of the man over there who just died on me."

"They brought her here ahead of me. She was stabbed. Her throat . . ."

"The movie actress? She's in surgery. You can find out about her later. Just let us get our job done, okay?"

The nurse swabbed Andy's right arm, and then quickly jabbed him with a syringe. Andy looked up, startled and angry.

"Tetanus," she said.

She jabbed him with another needle.

"Antibiotic," she said.

"You've got a couple of bad cuts on your forearm and a worse one above your clavicle—came close to going through the shoulder muscle," the intern said. "You're going to need a mess of stitches but I don't think any surgery. You've lost some blood. You want to be admitted?"

Andy shook his head.

"It's a fifty-fifty call."

He shook his head again.

"You right-handed?" The nurse had wheeled over a tray. The young doctor picked up a surgical needle.

Andy nodded.

"Good, 'cause for the next few days your left arm is going to hurt every time you move your little finger. Otherwise, I guess you're a lucky guy."

"Lucky guy," Andy repeated. "Emily . . ."

Someone in the crowded room was screaming. The doctor quickened the pace of his efforts.

"Gut-cut victim, doctor," said another nurse.

The intern glanced over his shoulder. "Okay, Ruth, finish this guy up." He disappeared into the mob.

Her hands moved quickly. Andy looked away, concentrating on dealing with his pain. She was done with the stitches much sooner than he expected, and began winding a dressing around his shoulder. She made it tight, numbing the hurt. His forearm got the same treatment.

"Can you walk?" she asked.

"I walked in here."

"Sugar, we have people pass out from a lot less." She turned to his forearm. "This'll just take another minute. Then I want you to go over to one of those chairs and rest a little. The police said they want to talk to you some more. And you've got to fill out some forms."

"Okay."

"You got a doctor?"

"No. Not in New Orleans."

"Well, you find one and go see him in the morning."

Andy staggered once going over to the chairs, but caught himself and made it to his destination without toppling over. Slumping into the seat, he leaned his head back against the wall and closed his eyes. The world began swimming.

When he finally regained his equilibrium he noticed someone sitting beside him—a woman, with tanned legs. It was Bleusette. She looked at him with concern, and disapproval.

"You alive, Andy?"

"If I'm dead, I never figured you for heaven."

"Fuck you. I come home and once again I find cops," she said. "Goddamn, Andy. You sure you're gonna live?"

"I think so."

"I got too many dead people in my life. I got no time to mourn for you, okay?"

"Okay."

"I thought you said that girlfriend of yours went to Texas."

"It wasn't her who was with me. It was someone from the movie."

"Goddamn you, Andy. You fuck every woman in this town except me."

He felt extremely wretched. "I'm sorry for the oversight. If you like, I'll make it up to you—if you'll give me a few days."

"You got too many women in your life, that's all. You see what happens? They're worse than booze."

"I'm not sure I still have this one. They cut her throat."

"I'm sorry. She someone you like?"

"Yes."

She placed her hand in his, and squeezed. "I am sorry, Andy."

He squeezed back. "Thanks."

"Why is this happening? What's going on?"

"I don't know. Wrong element moving into the neighborhood."

"Enough fucking jokes, Andy. I bet you didn't lock the goddamn gate, *n'est ce pas?"*

"No. Sure didn't. But I don't think that mattered much. The bastard was real athletic. Came in by way of my balcony."

"This scares me, Andy. Maybe I go away for a while."

"I don't think they're after you. It's something to do with me. I just don't know what."

"Maybe you should go away." She pulled her hand away. "Here comes Maljeux. I don't want to talk to him. You take care now."

He nodded. She hesitated, then leaned to kiss him on the cheek. She was away before Maljeux could shoulder his way through to where Andy was sitting.

"Never thought of Bleusette as Florence Nightingale," the lieutenant said.

"Good neighbor."

"They're still operating on Miss Shaw. A mess of doctors with her."

"Is she going to make it?"

"Tell you the truth, my boy, I'm amazed she's still alive."

The lieutenant heaved himself onto the chair Bleusette had just vacated.

"I've seen them pull off some major miracles here, though," he said. "Lord knows they get enough practice."

"Shouldn't have taken her back to my place, Paul. Might as well have killed her myself."

"Don't talk crazy. You're no more to blame than I am. But we've got to catch this guy before it happens again. Did you see him? Was it this creep in the black suit, or the one who kicked you in the balls before?"

"I just don't know, Paul. It was dark. No lights on. It all happened real quick."

"Could you see anything at all? You sure it wasn't that guy who did Ferrier?"

"I've absolutely no idea."

"You fired a weapon. Several times. Did you hit him?"

Andy started to shrug. The resultant, searing pain almost lifted him out of his chair.

Maljeux patted his knee. "Never mind. We'll have a talk tomorrow. We have to get some kind of statement from you tonight, though. I'll have one of the detectives here sit down with you. Won't take long. Then you can go home. Though maybe you'd be better off here for a while. We still have evidence technicians at your place. They're getting to know it real well."

"Find out about Emily, Paul. Please."

Maljeux patted his knee again. "Just as soon as there's something to find out."

He got to his feet and lumbered off. A moaning black woman with a huge bandage around her head was wheeled by. Andy sat motionless, waiting, hating this place. Finally, he could wait no more.

The nurse who'd worked on him looked up as he stumbled by.

"Men's room," he said.

He clumsily pushed through some swinging doors into a busy corridor. The hospital's main lobby was just ahead. He had no idea where the operating rooms were. He had the lunatic notion they'd tell him at the front desk.

Cooper was in the waiting area, along with several of his movie crew. Paris Moran was there, as were Hub Cleveland and D. J. Cosette.

Cooper looked a madman. He lunged up from his seat upon seeing Andy.

"You bastard! You killed her! You wrecked my film!"

He began swinging wildly, though he was several feet from Andy. Cosette jumped up and grabbed one of his arms. Cleveland took the other.

Paris was at Andy's side. "My God, Andy, are you all right? You look like somebody in a horror film."

Cooper was bellowing. They shoved him back onto the couch.

"Emily? . . ."

Paris shrugged. "They haven't told us anything."

"I've got to find out. I've got to see her."

"Not now, honey bunch. Let's get you out of here."

"The police. They want me to make a statement. Some forms . . ."

"Fuck 'em. Come on."

"You're fired, you son of a bitch!" Cooper shouted. "You'll never work on one of my pictures again! On anybody's picture."

Paris told the cab driver to take them to the Westin.

"I should go home."

"I don't think so, Andy. You'd better spend the night with me. It's no problem. I've got a suite, remember?"

"I can't walk into that hotel like this."

Paris was wearing a beige jacket over her blouse. She took it off and gently began to put it over his shoulders.

"I'll get it all bloody."

"No sweat, lover. Give you the shirt off my back anytime."

When she had the jacket in place, she sat back and lighted a cigarette.

"I hope you didn't leave New York just because of the high crime rate," she said.

"This is my home, Paris."

"Well, you sure must love it."

• • •

There was no one in the hotel lobby but a couple of bellmen and the night clerk. Andy and Paris got long stares from each, but no comment. By the time they reached the elevators, the staff people had returned their attention to their work. He and Paris were movie folk, after all, and presumed strange. Perhaps they'd just come from shooting a violent scene, and hadn't stopped to remove Andy's stage blood. In any event, this was New Orleans. *Laissez-faire*.

Once they were in her suite, Paris went to the bedroom door and opened it. "You take the bed, sweetheart. You're going to need some sleep."

"Not yet." After she'd taken her jacket from him, he went to the couch and collapsed upon it, tilting back his head. Paris tossed the garment onto a chair.

"You want a drink, honey bunch? Maybe you shouldn't have one. They gave you shots, right?"

"It still hurts."

"A stiff one, then," she said. "And one for me. I'm not sure how much movie work there's going to be tomorrow."

She filled two bathroom glasses with scotch. There was no ice, and she didn't bother ordering any. There were several bouquets of flowers in the room, and a basket with wine bottles with an envelope tucked in the side. Complimentary gifts, no doubt. Paris the VIP. Andy had gotten treatment like that when he'd stayed in fancy hotels on fashion shoots.

Paris handed him his drink.

"Please," he said. "Could you call the hospital? About Emily?"

She went to use the phone in the bedroom. He could hear her side of the conversation clearly. She didn't sound alarmed.

"Emily's still in surgery," she said, returning. "Still alive, I guess. Nothing more."

Andy's vision began to blur with the first of his tears. He set his glass down on the carpet and covered his face with his hand. The seat cushion sagged as Paris sat down beside him. Her arm went around him. Gently, she pulled him close, till his head was against her shoulder.

"So much for your world-famous sense of humor."

"I'm sorry, Paris."

"Life's a bitch, Andy."

"Why did I take her to my place? Why did I do that?"

"You took her home because she wanted you to. I could see that coming a thousand miles away." She stroked his face. "Maybe this will all work out. Maybe she'll make it. She's still with us. That's a good sign, after all this time. Let's just concentrate on getting through the night."

"I want to kill the bastard. I wish I had when I tried. I've never wanted to do that to another human being ever in my life."

"Well, honey, you haven't spent much time in the movie business."

She reached to set her cigarette in an ashtray, then slowly leaned down and kissed him, tenderly, her large blue-green eyes staring softly into his. She was wearing very little makeup, but looked more beautiful than he ever remembered.

"Better?" she asked.

He wiped away his tears with the back of his uninjured arm.

"I haven't done this since I was a little kid."

"What, cried?"

"Yes."

"That's bullshit, sweetheart. We all cry. People think I'm a tough broad, but I cry every time I start a new job. I get terribly frustrated, trying to figure out the part, wondering if I can possibly be up to it, asking myself 'Why am I doing this?' And I bawl like a baby. Every time. I'll probably do some crying tonight." She sipped some whiskey. "But not just yet."

"Would you call the hospital again?"

"It's too soon, Andy. That was D.J. I was talking to. He said he'd call as soon as he got the word."

"I think I love her, Paris."

"No you don't, honey bunch. You'd probably like to be in love with her. Maybe you might be someday. We all want to be in love. But don't get confused just because of what's happened to her. Don't get love mixed up in this. Not now. Won't help."

"She's like a beautiful child."

"She's a sweet kid, little Miss Muffet. Her brother belongs in this business, but she doesn't. Now finish your drink and get some sleep."

He gulped down some whiskey. It seemed to be having no effect, and then it did. After another swallow, he set down his glass and lay back.

"I'll just stay here," he said. "I don't need a bed."

"I'll get you a pillow."

She brought one, settled it underneath his head, then leaned down and kissed his forehead.

"I'll see you through this, Andy. I'll see you through anything that comes your way. God knows, you've held my hand enough when times were bad."

"I've never done anything for you like this."

"The hell you haven't. You made me believe I was beautiful when I was thinking I was a big fat lump. You gave me the courage to face that mob at Spago the night I won the Oscar. You put in a good word for me with the right people when I was in my crazy period. You've always been there when I needed someone to talk to late at night on the phone. Friends for life, honey bunch."

"Maybe I'll fall in love with you, Paris."

"Wouldn't that be a stitch." She turned off the lights, then paused in the bedroom doorway. "You're my friend, Andy. I don't have many. It means a lot to me."

"Me, too."

"You all right now?"

"I'm all right."

" 'Night then."

She left the bedroom door open. She went into the bathroom. When she returned, she was naked. She got into the bed, waved to him cheerily, then turned off the lamp.

• • •

When he awoke, it was to pain and the bright light of morning. New Orleans looked to be fixing itself a really hot one. He heard Paris talking quietly on the phone. He sat up. She hung up, then came to the doorway, this time wearing a robe.

"Gorgeous news, Andy," she said. "That was D.J. Emily's going to make it. It may be weeks before she talks again, if she ever does. But the son of a bitch missed her jugular. The worst is over."

"Thank God." His sudden relief made him feel exceedingly light-headed, floating.

"If it's any help, you probably saved her life. You and that gun of yours. Never figured you for that kind of stuff."

"Neither did I."

He was sinking back into wooziness.

"You get some more sleep," she said. "I've got to call Cooper. The son of a bitch wants to have a meeting. God Almighty. The poor girl nearly gets her head cut off and all that bastard can think of is his fucking picture."

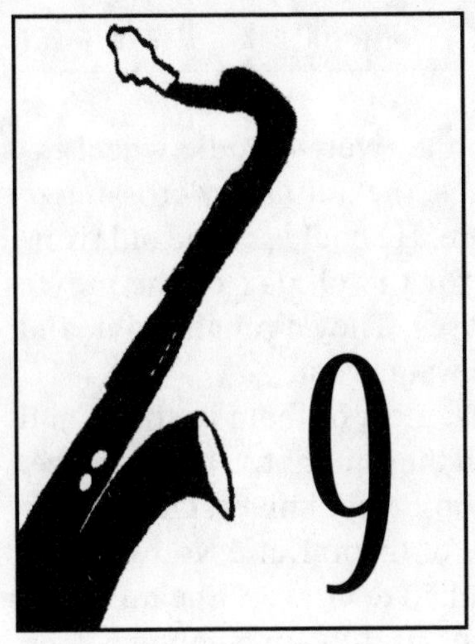

9

He slept again, and awoke this time to find Paris gone. Stirring himself, testing to see what movements caused the least hurt, he rose and went to the bathroom. A shower seemed out of the question, but he managed to wash his face and comb his hair. His eyes were bloodshot and there were dark circles under them. The flecks and smudges of blood on his skin looked like warpaint. If he could keep all this intact until Mardi Gras, he might win a prize. He took a mouthful of Paris's Listerine and, finding her razor, achieved a sort of shave. If not quite presentable, he at least no longer looked such a fugitive from Hell, though that was exactly how he felt.

Phoning the hospital, he learned nothing beyond what he'd been told by Paris. Calling the Vieux Carré station house next, he was told Maljeux was out on the street. Andy didn't want to talk to any other policeman. He didn't really want to talk to Maljeux. He didn't know what to do now.

A fruit basket, untouched by Paris, would provide breakfast. He ate an apple and part of an orange. He badly wanted coffee, but didn't want to put any room service charges on Paris's bill. He settled on another whiskey, this time with water.

There were two chairs by the big, wall-to-wall window. He pushed one close and gingerly sat down in it, wishing he'd stayed at the hospital long enough to have been given a sling. He hurt every time he twitched his arm.

There was a lot of traffic moving on the river—paddle wheel excursion boats, a tug with a raft of barges, the auto ferry crossing to the town of Algiers on the opposite shore. He could see the old riverboat Cooper had bought to blow up for the climax of the movie moored downstream by some warehouses. They'd repainted it, and it was the brightest craft visible on the waterfront.

The Quarter was acrawl with tourists, most of them in shorts and T-shirts. The town seemed so benign in the sunlight, a happy place.

Somewhere down there were the people with knives. Graves, the man in the black suit, was probably one of them. Katie Kollwitz was the only person Andy knew who had talked to Graves. She might remember something about him, something useful—presuming no one had taken a blade to her throat.

Andy had the scrap of paper with her phone number on it in his wallet. He went to Paris's phone and called, letting Katie's phone ring ten times before hanging up. Then he tried Henry Boone's New Orleans office. A secretary there told him Katie was with the senator and would be out for most of the day. They were scheduled to be at a rally that afternoon in one of the nearby upriver towns. She invited Andy to look for Katie there.

Clumsily setting the receiver on its cradle, Andy wondered if he was up to the drive. He wasn't sure he was able to stand up again.

Paris entered, carrying a plastic shopping bag.

"I brought you some clean clothes," she said. "I couldn't get into your place. The cops wouldn't let me. But D.J. came up with some decent things."

She produced a pair of jeans and a white dress shirt. It was about all Cosette ever wore.

"He's a generous man."

She set down her burden, then lighted a cigarette, seating herself in the chair next to his.

"How're you doing?"

"I'm just waiting for the plague of locusts. I'm sure that's next."

"D.J. thinks someone is trying to sabotage the movie," she said.

"You've been saying that for days."

"I was just being a smartass. D.J. thinks it's for real. A real serious effort to stop the picture or maybe get at Cooper, or the backers, or who knows, maybe Jim Ball. Or even me. Cooper's saying that you're to blame—that you're a jinx. Or that someone's after you. He wants you off this picture for good, as I guess he made clear last night."

"Maybe I am a jinx."

"Knock that off, Andy. It's not going to help anything feeling sorry for yourself."

"Is there still going to be a picture?"

"You wouldn't think so, but Cooper's convinced we can finish it. At least the backers haven't stopped the money. They called this morning. Cooper told them he's going on with it. He's got enough footage in the can to do without Emily. He wants to rewrite the ending, have the detective's wife get killed by the bad guys. So we won't need Emily anymore. Blowing up the riverboat and all that will be the detective's revenge. He'll save me at the last moment, before the explosion goes off, taking out the bad guys, and we ride off into the sunset—or more likely, off into the dead of night. Cooper's got *film noir* on the brain. Now, come on and I'll help you change clothes."

"I can manage."

She smiled again, with a little mischief in her eyes. "Skip the modesty, Andy. You've looked at me without adornment often enough. It's about time I had a gander at what you're made of." She laughed. "Don't get ideas. I'm not about to sleep with a man who might bleed all over me."

The hard part was the shirt. Paris was very deft, but pulling on the sleeve was agony.

"You need something else," she said. "Be right back."

She returned with a white silk scarf. In a moment, she'd outfitted him with a sling.

"Very elegant," Paris said.

"I could go to Spago like this, right?"

"You'd be overdressed. I've got to get downstairs. We're going over the script. You want to wait here?"

"I want to get on with my life. I want to see Emily."

"They're not letting anybody do that yet. Find me around dinner time. My treat."

"Okay."

"The cops are looking for you."

"I'm not the one they're supposed to be looking for."

• • •

He walked along the waterfront for a while, then crossed Decatur Street and joined the crowds around Jackson Square, pausing to rest against the square's wrought-iron fence. A black man in a multicolored beaded shirt—his face painted white and his long hair done in rainbow-hued corn rows—danced in front of him, looked at his sling, then spun and jerked away. A youth with a beer can affixed to his cap came by next, and then a fine-looking woman in shorts and halter, a small camera dangling from her wrist. It was sunny and bright, and very peaceful, except for someone playing drums on the other side of the street. Every artist in the Quarter seemed to be out here at work, along with several dozen fortune-tellers.

This was how he'd always thought of New Orleans when he'd daydreamed about it in New York. This is what he always talked to Candy about when he shared his homesickness with her.

Andy saw a police car moving along Decatur Street. It stopped. Wishing the police would just leave him alone, he moved into the crowd, heading up St. Peter. Then, turning onto Royale, he stopped in front of an expensive art gallery.

There were no customers inside, only the owner, a tall, thin, tanned, aristocratic-looking man, wearing gold-rimmed glasses and an immaculate white suit. He was standing by a desk in the rear. The gallery specialized in contemporary paintings and arty photographs. There were three of Andy's displayed on the rear wall.

"Good morning, Cousin," the man greeted. "The news of your misadventures precedes you."

Andy sat down in a chair beside the desk, grunting as he adjusted his arm in the sling.

"Has Paul Maljeux been in looking for me?"

"Not an hour ago. I informed him I hadn't seen you in two months, which is, as it happens, the absolute truth."

He had a slightly affected, deep and mellow voice—very much the Southern gentleman.

"Sorry, Vincent. I've been busy."

"You found occasion to visit my mother," he said, referring to Andy's Aunt Claire.

"Vincent, I haven't come by for the simple reason that I owe you twelve hundred dollars, and haven't the faintest idea when I'm going to be able to pay you back."

"I sold one of your photographs the other day, the picture of the three old musicians." He went behind the desk and opened a drawer, pulling out a hundred-dollar bill. "I'm afraid this is all I could get for it."

"Why don't you keep that on account."

"I'm not in need of money, André. I'm sure that you are." He set the bill on the desk, then leaned back, folding his well-manicured hands in front of him. "What can I do for you?"

"I need your advice. I'm wondering if I should leave New Orleans. I have the funny feeling that if I stick around, someone else is going to get hurt."

"Are you in trouble? A foolish question, looking at that arm."

"Not with the police, but someone doesn't like me. I keep thinking of Pancho Villa's last words after they gunned him down: 'What I done wrong?' "

"Are you afraid? If you are, then by all means, depart the city."

"Vincent. When I came back here from New York, you said I was making a mistake. I've never quite figured out what you meant."

His cousin sighed. "André, when you came home, you were talking like a man who had died and gone to Heaven, as though New Orleans was a vessel of redemption and salvation. All this nonsense about rediscovering yourself here, throwing yourself into real photography, into art, becoming another Ernest Bellocq. He wasn't an artist, André, and neither are you. His settings were decadent. His subjects were exotic. His plates were technically quite perfect, but in essence, they were snapshots. Candids. If they hadn't been Storyville whores, no one would be at all interested in them. You take very stylish pictures, sir. Very dramatic. But they're not art. They belong in magazines. When I sell one, it's almost always to a tourist, or someone who knows your magazine work, not a serious collector. If this is the fulfillment you seek, I'm afraid your ambition is misdirected."

Andy stared at the floor. "Thank you for your honesty, if that's what it is."

"There's no point in telling you what I don't believe."

"You won't mind if I get a second opinion."

"Suit yourself. I intend no insult, André. Nothing born of resentment. Your photographs . . . they need something."

"What?"

"You. The composition, the light, you're most accomplished at that. You have a wonderful eye, especially for the dramatic. You're obviously quite fond of women. But you're so damnably detached. There's nothing of yourself in your pictures. Never. Do you know Nicholas Nixon, the Boston photographer? I saw a traveling exhibition of his work not long ago. One series of pictures was of his wife and child in a bath. Another was of geriatric patients, all of them a wisp of life away from death. The third was of AIDS patients, and it was much the same. They were great art, André, because you sensed Nixon in every image, even the most grotesque. You sensed his love. It was overpowering. You're detached, dispassionate. Always the observer. Since you've come back, you've lived your life here in New Orleans the same way. It's your camera that lives here, not you."

"That's not true."

Vincent turned in his chair to gesture at a framed drawing on the wall. It was a piece of Freddy Roybal's prison handkerchief art—a finely detailed ballpoint sketch of a nude woman with a decidedly Mexican face, done in a manner that suggested the evilly decadent style of the previous century's Aubrey Beardsley.

"I sold that this morning," Vincent said. "Got fifteen hundred dollars for it, and I daresay it's worth more. It's art, André. It says everything that poor old bartender feels about women—everything he felt about them when he was locked away in whatever godforsaken jail they had him in. This is what you can't make your camera do, as celebrated as you are."

"I don't want to leave New Orleans."

"Then stay. It has its charms, Lord knows, but André, it's just another city. There are thousands of people here living lives as miserable as those of people in Detroit—or New York. It's not a fairyland—to use what I suppose is an unfortunate phrase. It's nothing at all like the place in the history and tourist books, or like that movie you've been working on. Take it for what it is. At the moment, it seems to be a rather frightening place for you."

"I have another question," Andy said. "That man who was killed at my place. Albert Ferrier? He had my name and address on him.

Do you have any idea what he might have wanted from me?"

"Why are you asking me?"

"You know why."

Vincent sat more stiffly. His voice took on an exasperated edge.

"None of my *friends,*" he said, "have ever had any association with Albert Ferrier. His former domicile in Faubourg Marigny has been much discussed in conversations in the Quarter, as the occupant seems to be a lady, and enjoys the company of gays. But Mr. Ferrier was not one of my friends or, to my knowledge, the friend of anyone in the community. If you're presuming some gay conspiracy is involved here, you should disabuse yourself of the notion."

"But Ferrier . . ."

"I would suggest to you that his lifestyle was irrelevant to his demise. I'd say 'unfortunate' demise, but I'm not sure that's appropriate."

"Why would he have my address?"

"I haven't any idea, but it's something I'd endeavor to discover, if I were you—and I'm rather terribly glad I'm not. That's all I know, André."

Andy said nothing.

"Does any of this help?"

"I don't know. Thank you, Vincent. I'll be back. And, Vincent, New Orleans is not just another city."

10

No one was in the Razzy Dazzy but Freddy Roybal, Long Tom, and Bleusette, who was sitting by herself at the bar, listening to that song again. She nodded a greeting, but did not beckon. Andy's business was with Tom, who was at a rear table, going over his accounts. Andy went to him, pulling out a chair.

Calhoun looked up, smiling warmly. "Andy! For a sorry sight you're a goddamn good one. You come real close to becoming a ghost this time. How's that poor girl?"

"Last I heard she's going to live."

"That's something to celebrate. Buy you a drink?"

Andy shook his head. "I need your help, Tom. I need a piece. I fired my dad's gun at whoever it was who got into my bedroom last night. The police have it now."

"Doubtless they do." Tom frowned. "Andy, I'd like to help you out any way I can, but I gotta draw the line at a firearm. The police can take that real serious nowadays. I can't be caught puttin' guns into circulation. Every one I got here is registered in my name. I'm running for public office again."

"Whoever these people are, they're playing rough, Tom. I don't know what to do."

"I know, boy. I'm looking out for you. We all are."

Bleusette turned around on her stool. "Andy, I am leaving now. You come walk with me."

"You take care, Andy," said Tom. "Sorry. Anything else I can do, you let me know."

"Right. Thanks." He paused at the bar as Bleusette finished her drink and gathered up her things. "Freddy, did my cousin Vincent tell you he sold one of your drawings?"

"Not a word did he say. Did he get a few bucks?"

"Fifteen hundred dollars, Freddy. You're a professional artist now."

"No shit?"

"Absolutely."

Freddy grinned. "Don't tell my bookie."

• • •

On the street, Bleusette turned in the opposite direction from her house, clattering along the sidewalk at a rapid pace. Andy struggled to keep up.

"The cops are looking for you, Andy. There're a couple outside my place. You want to talk to them?"

"No. They'll take me down to the station and make me fill out more statements. I've got more pressing business."

"They ask me all kinds of questions about you, about what you have been doing with yourself last few days. I tell them to fuck off. But this don't do me no good."

They'd come to a little alley. She glanced over her shoulder, then ducked inside. He followed.

She reached into her purse, taking out a small, silver-plated automatic. "Take this. It is only a twenty-two, so you have to aim *très precis.*"

"Bleusette . . ."

"I got another one, somewhere. It's all right."

He thought a moment, then gently slipped the little handgun into his sling. *"Je vous remercie, belle amie."*

"I found out something you will want to know," she said. "Your girlfriend in Texas. She is married to Ben Browley, that big rich guy."

"I already know that. And then some."

"What I am telling you is that I hear he has a girlfriend himself, here in New Orleans."

"You're sure? Who?"

"This I don't know. But I think you should stay far from him. And his wife. I mean it, Andy. I hear bad things about this fucker."

"I'll think about it."

"If you want to come home, call me first. I tell you if cops are gone."

"You said you might go away for a while."

"No. I decide I'm not going to let nobody make me do that." She touched his injured arm. "But you, Andy, I think you should go away. Far. Now."

"Right now, I'm going out to the boondocks. To a Hank Boone rally."

"What the hell for?"

"Look for somebody."

"He's a bad man to be around, Andy."

"Like someone said. We all are."

• • •

The old Cadillac's power steering still worked. Pushing the sling back on his arm, Andy managed to drive. Somehow getting the car through the city traffic and onto the freeway, he settled into the right-hand lane and headed west. If barely, he stayed awake, though he ran off the road twice when he was on the back highways.

The rally, fittingly enough, was held on a field used by visiting carnivals. Perhaps four or five hundred people had gathered—a large crowd for a town that far out in the country. Had they been wearing bib overalls, they might have passed for some of Huey Long's faithful. The men were mostly wearing tractor driver caps, some of them in camouflage fatigue pants. The women were in cheap dresses and shorts and halter tops.

A flatbed truck had been parked at the edge of the field to serve as a stage. A country-and-western band was playing next to it, warming up the folks. They didn't look as though they needed much exhortation. Some were nodding their heads and clapping in time with the music, but also to get themselves into the spirit of the forthcoming excitement. A Hank Boone speech was a religious experience, for the believers.

Boone was not in sight. There was a big tent set up behind the truck. Andy presumed the senator was in it—Katie Kollwitz with him.

There was a small roped-off area near the truck set aside for the press. Only a few reporters and photographers were present. Andy always kept a spare camera in his trunk. He brought it from the car with him, showing his New Orleans police press pass to one of the burly thugs standing sentry in front of the truck bed. Accepted, he ducked, somewhat painfully, under the rope.

Carl Bashaw was among the newsies. "Thought you were in the hospital."

"I'm all right."

Bashaw put pen to notepad. "You want to tell me something about what happened last night?"

"Not now. I'm working." Andy slipped his camera strap around his neck.

"You won't give me just a little something? It's a big story. Our city desk got a call from the *L.A. Times.*"

"No sir."

"Who you covering this rally for?"

"For whoever will buy my pictures."

The band broke into a noisy rendition of "Dixie" and people in the crowd began cheering. A moment later, Boone clambered aboard the truck platform wearing his country clothes—blue jeans, plaid shirt, and farmer's hat, a big red, white, and blue Boone button pinned just above the shirt pocket. He took off his hat, gesturing with it in homage to the crowd, and the cheering became a din.

"This is America—our America!" he said, then stepped back to wait for the whooping and hollering to abate. When it did, he came forward again. "You're here, and I'm here, because this is our country, and, by God, we're gonna take it back!"

The response this time was explosive. He was throwing raw meat to hungry lions.

"He's not even a candidate for reelection yet," Andy said, over the roar. "Let alone president."

"Hank Boone's always a candidate," said Bashaw.

"First thing we do," Boone said, "you and I and all the folks just like us, is take back the Democratic party. Our party. Your daddy and momma's party. Your granddaddy's party. The great Democratic party that got sold down the river by John Fornicator Kennedy and Lyndon Bull Johnson!"

"Ouch. Nasty stuff," Andy said.

"He was meaner than this up in Tallulah the other day," Bashaw replied.

"They started givin' America away and those who come after them have been givin' it away and that bunch of rascals we've got in Washington are givin' it away hand over fist. The District of Columbia has a shadow senator who's got more to say about what goes on in the Congress and the Democratic party than all the elected representatives of the state of Louisiana!"

The response this time was a succession of hoots.

"What's a shadow senator?" Bashaw asked.

"He's talking about Jesse Jackson."

Boone stepped closer to the microphone. He lowered his voice, but it came out of the amplifiers and loudspeakers like the whispers of a wrathful God.

"With your help," Boone said, "I'm not going to let them do it anymore. Their day is done!"

More wild cheering. Andy lifted his camera and, with some difficulty, aimed it one-handed at the platform. The telephoto lens had a motor-driven zoom. He touched the button that activated it, bringing Boone's dark, animated face into focus. He wanted to get at the messianic eyes, but was too far away.

"Was she your girlfriend, that actress who got cut up last night?" Bashaw asked.

"She was a friend." Andy snapped off three shots, then shifted the camera, using the lens as a telescope, looking for Katie's strange, beautiful face among the entourage arrayed behind the truck. She wasn't anywhere in view.

"Are you mixed up in something?" Bashaw asked.

"Just trying to do my job," Andy said. "Like I'm trying to do now. Let me do it, will you?"

"Sorry, Andy."

"I really have no idea why we were attacked last night. I wish I did."

"Whoever it was did you a kind of favor."

"What the hell are you talking about?"

"After the first one, people were saying you were mixed up in some gay thing, but I guess last night takes care of that. You and the girl were in bed, right?"

"Will you shut up?"

"Sorry. Just doing my job, too."

Andy wanted to move away from the reporter and the press pen, but he'd lose his vantage point. Up on the truck, Boone was talking about his growing up poor in a hardscrabble town, and how the America with the old values had made it possible for him to better himself. Nowadays, he said, no God-fearing Christian could get ahead. All the money was being made by New York shysters and foreign investors. Jobs were going to Japanese and Taiwanese and Mexicans. Americans who still had jobs had had their wages cut by Ronald Rip-Off Reagan's and George Boola Boola Bush's big corporation Republicans. And the government was taxing what was left and spending it on welfare recipients and boat people.

"I say send 'em back!" Boone thundered. "Send 'em all back where they came from! The foreign invaders on the boats and those thieving bums in Washington!"

More pandemonium. "This is becoming his stock speech," Bashaw said. "I'm getting tired of it."

"Why do you keep covering him?"

"Because my editor thinks that at one of these rousers he's going to let loose that he's an official candidate for president. I don't know how he thinks this kind of rhetoric is going to play up north."

"You've never been to Queens, have you?"

Andy stepped back and began snapping pictures of the crowd, scanning it through the lens for a glimpse of Katie. What kind of press assistant would stay so scarce? Usually at campaign appearances, they attached themselves to the reporters. They'd said she was coming to this rally. So where the hell was she?

He panned right, toward Boone's entourage again. There were several cars parked behind the tent, and a group of men standing near them—doubtless the drivers. Andy started to swing the lens away, then froze.

It was him, the man he'd chased down Burgundy Street, the man who'd killed Albert Ferrier. Andy couldn't be surer of it. The image in the viewfinder was clear. If it were a gunsight, he could have shot him dead—one round.

Andy clicked off a half-dozen pictures of the man, wishing he were closer. He glanced around. Everyone was staring raptly at Boone, who was ranting on about the Arabs taking away the jobs of Louisiana oil workers, despite all the American blood that was shed on their behalf in the Persian Gulf War.

Moving to the rear, Andy hit his rewind button, removed the film and put it in his pocket, then replaced it with a fresh roll. He started to slip out under the press rope. One of Boone's security guards stopped him.

"You can't leave," he said. "Not until after the speech."

"The hell I can't. He's not the president of the United States. Not yet, he isn't. And you sure aren't Secret Service."

"Nobody leaves. That's the rule."

"Look. I've got to use the john. You want me to use your leg instead?"

The man gave him a belligerent look, then relented, stepping aside.

"Okay. But if you leave, you can't come back."

"Fine," said Andy, getting to the other side of the rope. "I don't need to hear the rest of that speech."

"Maybe you won't get to next time."

"I'll survive."

He moved into the sweaty crowd, heading toward the row of portable toilets set up along the edge of the field. When the security man turned back toward Boone, Andy changed direction, making his way around to the back of the tent, then moving past it to the parked cars.

The man he sought was still there, leaning against a fender. Andy quickened his step. The man saw him, turned and ran.

"You!" Andy shouted. "Wait!"

His call was futile. The man kept running. Slinging his camera around to the side, Andy took off after him. He'd had little to eat, too much to drink, and had lost some blood in the punishment of the night before. The heat enveloped him like a heavy cloak. His breath shortened. His heart began to thump. He felt light-headed, then dizzy, then pained. But he somehow loped on, like some sick, hungry old wild animal desperate for a kill. His prey had an open field in front of him, but cut into the crowd, slowing as he pushed people out of the way. Andy staggered on after him, ignoring the startled and angry faces.

"Stop him! He's a murderer!"

The words, scarcely audible, came between Andy's struggling breaths. He stumbled, caught his balance, and trudged on, somehow drawing nearer the man, who had too many people in his way. A few feet more and Andy thought he might snatch at his shirt.

He'd done that last time, and the wretch had gotten away—had almost killed him.

A sudden blow at the back of Andy's head sent him sprawling to the ground. He tried to get up but everything seemed to be spinning, as though he'd fallen onto a merry-go-round. He couldn't make it stop. His shoulder burned with a pain like fire. He saw a man's foot just a few inches from his eyes, then everything disappeared.

• • •

He awoke to see a face peering into his, a woman's face, upside down, utterly expressionless, devoid even of curiosity. He thought it might be Bleusette again, but then realized where he was, more or less. He was lying on his back on the ground, but in a shadowy place, the sky above him a strange, gloomy, grayish white. It wasn't the sky. He was in the tent. The woman was Katie Kollwitz.

She touched his shoulder. He flinched.

"You're bleeding," she said. "Your shoulder."

"The locusts will be along any minute," he said.

"What?"

"I'm not having a good day." He sat up, slowly, supporting himself with his right arm.

"The man I was chasing," he said. "He's the killer. Stabbed that guy outside of my house. Ferrier."

"I don't know what you're talking about, Andy," she said. Her voice was soft, but without emotion. She was extraordinarily calm.

"He works for you guys."

She was kneeling. She rocked back onto her heels, and stood up, seeming to tower over him. Someone stepped up beside her—Senator Boone.

"What was all this about?" he asked.

"The guy I was after works for you," Andy said. "A driver or something. He was standing by your cars."

"All the people who work for me are in this tent or standing outside. You weren't chasing any of them."

"I've got him on film." Andy leaned forward, his hand going to his shirt pocket. The exposed roll was gone. He looked around. His camera was on a nearby card table; there was no film next to it.

The silk sling was still around his neck, although his injured arm was out of it. The bleeding had stopped, but there was a dark, red stain on his shirt.

"Help me up, please," he said.

Boone extended his hand, and pulled. The senator was very strong. Andy was surprised to find himself so quickly on his feet. He felt wobbly. Katie went to his side, putting her arm around his waist to support him. She was wearing her gargoyle earrings and another long, low-cut black dress. Her perfume was quite potent—a scent that made him think of the Orient, flowers and incense. She hadn't been wearing any the night they'd met.

"You should sit down," she said.

"I want to call the police."

"I'm the one who should call the police, sir," Boone said. "You were carrying a firearm."

"I told you he's all right, senator," said Katie. "I know him. He's Andy Derain, a photographer who does work for the newspapers."

"The press should not be carrying firearms, not around a United States Senator who's had threats made against his life."

"I'm sure he didn't know that," she said. "He was attacked in his home last night. A woman with him was almost killed."

"Damned criminals. Everywhere you look." Boone pronounced "damned" as a polysyllable: "damn-ed."

"Where's my film?" Andy asked.

"Our security people looked in your camera," Katie said. "I'm afraid they exposed it."

"There was another roll."

"We didn't find another roll."

Andy swore. Boone was staring at him intently.

"I'm going to let you go, sir," he said, finally, "since Katie vouches for you. But don't you come anywhere around me again with a weapon, you hear? My security men are authorized to carry firearms. You could have been shot."

"Someone hit me."

"With good reason, not knowing what you were intending, running like a wild beast into the crowd. I'm sorry if you suffered any injury, Derain, but you have only yourself to blame."

Andy gingerly touched the back of his head. There was a lump, but nothing too serious. His mind was clearing.

"I'll drive you home," Katie said.

"I have my own car."

"The way you look, you might have an accident. I'll drive it. It's all right. I came out here with the senator. My car's back in New Orleans."

Andy looked around at the others in the tent. He wanted to get out of there.

"All right," he said. "Be careful. It's an old car."

• • •

They gave him back his camera, but Katie put the pistol he had borrowed from Bleusette in her purse. She drove Andy's weary Cadillac about as fast as it could go, holding the wheel with one hand, her right hand resting on her lap. Andy lay back against the seat, fighting the urge to sleep.

"It was him," Andy said. "It was, Katie."

"Maybe it was. We get all kinds of characters at these rallies. But he wasn't one of our people. Nobody on the payroll. No one I know of, anyway."

"What was he doing standing by your cars? Your guys weren't even going to let me go to the bathroom, but you let him go where he pleased."

"Press don't have the same privileges as ordinary citizens. Not at campaign events. You know that."

"I'm going to tell the police about all of this."

"We'll be glad to talk to them. Everyone knows where Hank Boone stands on crime."

He studied her a moment. Her eyes were fixed on the road.

"How well do you know him?" Andy asked. "The senator."

"Not well. I only went to work for him a couple months ago."

"He's a racist and a bigot. He's stirring up a hell of a lot of trouble."

"Welcome to America. Anyway, he doesn't go around murdering homosexuals."

"He shot down two black kids."

"That was during a robbery. I believe you fired a gun last night at someone. Same thing."

"No it isn't."

"Andy, this talk isn't getting us anywhere. I like you. Knock it off."

"You went home with a man named George Graves the other night."

"I met him in the bar where I met you. He walked me home. I told you, I don't like to walk the streets alone at night."

"So you go out to bars looking for an escort to take you back again?"

"I was in that bar looking for you."

"Does Graves work for Boone, too?"

"No. I don't know what the hell he does for a living."

"He's a private investigator, out of Houston. A divorce specialist."

"How do you know that?"

"I'm psychic."

"Look. I left him at my door. I haven't seen him since. I'm not an easy lay, Andy. I don't go around trying to get picked up by strange men."

"You let me pick you up."

"That was different. I wanted to meet you. And you didn't sleep with me, remember?"

"I remember."

"Are you sorry?"

"About a lot of things. Including maybe meeting you."

"Ease up, Andy. I'm trying to be your friend. How's that girl, the movie actress?"

"She's going to live."

"Gives me the heebie-jeebies, what happened to her. Horrible. I'd hate to die like that."

"She's not going to."

"I'm glad to hear, though I wasn't glad to hear she was with you. Is she the reason you didn't want to go to bed with me?"

"No. As a matter of fact, after I left you, I decided I made a mistake."

"You could have come back up."

"It was late."

"Next time try early."

"You seem different today than you were that night. More cheerful."

"We all have our moods, don't we?"

The flat, green, swampy countryside swept monotonously by, flecks and slashes of water glinting in the hazy sun. The traffic was light. He wished she wouldn't drive so fast.

"You won't like it if the engine blows up, or a tire goes," he said.

"I wouldn't mind dying like that, you and me together. I'd like that."

She smiled.

"Now you're like you were before."

"Moods change."

"Did Graves ask you anything about me? He's been following me."

"Not a word. You lead an exciting life, don't you? I like that in you."

They picked up the interstate, heading east. She tried turning on the radio, but it didn't work.

"Get some sleep, Andy. You look like you need it."

The heat and his exhaustion compelled him to agree with her. He closed his eyes, listening to the thump of the tires on the pavement joints, then dozed away.

When he awakened, they were in the Quarter. She found a parking place a block or so down from his house.

"How do you know where I live?" he asked, rubbing his eyes.

"The bartender at the Razzy Dazzy told me."

She took the keys from the ignition and handed them to him, then got out of the car, leaning in on the door after she'd closed it. Her breasts bulged a little from the top of her deeply cut dress.

"You should see a doctor about your shoulder."

"I did. He sewed it up."

"You should see another one. You look like you need some more thread."

"I'll take care of it."

"Do you want me to come in?"

He wanted some food, a bath, and more sleep. But he owed her some hospitality. She had gotten him out of his scrape with Boone's torpedoes and driven him all the way home. And she might yet tell him something he didn't know. He didn't know much.

"There's a police car outside my house."

"An hour ago you were threatening us with going to the police. Don't you want to talk to them?"

"Not now."

"Do you have a back door?"

"Yes. There's a kind of alley."

"Let's try it."

A yellow police tape had been stuck across the kitchen door. Andy pulled the tape aside, turned the lock, and stepped inside. She followed him, then moved past him, heading into his studio. She stopped in front of the pictures on the wall.

"That's Paris Moran."

"Yes. In all her glory."

"Does she mind your having her up there like that, naked?"

"Did you see her movie *Sinners?* She showed the world a lot more than this, and you can rent it in any video store. I want a drink. You want to join me?"

"Sure. But should you have anything, after what's happened to you?"

"Yes. My shoulder's killing me. I need something."

He poured two whiskies straight. She sipped hers, looking at him over the edge of the glass. The window light touched upon a faint scar on her cheek he hadn't noticed before.

"I want to see your pictures—the ones you're taking for your books."

"I haven't decided which ones I'm going to use."

"Let me see."

He pulled two cardboard boxes out from under his worktable. She helped him lift them to the top, then opened the one on the left, which contained the prints he'd made up of his New Orleans street scenes. Like a child opening Christmas presents, Katie began to take them out, examining each carefully before turning to the next.

"You have pictures of dead people in here." Her face was rapt.

"A few. I do some work for the newspaper."

"And whores. And weirdos. Here's that woman with eyes tattooed on her cheeks."

"Local color. There are musicians in there, too."

"Very nice." She turned to the other box, pulling out a glossy print of a languorous, self-satisfied blonde reclining on a highly polished floor. "Is she a model?"

"No. She's a secretary from Schenectady who married a rich man in New York. She's the most egotistical woman I ever met."

"You can tell she really likes having her picture taken. But won't she mind this being in a book?"

"Not at all. She divorced him. Now she's rich. She does what she wants."

"Who's this? Another rich bitch?"

"She's a call girl. Used to live here. Moved to Miami."

"And this one?"

"The sister of a friend of mine. An artist."

"Do you have any of your girlfriend?"

"I had lots, but they were stolen the other night."

He watched for her reaction. There wasn't any.

"I mean the actress who was with you last night, the one who got hurt."

"No." He didn't want to talk about Emily.

"If you took my picture, which box would you put it in?"

He studied her. The correct answer was 'both.'

"It depends."

"Will you take my picture? I've wanted you to take my picture ever since I first saw your work."

"And where was that?"

"In a magazine. It was of a fashion model in a negligee. Will you do it?"

"Not now, Katie. I can barely stand up."

"Your shoulder."

"Everything."

"Take off your clothes, Andy."

"What?"

"Take off your clothes, and that bandage. You need a bath. And I want to tend to that wound."

"I can take care of it myself."

"Like you said, you can barely stand."

He let her unbutton his shirt and pull it off, then sat down so she could go to work on the dressing. Using a pair of scissors from his worktable, she cut the adhesive free, then pulled the blood-soaked gauze gently away from the cut.

"It looks nasty as hell," she said, "but there's no infection. Let's get you into the tub."

He shook his head. "I can take a bath by myself. You wait here."

"You're sure?"

"Yes."

Leaving her to look through more of his photographs, he wearily mounted the stairs, wishing he did not have to go into the bedroom to get to the bath.

The scene was as hideous as he had expected. The sheets and one of the pillows were streaked with blood and there were spatters of it on the floor. Nothing appeared to have been moved since the night before.

Letting the water run into the tub, he got out some fresh clothes—a clean pair of khakis, light blue dress shirt, and an old blazer—and set them on a chair. He was tired of looking like a derelict.

He took a long bath, wondering if she'd get impatient and leave. A few smudges of blood came off on his towel when he dried himself, but the deep cut did not reopen. He stepped in front of the mirror. He looked worse than he had that morning. There'd been touches of gray in his sandy hair for some time, but now there seemed to be a lot more of it.

A face suddenly appeared next to his in the mirror. Katie's eyes were wide and staring; the corners of her lips curled in a curious smile. She leaned close, and he felt her bare breasts against his back. He turned around and stepped back. She was as naked as he.

"Katie, I . . ."

Her eyes still on his, she lowered herself to her knees, then bowed her head forward. Before he could speak again, a sudden warmth enveloped his penis.

Andy went back against the sink, bracing himself with his right hand. He couldn't handle this now. He wanted to sleep.

"Katie . . ."

She kept on, relentless. The warmth spread throughout his entire body. His skin tingled.

Abruptly, she stopped, pulling back, looking up.

"Do you want more?"

"I . . ."

"Do you want me to finish?"

He closed his eyes. "Yes."

"Then promise me you'll take my picture. As soon as we're done."

"All right."

The warmth—now heat—returned. He was floating, swimming. Suddenly, he froze cold. There was the creak of a floor board out in the bedroom. Someone called his name. Andy opened his eyes, looking out through the open doorway at the startled face of Lieutenant Paul Maljeux.

Katie stood up, her face full of cold fury. Maljeux turned his back, pretending to cover his eyes.

"My apologies, mademoiselle," he said. "I didn't know Andy had anyone here."

Without pausing to speak, or to cover herself with a towel, Katie walked out of the room and down the stairs.

"For God's sake, Paul. This is my house."

"I'm sorry, Andy, but it's also a crime scene."

"How did you know I was here?"

"Got your house staked out front and back. For your protection, yes? The man out back gave me a call. Didn't say anything about a lady, though. Who is she?"

"Her name's Katie Kollwitz. She works for Henry Boone. I met her in the Razzy Dazzy."

"That makes no sense—someone who works for Boone hangin' around Long Tom's. She there scouting lynch victims?"

"She's not like Boone. She's okay. I like her."

"So I noticed."

Andy ignored this. "I found him, Paul, the man who killed Ferrier, the guy I chased down the street. He was at a Boone rally out in the country this afternoon. I tried to catch him but he got away from me again. I'm not much of a sprinter at the moment."

"Were you wearing clothes?" Maljeux eyes took in Andy's lack of them.

"Yes."

"Probably slowed you down. What was he doing at a Boone rally?"

"The senator said the guy didn't work for him, but he sure acted like he did."

"Can you add anything to his description?"

"Not much. He runs pretty good, for a stocky man."

Andy went into the bedroom and started to get dressed, with some difficulty.

"Can you come down to the station and give us a signed statement about last night?"

"What do you do with all these statements? You short of toilet paper? I want to go see Emily."

"They won't let you."

"They'll let you in. Take me with you."

Maljeux sat down on the bloody bed as Andy struggled getting on a clean shirt.

"What you say about that fellow maybe working for Boone is mighty interesting," Maljeux said. "We did a canvas of the neighborhood around Danielle Jones's house again today. Someone there said they saw a car with a Hank Boone bumper sticker on it the other night—a big, dark car, with a low number license. Could have been a senatorial plate."

"Henry Boone? Danielle Jones is black. And if he was fooling around like that he wouldn't use his official car."

"If it was Boone, wouldn't that be a fascinating development?"

"Fascinating? It could blow him out of politics. You going to talk to him?"

"Boone? Could get myself in a storm of trouble hassling a man like that with just this to go on. But I'm sure going to keep it in mind."

"You do that."

They went downstairs. Katie had left his pistol on his worktable. He quickly slipped it in his belt under his shirt.

"I saw that, Andy."

"No you didn't."

"You don't have a license for that weapon, do you?" Maljeux said. "Or, for that matter, one for the handgun you used last night."

"Look, Paul, some real bad people are making a habit of hanging around me—and you owe me one, if only for what happened upstairs."

"Hope you don't expect me to repay you in kind."

"Very funny."

"Lose your sense of humor, Andy, and you're in real trouble. Can't last long in the Quarter without a sense of humor."

• • •

Emily had been moved into a private room, just off a nursing station. A policeman, sitting in a chair by the desk, waved at Maljeux but gave Andy a suspicious look. So did the nurses. Maljeux went up to the one in charge.

"We'd like to look in on Miss Shaw," he said. "Is she conscious yet?"

"She was. Didn't like it much. We administered more tranquilizer. Should be asleep. Maybe she isn't."

"We won't take long."

"Is this necessary?"

"Yes ma'am. Have to do it sooner or later. Better sooner."

"She can't talk, lieutenant."

"Can she write?"

"I suppose—if she's awake. If she's asleep, you leave her be. Who's he?"

"Her boyfriend."

"Don't stay long."

"Yes ma'am. Thank you."

Emily was lying on her back. Her neck was swathed in bandages up to her chin. Her arms were at her sides, the tube of an IV extending from tape wrapped around her left wrist. Her eyes were closed. She was frighteningly pale, but still looked very pretty.

Maljeux stepped near, carefully leaning over the bed.

"Miss Shaw?"

Her eyes shot open. She focused on Maljeux's face with some difficulty.

"How are you?" Maljeux asked.

She shook her head slightly. The movement hurt. The lieutenant put his hand gently on her arm.

"They tell me you're going to be just fine," he said. "It'll take a while before you're back on your feet, but the worst is over."

Emily's lips parted. She made a faint croaking sound.

"Don't try to talk, honey. Just rest easy. We want to get the man who did this to you real bad, but we're going to need your help. Can you write?"

With some effort, she lifted her right arm and held her hand in front of her face, moving her fingers. Maljeux took out a pad and ballpoint pen from his uniform pocket.

"Anything you can think of," he said. "Anything you saw, or heard. Anything that can help."

He put the pen in her hand, and leaned forward to hold the pad. She stared at the pen, but didn't move it.

Andy moved around to the other side of the bed to help. Her eyes followed him, once again trying to focus.

"Emily?" he said.

Her eyes widened, straining, staring madly at his face. Then she abruptly turned away, her legs jerking, trying to roll over.

"Andy!" said Maljeux. "Get back!"

He retreated, moving to the rear of the bed. Maljeux was holding her arm so she wouldn't pull it away from the IV. Emily went over on her back again, her eyes still wild. She opened her mouth wide. More croaking noises and gurgling came out. Andy realized that, if she had a voice, she'd be screaming.

"All right!" said the nurse. She'd been standing at the door without telling them. "You're outta here."

Maljeux took Andy by the arm and led him from the room and down the hall. He didn't speak until they were in the elevator.

"She was scared to death of you, Andy."

"I don't blame her. It wasn't a fun date."

"I think now's a good time for you to come on in and give us that statement."

• • •

With a court stenographer present, Andy told them everything he could remember about the attack, which wasn't much. A homicide detective pressed him about his struggle with the assailant, for some reason wanting to know his and Emily's exact positions on the bed.

That was among the many things he couldn't remember.

He had to wait in Maljeux's office for the statement to be typed up for his signature.

"We took a mess of different prints from your bedroom and the balcony," Maljeux said. "Who all did you have up there?"

"Lately, just Emily, and my Texas friend. And Katie Kollwitz, the woman who works for Boone. Bleusette's in and out all the time."

"I'll bet she is. We've had a lot of calls from out-of-town reporters on this one—including some from those TV tabloid shows. They'll be after you, too. I'd advise you not to tell them much."

"I think what I have to tell them is called 'fuck off.' "

"These days, that might get on television."

A uniformed sergeant brought in the typed statement. Andy signed it quickly and got out of there.

• • •

He walked through the evening mobs of tourists to the Westin, ringing Paris's room from the lobby. There was no answer. He should have called her earlier.

He went into the cocktail lounge, where the movie crew spent a lot of their time when not working on the set. Two women he recognized—the film company's hair stylist and the wardrobe lady—were chatting over tall drinks at the big square bar. D. J. Cosette was on the other side, gazing vaguely at the television set, which had a baseball game on the screen.

"Have a seat," he said, lifting his martini. "I was wondering when I was ever going to see you again."

Andy sat down. "I'm looking for Paris."

"She went over to the hospital."

"I just came from there."

"You must have just missed her. She was here in the bar with us and got a call. Said she had to meet someone at the hospital. I thought it might be you."

"No."

"Paris did a good thing today," Cosette said, lighting a cigarette. "Cooper wanted to put a death scene in the script using Emily. In her hospital bed! Yeah, shoot it in her hospital room. 'She won't even have to act,' the son of a bitch said. I've worked for some real turds in my day but this guy floats to the top of the cesspool. Anyway, Paris queered the deal. She carries that contract of hers around in her purse like it was a can of Mace. She pulled it out, read the clause about script approval out loud, called Cooper a shameless prick, and said no dice. Great broad. I'd work with her in a Three Stooges picture. Cooper's going to settle for a murder scene. Exterior. Using a stunt woman. Jimmy Ball gets to cry over her body. Probably a three-drink shot."

He signaled to the bartender for another martini. Andy didn't want anything.

"They're really going ahead with the picture?"

"Cameras start rolling again tomorrow night. They dropped the car chase. Going to make do with everyone on foot instead. Got a night street shoot in the French Quarter. The baddies chase Ball and Paris, guns blazing. Somehow, they get away. Should have had you help with the site selection. I don't like the street they chose. Kind of a bad part of the neighborhood. Cooper likes it because there won't be so many tourists underfoot."

"You'll have a crowd of tourists the instant you turn on the lights."

"Well, that's one way to get an audience for this turkey."

"Cooper fired me."

"Paris tried to get him to change his mind, but no dice. You're better off, sport. Every day, he's got to have somebody to piss on and it's a good bet you'd be his boy."

Andy looked at his watch. "I'd better move along, D.J. If you see Paris before I do, ask her to call me at home tonight."

"You going to try to catch her at the hospital?"

"No," Andy said, thinking of the look on Emily's face. "Thanks for loaning me those clothes. I'm afraid I'm going to have to buy you a new shirt. I bled all over yours."

"Imagine that, real blood for once. Don't tell anyone about that shirt. Cooper will want to use it in the film."

• • •

Leaving a message for Paris at the hotel desk, Andy went down to the street and started across the Quarter toward home, stopping briefly on St. Peter Street outside Preservation Hall to listen to that venerable jazz ensemble go through part of a set. Cheered a little, he moved on, wondering if he might find Katie in his house when he got there.

Waving to the policeman parked outside, he entered through the front door, going directly to his studio. No one was there.

He hadn't checked his answering machine all day.

Most of the calls were from reporters, including one from "Entertainment Tonight."

Far back on the tape was a message from Candice.

"Andy! Are you all right? What the hell is going on? What was that woman doing in your bedroom? It's all over the goddamn news! You get me in all this trouble and then you turn around and shack up?"

There was a pause. He waited for the machine to click off but instead Candy's voice came on again.

"Ben hardly lets me out of his sight. I'll try to call you tonight. We've got to work this out, Andy. Please don't do anything to make things worse. I'm scared. I love you, Andy."

The machine clicked and went off. He lay back on his couch, shutting out the world.

The world wouldn't stay away. He awoke to someone pounding on his door. He'd forgotten to lock the gate again. Still exhausted, he got to his feet. When he turned the lock and pulled the door free, it was flung away from his hand, banging against the wall.

A large young man with long blond hair, muscles bulging beneath his T-shirt, fierce hatred burning in his eyes, burst in and lunged for him. Startled, Andy stumbled back, just as the youth's fist came swinging by his face. The next blow could not be avoided. It caught Andy on the chin. He fell sprawling, rolling over onto his back, his injured shoulder bringing a swift agony. The young man lunged again. Desperate, Andy cocked his knee and swung his foot, catching the man in the crotch with his heel. He knew exactly how that was going to feel.

The youth, swearing, rocked backward, then regained his balance and began kicking Andy in the side.

He rolled again, remembering the little pistol. Grasping at his belt, he yanked out the gun and thrust the barrel toward the young man's suddenly frightened face.

The youth backed up. Andy got up to his knees, keeping the gun aimed at the man's chest. His finger tightened on the trigger. He suddenly realized he recognized the stranger's face, but he couldn't put a name to it.

"Andy!"

He looked past the youth to the doorway, stunned to see Paris standing there.

"Don't shoot him, Andy! He's Emily's brother!"

• • •

It took a while for all of them to calm down. Andy put the pistol back in his belt. Richard Porter, hunk movie star, stood there meek and humbled, but no less angry. Paris was mad, too, at both of them.

"You said you wanted to talk to him," she said to Porter. "You didn't tell me you were going to try to beat his brains in."

"He got Emily into this."

"They cut him up, too, Richard. Can't you see the blood on his shoulder?"

Porter glowered, as though wishing Andy had been cut up more, then looked down at the floor.

"Go out and wait in the car, Richard," Paris said. "You're lucky that cop outside didn't come running in here."

"I'm holding you responsible," Porter said to Andy. "For everything. You haven't seen the last of me."

"Get in the car!"

When he was gone, Paris lighted a cigarette.

"You almost killed him, honey bunch. That would have been *finito* for everything."

"Sorry. I didn't know who he was."

"Look, Andy. I'm sorry, but I think maybe you ought to stay away from all of us for a while. At least until we finish this stupid picture."

"But we were going to have dinner. Your treat."

"Let's make that a rain check, okay? Maybe we can go to Spago the night I win the Oscar for *Street of Desire*."

"Are you mad at me, Paris?"

"Honey bunch, I'm just mad at my life. So please stay out of it for a little while."

12

Candice didn't call. When the phone did ring, it was early in the morning, and the voice on the other end was that of Katie Kollwitz, sounding husky, as though from too little sleep or too much drink.

"Hello, sailor."

"Good morning, I guess." Andy had slept on the couch in his studio. He sat up. "I'm sorry about yesterday."

"Things happen."

"Lieutenant Maljeux is a good friend, but sometimes he gets in the way."

"Cops do that. I have some news for you."

"I'd like a day without news for once."

"This is good news. I guess you could say that. I found out about that man you were after at our rally. His name's Frank Marengo. One of our drivers knows him—kind of knows him. Met him in some bar. He's not on our payroll. I never heard of him before. Neither has the senator. He just likes to hang around. You get people like that in politics. Can't be helped."

"Especially with your kind of politics."

"They're not my politics, Andy. This is just a job. The only other one I could find in this town was waitress. I'd rather turn tricks or rob banks than do that again."

"Does your driver know his address?"

"No. He just met him in a bar. They got to talking about Boone running for president. Marengo liked the idea and started coming around, hanging around. Leave our driver out of it. He doesn't know anything about Marengo."

"Does he remember what bar it was where he met this fellow?"

"He said it was some joint across the river in Algiers. The Acey-Deucey. Something like that. In a black neighborhood."

"What were two white guys doing in a bar like that?"

"I don't know. Looking for trouble maybe. Some people like trouble. How's Miss Shaw?"

"Not very happy."

"I wouldn't be either. I'd hate it if I couldn't talk. You'll tell your cop friend about Marengo, right?"

"Surc. Why don't you?"

"I'd get fired if Boone found out I did anything like that. It turns out the guy did some work for us. Volunteer stuff. Distributing leaflets or something. Errands. It won't look good when that gets in the papers. So, please, leave me out of it."

"Don't you care that it won't look good? That's your job, isn't it, making Boone look good?"

"Look, Andy, I'm trying to help you out. That bozo almost killed you. I want him to get what's coming to him, okay? I sure as hell want to get him off the street. Anyway, it's only a job. And with Hank Boone, there's only so much you can do to make him look good."

"Will you let me know if Marengo turns up again?"

"He won't. I think you spooked him pretty good. But call your cop friend, please. Right away."

"As soon as I'm done talking with you."

"I'll hang up then. See you 'round, sailor."

He'd been about to ask when, but the line went dead.

Andy had a cup of coffee, then called his "cop friend."

Maljeux was at home. The policeman's wife, a friendly woman named Jean, summoned him from the bathroom. He seemed startled by Andy's news.

"Do you know this fellow Marengo?" Andy asked.

"Never heard of him, but I'm not a habitué of Algiers—or Senator Boone's rallies."

"You going after him?"

"You bet. I'll put a couple of the boys on it, but I have to be in court this morning—maybe all day. And this isn't the only case that's got our attention at the moment—much as it seems to be preoccupying you."

"This guy should be your prime suspect—for murder, and attempted murder."

"I'll take care of it, Andy."

"Will you send somebody to look for him?"

"Soon as I can. But you stay away from there, okay?"

"I've got to go, Paul. Someone's at my door."

It was Bleusette, just home from work and wearing her customary slip. She invited Andy to come over for breakfast. He accepted.

As always, she had music playing in her house. Her taste was quite sophisticated and inclusive—she was as big on saxophonists like Richard Elliott and David Sanborn as she was on piano players like Mose Allison in his country-boy days and old-time music men on the order of Kid Oliver and Jelly Roll Morton. Andy had contributed a little to her extensive knowledge, but most of it came from the many musicians whose acquaintance she had made, in one way or another, over the years.

She'd brought home a bag of fresh, crisp *beignets*—the world's finest form of doughnut—and made some café au lait to go with it. There was no air-conditioning in either of their houses. As he sat at her table eating, she took off the slip, and went about her business naked. He still hadn't gotten used to this. The Storyville whores had been that way with Bellocq, once they'd gotten to know him. Bleusette was the only New Orleans hooker he counted as a good friend.

"I am thinking I will soon retire, Andy," she said.

"Why's that?"

"You won't tell anyone?"

"Friends who tell secrets aren't friends."

"I own four houses now, and I have nearly one hundred thousand cash. It's all mine. I don't have to beg some man to give it to me, like your Texas girlfriend."

He let that pass. "What will you do?"

"I think maybe I open a restaurant. Half the joints in the Quarter are named for working girls. I think maybe I'll open one and name it for me. I got a good name for a restaurant, yes? Bleusette's? Cafe Bleusette? I'll serve everything I like—beignets, chaurice, andouille, daube, crawfish, oysters, poboys, trout Nancy like at Brennan's, coquetiers, café brulot, chicory coffee, *le tout ensemble*. Maybe I stay open day and night. Get a good bartender."

"You'll need a liquor license, and a business permit. You might have trouble, given your present profession."

She sat down at the table opposite him, and lighted a cigarette. "Long Tom will fix it. This town is full of whores, Andy. Some of them hold elected office, *n'est ce pas*?"

He glanced at her breasts. They were as tan as the rest of her. She often sunbathed in the courtyard, an amenity Andy considered a *langiappe* of his renting the place.

"You'll have to wear clothes," he said.

She smiled. "Most of the time."

"It's sounds great to me, Bleusette."

"If I do this, will you come there? Hang out there, like Hemingway in Paris in the cafés? Maybe bring some artist friends? Maybe give me some pictures for the walls?"

"Sure."

"That's why I want this goddamn trouble to end. I don't want to fuck this up, Andy. I work *beaucoup* for this."

"It'll end. Maybe soon."

"*Bon*." She looked to the side, out the kitchen's screen door, then quickly got up and began pulling her slip on again.

"I don't mind you in the altogether," said Andy. "Really."

"There is a very handsome young man at your door, Andy, and I don't know him at all. We gotta get that goddamn doorbell fixed." She went to the screen. "Hey, you! André Derain is in here!"

It was Richard Porter. He stepped inside, at Bleusette's bidding, looking almost as unhappy as his sister had upon seeing Andy.

"Paris said I should apologize to you. Said you saved Emily's life and I shouldn't have decked you like that."

"Paris is big on good manners."

"Yeah. Well, I'm sorry. Okay? So now I've apologized."

"Accepted." The youth just stood there, a grimace set on his handsome face.

"You want some coffee?" Bleusette asked.

He looked at her as appreciatively as she had eyed him, then nodded.

"Sit down," she said. "I'm Bleusette Lescaut, Andy's landlady."

"This is Richard Porter, Bleusette," Andy said. "He works in the movies."

"I see his pictures. Very nice."

"Emily Shaw is his sister. That's why he's here."

Porter took a sip of café au lait, and found it agreeable.

"She's doing better," he said. "The doctors say she'll probably be able to talk again, but it'll take a long time. I don't know if she'll ever be able to work—in movies, I mean. She probably won't be able to sing. Her career's fucked."

"I am very sorry about her," Bleusette said. "This should not happen in a house of mine."

"My mother says Emily should sue. Maybe ask fifty million. That's not unreasonable for an actress with her potential."

"Well, I don't have fifty million dollars at the moment," Andy said. "To tell you the truth, I'd have a hard time scraping up ten."

"I have no money, either," Bleusette said, suddenly worried. *"Absolument rien."*

"Not you people. The movie company." Porter gave Andy a dark look. "But you, man, you got an obligation to Emily. I don't mean money. You've gotta do right by her."

"I will. In every way I can."

"You scared the hell out of her yesterday," Porter said. "She thought you were dead."

And he and Maljeux believed that had been fear borne of rage. It was a small consolation.

"For a while, so did I."

"I was supposed to start a movie shoot next week, but I told them to put it on hold until I take care of this. It's going to cost them some big bucks, but I don't give a shit. Emily comes first. I'm not leaving till they get whoever did that to her. That's what I came over to tell you."

"You picked a good day for it."

"What do you mean?"

Andy looked at Porter's arms and shoulders. "You get in fights a lot? I mean, aside from with burned-out, broken-down old photographers?"

"I got a Harley. I hang out with bikers a lot. I've been in some tumbles."

"Can you take care of yourself pretty good?"

"You would have found out last night if you didn't have that gun."

"Forget that, all right? I got a lead this morning on a guy. He killed somebody else a few days ago. Right out there in the courtyard. I caught up with him yesterday but he got away. The trail starts across the river in a place where people greet each other the way you did me last night, only with less etiquette. I'm going over there. You want to come along?"

Porter set down his coffee. "You're fucking A."

Bleusette leaned back against her sink, exhaling from her cigarette. "Remember, Andy, you gotta aim that pistol very careful."

"You're going to take that gun?" Porter asked.

"When in Rome," said Andy.

• • •

The bar was called Aces and Deuces. It had card games, a broken window, drunks sleeping on the floor, and no music. The bartender, a pot-bellied geezer with a mean face who had probably lived a lot longer than he'd expected to, was civil but suspicious. He was white, though most of the customers weren't.

Andy ordered beers for himself and Porter, and got immediately down to business since it was obvious they hadn't dropped in casually. He'd thought through his approach carefully.

"You seen a guy named Frank Marengo around?" Andy asked. "We've been looking for him all over the place."

"Well, you're looking in the wrong place."

"No we're not. We owe him some money. And we got another job for him."

"Didn't know Frank had a job."

"It's day work."

"Who are you?"

"We're day workers, too," Andy said. "Drivers. We've got a job for today. Same kind of work he's done before."

"You from the senator?"

"That's right. The senator."

The bartender looked at them doubtfully. Andy wondered if they should be better dressed.

"Well, if you know him, then you know where he lives."

"We tried there," Andy said. "Nobody answered the door."

"Well, try again. He's probably just sleeping off a bad night."

"We'll finish our beers."

"You say you owe him money?"

Andy nodded.

"You can leave it with me."

"You next of kin?"

"He's got a big tab."

"That's his problem. Not ours." The beer was warm. Andy took a small swallow of it, then looked at his watch. It was antique, and far too expensive to be flashing in a hellhole like this. "Forget it. We'll do it without him." He stood up. Porter did the same.

"Give him another try," said the bartender. "If you can't roust him, have the landlady do it."

"The landlady?"

"Mrs. Williams. Big black lady. Lives downstairs."

Andy nodded. "If it turns out he's not there, tell him to call in."

The bartender was looking at Andy's arm, once again in the sling.

"It's heavy-duty day work," Andy said.

They stepped out into the hot sunlight. It smelled as bad outside as it did in. A dead dog was lying on the sidewalk, amid a flurry of flies. They moved on toward where Andy had parked his old convertible around the corner.

"What do we do now?"

Andy glanced back. A large black youth had come out of the bar after them. He stopped, staring at them. It was then that Andy noticed another black man across the street. He was wearing a suit and sunglasses.

"Do you have any money?" Andy asked.

"Travelers' checks," Porter said.

"That won't do. Do you have any cash?"

Porter dug in his pocket. "A twenty and some change."

"Give me the twenty."

He went up to the black man, who seemed startled at Andy's approach, and held the twenty up in front of his face.

"This is yours if you can help us out. I'm looking for a guy, but I think I got the wrong address. You know Mrs. Williams?"

"You axing me where Miz Williams lives at?"

"Right."

"Shit. Gimme the twenty."

Andy did so, knowing full well the man might just snatch it and run off if he didn't.

"Around the corner and up two blocks. Place with a purple door."

They walked along the broken sidewalk quickly.

"We should have some cops with us," Porter said.

"I tried that, but didn't get much in the way of a satisfactory response . . ."

"I thought you said Marengo was wanted for another murder."

"Don't understand it myself. Maybe I don't have a lot of credibility these days."

"This place scares the shit out of me."

"You want to go back?"

"No."

• • •

The woman was indeed large. She stared at Andy and Porter as though they had come to murder her.

"We're supposed to pick up Frank Marengo," Andy said. "But he doesn't answer. Can you help us out?"

"You know Marengo?" She had a marked Caribbean accent.

"No. But we're supposed to pick him up. Got a job today."

She studied them both. "You look like that movie star. Dick Porter. Just like him."

Emily's brother smiled. "Never heard of him."

"You wait down here."

She began heaving herself slowly up the narrow stairs. Andy leaned back against the wall. His shoulder was hurting again, worse than the day before. Cooking smells were mixed with that of urine. He'd never been in such a place—not here, not in New York. If

Marengo was a hired killer, they sure weren't paying him much.

Unless he hadn't finished the job, and wouldn't collect until he did.

He heard her rapping on Marengo's door, far more gently than one would trying to rouse a drunk from deep sleep.

"Frank," he heard her say. "You hear me?"

There was a pause.

"You get out quick, mon. There's cops downstairs."

"Shit," said Porter.

They hurried up the stairs, Porter leading. The woman turned, her back to Marengo's door, barring it. Porter, with some effort, pulled her aside.

"Marengo!" Andy shouted. "Just want to talk to you. We're from Senator Boone. Got some work for you!"

There was no answer. The woman was trying to cast a spell on them with her eyes.

"What do we do now?" Porter asked.

"You're the guy who does this in the movies. What do you think?"

Porter backed up, then lunged at the door, shoulder first. Andy wouldn't have tried that even without stiches in his shoulder.

The door cracked, but didn't give. "You stop that!" screamed the woman. Porter gave it a more earnest try. The door creaked and cracked again and then went flying open.

Andy had pulled out his small pistol, but Porter went first. The room was surprisingly large and neat, and empty. The rear window was open, the screen hanging loose. Andy stuck his head out of it.

Marengo had dropped onto a pile of trash, scattering much of it. He was running across a vacant lot—barefoot, in dark brown pants and T-shirt. Andy stepped back.

"You go first," he said. "You may have to catch me."

Porter went out the window without hesitation. Following, Andy seated himself on the ledge, then jumped.

He landed feet first on an overturned garbage can, which went rolling, and he ended up on his bottom in the can's rotting contents. By the time he got up, Porter was thumping along across the weedy lot, gaining on Marengo. Suddenly, Porter stopped. On the sidewalk ahead of them were four or five black men, mostly young, among them the fellow to whom Andy had given the twenty. Letting Marengo run daintily past, they started forward. Porter began backing up. Andy felt helpless, utterly feckless. He had the little pistol, which was hardly enough to stop five big men coming at a rush. What if they were armed? In this neighborhood, it would be amazing if they were not.

Andy moved up to Porter's side, holding the pistol high. The black men kept coming, slowly now, but resolutely. Two of them flashed knives; another fielded a handgun that looked twice the size of Andy's. This one was grinning.

"You didn't tell me we were going to run into this kind of shit," Porter said. He looked nervous, but not frightened. Not yet.

"Should have checked the tourist guide first," Andy said. "Sorry."

"What you gonna do with that little piss-ant piece, motherfucker?" asked one of the black youths.

Andy did the only thing he could think of with it. He aimed it at the man with the big pistol. He might as well have had a BB gun.

"We don't want any trouble with you," Andy said. His mother's upriver accent was very strong in his speech now, as it had been when he was a boy. "We're after Frank Marengo."

"We don't know no fucking Frank Marengo."

"He just ran by you."

"We don't know you motherfuckers either. What are you, lost boys from New Orleans? Maybe you willin' to pay us a little somethin' to find your way home."

"Maybe they don't need to go home," said another.

The one with the big handgun held his ground, but the others began to spread apart, moving around to either side of Andy and Porter.

"Just let us go on our way and nobody'll get hurt," Andy said.

"We don't figure to get hurt no way, man."

They kept coming. Just as one of those with a knife was almost in reach of Porter, there was a gunshot as loud as a Fourth of July cannon. The report rattled a nearby window and echoed all over. The grins disappeared.

The shot had been fired into the air. It had come from another black man, the one in the suit and sunglasses Andy had seen across the street from Aces and Deuces.

"You drop that piece and the blades," he said, coming closer. The youths turned to face him, then resentfully but obediently did as he said. "Now move aside and let these gentlemen by."

"You dissin' us?"

"You been disrespectin' my friends here. So we're even. Now move."

They obeyed. When they had gone, the man in the suit stuck his revolver into a shoulder holster under his coat.

"We got a little time," he said. "But don't waste it. You get in that wreck of a Cadillac of yours and, if it'll start, find yourself another place to be in a real hurry. Like that nice big city across the river. I'll follow you."

"Not that we're not grateful," Andy said, "but who are you?"

The man smiled. "I'm a business associate of Long Tom Calhoun's. He asked me to keep an eye on you. I didn't figure you'd head straight for the deep shit like this."

"Well, thank him for me."

"You can do that yourself."

Andy and Porter started walking. The man followed, finally getting into a long dark Pontiac parked down the street from Andy's old heap. He followed them onto the Algiers car ferry for the short trip across the river to the city. Andy and Porter got out and stood by the rail, but the man stayed in his car. The river water was a muddy, turgid, greenish brown.

"You enjoy all that?" Andy asked.

"Yeah. Kinda. Once we were out of trouble."

"Just like in the movies."

"Learned some shit. I can use it in my next picture."

"Otherwise, we don't seem to have accomplished much."

"That girl who told you about Marengo, did she tell you to come out here?"

"No. She wanted me to tell the police. Which I did."

"Then where the fuck are they?"

"Maybe they don't like messing around in Algiers."

"You trust this fox?"

Andy was about to say Katie wasn't a "fox," but, in Porter's sense of things, she was exactly that.

"I trust her enough. So far, she's done me nothing but good turns."

When they reached the New Orleans side, Porter asked Andy to drop him at the hospital so he could look in on his sister again. Andy decided to take advantage of the opportunity to have someone in the emergency room check out his shoulder. The attendants declined to do so until he paid his bill for the treatment he'd received the night of the attack. He wrote them a check for which he had no funds.

The nurse who examined his shoulder clucked when she looked at the wound, but said that at least it didn't seem gangrenous. She cleaned it again, then added some new stiches and replaced the dressing, sending him back to the bookkeeping office. He went instead to the main waiting room, where Porter was sitting on a couch, staring at a scrap of paper.

"You don't look happy," Andy said. "Is Emily all right?"

"The doctor said she's doing as well as expected, but it's hard for me to tell. She wrote this for me. I'm trying to figure out what it means."

He handed the paper to Andy. She had scrawled one word: "Woman."

Andy frowned. "That's all?"

Porter shrugged. "She went back to sleep. They have her under a lot of medication."

"Can I keep this? To show to the police?"

"Sure. I mean, 'Woman.' I can remember that. When we make movies, you know, sometimes we have to memorize whole sentences."

Andy took Porter to the Westin, where he was staying in his sister's room. The young man lingered by the car door.

"I want to keep on with this," he said. "What happened across the river, I'm not sweating it. I want to get that son of a bitch."

"I really don't know what to do next," Andy told him.

"Well, you better think of something. I'm sticking with you, man. Until we find him."

"I need sleep."

"So get some. I'll come by your place tonight after dinner. Maybe you'll get a bright idea."

"Are you still mad at me?"

"That's up to Emily."

Maljeux wasn't at the Vieux Carré station. Andy left a message there for the lieutenant to look him up at the Razzy Dazzy, and then went there. No one was in the place except a couple of drunks about to go under. Freddy had put a tape of drinking songs on Tom's machine, as if to encourage them. Andy sat through John Hiatt singing "The Usual," Jerry Lee Lewis doing "Drinkin' Wine Spo-Dee-O-Dee," Ry Cooder and "I'm Drinking Again," and Bonnie Bramlett with "Let's Get Stoned"—slowly sipping a warm whiskey. Finally, he went over to the pay phone and called Katie. He wondered if he was pushing things with her too much.

"We found Marengo," Andy said. "But he had a lot of friends there. Black friends. How do you figure that?"

"I don't know anything about him, except what I told you. Did the cops take him out?"

"No cops. Just me and Emily Shaw's brother."

"Where were the cops?"

"Press of other business. Marengo's still a free man."

"I should have called them myself."

"Too late now."

"Are you all right, Andy?"

"Not a scratch. Not any new ones, anyway."

"That took a lot of guts, going over there on your own. You amaze me."

"Maybe I'm just going crazy. Seeing Emily in the hospital provided some motivation."

"Take me with you next time you go see her. I know what that's like, being trapped in one of those joints, connected to tubes. It's a bitch."

"I'm not sure Emily wants there to be a next time."

"Oh." Katie sounded tired.

"I'd like to see you again," Andy said.

"Me, too, sailor. But I can't. I'm working. On my computer here. It's going to take all night."

"You're sure?"

"The senator isn't too happy with me, after what happened at the rally. I don't want to make it any worse."

"Okay."

"Soon, Andy. But not tonight."

"Okay."

"You want another?" Freddy asked, when Andy returned to the bar.

"Not yet. Has Bleusette been in?"

"I woulda noticed."

"How about the guy in the black suit?"

Freddy shook his head. "It's been a real slow day, Andy."

"That's funny, it was jumpin' over in Algiers."

Jerry Lee came on again, this time singing "It Was the Whiskey Talkin'."

"That's enough of that," Andy said. "If anyone comes in looking for me, tell them I'm back at my place."

Moving toward the door, he hesitated.

"Not 'anybody,' " he said. "Just friends."

"That include Lieutenant Maljeux?"

"I guess."

• • •

Andy eased himself onto the couch in his studio, and stayed there until the day died, staring up at the cracked and dingy ceiling, feeling unsatisfied and lonely again.

He didn't like being there alone. He needed to get away from Smoky Row, back among people. He brushed his teeth and dressed, once again in blazer, khaki pants, and dress shirt. Locking his house and the courtyard gate, he went over to Bourbon Street, deciding to have dinner at Captain Al's Seafood and Oyster Bar, hoping the noisy crowd that was always there and the jazz from Maison Bourbon next door would distract him from his troubles.

They didn't. A long walk to the river wasn't any help, either.

He was near Katie's building. He walked over to it, hesitated, then rang her bell. When there was no answer, he stepped back out into the street, so she could see who it was.

Nothing moved in her window, but a moment later, the building door buzzed open. He hurried to it.

She looked quite weary, but not displeased to see him.

"I kinda thought you might turn up," she said. "Run out of friends, sailor?"

He could see the green glow of her computer screen in the other room. The table was piled with papers.

"I'm just sorry. About yesterday."

She sat down on the bed. She was barefoot. He stood in front of her, staring at the tattoo on her ankle.

Her eyes lifted. They offered no clue to her thoughts, showing only fatigue.

"You want me to finish what I started," she said, matter-of-factly.

"No. I just don't want to leave things like that. You were so angry."

"I'm not now." Her eyes lowered. "Okay. Come here."

"Not that. I want to make love to you, Katie. I want to please you."

"What about Miss Emily Shaw? You're not a very faithful gent, are you? Kind of an alley cat."

"I've got a lot to answer for with Emily, but this has nothing to do with that. I want you, Katie."

He did. He wished he could keep his wants under control.

"A lot of men do. Sometimes it gets to be a real pain in the ass." She smiled—her tough, worldly broad-in-a-bar smile. "I don't mean you. I don't think you want me, Andy. You just want someone to make you stop feeling bad. I don't mind. I feel that way myself sometimes." She stood up and unzipped her dress. Her abdominal scars were more visible in the brighter light, but she was no less beautiful. He wished he were a painter.

She moved close to him, looked questioningly into his eyes, then carefully lifted his arm from the sling.

• • •

It wasn't very good, for either of them. He was in too much discomfort and she was unable to hide her weariness. At the end, she was lying on top. Her body clenched his tightly at the moment of release, then she leaned back, sitting up, closing her eyes.

"Oh, God," she said, making the words sound bleak.

"You okay?"

"I'm fine, Andy." She eased herself off him, then shifted to the edge of the bed, sitting hunched forward.

He stroked her back. She gave a shudder of her shoulders. He tried to bring her close to him again, but she pulled away.

"Are you crying?" he asked.

She shook her head, keeping her face turned away from him.

"I'm scared, Andy."

"I guess we've all got good reason to be."

"I'm scared for you. I'm scared for me. I'm scared for the whole goddamn world."

"Katie . . ."

"I should never have taken this job." Her shoulders quivered again. She put her hands on them, long fingers, the grotesque ring. "Shit."

"There are other jobs."

"No there aren't. Not for me. I'm lucky to have it. I don't want to screw it up, like I . . . You've no idea. I hate to get up in the morning. You just don't know what a thoroughly bad man he is. He's as fucked up and evil as the sons of bitches who vote for him."

"Why don't you quit, for God's sake? Try one of the TV stations here. If nothing else, they like people who work cheap. I know a guy who runs one of them."

"It's no good. My health problems. I'm stuck, Andy. It's my own fault. Like everything else in my life." She gave another shudder, then turned to look at him over her shoulder, her smile made weird by her sadness. "I'm sorry. I'm just so damned tired. You shouldn't have come."

"I thought somehow I'd be welcome."

"If you weren't welcome, I wouldn't have let you in. But you shouldn't have come. I've got all this work. You'd better go."

He got dressed. She stayed where she was, waiting patiently.

When he was ready, he leaned down and kissed her. She responded with just enough warmth to impart affection, to show there was no hostility.

"You want me to take your picture?"

She took his hand. "Yes. Very much. But not now. Not tonight, okay?"

"Okay."

"I'll do what I can for you, Andy, with Marengo and Boone and everything. I'll try."

"Katie, I . . ."

"Don't say it. Good night, sailor."

• • •

Down on the street, he looked at his watch. The movie shoot D. J. Cosette had mentioned would probably still be under way. Perhaps he could get close enough to draw Paris aside without Cooper noticing, arrange to meet her for a drink. She couldn't have meant what she'd said the previous night. She'd just been upset by his gun.

A short, scrunched-down man everyone knew as Squatty came along the sidewalk, nodded to Andy, then hurried on, as if to avoid conversation. This was unlike the Quarter. He felt lonelier now than he had before. Except for Bleusette, Long Tom, and Maljeux, his New Orleans friends were largely avoiding him. After what had happened to Emily, he didn't much want to talk with them anyway. He'd have to explain things, and he couldn't, not even to himself. Especially to himself. With Paris, he never had to explain anything.

Despite the out-of-the-way location, there was a substantial crowd of spectators—mostly tourists from the look of them—enough for Andy to remain inconspicuous if he kept in their midst. He edged forward until he could get a clear view of the actors, who were seated in canvas chairs by a big van parked at the side. Ball was slumped wearily in his. Paris sat next to him, legs crossed and smoking a cigarette, ignoring everyone. One of the actors playing a bad guy was walking around in circles, talking to himself, apparently working himself up for the next take.

Cooper was over by the lighting crew, waving his arms about, his back to the spectators. It occurred to Andy this might be his best opportunity to get near Paris, but that would take luck, and he wasn't having much this day.

The crowd was pressing fairly close to the equipment, some of the onlookers standing among the technicians. It wouldn't take much more of that for Cooper to start screaming to have the street cleared.

Andy edged back toward the rear, deciding to work his way around to the side, by the trailers and vans. As he started to move, he caught sight of a figure standing by the open door of the prop truck.

Black suit. Panama hat. Dark glasses. Little cigar. Why didn't the bastard wear a neon sign?

"Son of a bitch," Andy said.

A teenage boy in front of him turned around.

"Not you," said Andy. "Sorry."

Andy didn't think he'd been seen, but George Graves was moving on, taking a last drag of his smoke and turning and heading for the open street.

He walked fast. Andy had to shove his way clear of the crowd, and then get around some cables and light stands. By the time he was again on empty sidewalk, Graves was most of a block away, on the other side of the street.

If Andy ran, he might only spook the man and set him to running. Even a chain-smoker of cigars could outdistance Andy in his present condition.

Graves was hurrying now. Before Andy could close the distance, the man turned the corner.

Now Andy did run. He was winded by the time he reached the intersection.

Nothing. No one in view but a black musician carrying a large bass viol in a case down the street. Graves had vanished.

Andy returned to the shoot, glancing over his shoulder all the way. This time, he headed straight for the trailers, taking a position just to the side of the van near Paris's chair.

Cooper had set up his shot, and his assistant was moving the actors to their marks. Ball was holding his stage gun. The actors playing the bad guys went to the prop truck to get theirs. A couple of the pistols they came back with were as big as the one Andy had faced in Algiers.

The cast took their places. As Andy recalled from the script, Paris and Ball would be walking along the street when the bad guys would take a shot at them. They'd run, the villains would chase after them, firing, and Ball would do something heroic to get them out of their jam.

Cooper delayed the camera roll a moment to have a light adjusted, then took to his chair. The assistant with the slate board stepped in front of the camera.

Prop guns. Graves had been standing by the prop truck. With the big crowd, the usual street location confusion, and all the worrying about the lighting, Graves might have had an opportunity to get into the truck without anyone noticing.

Someone had tampered with the Mercedes' brakes. Someone had cut the ingenue's throat.

"Action!"

One of the bad guys fired a shot. He aimed it slightly above the stars' heads, even though he was shooting blanks. Or was he?

Paris and Ball began running, she with some difficulty in her high heels. The bad guys started after them, the one in the lead leveling his pistol again.

What if Graves had gotten into that truck?

"Hey you!" Andy shouted. "Stop!"

Heads turned. Andy vaulted over an equipment case and ran into the scene. Cooper began screaming. Two of the actor villains stopped and stared blankly at Andy but the one in the lead trotted on relentlessly, aiming his weapon.

What was the word? The magic word?

"Cut!" Andy bellowed.

The actor hesitated, then looked back. Not wanting to risk anything, Andy ran on and piled into him. They hit the pavement hard, the pistol skittering out of the guy's hand.

Bedlam erupted everywhere. The fallen actor sat up, looked at his skinned hands, and began calling Andy foul names. Someone pulled

Andy rudely to his feet. The crowd was hooting. He could hear Cooper raging. Paris, her face flushed, was storming back toward him. "Have you lost your fucking mind?"

Then Cooper was in front of him. A million words a minute seemed to roar from his mouth. Andy was a lunatic, a jinx, a saboteur, a one-man disaster. Cooper was going to have him run over with a sound truck, put through a shredder, drowned in the film processing tank.

"You'll never work on this planet again!" he screamed, using up the last of his fury. He stood there twitching, his eyes bulging, veins standing out at his temples.

Andy took a deep breath, then stepped past the director, going up to where the pistol had come to rest. Before anyone could take it away from him, he lifted it high, aiming at one of the big klieg lights. A blank shell fired a harmless, thin cardboard wad that couldn't cut human flesh at ten yards and probably wouldn't even reach the light. A real bullet would prove his point as dramatically as any Hollywood scriptwriter could wish.

Andy didn't even check the revolver's cylinder. He was absolutely certain what it contained.

He fired, and the light went out in an enormous explosive burst of incandescence—the force of the bullet making it rock back and forth on its stand.

"That's what was about to happen to Paris," he said.

There was silence. He walked back to a stunned Cooper.

"Here," he said, handing him the gun. "Shoot me. I prefer it to the shredder."

"I told that director I'd take you to the station house, but I didn't say I'd keep you there," said Maljeux, steering his police cruiser carefully through the Quarter's night pedestrians. "Indulge me with one more of those statements and you can be on your way."

Andy was sitting up front beside him. "What about Graves? That was a goddamn live round in that gun, Paul."

"He's a wanted man. Put a pickup order out on him. The pistol you say he fooled with is in the trunk. I'll turn that over to evidence. Too bad you got your fingerprints all over it."

"It was Graves. It was him, Paul."

"We'll find him, Andy. But you've got to stay away from those movie people. Cooper said he's going to get a judge to issue a restraining order against you. He wanted to file charges 'cause you shot out his light."

"What about Marengo?"

"We're looking for him, too. State police. Everybody. But keep in mind we can't charge him with a goddamn thing until such time as you identify him in a lineup."

"You just find him. And Graves."

"Shouldn't take long. Graves would stand out in Mardi Gras, with that Leon Redbone outfit of his."

"That's something I just don't get, Paul. He's supposed to be a private investigator, a snoop, a sneak. But he goes around in that undertaker's suit all the time making himself unmistakable."

"He's a self-confident son of a bitch, all right."

"Maybe he's dealt with you guys before. Got the idea he could stroll around dressed up like the Devil and you wouldn't notice him."

"Be nice, Andy." Maljeux laughed. "What if we picked up Leon Redbone himself by mistake?"

"Is he in town?"

"No, but I meant to tell you, Alan Toussaint'll be back here next week with his R-and-B band. Did you know he wrote 'Southern Nights?' My favorite song."

"I used to play it on my stereo all the time in New York. Made me homesick."

"Did you know he's from Toronto?"

"Alan Toussaint?"

"No. Leon Redbone. Sure sings good New Orleans for a Canadian."

A voice crackled onto Maljeux's police radio. It was one of the detectives he'd sent over to Graves's hotel.

"Shit," Maljeux said, when the brief conversation was over. "He's checked out."

"Let's go over there anyway."

"What for?"

"Look in his room."

"I assume our boys did that."

"Let's us look."

If the detectives had conducted a thorough search, there wasn't much evidence of it. As Maljeux stood shaking his head, Andy started going through the dresser drawers himself. Finding nothing, he went to the closet and looked up on the shelf. Then he peered under the bed.

He stood up. "Not a thing," Andy muttered.

"I said he was self-confident," Maljeux said. "Not stupid. Paid his bill with cash. Bet he's on the road as we stand here. The highway troopers are watching for that black Cadillac of his. But if he's real smart, he's using the back roads. You can make good time on those bayou roads at night. Wish we had some idea where he might be heading."

"He's from Texas. You might give the Houston cops a call."

"Did that, friend. Have to get a warrant out for him, though, if we want them to pick him up."

"Have you been to the hospital today?"

"No."

Andy handed him the scrap of paper with the word "Woman" on it. "Emily wrote this down and gave it to her brother."

Maljeux pondered it. "What the hell do you suppose this means?"

"You asked her to put down anything she could remember."

"She thinks a woman did that to her?"

"If she's conscious again, you might ask her."

"Who the hell could it be? Your Texas lady friend? Maybe jealous?"

"My Texas lady friend is in Texas."

• • •

There were several people gathered on the street outside Andy's house as Maljeux pulled up at the curb. They were tourists, and in their midst was Richard Porter, signing autographs, with Bleusette at his side, looking star-struck.

"Where the hell have you been?" Porter said, scribbling his name on the cover of a kid's New Orleans guidebook. "I was about to split. I've been waiting for you almost an hour."

"We were going to the Razzy Dazzy," said Bleusette. "I'm gonna take the night off."

"There was trouble at the movie set," Andy said.

He waited as a boy perhaps eleven gave Porter a big marker pen, and then turned around to have the movie star autograph the sweaty back of his T-shirt. Porter finished, and stepped back, smiling as the boy told him how much he had liked Porter's last movie. The tourists began to walk away.

"Someone put a loaded revolver in with the prop guns. Paris almost took a slug in the back," Andy said.

"This fucking town is going crazy," Bleusette said.

"Is she all right?" Porter asked.

"Yes. But it was close."

"I've always worried about that happening to somebody one day," Porter said. "Had a dream once where it was me. You save Paris's life, too, like Emily?"

"You could say that. It was George Graves, the guy in the black suit I told you about."

Porter looked over to where Maljeux still sat in his car, talking on the radio. "The cops get him?"

Andy shook his head. "No such luck, today."

"I went over to the hospital again," Porter said. "She's still the same. Every time I look at her, it makes me cry."

"Let's go get a drink. I'm tired of trying to think."

They started down the street. They were just about to turn into the Razzy Dazzy when Maljeux's cruiser came roaring up to a stop beside them.

"Andy!" the lieutenant shouted. "Man just went into Danielle Jones's place. Think it's this guy Marengo. Get in. You can tell us for sure."

Andy put his hand on Bleusette's bare shoulder. "Go home. I'll be back as soon as I can."

"You be careful, Andy. You're no fucking good at catching bad guys."

Andy slid into the back seat of the police cruiser. "Your men go in after him?" he said to Maljeux.

"They're waiting for me. I've got other units en route. We're going to try to take him without anyone getting hurt. Especially him. I want to talk to that boy."

Porter went around the other side and got in next to Andy.

"He's coming too?" Maljeux said.

"Consider him backup," Andy said. He looked at Porter. "You don't want to stay and play house with Bleusette?"

"First things first, man."

The lieutenant accelerated down the narrow street, squeezing past a stopped taxi without slowing. Andy had never before seen the lieutenant so enthusiastic about his work.

"You still carrying that firearm?" Maljeux asked.

"Yes. I almost forgot about it."

"Do us all a favor and keep it in your belt, okay?"

"I hope you blow that bastard's head off," Porter said.

"And keep the hero out of the way," Maljeux said to Andy. "This ain't the movies."

• • •

The lieutenant got to Faubourg Marigny in a handful of minutes. He slid the cruiser to a stop at a brightly lit street corner, bouncing it up onto the sidewalk. Andy could see policemen hunched behind parked cars further down the street.

Maljeux reached under the seat and pulled out what he called his "serious weapon"—a long-barreled .44 Magnum.

"Don't you have a bullhorn?" Porter asked.

"Like I said, this ain't the movies. We don't tell him to come out with his hands up. We wait for him to come out on his own, unsuspecting. If he don't come out, we go in." He checked the load of his pistol. "We'll talk to Marengo after we get him cuffed. Right now I want to try to figure out what's going on in there."

"He killed Ferrier," Andy said. "He may not be paying Miss Jones a friendly visit."

"Just hush up, Andy. We're not even sure yet this is Marengo."

They followed Maljeux to a vantage point opposite the front door of the woman's house, hunching down beside him by the fender of an old Chevrolet sedan. The downstairs windows were well lit, but they could see no one moving inside.

The lieutenant called over a detective, a burly young man wearing white jeans and a polo shirt.

"Who you got in back?" Maljeux whispered.

"Zabriskie and Bishop. Either side of the rear gate. He tries that way, he's gonna be in custody or dead."

"Get back there with them. Go easy. We want him breathing. And I don't want any chatter on the radio. This street's real quiet tonight. He might hear us."

Andy felt exhilarated. At last they were about to do something meaningful. He began to think that all the horrors that had been vexing him might indeed soon be over, that he might at last resume a normal life.

The primal scream from an upstairs window surprised them all.

Andy thought of Ferrier's last moments. The sound was virtually the same.

Maljeux threw himself across the trunk of the sedan, lifting his pistol and aiming at the house. To the left and right, other policemen readied their weapons.

A man appeared in the doorway. Andy had no doubt.

"That's him," he said.

Marengo glanced about, then looked back to the house. Satisfied with its silence, he began walking quickly toward the street.

"Stop!" Maljeux shouted. He cocked the hammer of his big revolver. His thumb slipped and the weapon went off, echoing all around them. The shot went high, striking the house's facade, but the other cops immediately began firing.

Marengo did a jittering little dance, then fell back in a heap on the lawn, his left leg twitching. His body arched, then went limp. He never once cried out.

Porter, running, got to him first. Andy wondered if the actor had ever seen a real dead man before.

Apparently not. He turned aside, and threw up.

A detective rolled Marengo over, taking a pistol from underneath the man's shirt in back. From Marengo's back pocket, he gingerly pulled out a long bloody clasp knife.

"Looks to me like you're real lucky he got away from you before," Maljeux said.

"This guy stabbed Emily?" Porter asked, after wiping his mouth. "We're sure now?"

"Maybe," Maljeux said. "Forensics will have to tell us that." He looked to his men. "Let's go! Into the house!"

They found Danielle Jones in a darkened upstairs room, lying face up in a silk robe on a bloody bed. She'd been stabbed and her throat had been cut, much more thoroughly than Emily's. Her lipstick was as red as the blood.

" '*Tableaux vivants,*' " Maljeux said. "*Vivant soit morte, maintenant.*"

Andy began to feel sick himself. Maljeux noticed. He led them out into the hallway.

"Go on home, Andy. Or to the Razzy Dazzy or wherever. We'll come by later and get a statement."

"You're going to have enough of those to make a book."

"Let's hope this is the last chapter. We got the doer this time. You're going to have to identify Marengo—officially—as the man who said good-bye to the late Albert."

"Consider him identified. I don't need to look at the body again."

"Run along then. We'll tidy this up. Seems to me like it's all over."

"How can you be so sure about that?"

Maljeux took off his hat and scratched his head. "Well, I don't know what forensics is gonna say or what the district attorney will want to do, but it all seems pretty clear to me. The late Albert was shaking down Danielle here and her sugar daddy. For reasons we haven't exactly determined, Albert went to you with the information. Maybe because you do work for the newspapers. Maybe because you know someone who would want to know, like maybe your Texas lady friend. Marengo stopped him—forever—doubtless hired to do so by Danielle's mysterious beau. To be on the safe side, he took care of Danielle, too, and earlier he tried to do you—wounding Miss Shaw in the process."

"But you don't know who the sugar daddy is. You sure don't know it's Ben Browley."

"Nobody knows now. I'm just guessing."

"What if sugar daddy is Henry Boone?"

"Strikes me as a remote possibility."

"What about George Graves?"

Maljeux shrugged. "That's another matter."

"Well, let's take care of it."

"In time. Gotta clean up things here."

"What I think, Paul, is that you're stretching good old *laissez-faire* pretty far."

• • •

Porter came back with Andy to his Smoky Row house, going to the kitchen to get a beer for himself while Andy took some gin from a bottle in his studio. Bleusette, seeing his lights go on, came over, still fully dressed and carrying a glass of Pernod.

"I was worried about you guys. You get this Marengo?" she asked.

"The cops did. He's dead," Andy said.

"*Bon*. Maybe now we get some peace and quiet."

Andy sat down wearily on his studio couch. His shoulder cut was beginning to itch beneath the bandage. Was that a good sign, or a bad?

Something in the studio was wrong. He looked about. Nothing seemed to be missing.

Porter strolled in with his beer. "No one in L.A.'s going to believe any of this when I tell them. 'Hard Copy' wouldn't believe this. The *National*-fucking-*Enquirer* wouldn't believe this."

"You are all right, too, Richard?" Bleusette asked, pronouncing his name as 'Reechar.' "Everyone is all right?"

"A woman was killed over there. This Marengo guy did it."

Andy stared at the opposite wall, at his assemblage of framed photographs. Everything was where it should be. His picture of Paris was there. His picture of the crazed hooker with eyes tattooed on her cheeks was there. The problem was that nothing was missing.

His nude of Candice was back in its place, as though it had never been gone.

He stood up, and drank the rest of the gin. "That does it."

"What's wrong?" Porter asked.

"I'm leaving town."

"You're going to bug out now, right at the payoff?"

"Payoff, hell. I'm going to Houston. I'm going to find George Graves, if he's there. And I'm going to see a man named Ben Browley."

"Who's he?"

"I think he's the cause of all our troubles."

"I told you that woman is no fucking good for you, Andy," Bleusette said. "You always pick the bad ones."

Porter took a swig of his beer, then set down the bottle. "I'll drive."

"You want to come? All the way to Houston?"

"Like I said, man, I'm enjoying this. Some of the time."

"Emily's not."

"That's why I'm enjoying this."

15

Andy liked Texas, for many of the same reasons he was so fond of New Orleans. Every dusty little town in the sprawling state was a reminder to America of what it was really all about, yet Texas was a country unto itself. He liked the rough edge of the faces, the bigness and raw colors, the raucous border towns, the beautiful city of San Antonio, even that painted woman of a city called Dallas.

But he hated Houston. It was the nation's fourth-largest metropolis, with nothing really to justify its size—a hot, ugly, ill-conceived city built too big by people with too much money. For all its immensity, it was a depressingly empty place. Andy had gone there once to do a fashion shoot. On an idle morning, he'd walked from his hotel across downtown, strolling aimlessly at first. Curious at the lack of shops and stores, he'd turned his perambulation into a search for one—and one was all he'd been able to find, a dime store eight blocks from the hotel. The rest was all monstrous, glassy high-rise office buildings, sterile monuments to corporate ego and greed, embellished only with fountains, bits of shrubbery, and heavy junk sculpture on their plazas. Ben Browley's, he was sure, was just such a building.

They roared off the expressway into the city center late the next morning, throttling down with noisy rumbles coming from the high-powered car's exhaust. Instead of something circumspect that would attract little attention, Porter had rented a Corvette—to make time, he said. He'd laughed at Andy's suggestion of taking the old Cadillac.

It was a workday, but the streets had little traffic. Porter was driving, as he had been for most of the journey. Andy lowered his window, admitting a suffocating billow of superheated air.

"As bad as New Orleans," Porter said.

"With New Orleans, you get good food." Andy raised the window again and turned up the air-conditioning.

"So what now?" Porter asked.

"Graves must have an office. We'll have to find it."

"How do we do that?"

"The Yellow Pages?"

"I'll look for a drugstore."

"You won't find one downtown. I should have told you. We'll have to go out to the neighborhoods."

"Do you know anyone in this stupid town?"

"Yes. Ben Browley's wife."

"You like to fuck around with trouble, don't you?"

"I didn't used to look at it that way."

They found a convenience store in a dingy district just west of downtown. Porter bought some junk food and soft drinks while Andy looked through the phone book. He found a "Graves Investigations" on Lubbock Street. It proved to be just a few blocks from the central police station.

"Do you think they might have already picked him up?" Porter asked. He had pulled to a stop in a "no parking" zone and was munching a Twinkie.

"I don't know. We're not sure he's even here, are we?"

"Do you want to stop by the cops and ask a desk sergeant or something?"

"I don't want to get involved with the police. In any case, I'd rather check out Graves's office first."

"What if he's there?"

"All the better. We'll have a chance to talk."

"You still have that little handgun?"

"Yes. Want to back out?"

"No. Why should I?"

"Maybe you're sane?"

"Let's go."

Graves's office was on the third floor of an old four-story building that housed an odd variety of enterprises, including a chiropractor, a faith healer, a couple of shady-looking law firms, and a small alcoholic treatment clinic. The building's janitor, apparently, took a lot of time off.

"Graves must not make very big money at his work," Porter said, as they started up the stairs.

"If he's working for Ben Browley, he's making money."

"You'd think a guy that rich would hire one of those slick, big-time outfits."

"I guess that would depend on what he wanted done. The big-time outfits probably don't do a lot of murders."

Graves's office was at the end of a dimly lit corridor. All the doors had opaque, beveled-glass windows. A few doors were open. Graves's was closed; the interior, dark. Andy turned the knob. It was locked.

"I can't believe this," said Porter, staring at the lettering on the glass. "It's like something out of a forties movie. Philip Marlowe maybe."

"Just what you'd expect from somebody who goes around in black suits."

Andy rapped on the door.

"What are you doing, man? You can see nobody's there."

"I want to make sure."

"Ain't nobody there." It was a woman's voice.

They turned around to find a young Hispanic woman standing in a doorway down the hall.

"We're looking for Mr. Graves," Andy said.

"Ain't been nobody in there for a week or more. Maybe they closed down or something. He's gone. His partner's gone. His secretary, the two big guys he has come around all the time. Ain't seen none of them. For weeks."

"Let's split," said Porter.

"Do you know where Mr. Graves lives?" Andy asked.

"Hardly know the man," said the woman. "Never talks to me." She went back inside.

"You want to stop by the cops now?" Porter asked, when they were back in the car.

"I want to look in that office."

"That woman might notice if we tried to break in."

"Not if we came back tonight."

"So what do we do in the meantime? I mean, we drove like hell all night to get here so we could catch up with the bastard. Now we're here in this big, hot fucking city and we don't know where the hell he might be."

"We can try some of these bars along the street. They might know something. Then I thought we might drive out to Browley's place."

"Why do that?"

"Just take a look."

"Do you know where he lives?"

"Not exactly, but I'm sure it's in the most expensive neighborhood in town."

• • •

The bartenders in the three joints they checked out were about as friendly as the one in Algiers. Two of them acknowledged that they knew Graves and the other recalled a customer who always wore black suits, but none admitted to having seen him in recent days.

"I had to throw away his bottle of milk," said one.

"Milk?"

"Yeah, milk. That's all he drinks."

"Not whiskey?"

"Not for a couple years now."

"Milk?"

"Yeah. Milk. You want some?"

They left.

"Maybe Graves got an ulcer," Porter said.

"Last time I saw him he was drinking double bourbons and smoking little cigars. That's not easy with an ulcer."

"Maybe he's just a drunk and fell off the wagon."

"Let's hope so. Might make him easier to deal with."

"If he drinks milk, why would he keep going to bars?"

"You form habits. I went on the wagon for a while last month and went to the Razzy Dazzy every night."

They found Browley's place easily, driving out to wealthy River Oaks and inquiring at the first real estate office they encountered.

The house, set far back from the road behind a pike-topped fence, was bigger than Candy had described it. With the central tower, it was three stories high. The garage had doors for five cars. There was no vehicle in the circular driveway.

"Looks like something you'd find in Bel-Air," Porter said.

"Just as tasteless. What kind of house do you live in?"

"I live in Venice Beach, man. My place is just big enough for, you know, parties. Have friends hang out."

"Pool and tennis court?"

"Nope."

"Bet Mr. Browley has both. Maybe a little golf course."

"The gate's open. You want to go in?"

"That can wait until tonight, too. Let's find a motel and get some sleep."

• • •

They took two adjoining rooms in a clean place just off the Southwest Freeway. A nearby Kentucky Fried Chicken outlet provided a lunch of sorts. They bought some whiskey and beer, but Andy didn't want any. He was asleep almost the instant he lay down on his bed.

Porter awakened him by shaking his shoulder. As the actor picked the wrong shoulder, Andy awakened very quickly, swearing as he sat up.

"Sorry," Porter said. "Paris wants to talk to you."

"Paris?"

"On the phone. I called her."

Andy stumbled into the other room, sitting on the bed and waiting for his head to clear before picking up the receiver.

"You want a drink?" Porter asked.

Andy nodded. "Thanks."

Paris sounded grumpy. "What are you doing in Houston?"

"You told me to stay away from the movie shoot."

"I didn't mean you should change states. Now I wish you were here."

"Are you having more trouble?"

"Nothing involving guns or knives. We have a lot of reporters bugging us and the city fathers have decided to give us a hard time."

"What do you mean? They don't give anyone a hard time. You should see the place during Mardi Gras."

"I did once. Must have taken ten years off my life. No, they're hassling Cooper about the riverboat scene. Having serious second thoughts about the special effects."

"You mean blowing up the boat?"

"They think that with all the trouble we've had, we might get more. Cooper thought he had them convinced that it won't be anything more frightening than a big fireworks display, but all this bad shit that's happened has them spooked. I mean, we're not going to sink the thing. Just set fire to—what do you call it?—the superstructure. I don't know what to do. Cooper's idea is to wine and dine them, throw a big party, let them mingle with the stars, but I don't know what that will accomplish. Give them a dose of what goes on at Spago or Morton's and we might queer the deal for good."

"The cops got the guy we think hurt Emily."

"I know. It was in the paper. We all cheered. But the city fathers aren't cheering."

"Parties don't exactly impress people in New Orleans. It would be like taking someone from Las Vegas out for a night of bingo."

"Cooper wants to throw the party on a boat."

"The one you're going to blow up?"

"He's not quite that crazy. He's going to charter one of those tourist paddle wheelers for an evening. I guess I'm supposed to wear a low-cut dress and make bedroom eyes at City Councilmen."

"A little of that and they might let you blow up City Hall."

"Aren't you sweet. Seriously, Andy, you know anybody in this town who might give us some help?"

Porter brought him a whiskey and water. He took a sip.

"As a matter of fact, I do. A former state senator who owns a bar in the French Quarter. His name is Tom Calhoun and the bar's the Razzy Dazzy. Tell him I suggested you talk to him. At the very least, he can tell you what's possible."

"I'll do that. Emily's taken a big turn for the better, but they can't take her off that IV until she's able to swallow. She's going to come out of this as thin as Marisa Berenson."

"Give her my best."

" 'Your best.' Right. Just what are you guys doing out there?"

"Looking for the creep who put live ammunition in that prop gun." Andy stared at the floor. There were cigarette burns on the carpet.

"It might be a good thing if you could be at that party, Andy. Local hire and all that. You know these people. It might help. I'll see if I can get Cooper to put you back on the payroll. At least for the night."

"Don't do me any favors, Paris."

"It would be a favor for me."

"That's different. But Cooper won't take me back. I'm not very keen on the idea myself. In fact, I never want to work for that man again. On any planet."

"Come as my guest, then. I have another two hundred thou coming when this thing's a wrap. I'll make it worth your while."

"Paris, I wouldn't take a dime. But I really don't think your riverboat soiree will make the slightest damn bit of difference."

"Your parents were some sort of big deal in society here, right? Prominent family, that bullshit? Connections? Please, Andy. Play the card. I want to win the hand. I want to get this picture made."

"Why don't you finish it without blowing up the boat?"

"What do you think this is, an art movie?"

"I don't know when we'll be coming back."

She paused. "All right, honey bunch. Call me soon. And be careful."

"You, too."

He looked at his watch. It was past eight o'clock. Through the gauzy window curtains, he could see that the sun was setting.

Porter came in with a can of beer, dumping himself in a chair.

"Paris says your sister's doing better."

"I know. Talked to her."

"The movie company has a problem. The city may not let them have their big pyrotechnic finale."

"I know."

"Cooper plans to throw a big party to reassure them."

"Know that, too. You had enough sleep?"

Andy finished his drink.

"For now."

• • •

It was just coming on to twilight when they pulled up outside Graves's crummy old office building again. There were no lights on in any of the windows they could see, but there were people on the sidewalk.

"Here we are," Porter said. "Let's go."

"Wait till the street clears a little. You ever pick a lock before?"

"No."

"I haven't either."

"Maybe this is dumb."

"Isn't this the sort of thing you do in your movies?"

"Nope. Always kick the doors in. Nice balsawood doors."

The downstairs door, at least, was unlocked. Andy wondered if derelicts came in here to sleep at night. The place smelled as though they might.

They walked the full length of the dimly lit corridor on Graves's floor to make sure none of the other offices were occupied, then returned to his door.

"Still locked," Porter said, turning the knob.

"Amazing."

Andy took out his pen knife, pulling out the smallest blade and slipping it into the keyhole. He jiggled it, then sawed it back and forth. He didn't really know what he was doing. Nothing happened. If he wasn't careful, he could break off the blade and then jam the lock for good.

"Well, it's only glass, right?" Porter said. "Step back."

It shattered with the first blow of his heel from a sideways kick. Porter grinned.

There was a tiny reception room, and two glass-windowed doors leading off it, both of them open.

"Take the one on the right," Andy said. "I'll look through this one."

"What do I look for?"

"Anything to do with a Ben or Candice Browley. Or me. Pictures. Files. Anything."

Porter went into the side office and turned on a light. With the front door glass kicked out, Andy supposed it didn't matter.

There was a goosenecked lamp on the desk of the office Andy had selected. He clicked it on, turning it away from the window.

He went first to a row of four file cabinets against the wall. None were locked. Most of the files were for divorce cases and many contained compromising photographs, some with very attractive women. He studied a few, then reminded himself of the need for haste.

Finding nothing under "Browley," or "Derain," he kept looking, in case something had been misfiled. At length he came to a folder marked "New Orleans." It was empty.

The window was closed, but he could hear a siren. It was a big city.

Porter came in.

"Nothing at all in there," he said. "Just a couple of chairs and a desk, and all the drawers are empty. There're some weird pictures on the wall. That's all."

"What kind of pictures?"

"Paintings. Prints. Stuff like that."

Andy glanced around the walls of this office. There was a calendar, showing the previous month, and some cheap Frederic Remington prints, including one Andy recalled of some cavalrymen defending a water hole. He went back to the file cabinets.

The siren was now very loud.

"That could be for us."

"Maybe."

Andy slammed shut one drawer and pulled out another. It contained nothing but a stack of canceled checks.

The siren stopped. Downstairs.

"I think that maybe is for us," Porter said.

Andy hesitated a moment, thinking, then grabbed the checks.

"We'll take these."

"Then what?"

"I don't know. I never committed a burglary before."

"In some movies, the bad guys make for the roof."

"Let's try it."

With movies, there were always people who scout locations ahead of time. No real fugitive would have liked this roof. The building to one side was two stories higher than theirs. On the other side was a ten-foot drop below. They went to the ledge facing the street, and peered over.

There was a police car out front. It was parked half on the sidewalk outside one of the bars. People were gathering, watching whatever was going on inside. A moment later, two cops emerged, dragging a man between them. Andy could hear shouting.

"Bar fight," Porter said.

"Let's get out of here."

"Where to?" said Porter.

"Just get on the freeway."

They hurried down the stairs.

In the Corvette, Andy turned on the dash light and began looking through the checks. He recognized none of the names. Most of the checks were written for small, routine amounts, but a few were in four figures. One, made out to a Marlene Krauser, was for $10,000.

He began looking at the cancellation stamps on the backs. There were no New Orleans banks.

"How long do I stay on this freeway?" Porter asked.

"Keep going."

"A car followed me onto the ramp. It's still behind us."

Andy glanced out the rear window, seeing only a stream of headlights.

"Slow down. See if he goes by."

Porter had been going seventy. He eased his foot off the accelerator and it quickly dropped to fifty-five.

"He's sticking back there."

"Who wrote this script?"

"Think it's a cop?"

"Hope not. I don't imagine the police here have quite the same charm as those in New Orleans."

"We committed a burglary, man. We're criminals."

"Always wondered what it was like." Andy glanced down at the checks in his lap. "See if you can lose him in traffic, at least for a couple of minutes."

Porter hit the gas pedal and the Corvette began gathering speed like a jet plane on a takeoff roll. Nimbly, he veered to the right, slipping around a station wagon, then, back in the fast lane, foot to the pedal, moved rapidly along a line of trailer trucks.

"Son of a bitch is still with us. This is turning into a fucking James Bond movie."

"Bond always wins in the end. When you get ahead of that lead truck, pull over in front of it."

"Not much room."

"Do your best."

Andy lowered his window. The blast of hot wind snatched at some of the loose checks. He retrieved them from the floor, looking up as they drew even with the trailer rig's tractor. The driver, drinking from a can of beer, glanced down at them curiously.

"Hurry up," Andy said.

There was a car in the lane ahead of them, moving too slowly. Porter gunned the engine and jerked the wheel to the right, sliding in front of the trailer truck with just a few feet to spare. They were greeted with an angry, deafening blast of the rig's air horn.

Andy tossed the wad of checks out the window, looking back to see them whirl in a small blizzard up over the hood of the truck tractor. The horn protested once more.

"Why'd you do that?" Porter asked.

"Evidence. Got rid of it. Just in case that is a cop back there."

The sudden flurry of paper in his windshield caused the truck driver to hit his air brakes. They could hear those of the other trucks all the way down the line.

"That was a mistake," Porter said. "Now he's got around the trucks. He's on our tail again."

"Get off at the next exit."

"I don't know why I'm following your orders."

"Because you think I know what I'm doing."

"Do you?"

"Haven't a clue."

A green highway sign flashed overhead, its red, white, and blue federal logo bearing the number "610."

"The next exit is another freeway," Porter said.

"Take it. I know where we are."

Porter slowed only slightly for the curving ramp, the Corvette's tires protesting loudly.

"You know this town?"

"A little. I did a magazine shoot once at the Bayou Polo Club. We're near there."

There were high sodium-vapor lamps above them, illuminating the roadway with something akin to daylight.

"He's still with us, and I don't think he's a cop."

"How do you know that?"

"He's driving a Caddy."

The word jarred Andy's memory. "Is it black?"

"Black, maybe dark blue."

"It's Graves. It has to be."

"Hey! You're pretty smart after all. We found him!"

They snaked at high speed through traffic, passing an exit.

"Take the next one," Andy said. "Woodway Drive."

"Where does that go?"

"It leads to Memorial Drive. A parkway that goes back downtown. Maybe we can lose him."

Porter followed Andy's directions and soon they were on Memorial.

"He lost ground, but he's still coming."

"Look for a sign. For the Polo Club. When you see it, kill your lights. There'll be a dirt road just beyond it."

"How am I supposed to make a turn like that without lights?"

"I have great faith. I've seen your movies."

"Shit."

Porter saw the sign before Andy did. He hit the headlight switch and the brakes simultaneously, skidding and bumping the car off the pavement and onto the access road.

"Go like hell now."

Headlights flared behind them.

"Double shit," said Porter. "He must have seen the brake lights. Dumb idea."

"Keep going. Maybe we can ditch him. There are a lot of stable buildings just ahead."

"Is there another way out of here?"

"I don't think so."

"Do you know where you're going in here?"

"Not really. I'll leave that up to you."

Porter did a superlative job, holding the Corvette steady even when they smashed through a wooden barrier bar, expertly bounding the car over a shallow ditch—all this in the faint, jouncing light of the headlamps behind them. Long silhouettes loomed ahead: the stable buildings.

Andy gripped the dash as Porter skidded around the nearest structure, scattering gravel as he roared through a parking area and hurtled on toward a wide expanse of grass.

"It's the polo field. Careful. There's a low wooden barrier around it."

Just as Andy spoke, the wheels thunked against the wood. The front end lifted and fell, as did the rear. Somehow, the tires and axles survived. A line of trees beckoned in the distance.

Porter sped toward them, then, realizing there'd be another barrier on the other side, spun the wheel and headed left. They coursed around the field in an arc, the headlights behind them fading away, then slowed to thump over the barrier again at a minimal speed.

They were at the far end of the line of stables.

"Kill the engine," Andy said.

Porter obeyed. Instead of silence, they were greeted by a huge chorus of Texas insects. But they could hear no other vehicle. No headlights were visible at all.

"I guess we confused the hell out of him," Porter said.

Andy listened. "Okay. Let's leave this place. While we can."

Driving slowly, lights still off, Porter made his way back over the ditch, through another, larger parking area, and past the club house, which unfortunately was well lighted. Just as they turned onto the dirt access road, a pair of headlights flicked on and jolted forward.

"Fucking brilliant," Porter muttered. "Here he comes again."

Andy clenched his fists, but that didn't make his brain work any better.

"Take Memorial east. We'll go back downtown."

"To do what?"

"I don't know. Pull up at the police station. That'll stop him."

"We've got to get there first."

Porter churned more gravel and dirt swerving onto the paved highway. There was no traffic ahead and he drove flat out. So, unfortunately, did Graves.

"He's keeping pace," Porter said.

"I thought this was a sports car. He's got a big tub."

"Powerful engines are powerful engines, no matter what you put them in. You got any more bright ideas?"

"Absolutely none."

"Well I've got one." He eased back on the gas.

"What're you doing?"

"Letting him get a little closer. These 'Vettes got great antilock brakes, as I'm about to make him discover."

The parkway led along wide-open meadow interrupted by clumps of trees. Ahead to the right they could see the lights of the downtown high-rises. The glare from the following headlamps grew brighter.

"Tighten your seat belt," Porter said. "Here goes."

He jammed the brake pedal down hard. The tires screamed, but the Corvette stayed pointed straight ahead as it shuddered to a stop.

Before Andy could turn his head, he heard the gathering squeal of the other car's tires. Its headlights flared left, then right, then left again. Moving sideways in an uncontrollable skid, it flashed by, then struck the shoulder rear-end first, bounced and tilted, and, still turning, slammed on the driver's side into a large tree. The sound of the crash was rendingly explosive, but, unlike in the movies, there were no flames.

16

The Corvette's engine had died. They sat there in the middle of the road. Andy found he was shaking.

"I didn't mean to kill him," Porter said. "I just wanted to get him off our tail."

"Damn near killed us."

"I never even met the guy."

"You wouldn't want to," Andy said. "Don't worry about it. Think of your sister. I am."

"Maybe he's still alive."

"Pull off the highway. We'll take a look."

The engine restarted, with some difficulty. Porter spun the wheel, moving the Corvette off the road so that it faced the wreck, the headlights revealing a scene that might have been used for an auto safety scare poster.

"I don't think he's alive," Porter said, softly.

Andy sighed. "Let's make sure."

They approached the devastated Cadillac slowly. Steam was hissing forth from beneath the crumpled hood, but Andy could smell no leaking gasoline.

Graves's body was wedged in a crush between the steering wheel and a crumpled piece of door metal, his arm sticking bent out the window. The windshield was missing. There was something odd, something wrong.

"Where's his head?" Porter asked.

Andy gagged, then took a deep breath. Porter went up close to the car, finally looking in the rear seat.

"There it is," he said. "Oh shit." Once again, he threw up.

Steeling himself, Andy came up close. There was enough light for him to recognize the face he had looked into on the movie set. The eyes seemed to be staring at him, sideways. He told himself it was only a photograph, that it was the same as if he had a camera. He'd taken dozens—hundreds—of photographs of dead bodies. He kept himself from following Porter's unfortunate example.

"Oh boy," said the actor.

Andy reached in through the window, amazed at his fortitude. Graves's body was still warm, his shirt front sticky with blood. Andy groped beneath the man's suit jacket, his fingers finding the victim's wallet. He pulled it forth.

"You need money? What're you doing, man?"

Ignoring Porter, Andy turned to hold the billfold to the light. He took out the driver's license. It was issued by the state of Mississippi, and bore the name "Charles Meeker."

"This isn't right," he said.

Porter peered over his shoulder. "Maybe it's a phony."

They could hear a car approaching at high speed.

"Let's get out of here."

"Wait," Andy said. He opened the money compartment. It was thick with hundred-dollar bills.

"Come on, man."

Andy closed the wallet. The approaching headlights brightened the roadway. A moment later, the car came by, slowing, then braking sharply.

It was a police car.

Porter and Andy stood there, neither knowing what to do. The cop car backed up rapidly, rooftop Mars lights whirling, then swiveled up onto the shoulder. A very big policeman, hatless and sporting a military-style crewcut, strode toward them. He took the wreck in with a quick glance, then turned his eyes to Andy.

"What happened here?" he said.

"We saw this accident, and stopped to see if we could help."

"The driver's dead," Porter said. "There aren't any other passengers."

"Stay where you are," the policeman said.

He went back to his patrol car, spoke a moment into his radio microphone, and then fetched a big flashlight and a notebook. Going over to the wreck, he played the light over the interior, shook his head, then stepped back to take note of the license number.

"How long you been here?" he asked, when he was done.

"Just a couple of minutes," said Andy.

"I was responding to a call of two vehicles traveling on Memorial at high speed," he said. "Was yours one of those vehicles?"

"Like I said. We were just passing by and saw the accident."

The cop looked at the Corvette's license plate. "You from Louisiana?"

"I rented the car there," Porter said. In his jeans, T-shirt, and long hair, he looked like a biker.

"What're you doing in Houston?"

"Passing through," Porter said.

"May I see your driver's license and registration, please?"

Porter pulled out his license and the folded rental car agreement. The policeman examined these as he might counterfeit money.

"You're from California."

"Yes."

The cop sniffed. "You been drinking?"

"I had a beer earlier."

He sniffed again. "I smell whiskey."

"That's me," said Andy, "but I wasn't driving."

Studying Andy for a moment, the policeman then walked out onto the highway. "Two sets of skid marks there."

"I hit the brakes hard when I saw the accident."

The cop had made up his mind. "Step over to your car, please, and place your hands on the roof. Both of you."

Reluctantly, they complied.

"I'm going to ask you to submit to a Breathalyzer test," the cop said. "As I don't have that equipment with me, you're going to have to come with me to the station, where they do."

"Look," said Porter, "we just stopped to help."

"Spread your legs, please."

He searched Porter quickly, then moved to Andy.

"What's that in your hand?"

Andy felt very stupid. "It's the man's wallet."

"You took the guy's wallet?"

"I was just looking to see who it was."

The cop's hands began moving down Andy's sides, stopping abruptly at his jacket pocket. He reached inside, taking out the small pistol.

The next thing Andy knew, his hands were cuffed behind him.

• • •

"Shit happens," Porter said.

"I think that's Houston's municipal motto."

"At least we got a cell to ourselves."

He and Andy were seated on a small cot affixed to the rear wall.

The corridor outside was lighted but the cell was not. It smelled as though it had been drenched with disinfectant, a substance that had no effect on the insects skittering along the floor. Andy thought of stamping on one that came near, then changed his mind. Enough death.

It had been more than an hour since they had made the one telephone call allowed them, which to the astonishment of the lockup officer was to Lieutenant Paul Maljeux of the New Orleans police. Maljeux was not in the station, but Andy's patrolman friend Hernandez got on the phone and promised to inform the lieutenant of what had happened in a big hurry.

"I passed the fucking Breathalyzer," Porter said. "Why the hell are they holding us? They haven't charged us with anything."

"I guess they're trying to work something up. At the least, they'll probably hit me for carrying a concealed weapon."

"It's illegal to have a gun in Texas?"

"I imagine it is if you have it in your pocket. Especially if you're not from Texas."

"Why hold me then?"

Andy shrugged. "Reckless driving?"

"Shit."

"I'm surprised you didn't pull stardom on them."

Porter smiled. "No thanks. I'd get my name in the papers, sure as shit. I still might. Not a smart career move—getting written up for involvement in a fatal accident on a drunk-driving bust. Even if it is bullshit."

"With your fans? They'd love you all the more."

"The trade press has been calling me a goon as it is. I don't need any more of that. My agent has been trying to get me some serious parts."

"Your last film made fifty million."

"It wasn't *Romeo and Juliet*." Porter stretched out his legs and arms, yawning. "I wish they'd allow us another call. I'd like to check on Emily."

"Me, too."

"Do you really like her?"

"It's all mixed up with a lot of guilt at the moment, but, yes. I just wish I'd met her under different circumstances."

"So do I, man. So do I."

"Whether it was Graves or Marengo who did it, they're both dead. There's that."

"I don't blame you, Derain. Not anymore."

"Thanks."

"But I'll never get over it. Of all the people in the whole fucking world, why did that have to happen to her? She's really nice, you know. I mean nice through and through. Nicest damn woman I ever knew. Smart, too. She had a three-point-five average in college, before she dropped out. Reads all the time. A lot of poetry. Writes poetry. They make good songs."

Andy stared glumly at the sour floor.

"She didn't want to get into movies," Porter said. "Hated having to go around trying to sell herself to the producer types. But my mom figured that, with her looks, she'd be crazy not to make some money with them. My mom's a hard person to say 'no' to. She had me going around for auditions when I was ten."

"A lot of people like your mother around. You find them in the modeling business, pushing their kids."

"She's all right. Just kind of hard-driving. Emily's not like that. Always trying to please other people. If she pushed more, if she was tough like Paris, she might do better in the business. It wouldn't matter that she's . . . that she's not such a hot actress."

"She does fine." It occurred to Andy that he more accurately should have used the past tense. It was no certainty she'd ever work again. He owed her—for the rest of his life.

"She goes with a friend of mine, but . . . well, he's kind of a lunkhead. I was hoping she'd find somebody nice."

"Instead she found me."

"It's okay, man."

"It's not okay with me."

"You got a lot of broads on the line, don't you?"

"Much to my amazement. Up until a few days ago, I only had one."

Porter looked down at his hands. "How come you never got serious with Paris?"

"Paris?"

"The way she talks, I get the idea she's a little nuts about you."

"We're good friends, that's all. I never gave any thought to anything more."

"Bet every man in America has at one time or another. Including me. Why not you?"

"It just didn't work out that way. She's a big-time movie star."

"So am I. It's no big deal. Except the money."

"You could probably afford to bail us out of this trap."

"If I call anybody in L.A., the whole fucking world's going to find out about this."

They sat in silence for a moment.

"You still got the hots for this Mrs. Browley?"

"That's old news now," Andy said. "I guess."

"Anyone else?"

Andy didn't want to talk about Katie Kollwitz in this context. "Maybe. Someone I don't know as well as your sister."

"Bleusette likes you. Hell of a fine-lookin' woman."

"She's a prostitute."

"She is?"

"That bother you?"

"I don't know. I guess not."

"Doesn't bother me."

"You got a fucked-up life, man."

Andy looked around the cell. "Don't know why you say that."

A clanging sound startled them. A policeman, bigger even than the one who had arrested them, was opening the door.

"Come with me. Got a detective wants to talk to you."

• • •

It was a good sign that the lockup officer let them walk behind him, and that he was taking them out together. Usually when cops wanted to quiz suspected criminals, they did so individually—one on one.

It was an even better sign that he led them to a squad room, and not one of those two-way mirrored interrogation chambers.

The detective, a thin, lanky, dark-haired man in his mid-forties with a face like saddle leather, motioned them to two chairs by his desk. He had a weary, haunted look to his eyes that Andy associated more with New York cops, but when he spoke, it was with the accent of a lifelong Texan. He was polite, but not friendly.

"We talked to Lieutenant Maljeux of the New Orleans Police Department," he said. "He vouches for you."

Andy and Porter grinned. The detective did not.

"But he didn't exactly explain what you're doing in Houston."

Neither of them responded.

"You're Dick Porter, the movie actor?"

Porter nodded.

"Who's this guy?"

"My sister's boyfriend."

The detective looked down at his notepad. "She's Emily Shaw? The actress who got her throat cut?"

"Yes."

"Shouldn't you be with her at the hospital?"

"Like to be."

"So what're you doing here?"

Andy hesitated. "Well, we were looking for someone. A guy who I think was involved in what happened to Miss Shaw, and some other trouble back there."

"And just who is that?"

"George Graves. He's a private investigator here. He's the guy in that wrecked Cadillac."

The detective was looking at him as though he were babbling incoherently.

"George Graves?"

"Yes. Has a thing for black suits and Panama hats. He put a loaded pistol in with some prop guns at a movie shoot back in New Orleans. The leading lady almost got killed."

"You can't be looking for George Graves."

"You're supposed to be looking for him, too. He's wanted by the New Orleans police. Maljeux called you people about him. You were supposed to arrest him."

The detective leaned back in his chair, tapping on the table with a ballpoint pen.

"We got an inquiry from the New Orleans police, all right. But nobody asked us to pick him up. Good thing, too. George Graves is dead."

"I know. He was wrapped around that tree back on Memorial Drive. Most of him, anyway."

"That isn't George Graves." The detective glanced at his notepad. "That's one Charles Meeker, of Pascagoula, Mississippi."

"His license is a phony. It's Graves. Black suit and everything."

The detective stared. "We found Graves yesterday afternoon out toward Galveston—in a fifty-gallon drum that didn't stay buried. He was real ripe. Cause of death was puncture wounds to the chest. Knife wounds. We got a positive ID from the teeth."

"There must be a mistake. That can't be Graves. He was in New Orleans night before last. I saw him."

"It was Graves in the drum. Positive ID."

"I don't understand. Who was that in the car then?"

"Charles Meeker, of Pascagoula, Mississippi. You should know that. You lifted his wallet."

"This is crazy."

The detective sat forward. "All right. Let's end the bullshit. You weren't just driving by when you saw the accident. Either you were chasing him or he was chasing you. Which is it?"

"He was after us."

"Why?"

"I told you. He was part of what happened to Emily Shaw. And another murder. The New Orleans police should have told you that."

"They told me they nailed a guy named Frank Marengo on the Shaw rap. They never charged George Graves with anything. Or this

Charles Meeker. How long have you been in Houston?"

"Just since yesterday morning," Porter said. "You can check with the car rental."

"If I try to hold you," the detective said to Porter, "I suppose you'll have a dozen high-priced L.A. lawyers down on our backs, right?"

"I'm not trying to make any trouble."

The man tapped his pen again. "Either of you know George Graves, the real George Graves? Have any business with him?"

"Our business was with the guy in the Cadillac."

He looked to Porter. "I'm going to let you go. You can go on back to New Orleans and look after your sister, but let us know where you're staying there."

"Sure. What about him?"

The detective gave Andy a serious look. "He stays—for now."

"Why?"

"Just go on about your business, Mr. Porter. Before I change my mind."

Porter rose, turning toward Andy. "Should I call anyone for you? Paris?"

"Don't get her mixed up in this. Try to get Paul Maljeux again. Or Bleusette."

"Do my best. I don't want to leave you hanging."

"Get back to Emily, Richard. I'll be all right."

• • •

The charges were unlawful possession of a firearm and attempted theft. They took Andy's picture and fingerprints, booked him, then returned him to the cell. He sat morosely in the gloom for a long while, then lay back on the cot and went to sleep. There was nothing else to do, except to ponder his troubles, or think upon all the women who were now in his life. That didn't make him very happy, either.

As they'd taken his watch along with his other possessions, he had no idea what time it was when he awoke. It seemed to be day, but there were no windows in view. He could hear a number of voices down the corridor. A couple of policemen came by, leading a prisoner. He didn't return with them when they came back. Later, another lockup officer stopped at his cell and asked if he wanted anything to eat. Guessing at what that might consist of, he declined.

There were more crawly insects in view in the daytime than there had been in the night. Andy tucked his feet up on the cot and leaned back against the wall. He felt stiff, sore, and tired—and very dirty. He and Maljeux had been friends, off and on, since childhood. The man had never failed him.

But then, Paul hadn't asked him to go off and get put in jail in Houston.

He slept again. The lockup officer awakened him with a rattle of the cell door.

"You've been sprung," he said. "Come on."

"Sprung by who?"

"I don't know her name. Some woman with a thousand dollars U.S. currency. That's your bond."

When Andy had retrieved his personal effects, he was taken back to the squad room. Standing by the desk was Candice Browley, looking coolly beautiful, as always, but somehow thinner, and very nervous.

She sighed. "The things I do for you, Andy."

Candice's car was a long, cream-colored Infiniti convertible, which she drove with the top down despite the suffocating Houston heat. She wore a matching cream-colored, loose-fitting, and very chic silk pantsuit, with Hermes scarf and only a few pieces of jewelry. As she sat behind the wheel, car, clothes, and woman all seemed part of the same color-coordinated ensemble. Only in Los Angeles and Texas did automobiles figure as part of your wardrobe.

"I thought you weren't partial to the heat," he said, as they pulled away from the police station.

"It's a convertible. It's what they're for. Anyway, I'm in a hot mood."

"How did you know I was in the slammer?"

"Your charming landlady Bleusette called me," Candice said. "Got my phone number from your studio. She threatened me with all kinds of unspeakable things if I didn't get over here and bail you out."

"Your husband didn't interfere? I'd have thought he'd have you chained up in a dungeon by now."

"He's out of town. On business. Sometimes God is merciful."

"I'll pay you back the thousand."

"Just show up in court. Then I'll get it back."

"I'm not sure I'm of a mind to do that. They might put me back in that zoo cage on a long-term basis. Texas law isn't as merciful as God."

"Zoo cage?"

"Insect zoo. They have quite a number of interesting species in there."

"God, Andy. The trouble you get in. For no reason. Why were you carrying a gun?"

"I thought they were *de rigeur* out here." He slid down in the seat a bit. "Do you suppose your husband's having us followed? We're kind of obvious with this top down. Or would you like me to stand up on the hood?"

"I told you he's out of town."

"I guess there's not much about us he doesn't already know."

"He was almost nice to me when he left. It's spooky. But I'm grateful."

"Why did you come for me, Candy?" Andy asked.

"You mean, aside from your friend Bleusette's threats to have me beaten up in an alley?"

That surprised him. "Yes. I thought we were through."

She didn't address that question. "I was afraid for you. The idea of your being in Houston, but locked up behind bars. It bothered me. I wanted to see you."

He sat up again, using both arms to push himself up. The police had returned the scarf Paris had loaned him to use as a sling, having confiscated it as a precaution against his trying to escape their lovely jail in a casket, but he'd stuffed it in his pocket and now left it there. His arm was getting stiff. He needed to start moving it.

"How long will your husband be gone?"

"He didn't say. I'm supposed to meet him in New Orleans at the end of the week. There's some big party he has to go to. Sometimes I think that's the only reason he married me—to drag around to parties."

"What kind of party?"

"It's for that movie you were working on. *Street of Desire*? He's one of the backers. I think the biggest."

Andy sat up very straight. "He's bankrolling Cooper's film?"

"He wants to get into movies—in a big way. I think he has it in his mind to go to Hollywood and become a big deal. They like Texas money in L.A. And Texas money likes the beautiful women in Hollywood."

"They like anybody's money in L.A." He frowned. "I'm supposed to go to that party, too."

"Great."

"You've just given me another reason not to."

"Are you afraid?"

"Last time we talked you sounded like he was after you with a chainsaw."

"Ben scares me. He always has. But now that he's calmed down—well, enjoy the interlude, I guess."

Andy had never seen Candice drive an automobile before. She seemed very self-possessed, very elegant behind the wheel. He'd been asking himself what had attracted him to her so much in the beginning. There it was. Down-home Texas girl that she was, Candice was born to be on *Town & Country* magazine covers.

But so, when you looked at her, was Bleusette.

"You know a man named George Graves?"

She glanced at the rearview mirror. "No. Should I?"

"Man in a black suit, black tie, sunglasses, shiniest shoes this side of West Point? He ever come to your house?"

"I think I remember someone like that. But, I don't know. All kinds of weird people come to our house. Why? Who is he?"

"Private investigator. He's dead. Your police found what was left of his body yesterday. Another man, also given to the same somber color, was using his name. He's dead, too. Car crash. I won't bore you with all the complicated details, but the phony Graves was causing all kinds of trouble around the movie set in New Orleans. He almost got Paris Moran killed."

"I'd no idea."

"He might have been working for your husband."

"Which one? The real Graves, or the phony?"

"I don't know. Maybe both."

She gave him a funny look. "They said in the newspaper that the New Orleans police caught that man you chased out of your courtyard."

"They didn't catch him. They shot him into muffuletta. He was the one who attacked Emily and me. At least, that's how the cops see it."

"Emily Shaw. The lady you took to your bed." The words came out more sad than angry.

"He killed another woman before they got him."

"So all these bad people are dead now."

"Yes. Maybe that's why your husband is so calm."

"What do you mean?"

"Forgive me for saying this, love, but I'd be a lot calmer myself if Ben Browley were among the casualties."

"Don't say that."

Andy shut up. He rubbed his chin. He badly needed a shave and a bath. He supposed he looked a little like the hard-eyed building-front loungers they were passing along the street.

"Where the hell are we going, Andy?" she said, after a moment.

"Back to my motel, I guess. Pick up my things. It's a couple of stops out on Interstate 10."

"East or west?"

"East."

She glanced over her shoulder, then spun the long car around in the street, reversing direction with a squeal of tires.

• • •

Leaving Candy in the Infiniti, Andy went to the door of his motel room, finding it unlocked. The bed had been changed and made. Everything of his was gone, including the bottle of whiskey. He went through the connecting door to Porter's room. It was also empty.

"I'm going to check at the office," he said to Candice. "Be right back."

When he returned, he slumped into the passenger seat and sat there, staring through the windshield, leaving the door hanging open.

"What's wrong?" she asked.

"Dick Porter's gone, checked out, took my bag, too. Maybe he's safeguarding it for me. It was that nice, hideously expensive Prada one you gave me for my birthday once."

"Who's Dick Porter?"

"A movie actor. He came here with me."

"You mean Dick Porter the movie star? You know him?"

"He's Emily Shaw's brother. I guess he went back to New Orleans. She's still in the hospital."

"So what do we do now?" She glanced at the row of motel rooms.

He thought he recognized the look on her face. It pleased him.

"What do you think? Should I get my room back?" he asked.

She flushed. The car's engine came roaring to life.

"No."

"Sure?"

"Andy . . ."

He leaned over, sliding his injured arm around her shoulders, and kissed her. The look he thought he recognized came back strong.

"Not here," she said. She put the car in gear and backed out into the parking lot, spinning the wheel and heading out to the highway.

"I have a perfectly ridiculous wonderful idea," he said. "Let's go to your house."

"That's insane!"

"No it isn't. There won't be any cops, private eyes, or street riffraff watching us there, and it's the last place your husband would expect to find me."

"I don't know what he expects."

"I suppose you've got an army of servants at your place."

"Not really. There are groundskeepers and a chauffeur and all that, but they never come into the house. He has an assistant, a sort of valet, but he always travels with Ben. Otherwise, there's just the maid and the cook."

"When's their day off?"

"It was yesterday."

"Give them another."

"Andy . . ."

"You and me, Candy. Like always."

She bit her lip. "I hated it, the way I had to leave you in New Orleans."

"Me, too."

Candy looked to the lowering sun.

"We're not going to do anything he doesn't know we've already done," he said.

"He pisses me off. He's put me through a lot of hell these last few days."

"So why not?"

"This is crazy."

"We're crazy."

• • •

After so many years, they knew each other's bodies as intimately as their own, and managed to accommodate his injured shoulder without interfering with their pleasure. Candy made love carefully but hungrily, not letting him go until she had all she wanted. Then she collapsed upon his chest, lying flat against him, stretching out her long legs, her hair falling across his face.

"I love you, Andy." The words were whispered into his ear. "I was so goddamn stupid to marry Ben."

He stroked her back, his hand coming to rest finally on her silky buttocks. After a moment, she eased herself off him, and they slept. They awakened to what appeared to be the end of the day. He sat up.

"Before another minute passes," he said, "I've got to have a shower. I'm surprised you let me into your bed."

She smiled, with dreamy content. "Wait a minute."

Candy went into another room, and returned with a brand-new toothbrush and a plastic disposable razor. Showing him the bath, she then went downstairs to get some food for them. The bathroom she'd led him to was nearly as big as his studio, and filled with feminine things. Andy gathered she and her husband had separate baths—and bedrooms.

When he was done, he lingered a moment at the large window next to the basin. The view was of Texas's immense flatness, the sky a hazy gold in the setting sun. He looked down at the grounds. A dog was resting beneath a scrubby bush. A German shepherd, not a Doberman. He wondered which breed was worse.

Candy was waiting for him on the bed, sitting cross-legged, unmindful of her nakedness. She'd called ahead to tell the maid and cook to go home, and the two servants had left by the time they'd arrived. They were alone.

She'd made sandwiches and brought a cold bottle of white wine. When they were done with the meal, he felt sleepy. He prodded himself to stay awake.

"I was just thinking of the first time we made love," she said.

"It was on the floor," he said, "in the corner of some wretched loft in SoHo, at the tail-end of an all-night party."

"No one noticed," she said.

"Just like New Orleans."

She smiled. "You and New Orleans."

"You'll learn to love it."

"We'll talk about that later."

He didn't want to think about 'later.' Neither did she. Candy lay back and stretched out, spreading her legs slightly.

"Andy, Andy, Andy." She said it softly. He rolled over and kissed her breast.

• • •

He waited until he heard her gently snoring, then carefully eased his uninjured arm from beneath her head. Sitting up slowly, he slipped off the bed onto his feet. His pants were on a chair. He took them up with great care, to keep his keys and change from clinking, then carried them out into the hall, not putting them on until he was on the stairs.

It was quite dark now. The huge house was silent, except for dull, innocuous background sounds one would expect. Barefoot, he made his way downstairs and went searching through the rooms until he found what had to be Browley's study. It was as outsized as the bathroom, expensively but tastelessly furnished, big enough to accommodate a small insurance company. Only William Randolph Hearst would have considered it cozy.

He turned on a lamp, then stopped to think. If Browley was as involved in all the New Orleans nastiness as he suspected, he would have the things Andy was looking for close at hand, for easy perusal. Certainly he would if he enjoyed what he was looking at, and Andy presumed that he did.

The logical place then was the desk, a burnished mahogany, slablike piece of furniture as large as a pool table.

It had nine drawers, and they were all locked. Andy looked around the room, noting the baronial fireplace and the gleaming set of hardware in the stand by the hearth. Taking up the poker, he jammed its point in the crevice above the desk's wide center drawer, and shoved upward carefully.

Nothing budged. He thrust the point in more deeply, worked it back and forth, then shoved again, this time with all his strength.

There was a loud creak, and then a crack, but not the sound he was waiting for.

Taking a deep breath, he inserted the poker again and got his good shoulder under it, pushing hard.

The lock broke with a snap. The draw whizzed open and Andy went sailing onto the top of the desk, the poker rolling off onto the carpeted floor. He stood up, noting that he had carved a shallow gash in his right side. He waited, listening.

Candy was miles away upstairs. He'd be amazed if she'd heard anything. He pulled up Browley's big leather swivel chair and sat in it. Candy would have to explain all this to Browley, but, hell, even billionaires got burgled.

Anyway, it was tit for tat for the sneak thievery that had gone on in his studio.

As he hoped, the center drawer lock controlled all the others. The side drawers slid open with ease, as though on well-oiled ball bearings. There was nothing of interest in the first three he went through—unless one counted a .357 Magnum revolver something of interest—but in the fourth, in a thick, Mark Cross cowhide briefcase, was everything he wanted to find. And a little bit more.

One file contained minute reports, all signed with the name George Graves, on various aspects of the movie shoot and its progress, along with clips from *Variety* and other trade publications of stories relating various problems Cooper was encountering with the unlucky film. Another file was thick with biographical material on Senator Henry Boone, and an attached manila envelope contained newsclips concerning Boone's trial for manslaughter. In there also was voter analysis data from all of Boone's elections—the figures relating to the black vote circled in red.

The sheaf of photographs was the most fascinating. There were copies of all the shots he had taken of Candice, including those of the two of them in their shameless, divorce court–perfect naked embrace, as well as several Andy hadn't seen before of the two of them walking about in the French Quarter, mostly hand in hand.

But he and Candy weren't the only photographic subjects in this collection, nor the only illicit lovers. To his amazement, he found two other pictures—professional-looking eight-by-ten glossies—of Ben Browley and a woman in bed. He could only half-see her face in the first, but in the second, she was all but leering at the camera. She was small-breasted, long-limbed, and attractive, with long, lustrous black hair and skin more deeply tanned even than Bleusette's.

It was Danielle Jones—the late Danielle Jones.

What the hell was Browley doing with pictures of himself and such a strange and notorious woman? What were they, trophies?

There was a small piece of torn paper clipped to the back of the second photo. It bore only a figure—$75,000.

He looked further. There were more photos, mostly obscene or at least compromising. One was of Alan Cooper, in what looked to be one of the location trailers, having fellatio conducted on him by an actress who had a bit part in the film. The others were of people he didn't recognize—straight couples, and a few of homosexuals.

One picture struck him with a jolt. It was Danielle Jones again, in the same French bed, only the man with her wasn't Browley. It was United States Senator Henry J. Boone—from the looks of it, having the time of his life.

"Andy!"

Candice hit a switch that turned on lights all over the room.

"What the hell are you doing in here, Andy? Good God Almighty, what are you doing?"

"Candy! Look at this stuff! It explains everything!"

"Is this why you wanted to come to my house? So you could break into his things? So you could steal? Fuck me to sleep so you could creep down here and play CIA agent?"

"Candy . . ."

"You bastard! You son of a bitch!"

"Just look at it, will you? Look at it!"

"Get out!"

"Please, Candy."

"Get out! Before I call the cops."

"Don't be crazy. Candy."

"You're the one who's crazy. Out of your bloody mind. Now get out!"

Andy hesitated, then shoved the files into the briefcase, and snapped the lid shut. He'd broken the lock to open it, but the clasps held.

"Put that down! That's my husband's!"

"It's coming with me."

She moved toward him, still naked. With a quick move, he opened one of the drawers and pulled out the big pistol, holding it clumsily in his left hand.

"You're pointing that at me? At *me*?"

"Just get out of the way, Candy. Please."

She stepped back, furious, her rage almost beyond control.

"Jerk! Prick!"

"Think this over, love," he said. "I'm doing the right thing."

"Get out! Go away! Get out of my life!"

He hurried past her, going through the front door nearly at a run.

Lights came on, illuminating the grounds all the way to the pike-topped metal fence. The driveway gate was still open. He wondered if she had some electronic means of closing it from the house.

He had more immediate worries. Bells began to ring, their insistent clatter suddenly mingling with the raucous whine of a siren. She'd hit the burglar alarm. She'd completely lost it.

Andy pounded down the walk, his bare feet suddenly stinging as he came upon the gravel drive. It seemed to take a hell's forever getting across it and onto the coolness of the lawn.

Then a new, terrifying problem: a barking dog. One dog? Two? More?

He ran on. The barking drew nearer. He imagined huge jaws slicing into his leg.

A few steps more, then he whirled around. The shepherd was streaking toward him from across the side lawn. He remembered a command he'd heard an actor use in a movie scene much like this.

"Release!" he shouted. "Release!"

He might as well have bellowed, "Come get me!" The dog's pace did not abate.

Andy truly loved animals. Even when broke, he always managed to send a check every year to Cleveland Amory's Fund for Animals. For all the irregular meals he served her, he passionately loved his cat, Beatrice. He was fond of dogs, too. Even German shepherds.

But he didn't want to die.

Sticking the pistol he'd taken in his belt, he swung the big briefcase just as the shepherd made its final bound. A corner of the case caught it in the shoulder. It yelped, skewed sideways, and hit the ground rolling. Andy hoped he hadn't seriously injured it, but sure as hell hoped he'd changed its mind.

The animal recovered, getting back onto its feet, snarling, growling, its eyes fiendish. Andy backed away, then ran. The gate was about a hundred feet away.

More barking and snarling. The dog came lunging on. Before Andy could turn to attempt another riposte, it made its attack, leaping toward its target. An instant later, its teeth sunk into the soft leather of the briefcase, nearly wresting it out of Andy's hand.

He tried to jerk it away, but the dog came with it, growling furiously. It dug in its feet and pulled back. Andy yanked again, but the beast did not relent. A brief game of tug of war followed, the creature eventually giving ground, but not giving up, its teeth gripping the briefcase leather like rivets.

Andy looked ahead. The driveway gates were moving, closing. Candy was really mad.

He took a deep breath, then plunged on, dragging the noisy, writhing beast behind him.

Somehow, he made progress. The dog's single-minded tenacity was probably saving Andy's life. A wonderful thought occurred to him. He would slip through the closing gate just before it shut on the dog.

It was a stupid, stupid notion. He got through the gate all right—briefcase, German shepherd, and all.

In the same fashion, he struggled along the sidewalk. If he released the briefcase, he'd lose what he came for—and the dog might attack him anyway.

If it came to it, he could shoot the animal—a last resort. But he didn't want to do that. Bleusette had wonderful words in two languages for what he felt.

He urged himself on, the growling dog now seeming to enjoy this. Lights were going on in houses along the road. Then there were bright lights behind him, headlights. The cops?

A car roared up beside him. A red car. A Corvette. Richard Porter stuck his head out the window.

"Don't just stand there, you stupid idiot," he said. "Get in."

Andy hurried around the front of the car.

"Don't bring that dog!"

The shepherd didn't like having a car door for a necklace. As Andy increased the pressure, its jaws came open, and, free of the briefcase, it backed away, barking insanely.

"Floor it!" Andy shouted, closing the door completely, but Porter was already doing that.

• • •

They got clear of River Oaks without encountering any police. Perhaps Candy hadn't called them after all—contenting herself with the prospect of Andy being chewed to bits.

"Thought you'd be in New Orleans," Andy said.

"Thought you'd never come out of that house. Didn't expect you'd be treated to an all-night shack job."

"Wait till you see what I've got in here."

"Let's not stop and look right now, okay?"

"How come you're still in Houston?"

Porter made a sharp turn off the highway onto a dark side street, taking what Andy presumed was evasive action. "I started for New Orleans. Got as far as that bridge across Galveston Bay, then figured I wasn't going to accomplish much sitting around holding Emily's hand, since all the action seemed to be here."

"More than I figured on."

"I called that policeman Maljeux, but couldn't get through to him. So then I called Bleusette like you said, and she said she'd take care of getting you the bail money or whatever. So I came back and parked outside the police station and waited for you to come out. It seemed like it would take fucking forever, and then all of sudden out you come with that foxy lady and zoom off in that Japanese Rolls-Royce. That's Browley's wife? Your main squeeze?"

"An hour ago she was telling me she loved me."

"And now?"

"You met her dog."

"I followed you back to the motel, but I didn't know what was going down. Figured I'd wait to ask you when you were free to talk. Next thing I knew, you were off to this Texas version of Beverly

Hills. I fell asleep. All those fucking bells and sirens woke me up."

"I guess she did me a big favor then, setting off that alarm. You know where you're going?"

"More or less. What's in that briefcase?"

"Among other things, some very dirty pictures. I didn't get a chance to look through all of it, but there's one of Ben Browley and another of Senator Henry Boone, and they're both with that woman Marengo cut up in Faubourg Marigny."

"Let me see."

"Just keep driving. Can you get us back to New Orleans without getting arrested again?"

"I'll get us back there, but I think I'd better find us some back roads. You know East Texas?"

"Not really."

"Well, you will by the time we get to the Louisiana line. Browley and Boone? Who was spying on who? Which one was Graves working for?"

"Maybe both. Maybe just for himself. Hot stuff like this on two big guys like that, a man could turn a pretty penny putting the squeeze on both of them."

"So which of them killed Graves?"

Andy was getting confused. He'd been as unnerved by the fact that he'd actually threatened Candy with a deadly weapon as he had been by the snarling dog she'd loosed on him. "You mean the real Graves?"

"I don't mean the guy we sent into that tree back on Memorial."

Porter slowed down. A police car came by from the opposite direction, but the officer paid them no attention.

"I wish he were still with us," Andy said. "He might have answered a few questions. Like why he was masquerading as Graves."

"Maybe the real Graves just wouldn't go along with all the shit his client asked him to do, so they whacked him and hired this other dude to take his place," Porter suggested.

"Just do what he was told."

"And in the end," said Porter, "when all was said and done, they could blame everything on the real Graves, who'd be dead."

"Neat idea, except the cops found his body too soon."

"Bad guys always fuck up. It happens in all my movies."

With the police car long gone behind them, Porter put the gas pedal down. They were passing from suburbs into the country now.

"We still don't know why they came after you and Emily, or why someone's been trying to fuck up Cooper's movie."

"No, we don't."

"There could be a lot more of these people around."

"Wouldn't surprise me."

Porter stepped harder on the accelerator. "I'm going to get us to New Orleans, but I'm not sure I should."

When they reached the town of Gretna on the south bank of the Mississippi, Porter pulled into a gas station. Andy went to a pay phone and called Bleusette. It was nearly five o'clock in the afternoon. She'd be up.

"You are alive, Andy?"

"If I was a ghost out to haunt you, I wouldn't do it by telephone."

"You are out of jail?"

"Yes. Thank you very much. But I'm still charged with a couple of crimes, and last night I committed another one."

"What are you talking about, Andy? Where the fuck are you?"

"In the fabled city of Gretna, Louisiana. Is my place crawling with officers of the law? For all I know, I'm wanted in four states."

"It is probably crawling with cockroaches, like always. Maljeux was in there today. I don't know what he was doing."

"He say anything to you?"

"He said, 'Good mornin', Bleusette,' and he smiled."

"Maybe he's happy because he thinks I'm out of New Orleans and won't be back for a while. Are there any other cops hanging around?"

"There are always cops hanging around. This is the French Quarter. Anyway, I thought Maljeux is your friend."

"My circle of friends seems to be rapidly diminishing. I need a place to stay where they won't be looking for me. For a few days, anyway."

"One of my houses is vacant. But I don't think you would like it very much. It's my worst one—up by old Congo Square."

"Does it have a telephone?"

"No, it does not have a telephone and it does not have a microwave and it does not have—what you call it?—a sauna. But it has a toilet."

"I'll take it." He paused. "Bleusette, I'm afraid the Houston police took that little pistol you loaned me."

"No big shit. I took it from a client—a cop who did not want to pay cash for enjoying a very good time with me."

"I brought another one back for you. You'll love it. You don't have to aim it so carefully."

"You go use my little house." She gave him the address. "I will come by and see you tonight. Late. After work."

• • •

Porter drove him to the house Bleusette had provided, a sagging one-story frame separated from the street by a chicken-wire fence and a weed-choked yard. The key was hidden behind a shutter, as Bleusette said. She might as well have left the door unlocked, for all the prospect the place offered a burglar.

"What a fuckin' dump, man," Porter said.

"This is *real* New Orleans decadence," Andy said, tearing off a swatch of peeling wallpaper.

"You're going to hole up here?"

"I guess there are worse places."

"If there are, they must be on this street. What're you going to do now that we're back?"

"Go through all this stuff in the briefcase again and think."

"You want some help?"

"I wouldn't mind if you got us some food and something to drink. Maybe that'll help. I don't mean to make you an errand boy, Dick, but if Candice went to the police about my taking the briefcase, it's probably not wise for me to go strolling around the streets."

"You don't mind if I go to another neighborhood to shop?"

"I don't think you'll have much choice."

• • •

Andy turned on the one lamp that worked in the small living room of the house, then pushed the cheap coffee table aside and spread the contents of the briefcase out on the grungy carpet. The most intriguing item in the collection was a small notebook. There was writing on only three pages—a handwritten list of entries, each line containing a monetary amount, a date, and the initials "G.G." Halfway down the second page, the initials changed to "M.K."

The last dollar amount was a most intriguing "$75,000."

He read over the list again. G.G. M.K. But the name on the accident-victim's driver's license had been Charles Meeker—initials C.M.

Unless "Charles Meeker" was a phony. Everywhere he'd turned in this *Alice in Wonderland* adventure, reality quickly became something else.

He spread the photographs out further, then shoved aside those of him and Candy, Cooper and his actress friend, and those of Browley and Boone at play with the late Miss Jones. Wishing he could use his darkroom magnifier and enlarger, he began examining the others one by one.

The couples in them were complete strangers to him, but he suddenly realized one of the women was not. She was a Texas society type who spent a lot of time in the East, and sometimes turned up on the gossip pages of fashion magazines—usually at parties and seldom with her husband. Her face was a plastic surgeon's masterpiece. Looking closer, he guessed she'd probably had a lot of remedial body work done as well. Her love partner's haircut was what you'd find in a cowboy bar.

Perhaps squeamishly, Andy saved the homosexual couplings till last. There were only three such photos, and he didn't recognize the individuals. With two of them—both shot through windows—he couldn't even make out the faces. Graves/Meeker was a lousy photographer.

He studied the body of one of the men. He was plump, though not quite fat, and looked to be nearing middle age—though that might only be because of his thinning blond hair. The man with him, half-hidden by the other's body, was much younger. He wore a bracelet, one Andy thought he might have seen before.

Bracelet.

Thinning blond hair.

Andy sat back on the couch, leaning his head against the wall. He wished Porter would hurry. Now he could really use a drink.

• • •

Porter rapped twice on the screen door, then pushed it open. He was carrying a large paper bag and a small one.

"I got some potato chips and Cheetos," he said. "And some lunch meat and Wonder Bread."

Andy shook his head sadly. This was New Orleans, where you could do a little better than Wonder Bread. Porter would probably order a grilled cheese sandwich at Le Cirque.

"What else?"

Porter opened the other bag and pulled out a fifth of Wild Turkey.

"Richard," Andy said, "there are people in this neighborhood who would gladly kill you for a shot of that."

"So don't invite them in. I'll get a couple of glasses."

"Don't. I took a look at the kitchen. Nothing's very clean."

"I'll wash a couple."

"With this plumbing, I think that would only make them worse. Just hand me the bottle."

Porter did so. Andy drank. He let the first sip spread its magic through his system, then took another. He wiped his mouth and the top of the bottle, then offered it to the actor.

"I've got some real good news," Porter said, taking a seat in an ancient stuffed chair that gave off a fluff of dust. "You ready for it?"

"Couldn't be readier."

"I went over to the hospital. Emily can talk! I mean, she can't say much, and she sounds like Brando in *The Godfather,* but Andy, real fucking words! She spoke my name. Yours, too. It was like she was asking for you."

"I wish I could be there."

"Better hurry. They got her off the IV. The doctor said she'll be able to go back to California in a couple of days. My mom's going to come out to get her."

"She's not here yet?"

"She's busy, man. They're casting some TV pilots. But she'll be here, don't worry."

"Did Emily say anything else?"

"Not much. Something she already wrote down for the cops. She said whoever attacked her was a woman."

"How could she tell?"

"I don't know. Maybe perfume or something. Emily's got a great sense of smell. She knows wines."

"I didn't smell any perfume. And Frank Marengo was no woman."

Porter shrugged, then glanced around the room. "What kind of people live in this dump?"

"I think Bleusette rents it to her fellow Followers of Venus."

"What?"

"Hookers. Low end of the scale. Bleusette's the high end—about as high as you can get in this town, at least till you get into trophy wives."

"Do you suppose they take their johns back here?"

"Only the lunatics and morons. Why don't you go back to Emily? I'll get you at your hotel tomorrow."

"You'll be all right here, man?"

"If you leave the whiskey. Don't worry. I've got Mr. Browley's pocket howitzer here. It's enough to make an impression on the local Welcome Wagon."

Porter stood up. "You want me to say anything to Emily for you?"

"Tell her I'm sorry, that I'm really, really sorry—that I'll find a way to see her before she goes, that I'll do everything I can for her. Tell her I plan on hearing her sing 'Skylark' in that club in Venice Beach."

"She'd like that."

"So would I."

• • •

Andy and the Wild Turkey fraternized for an hour so, then he went to sleep on the couch. He stirred from his slumber when he sensed that someone was sitting on the other end by his feet. As he should have expected, it was Bleusette.

"It seems that every time I close my eyes, there's a fifty-fifty chance I'm going to see you when I open them again."

"So? This is a bad thing?"

She was wearing a black cocktail dress with a single strand of fake pearls. She could have just come from a Junior League reception.

"It's a wonderful thing," he said, "especially when I think of who else it might have been."

He sat up, swinging his feet to the floor. It was dark, well into the night. "What time is it?"

"Almost three. I quit early. In fact, I walk out on a guy, the son of a bitch." She was holding the big Magnum pistol, which he'd left on the table. "This won't fit in my purse, Andy."

"I'll get you a shoulder holster." He fetched the bottle up from the floor. It troubled him that it was nearly half gone. He'd been drinking like this during those last days in New York.

But it didn't trouble him that much. He took a swig. "You want a belt, Bleusette?"

She made a face. "I drink only Pernod. You know that."

"Forgot."

"So what you going to do now, Andy?" She nodded toward the papers and pictures on the floor. "These things help you figure everything out?"

"Figured out a few things. Bleusette, do you suppose there's any way you could get in touch with Paul Maljeux tonight?"

"That depends. If he's at One-Legged Duffy's or the Razzy Dazzy, then *bien sûr.* If he's at home with his wife, maybe she won't like that so much, and tell me to go to hell like the last time I talk to her."

"If you don't mind going to one of your houses that has a telephone, would you try? Tell him I want to see him in the morning—early in the morning. Say six A.M. Maybe down by the river. Past the Moonwalk, by the end of Nicholls Wharf. I'd call him myself but I don't want to talk to him until I can do it face to face. It's important."

"Okay."

"And tell him he's got to come alone. Private business. Just us. Any warrants he's got for me from Houston will have to wait."

"I'll tell him."

"I owe you, darlin'."

She smiled at him, then looked down, almost demurely, at her neat tan hands.

"You know something, Andy. I have decided to quit the life."

"You told me."

"I mean now. Tonight. That's why I walk out on this guy—some big slob from the car dealers convention. I've got ninety-seven thousand, three hundred fifty dollars. I say, why wait to make it an even hundred thousand, Bleusette? You got enough. That's stupid. No more fucking, Andy. Never again for money. Except, well, maybe just one last time." She looked at him a little mischievously. "The last time, Andy, I think it should be something special. Not some jerk from Louisville who uses goddamn Aqua Velva. I should go out in style, yes?" She leaned back, putting her hands behind her head.

"Bleusette . . ."

"What do you say, Andy? Will you be my last fuck? You never sleep with me. Not once. I am the cleanest, healthiest whore in New Orleans. I don't do dope. I go to the doctor's office every month. I buy the finest condoms. I pick my clients with discernment. Yes, discernment."

"I know . . ."

"And I like you very much. You are maybe my best friend in all the world. My last time for money. So I have a nice memory."

"I'm honored and flattered, darlin', but I'm beat to hell and half-drunk and my shoulder hurts." He looked around the room. "And this is not exactly the Royal Orleans Hotel. I just don't think this is our night of nights, okay? Let me take a raincheck."

"It's not raining, Andy."

"In my soul it is."

"Okay, Andy. You don't want me? You don't want me. I'll go try to talk to Maljeux. If I find him, I'll come back *tout de suite*."

"Be real careful out there."

"Always careful, Andy. Not like you." She put the big revolver into one of the paper bags Porter had brought, then stuck it under her arm.

After she left, he sat without moving for a long time, then gathered up the papers and pictures and put them in the briefcase. He felt vulnerable without the gun. The night outside the screen door was full of strange noises. He turned off the light.

• • •

He heard Bleusette come up the steps. She paused at the door, then rapped on it loudly three times before swinging it open and stepping inside into the dark.

"You there, Andy?"

"Yes."

"Maljeux wasn't in any of the joints. He was at home with his wife, but I talk to him anyway. She answered the phone—not very nice to me, goddamn it—but I told her it was a police emergency, so she wakes him up. He'll do it, Andy. He said to tell you he's glad you're back safe and sound from Houston and that he's been looking to talk to you anyway. He'll be there at the river. Six A.M. Okay?"

"Did he say if I'm wanted?"

"You mean like public enemy number one? No, he just say he'll see you." She turned on the light and held up Browley's big pistol. "Two muggers come at me over on Rampart, Andy. I scare the fucking shit out of them with this."

"That's what it's for, I guess."

"Andy, you have on no clothes."

"Well, I've been thinking. You are about the most beautiful woman I know, and, hell, a night of nights in the hand is worth two in the bush."

"In the bush? In the hand?"

"What I mean is . . . never mind. It's a special night for you and so it's special for me. But let's not use the bedroom. I don't like the looks of it in there. Or the funny little noises."

"Any way you want, but, remember, this has got to be for money."

"There's a hundred-dollar bill on the table, Bleusette. It's from the first sale of a serious photo of mine in a New Orleans art gallery. This'll be a special occasion for both of us."

She smiled, a happy child, then turned off the light.

"We will make this a very grand special occasion," she said. "No one knows how to do that like me."

• • •

Afterward, Bleusette slept, but Andy could not. She'd been more than true to her word. Sex was her art, and for him she had produced a near masterpiece, flawed if at all only by his fatigue and, in her terms, inexperience. But there'd been more than a prostitute's skill and knowledge and practice in this. There had been an almost uncanny happiness, enough for them both to share. And maybe something more. She'd used the word "love" several times. He'd thought it part of her routine, but now he wondered.

They'd always been friends, a bond in its way as strong as the one he'd had for so many years with Candice. He was devoted to Bleusette. He'd been at what they'd both thought might be her deathbed and he hoped that, whenever it came, he might find her at his. But "love"? What could that ever be to a whore—even a whore who was otherwise such a special person? Could a model be capable of a truly natural smile, or an actress of a genuine emotion?

He felt terribly confused, then stopped to consider something. With this night, Bleusette was finally leaving the life. It couldn't have been love, but simply a joyous act of self-liberation, of transformation—and, doubtless, gratitude.

Andy took comfort in the logic of this explanation. It removed so much complication. Bleusette could remain what she had always been to him.

Turning, he gently slid his arm around her bare shoulders, and found sleep.

19

Andy got to the wharf early, just as a gooey pink sun began to emerge from the top of a low cloud bank rolling slowly off to the southeast. He watched as an old tug pushed a long line of barges around the bend of the river, then turned around to wait with his back to the water so he could observe the approaches from the street.

Maljeux came alone, wearing his policeman's uniform, crossing North Peters Street as nonchalantly as he might on an idle morning's stroll.

"Welcome back to the city of good times, Andy."

"Hello, Paul."

"How's the shoulder?"

"Still there. Sort of."

"You look a little peaked."

"I guess it's those good times."

Maljeux went to the railing, leaning his elbows on it and gazing across the river at Algiers.

"Best time of day to be out and about in New Orleans," he said. "Everything's so nice and clean and quiet."

"A regular Indianapolis."

"Before you tell me what's on your mind, my friend, I want to tell you that you've got nothin' to worry about anymore from those cops who hassled you in Houston."

"How can you say that? They booked me—fingerprints, mug shot, *le tout ensemble*."

"I had a talk with those boys. Took a while, but the charges have been dropped. That wallet thing was bullshit, as they goddamn well knew. As for the weapons beef, they ran the numbers off that little gun through the computer, and, wouldn't you know it, they traced it right back to our department's property section. A considerable embarrassment. I don't know who lifted that piece from there, but I claimed jurisdiction. Told them we'd take care of everything. Which means, I'm going to forget all about it. Anyway, they won't mess with you anymore. I get the idea they were real impressed when no less than Benjamin Browley's wife turned up to bail you out."

"They don't have a warrant out for me on armed robbery charges?"

"Not a word about that. Robbery of what?"

It was comforting, at least, that Candy hadn't wanted him back in jail. She could have put the screws to him hard. He'd try to figure out later why she didn't. Andy picked up the briefcase. There was a low concrete ledge running along the walk behind them. "Let's go sit down, Paul. My shoulder hurts. So does my back."

"Sure."

The concrete was cool. In another hour, they'd be able to fry beignets on it.

"I turned up a George Graves in Houston, all right. A licensed private investigator, just like you said. Only it was the wrong George Graves. They found his body, and he'd been dead for a while."

"So I was informed." Maljeux sounded a little more serious now. "Couple days is quite a little while for a corpse in that Texas heat."

"The man who was causing us so much grief here was posing as Graves. His driver's license says he's a Charles Meeker, out of Mississippi, just like Albert Ferrier and Danielle Jones. He's also deceased, after stopping his Cadillac with a tree."

"They told me that, too."

"One or both of those George Graves was working for Ben Browley, Paul. I think Frank Marengo and Ferrier were, too." He patted the briefcase. "I've got all sorts of stuff in here. Browley's files. Some of them anyway."

"And how did you come by those?"

"Let's just say a serendipitous visit to my lady friend. Browley was spying on all kinds of people. Me, Alan Cooper, even Senator Boone.

A lot of people. Not just spying, but having compromising pictures taken, digging into financial records, digging up dirt. A regular one-man CIA."

"You hear about rich guys doing this all the time. PI's make a lot of money working that kind of trade."

Maljeux kept his eyes away from Andy's, pretending to watch the progress of a car ferry whose river crossing he must have seen a thousand times. Then he shifted his gaze down the wharf to the old riverboat Cooper was planning to blow up.

"Those movie people of yours sure have that old hulk looking pretty. Seems a waste to make it go kaboom."

"Browley's coming to New Orleans," Andy said.

"He comes here a lot, I hear. You and his wife should have picked another town." Maljeux slapped at a fly. They were beginning to stir in the warming air. "You said something about dirty pictures?"

Andy nodded, patting the briefcase. "Got a regular porn shop in here, including one of Senator Boone at play with a bimbo—and she isn't just another Jackson Square hooker. It's Danielle Jones."

"No shit? With Hank Boone?"

"Yes sir. Right here in black-and-white."

A young woman jogger in very brief shorts and a T-shirt was huffing and chuffing toward them down the wharf, a black Labrador retriever on a leash trotting along beside her.

"Danielle Jones would be trouble for Boone all kinds of ways," Maljeux said. "Turns out she was a threefer. A business girl. A lady of color. And a transsexual."

"Transsexual?"

"They did the autopsy yesterday. Those sex-change operations are a lot of bullshit, you know. Just cosmetics. They don't change anything inside, and men and women are as different inside as they are out. A lot more, really."

The girl jogger, eyes fixed straight ahead, pounded past. She had the kind of figure that belonged in Andy's picture book.

"Something else you'll be interested to know," said Maljeux. "Those fingerprints we took off your balcony? We got a clean set belonging to the selfsame Miss or Mister Jones. You never had this person up to your place before, right?"

"You know I haven't. You said she's a transsexual?"

"Yes, indeed. Explains her athletic prowess in monkeying up to your bedroom."

"Emily said she smelled a woman. Surgery couldn't have changed that."

"Did you smell anything?"

"No."

Maljeux shrugged. "Might have been the residue of some perfume. Who knows? Never heard of a case settled because of what a witness smelled. Fingerprints have sent a lot of folks to death row, though. We would have picked up Jones if Marengo hadn't done her that night. Easy damn conviction, I figure. Anyway, you should rest easy now on that score. Miss Shaw's doer is broiling in Hell, if there is a Hell, and after what happened to Miss Shaw, you sure want to hope there is."

Andy stared at the briefcase. "I'm not resting easy."

"Well, I'm feeling a lot more comfortable about matters than I was."

"There's an even better picture in here," Andy said. "One of Miss or Mister Jones servicing Browley himself."

Maljeux whistled. "Maybe he's the one who set her up in Faubourg Marigny. Maybe he's the sugar daddy we were looking for."

"Why would a guy like that have his own PI take pictures of him *flagrante delicto*?"

"Maybe it was some other PI. Or someone shaking him down. Could be that's what set off this whole damn thing. Though that's just speculation."

"I think you ought to bring Browley in for an official conversation, Paul. Maybe Hank Boone, too. And Alan Cooper. It turns out Browley's got big money invested in his movie, and Graves or his impersonator or God knows who was doing every fiendish thing possible to shut the shoot down."

"Wouldn't want do that. Bother those gentlemen now."

"Why not? Five people are dead, and Emily's in the hospital. The questions still to be answered in this could run a quiz show for a year."

"With important men like that, I'd need a warrant from a judge pretty close to God just to have them come in for questioning—especially if they'd rather not. And I don't think Browley or Boone would appreciate that kind of indignity, do you?"

"I don't care what they'd appreciate."

"Unless you got some real hot, incriminating evidence in that lawyer's lunch bag of yours, what you've told me so far doesn't connect Browley to anything criminal. No sir. The man's wife's been cheating on him. He's trying to keep an eye on his movie investment. He's checking out a dangerous politician—in fact, a politician who's been screwing his girlfriend. So he hires a PI. Happens every day. Just because the PI firm turns out to be involved with a lot of squirrelly slimeballs, who turn up dead, well, you can't indict him for that. He may be just as nervous about what's been going on as you are. And it sounds like Boone's nothing more than a blackmail victim. I don't know what Cooper would tell us, except to arrest you."

"Marengo worked for Boone."

"And Graves, or what's-his-name, was working for Browley, you say."

"They were both from Pascagoula, Mississippi. Just like Albert Ferrier and Danielle."

"They're all dead, Andy. As far as I'm concerned, this case is in the grave, too."

"I don't think you're getting the picture, Paul. Maybe you're very deliberately not getting the picture."

"What the hell do you mean by that?"

"I think you're going far beyond *laissez-faire* on this one. I think you're lying down on this case. If you'd gone after Frank Marengo over in Algiers right after I told you about him, he'd be behind bars now—alive, and maybe talkative. You and your boys just sat there outside Danielle Jones's house while Marengo was putting a knife to her throat. You didn't lift a finger to stop him. You just waited for him to come out, and then you shot him to ribbons before he had a chance to even say 'fuck you.' "

"Police work ain't perfect, Andy. That was an accident."

Maljeux was beginning to perspire. He took off his hat and patted his head with his handkerchief.

"Emily wrote you a note saying her attacker was a woman, and you didn't do anything about that, either."

"What would you want me to do, arrest all the women in New Orleans? Starting with the charming Bleusette, who lives right across the courtyard from the crime scene? Anyway, the 'woman' was Danielle Jones."

"What bothers me most is that you didn't do anything about Graves—or the man we thought was Graves. Even after that pistol switch he made, you just fooled around like he was some guy who owed back parking tickets. You didn't even ask the Houston cops to pick him up. They said all they got from you was an 'inquiry.' "

Maljeux stared down at the pavement.

"There's a little notebook in here," Andy said, "a kind of paybook. The entries include some initials I can't identify, but the figures represent pretty serious money. Did some of that come your way, Paul?"

The lieutenant didn't move an eyelash. "Andy, in all my years in this uniform, the only thing I ever took was some on-the-house refreshment." He looked up. "What else you got in there?"

Andy pulled the briefcase up on his lap and snapped open the lid.

"Is this you?" He handed Maljeux the photograph of one of the homosexual couples. "And is that maybe Bobby, the pretty little waiter over at One-Legged Duffy's? That bracelet's kinda familiar-looking, isn't it?"

Maljeux looked at it as if he could burn it up with his eyes. Then he turned away. "Don't know how they managed to take this picture," he said, finally.

"Come on, Paul. This is New Orleans, the city of open doors—and windows. Were they putting the arm on you over this? Do what they told you to, or else?"

The lieutenant nodded. He let the photo hang loose in his fingertips.

"It wasn't as bad as it sounds," he said. "They offered me a deal. If I laid off of Graves till he got his business done and got out of New Orleans, they promised to let me take the guy who did Ferrier—and Miss Shaw. That night at Danielle Jones's place, that's just what happened. We make deals of that nature all the time—let a bad guy or two go if they turn some worse ones for us. Marengo was a worse one, sure enough."

"This wasn't a deal. They gave you no choice."

"They said if I didn't go along, they'd have it all over New Orleans about me and Bobby."

"What if Paris Moran or Jim Ball had taken a bullet from that loaded prop gun, Paul? What about your fucking deal then?"

"Then all bets would have been off. That was the only condition I made—that nobody else was to get hurt. Especially you, Andy."

"Look, Paul, everyone in the Quarter knows you've got an eye for more than the ladies, that you've played more than trumpet sets with Loomis Demarest. I've understood that about you for years, since before I went to New York. It was kind of obvious the way you kept turning up at my cousin Vincent's parties. I assumed your wife knew, and went along because otherwise you've kept her happy. But so what? Who the hell would care? This is the French Quarter, like you always say. You've got a couple guys on the force who are out-of-the-closet gays."

"Loomis would care, Andy. And, no matter what this picture shows, I love Loomis." He stared bleakly at the photo in his hands. "Loomis doesn't know about me and Bobby."

They sat without speaking.

"Was it Browley who yanked your arm on this?" Andy said, finally. "Was he the one who offered you this deal?"

"Wasn't Browley I talked to. God's truth, I don't know who it was. I didn't recognize the voice over the phone. There were only a couple of calls. But they sure knew what they were talking about."

"And where does your deal stand now?"

"The deal? The deal is done, Andy."

"I'm not going to let this drop."

"Suit yourself, my friend. But I'd strongly advise you to stay on the good side of trouble. Let things settle down now, boy. Let life get back to what passes for normal down here. *Les bonnes temps,* Andy. *Laissez les bonnes temps rouler encore.* And I sure as shit wouldn't do anything rilesome about Senator Boone and his indiscreet love life. You want to see the bad side of trouble, a man like that's got all kinds of ways to make sure you do."

He handed Andy the picture he'd been holding.

"You keep it," Andy said.

• • •

When Andy returned, Bleusette was still in the house he had borrowed for the night, curled up on the couch, asleep. She sat up at the sound of the screen door closing.

"So," she said. "How was it with Maljeux?"

"Enlightening. I'm going back to my place. The good news today is that I'm no longer an official criminal."

She stretched and yawned. "I will go with you."

"Better put on some clothes."

"Okay, just for you," she said, but took her time doing so.

They walked back to the Quarter. For part of the way, she put her hand in the crook of his arm—the gentleman and his lady, out for a morning's promenade. He wondered what they must look like. It might make a good photograph, the two of them walking through the slum. It seemed such a long time since he had used a camera.

"It feels funny, being out on the street this time of day," she said.

"You're a free woman now. You've got to get used to real life."

"Andy, what if real life sucks?"

"Sometimes it does."

"What do I do then?"

"You give it a good kick in the ass."

"You still like me okay? We are still friends?"

"For life, Bleusette."

"Maybe I will frame the hundred-dollar bill."

They crossed Rampart Street. The French Quarter beckoned like the gates of Heaven.

"Bleusette, you wouldn't know of a real good place to hide this briefcase?"

"Sure. I got a place where no thief or fucking tax man is ever gonna find it—right next to my ninety-seven thousand dollars."

"When we get home, would you mind putting it there?"

"Okay. But I'll need a car. This place I got isn't in my house. It's in the bayous."

"All the better. Use my Cadillac." He dug the keys from his pocket.

"That old heap runs? I got to go pretty far, Andy."

"Sure it runs, if you're nice to it. Just treat it like you did me last night."

She smiled. "What are you gonna do now?"

"Take a shower. Dress up a little. Get on with my business."

"See a woman? In the hospital?"

"Yes."

"That gonna be real hard for you?"

"You bet."

"Like you say, Andy. Sometimes real life sucks."

20

Emily was propped up in her bed, the IV and other tubes gone, her face very pale and thin. Fresh bandages were around her neck. Her green eyes flicked over to Andy when he entered the room. She didn't smile, but accepted him calmly.

Andy shoved a chair close to the bed and sat down. To his surprise, Emily moved her hand toward him. When he took it, she held it tightly.

"You look better," he said. "A lot better. I can't tell you how happy that makes me."

Now she gave him a small, weak smile.

"Do you feel better?"

She nodded, almost imperceptibly.

"I don't scare you anymore?"

A tiny shake of her head.

"You told the police you thought it was a woman who did this to you. Emily, there's a woman—a sort of woman—who probably did this. She's dead. The police shot the man who killed her. All the bad people we know about, they're all dead. You're safe now. It's all over." He hoped he sounded convincing.

"Good."

The sudden sound of her voice startled him. It was close to hideous, a low, husky, painful groan.

"Your brother says your mother's coming for you. You're going home soon."

Her eyes blinked rapidly, but she made no other response.

"They're almost finished with the movie. They've rewritten the ending, so your work is done. It's going to be a big hit."

Another smile, almost mocking. He sat back, still holding her hand. The room was full of flowers, the strong mixture of scents probably giving her much pleasure.

"I've been spending a lot of time with your brother. He's a nice guy. I like him."

There was no radio in the room. Why hadn't anyone thought of that? All these days and nights without music. He'd get her one.

"Emily, I had no idea we were in any danger. I would never have let this happen to you. Please believe me."

Another nod, with more discomfort.

"I should let you rest now."

He started to release her hand, but her grip became insistent. She pulled him close, turning her head slightly. She wanted to speak again. He leaned very near, to minimize her effort.

Her voice was so deathly. "You . . . helped me."

"I tried. I didn't do enough."

"Come . . . see me."

"I will. Every day, till you leave."

She pulled him closer, then spoke again. "See me . . . in . . . L.A."

He looked into her eyes, then gently kissed her forehead. She released his hand, then abruptly began coughing, uncontrollably.

The door to the room was open. A nurse came rushing in. "Okay. That's enough."

Politely but firmly moving Andy aside, she bent over Emily and turned her onto her side, facing away from him. He watched her body shudder with each cough. It must be agony.

He backed up. There was nothing he could do. Not here. He left the room, putting his hand to his face so the nurses outside wouldn't see the tears in his eyes.

He'd hear that mournful half-human voice of hers the rest of his days.

• • •

Porter met him in the bar of the Westin. As Andy entered, he was sipping a Heineken and trying to watch a Cubs game on the large color television set, while fending off the unsolicited conversation of a couple of tourists. He and Andy moved down a few stools.

"I went to see your sister," Andy said.

"It go better than last time?"

"A lot."

"I told you. She likes you, man."

"We've got to get her a radio."

"Good idea."

"Are you going back to L.A. with her?"

The actor took a deep swallow of his beer. "I'm going back when you tell me it's all over here."

"It's not. Where's Paris?"

"Up in her room. I called her a little while ago. She sounded like she was still in bed, like maybe with somebody named Johnny Walker."

"Let's go rouse her."

• • •

She answered the door wearing a robe, and not much else. Porter was right. She had been drinking, but her eyes still focused.

"It's you, honey bunch. Come on in and pour yourself some breakfast. I guess you had enough of Texas."

"We were in jail," Porter said.

She went back to the chair where she'd been sitting, rubbing her eyes, and then picked up her glass.

"Jail sure calls for a drink," she said. "Make yourself one."

"No thanks. I'm trying to stay awake," Andy said.

"Why?"

"Paris, I want to see Cooper."

"You've got bad taste in wants, sweetheart. He said he'd be in his trailer working on the script. But I think he's jumped in the jug, too. He's not shooting another frame until he's got a firm green light from the city on his big boat scene."

"Come with us, Paris. He'll let you in."

• • •

Cooper took a long time answering the door to his RV. He was in his underwear. Failing to notice Andy and Porter, he let Paris climb inside. They swiftly followed before Cooper could shut the door.

"What do you assholes want?" he said.

He'd not only jumped in the jug, but into the coke bowl as well.

"I want you to consider finishing your picture in L.A.," Andy said. "I don't think New Orleans is a safe place for you."

Cooper lifted a pint bottle of vodka to his lips. Andy couldn't tell if he had neglected to shave or was growing a beard.

"That's not what the police say."

"They don't know. Or don't want to. Paris and Emily are lucky to be alive. I'm not sure you've got a lot of luck left. One of your backers, Ben Browley, has had a private investigator haunting your shoot here. It was the same off-the-wall guy who switched the load in that prop gun. He's dead, but Browley isn't. I think you have a problem."

"That's crap! Browley's got like five million in this project. He's not going to fuck that up. Why should he? I've got the picture of my life working here. I've got the right town, the right atmosphere, the right cast, the right script—and a fantastic climax. Shit, some of my scenes would make Scorsese drool." He looked over at Porter. "If I had you as the cop instead of Jimmy Ball, I'd have a guaranteed blockbuster."

"Sorry," Porter said. "I don't do love scenes with my sister."

Cooper wasn't through. "You're the one who's been fucking up my movie, Derain. Why don't you get the hell out of here? Go back to New York and those fruitcakes where you belong."

"Alan," Paris said, "you haven't had a screen credit in nearly two years. If this flick goes belly up, you're going to end up shooting those hotel hand-job pay-TV movies for a living. Listen to the man. Maybe he's right. There's nothing wrong with winding this up in L.A. They still make pictures in Hollywood, you know."

Cooper stared at her. "Sure, I could do that. If I wanted a garbage picture. Location is the whole goddamn concept of *Street of Desire*. It's all built around the river and the French Quarter. And the riverboat blowup is the payoff. It's fucking obligatory! It's what the audiences are going to pay to see—that and your bare ass and boobs."

She looked away, shaking her head. "Come on, Andy. You said your piece. You got your answer."

They stood up.

"Porter," Cooper said. "Is your sister doing okay?"

"Doing better."

"Good, good. Super. Give her my love."

Paris rolled her eyes.

• • •

Paris went back to her room. Andy hoped it wasn't to her bottle. Porter came back to Andy's place with him. The Cadillac was not among the many old cars parked along the street. The gate leading to the courtyard was open and so was Bleusette's back door. Andy pushed open the screen and called her name, several times, but there was no reply. When she was at home, she almost always had some kind of music playing. There was silence.

"Maybe she just went to the store or something," Porter said.

"She wouldn't leave the door open." He closed it, but left it unlocked.

Back in his studio, Andy went to his telephone answering machine while Porter studied the photos on the wall.

"This one's Mrs. Browley, right?"

"Yes. A very popular photograph these days."

"You got any pictures of Bleusette?"

"In that box underneath my worktable, the one on the right."

Porter lifted it to the top of the table and began sifting through the prints. Andy turned to his machine. There were more messages from "Entertainment Tonight," a couple from Carl Bashaw at the newspaper, about a half-dozen from assorted creditors.

And one from Katie Kollwitz.

"Andy. I've got to see you. That Graves guy came by my place after you left. Kept ringing the bell. Then he hung around across the street. He may still be down there somewhere. Boone got another death threat today. I don't think it was a kook. I'm afraid to go out. I'm really scared now, Andy. I've never come up against anything like this. I don't know why I ever came to this fucked-up town of yours. Call me, Andy. Please. As soon as you can. I need you."

The playback tape stopped. It was the first message recorded since he reset the machine. She must have called the night he'd gone to Texas, the night they'd made love, the night she'd been crying. He could hear tears in her voice on the tape.

He took her number from his wallet and dialed, quickly. There was no answer. He let the phone ring long enough for her to run up ten flights of stairs to get it.

"This one's terrific," Porter said, holding up a nude of Bleusette curled up in the sunshine of the courtyard. "You wouldn't want to part with it, would you?"

"I'll print you up a copy."

Andy called Boone's office. The receptionist told him Katie wasn't in.

"Is she traveling with the senator?"

"She didn't come into work today. Didn't come in yesterday, either. Maybe she's sick. She gets sick a lot."

It was nice of the girl to tell that to strangers on the phone.

Andy sat a moment, considering the possibility that Katie might turn up in a rusty drum, just like the real George Graves. He remembered how Danielle Jones's body had looked, how the cut across her throat looked like a big red grin.

"Is the senator in?"

"I'll inquire. Who's calling, please?"

"André Derain. I'm a journalist."

"Then you want to talk to the senator's press assistant."

Andy swore, silently. "You just told me she didn't come in today."

"I'll see if the senator's available. What did you say your name was?"

"Derain." He spelled it.

"And what is it you wish to talk to him about?"

This time Andy swore aloud. "The state of the oil and gas industry."

"One moment, please," she said curtly.

Porter was gazing at the picture of Bleusette like a kid taking his first peek at a *Playboy* magazine.

"I'm sorry, sir. The senator can't take your call. If you'll leave your number, I'll have his press assistant call you as soon as she comes in."

Andy hung up, and sat brooding.

"Has she ever thought of trying her hand at acting?" Porter said.

"What?"

"Miss Bleusette."

"No. Not her hand anyway."

"She could do biker pictures."

"She doesn't like bikers." Andy got up. "I'll get you that print later. I'm going out, going to call on a U.S. Senator."

"Boone?"

"No, Claiborne Pell."

"You want me to come along?"

Andy rubbed his still painful shoulder. "Yeah. I sure do."

"I turned in the Corvette. And Bleusette's got your car."

"Unlike L.A., this town has cabs."

Porter reluctantly set down Bleusette's picture.

• • •

Andy had feared Boone's office might be full of the same kind of security louts that had been so numerous at his campaign rally. He was relieved to find only the receptionist and a middle-aged, bulbously overweight lout dozing in a chair in the corner. Porter identified himself as the famous movie star, which wasn't necessary, as the young woman recognized him immediately and became quite flustered. Porter said he was visiting New Orleans and thought he'd stop by and pick up some Boone bumper stickers to take back to Hollywood, where the senator had a lot of supporters among right-thinking movie people. Utterly twitterpated, she bought the stupid line, and hurried off to an adjoining room to fetch what he requested. Andy, who'd been standing behind Porter, simply proceeded past her desk and into the corridor beyond. The Humpty Dumpty lout protested, but by the time he got out of his chair, Andy was walking swiftly past Boone's secretary and into the senator's office.

Boone looked up from the magazine he'd been reading and blinked, unbelieving.

"What the hell are you doing here, Mr. Derain?"

"Five minutes," said Andy, closing the door. "I've got something to tell you."

"Get out."

"Two words: Danielle and Jones."

Boone's face went blank. "What are you talking about."

"The lady who was murdered in Faubourg Marigny the other night—by the guy I chased around your campaign rally, Frank Marengo. It was in the papers. You read newspapers around here, don't you?"

"This is a federal office building, Derain, and you're trespassing. I'll call in the FBI."

"I'm not here to give you a hard time, Senator. I'm here to do you a favor. Danielle Jones was working for Ben Browley, or at least for a guy who was working for Browley. You were set up. There's a picture. I've got a copy. Browley may have others. You're a prime candidate for a sex scandal, a doozy."

"I don't know what you're talking about. If there is such a picture, it's a goddamn fake. It's very easy to falsify photographs with the technology they have today. They use computers, digital images. You can't tell them from the real thing. I have a lot of enemies, Mr. Derain. They don't stop at much. You said you had this picture. Where is it?"

"A nice safe place."

"What do you want from me?" Boone's face was twitching.

"I'm not blackmailing you, Senator. I'm trying to make you understand what's going on."

"I know about you, Mr. Derain. You're a notorious pornographer. And you're a friend of that nigger crook saloonkeeper politician, Thomas Calhoun."

Andy turned to leave. "Fuck you very much, Senator."

"Wait a minute. What are you going to do with that fake picture you got?"

Andy moved toward the door. "I don't know. Maybe I'll just add it to my vast pornography collection, though I'll bet it's not as big as yours."

He opened the door, then hesitated. "By the by, they did an autopsy on Miss Jones. She was a he—a transsexual. Amazing what those plastic surgeons can do these days."

The look on Boone's face made him wish he'd brought a camera.

• • •

"Now what?" said Porter.

"Let's head over to the French Market. Maybe Miss Kollwitz is back at her apartment now."

"You're worried about her, too?"

"Last time I heard from her, she was worried about her."

There was no response at all when they rang Katie's bell. Andy tried some of the others. An old woman finally came to the door, for some reason holding a pot of something she was cooking. Unlike the hallway, it smelled very savory.

"Haven't seen her. Not for days. She goes out a lot."

A young man with wild eyes in jeans and a dirty T-shirt half-stumbled down the stairs from another apartment. He took a long look at Andy and Porter, his face sinking in profound disappointment, then stumbled back up again.

"When you last saw Miss Kollwitz," Andy said, "was she with anybody? A man in a black suit?"

"She's never with anybody." The woman peered into her pot, then shuffled away.

"I think that guy was expecting his dope dealer," Andy said, as they walked away.

"I played a dope dealer in my first movie."

"He didn't find you very convincing."

They walked around the Quarter through the milling crowds of tourists. Many good-looking women, but no Bleusette, and no one whatsoever wearing a long black dress.

They stopped in at a store and bought Emily a small Sony portable radio.

There was still no old Cadillac outside Bleusette's place.

"She said she had to go far," Andy said. "I wish I'd been bright enough to ask where."

"Let's check out the house, just in case."

Several of Bleusette's rooms Andy had never been in before. The place was cheaply but elaborately furnished, including nicely framed magazine pictures on the walls. Bleusette had one of the nudes Andy had taken of her hanging above the mantel of her dusty fireplace.

They stood looking at it.

"We better find her, man."

"All right. Back on the streets. Maybe one of the working girls has heard something."

They had gotten no farther than Dauphine when Porter glanced back, then caught at Andy's arm.

"A couple of big guys are following us."

"Maybe they're cops," Andy said.

Before he could turn to look, a sharp pain exploded in the small of his back at the kidneys. Next came a kick into the back of his knee that sent him crumpling to the sidewalk. Then more kicks. He covered his head. He had no idea what was happening to Porter. This was Dauphine Street. There were people all over the place. How could this be happening?

He began shouting. Two more kicks, then someone strong pulled Andy up to his feet. He found himself looking into a very ugly face.

"Message from the senator," the face said. "He'd appreciate your vote. And that picture you got."

The man whirled Andy around and shoved him face first against the building wall. Andy slid once more to the ground. He heard a car drive off, but when he turned around to look, his vision was blurred. He rubbed at his eyes. The back of his hand came away sticky with blood.

21

Paris and several other of the movie people were in the Westin bar. She smiled brightly upon seeing Andy and Porter enter, and then the expression disappeared.

"Aw shit, Andy," she said. "Not again."

Andy lifted himself gingerly to the stool next to her. Porter just leaned against the bar. He'd hardly been touched.

"Political discussion," Andy said. "Would you believe that in all the years I was in New York, I never so much as cut myself shaving?"

Paris gently touched his face. "Come on upstairs. You need some fixing."

• • •

Paris's scotch took care of the pain for the night, but it was back waiting for him in the morning. He was on her big, luxuriant bed, her soft, bountiful, and quite naked body next to him. What did this mean?

"Morning, honey bunch," she said. "You feeling remorse for a night of wickedness?"

"I'm feeling remorse. Was there wickedness?"

"Afraid not, sport. We thought about it, briefly, much as we were in condition to think about anything, but you weren't much of one for moving around a lot, and I got cold feet, warm as they are now."

He rolled over and raised himself on an elbow, feeling incredibly dizzy. "How much did I drink?"

"Everything you could. What's that Spanish proverb? 'Take what you want,' said God, 'but pay for it.' "

His forehead hurt to the touch. So did his right cheek.

"I got a couple of receipts."

She slid off the bed to her feet, giving him a chance to admire her exquisite bottom. "Andy, I want you to think seriously about coming out to L.A.—getting out of here and getting into the movie business."

"I do think about that sometimes—in the middle of the night. Then, thank God, I wake up."

"I don't mean half-assed work like shooting publicity stills. I mean become a director. You know how to frame a shot better than most of the losers in the business. And if you can work actors like you do your photo subjects, well, hell, what else is there?"

"There's knowing what you're doing."

"A lot of actors become directors, and some of them don't know looping from splicing."

"I don't even know looping."

"If I ever manage to get another project after this fandango of Cooper's, I could get you signed on as an assistant director. Couple of those trips—learn the little details—and you'd be in business. All you'd have to do is join the Director's Guild. I mean it, Andy. A man with your talent should be a somebody in this world. You sure were once. You're never going to get that back hanging around these gumbo joints shooting snaps of whores and weirdos. Anyway, we've got whores and weirdos in L.A."

"Not like those in New Orleans. We've got the finest whores and weirdos in the world."

She gave him a funny look, then headed for the bath. "If you need a john there's another bathroom off the living area." She paused in the doorway. "If Cooper still means to go through with it—and I guess he does—the riverboat party starts at eight tonight. You want to grab something to eat beforehand?"

"If you'll charge it to Cooper, I'll take you to Antoine's."

"Dinner at Antoine's. I like the sound of that. Order us some coffee, will you?" The door closed behind her.

He rang up room service, then called Bleusette's and Katie's numbers. Nothing again. He tried the Razzy Dazzy. Freddy Roybal took a long time telling him he had nothing to tell him.

When he was done in the other bathroom and dressed, he knocked on Paris's door. She was taking a shower, and a gauzy cloud of steam floated out when he opened it.

"I've got to go, Paris. I want to look for my friend Bleusette."

"Hope you find her, sugar. If nobody kills you in the meantime, I'll see you at six."

• • •

He wandered the Quarter for most of the morning, trying Katie's place again, without success, then going from café to café and shop to shop asking after both women.

Drifting over toward Canal, he turned down a tawdry street where the derelicts tended to congregate during the day, and encountered, in its usual parking place at the head of littered alley, a pale gray, rusty Chevrolet van that was the more or less permanent home of an artist friend named Gustave Heinckle, one of the caricaturists who plied their trade among the tourist throngs down at Jackson Square.

Andy rapped on one of the van's back doors. The rear windows were painted over with a brightly colored tropical scene featuring two voluptuous, dark-haired nudes. The side of the van bore ornate lettering that said: "Expert Sign Painting, Inquire Within."

When Gus Heinckle wasn't working, which was often, he was drinking. The van's side door opened and Heinckle's bearded, bleary face appeared. He blinked at the sun. A sour smell from the van's interior drifted out into the muggy heat.

"Andy," Heinckle said, squinting. "Shit, man. Thought you were dead."

"I just feel that way. I'm looking for Bleusette. She hasn't come home, and I'm worried."

Heinckle, who was on his hands and knees, blinked some more and scratched at his beard.

"Heard she left town," he said, sitting up. "Heard you got your throat cut and she split. Thought maybe you two had an argument about the rent, and she won."

"Where'd you hear that crap?"

"Down at the Square. Around. You want some wine? Got a fresh jug. Good stuff. Almaden."

He started to decline, but with Gus Heinckle, that would be rude. The artist liked to share.

"Okay."

"Let's go out on my terrace."

Heinckle struggled to his feet and went around to the back, opening both doors. He was barefoot, wearing a black T-shirt and jeans, and the hot pavement caused him to hop a little.

He pushed himself up onto the van's rear, dangling his legs over the bumper. Andy took a seat beside him. The wine was Mountain Burgundy, which Andy didn't mind this warm.

"Gotta get a new battery and move my van," Heinckle said. "The cops are getting bad over here. Had some crackheads move in. How's it on your street?"

"If you don't like cops, don't come over my way. They're in permanent residence. Had a lot of trouble lately. I'm kinda at the end of my rope."

"Least you're not dead. Wish I could remember who told me that. My mind's going. Gettin' old."

They both drank from the jug. Andy wondered when Gus had last washed his feet.

"I think Bleusette did go out of town," Andy said, "but she was supposed to come back."

"You know Rochelle? The girl who's got eyes tattooed on her face? She's the one who told me. I remember now. She said Bleusette was fixing to leave the life and that pissed you off because you've been living off her. Said you two had a big fight and she chased you out of the house buck naked. Said you two had another bust up that ended with you breathing your last through a new mouth cut in your throat."

"She got what happened all screwed up. Doesn't that girl read the newspaper?"

"Rochelle can't read."

"Well, the truth isn't much different—not a hell of a lot better, anyway."

There was a small pile of dog excrement on the sidewalk, neatly centered in a square of pavement. Andy smiled.

"You ever hear of a photographer named Lyn Welland?" he asked.

"In New Orleans?"

"No. New York. He was a big deal in SoHo, even had a one-man show once in a gallery up on Fifty-seventh Street. He specialized in nudes that showed blemishes and underarm hair. Liked to shoot fat women. He went through a period where he did a lot of equally disgusting still lifes. One was a shot just like this—a pile of dog shit on a sidewalk. He used a deep-field view camera. Every detail perfectly in focus, like a pretty piece of sculpture. He called it *Life.* I thought it was a lot of crap—like everything he did. But it occurs to me now that the man was probably a genius. He got it just right."

"I don't like that allegorical stuff. I'm a Realist."

"I thought you were an anarchist."

"Same thing." He passed the bottle. "You want some breakfast? I've got some bologna and bread."

Andy declined the offer. "You need money for that battery, Gus? You tapped?"

"You got some?"

"Not at the moment, but I've got a couple of weddings to shoot this month. I can help you out."

"I'm all right. I can always get money. As long as the world keeps sending us tourists."

Andy glanced back at the piles of old clothes in the van. "Why don't you give up this wreck and get yourself a room somewhere?"

"No way, man. Don't want to be tied down. I tried that. It sucked."

Andy got to his feet. "Got to go, Gus. Bleusette has to be somewhere."

"Don't worry about what Rochelle said. Shouldn't believe that girl about anything. Last week she was bragging about sucking off a U.S. Senator."

"A senator?"

"Yeah. Henry Boone. Can you believe that?"

"As a matter of fact, today I might. You haven't by any chance seen a good-looking woman in a long black dress around?"

The artist scratched at his beard again, then ran his hand through his long, dirty hair. "You know, I think I did. Down by the Square. She stopped to watch me do a picture of some guy. I remember 'cause he started talking kinda dirty to her and she got real pissed off."

"Dark hair? Big funny earrings?"

"Yeah."

"Did she have a limp? Tattoo on her ankle?"

"Didn't notice. Real beauty, though. Tiny thing. Chinese or Vietnamese or something. The hair dye looked funny."

Andy shook his head. "See you, Gus. Enjoy the day."

"Sure. Why not?"

• • •

Inevitably, he ended up at the Razzy Dazzy, late in the afternoon. As he stepped through the open door, Freddy Roybal's eyes lighted up.

"Hey, Andy! Bleusette's back. She's looking for you and she's mad as hell."

"Where is she?"

"Home, I guess. Maybe you don't want to go there."

• • •

There was music coming through Bleusette's screen door—a saxophone piece recorded by her dead boyfriend, though not "Bad Girl Blues."

Bleusette was at her kitchen table, sitting as still as a piece of sculpture. She'd taken off all her clothes, *comme toujours,* and her long dark hair was a mad tangle. A bottle of Pernod and a glass stood before her. She was staring into the latter with reddened eyes.

Andy let the screen door close behind him.

"Bleusette. I was scared to death about you."

She lifted her head slowly.

"They took my fucking money, Andy."

22

"Ninety-seven thousand dollars," Bleusette said. "Everything I got except for the houses. They got your briefcase, too. Goddamn you, Andy. It was that briefcase they were after."

She drank, a sip at first, and then she drained the glass.

"What the hell's happened, Bleusette? Where have you been?"

Her dark eyes flashed at him as she lighted a cigarette, her expression now slightly less sad; more mocking and familiar.

"This hiding place I have. It is out in the bayous, in the parish where my father's people live. You think I would keep so much money in New Orleans? All these thieves? No wonder there are so many poor people in this fucking town. Only way to be safe from the thieves. So I drive out there with your briefcase to put it with my money.

"There was this car—a black car. It showed up in my mirror, like two, three times, a long way out on the old highway. I get pissed off by that car, so I pull off quick and it goes by. Speeds off like hell and *disparu*."

Andy sat down. She didn't object. He was surprised she wasn't throwing things at him.

"*Alors,* I forget about it. Highways are full of fucking creeps," Bleusette continued. "So I go on to my cousin's place, this old farm. I got my stash in his chicken coop. Under the floor, under like three feet of old chicken shit, you know? Who'd go in there? I stick your briefcase in there, have a coffee with my cousin, then start back. I'm a few miles into the next parish, and I get this itchy feeling. Something wrong. I don't know what got to me. Something. So I turn around to go back and make sure everything's okay, and this goddamn car come by again, from the other way. Scare the shit out of me it's going so fast.

"I get back to my cousin's place, and it's gone, Andy! *Tous les choses*. Ninety-seven thousand dollars! You know how much fucking goes into that money? You know how I earn that money?"

"I know."

"All I got to show for all these years on my back is your hundred-dollar bill."

"I'm sorry, Bleusette."

"You are sorry a lot, lately, you unlucky son of a bitch. Now, me too."

"You'll get your money back. One way or another, I'll see to it."

"Andy, you can't even pay your goddamn rent."

Abruptly, she stood up. She went over to the sink and stood with her arms folded, looking out the window.

"Did you see who it was? In that car?"

"Hard to say. Goin' maybe ninety miles an hour. Scared the shit out of me."

"You've been gone for more than a day. Where were you?"

"I got busted. That's what else happen to me. When I find my money gone, I burn up that old road, as fast as that old wreck of yours go, lookin' for that black car. Goddamn sheriff's deputy pull me over. He was gonna hit me with speeding, reckless driving. He don't like that your car got an expired license tag, and that I got no driver's license. My fucking lucky day, right? Then he gets a bright idea. Why don't I hop in the back of his police car and help him forget the whole thing. I tell him to go to hell. I spent the goddamn night in jail."

"Why didn't you call me?"

"I figure I talk to you and then maybe the goddamn jail catch fire, Andy. My cousin come this morning and get me out. If that white trash cop pulled that shit in my family's parish, he'd be a dead man now, I swear. Dirty fucker. Only good cops are New Orleans cops, only they're not worth much as cops."

Andy got up and went to stand behind her, putting his hand on her shoulder. She shook it off.

"Everybody in the Quarter likes you, Andy. We liked you back in the old days when you first started hangin' around the joints. You didn't act like a *grand homme* from the Garden District. You treated us all real nice, with respect. And you took care of some heavy shit for us. I'll never forget how you take care of me when I got so sick from that bad abortion. But I tell you, Andy, right now I'd like to take this bottle and smash you over the head."

"You'll get the money back, Bleusette. No matter what I have to do."

"Okay." Her voice was somber. "Forget it for now."

"Is there anything else I can do for you? Anything I can get you?"

"No. I'm just going to sit here and listen to the music. And maybe get a little drunk."

"I have to go to that party on the riverboat tonight with Paris Moran. Do you want to come?"

"What? To pick up some movie guy? Work the crowd? Fuck you, and your fucking party."

"I didn't mean that."

"When I quit the life, I quit for good. Whatever's gonna happen, I'm not goin' back to that, understand?"

"That isn't what I meant."

She went back to her chair, refilling her glass. "Maybe I should go. Meet some rich guy who maybe marry me so I don't have to worry about this shitty life no more. You think some guy like that would marry a whore, Andy? You think that is possible?"

Andy had known Bleusette since he was twenty-one-years old. Ninety-seven thousand dollars or no, he guessed she was still his friend—like few others.

"My mother was a whore," he said.

"Do not talk about your own mother that way. God rest her soul."

"It's true. She didn't grow up on one of those upriver Baton Rouge plantations like my father. She was a waitress in a roadhouse and she entertained on the side. That's how she met my father, when he was in the legislature. He fell in love with her and brought her home at the end of the session."

"How do you know this? She tell you?"

"God no. My cousin Vincent brought it up, in unpleasant fashion, when he got fed up one night with her giving him a hard time about being gay."

"But she was such a *grande dame*."

"The worst snob in the Garden District. It happens that way. You should meet some of the high-priced floozies on the Upper East Side of New York."

"I would not be like that. A goddamn snob."

"I don't suppose you would."

"Was she accepted by those other ladies? Those ladies in the hats and gloves?"

"No, but it didn't matter. Snobs don't care if other people like them. I think that's mainly why they become snobs, so they don't have to worry about that."

"You help me get my fucking money back, Andy."

• • •

Paris Moran liked to dress up in all sorts of different ways—L.A. cool, New York chic, Miami hot, Junior League prim, sexpot outrageous, Edwardian strange. Andy had once escorted her to a Kennedy Center Awards reception in Washington for which she had worn a long, black, high-collared velvet evening gown that Mary Queen of Scots might have chosen for her burial. Paris had worn little make-up, no jewelry, and yet had been the most smashing woman there.

For this warm but breezy evening she had selected a simple, low-cut, white cocktail dress with white high-heeled sandals and a thin turquoise and gold necklace that fell almost to her well-displayed bosom. If they'd been going anywhere else, Andy would have felt like strutting, but now his mind was on their destination. They were walking down the street from the restaurant to the riverfront. Paris had one arm in his. With her other hand, she held a cigarette.

Paris didn't like his mood.

"You're not going to spoil Cooper's party for him, are you?" she asked. "You look like a hit man on the way to work."

"Browley's going to be there."

"If I had known you were going to make a big deal out of that I wouldn't have asked you to come. Maybe I should just leave you on the dock."

"Ninety-seven thousand dollars, Paris. It took Bleusette forever to put that together."

"How do you know Browley's got anything to do with that?"

"He sure as hell must have wanted that briefcase back. The money was with the briefcase."

"Ninety-seven thousand to him is like a stick of gum."

"He's a prick, Paris. Pricks are mean."

"Tell you what," she said. "I'll loan it to you. I've got some rainy-day money left. A few investments. I can swing it."

"I don't know how the hell I'd ever pay you back."

"Easy, honey bunch. You can come back with me to L.A. And earn it."

• • •

They had cordoned off a walkway across the wharf with ropes and stanchions. At the street end was a woman usher checking invitations, with two security guards standing next to her. At the river end were more security guards and ushers and a few uniformed policemen. There was also a metal detector.

One of the policemen was Paul Maljeux.

"Oh, shit," said Andy, stopping.

"Forget something, honey bunch?"

He reached beneath his jacket at the back. Of course the pistol wasn't there. Bleusette still had it—or had had it.

"What's wrong, Andy?"

"Nothing, Paris. My back hurts." It wasn't a lie. "Let's join the party."

Maljeux stepped up to them after they cleared the metal detector.

"The president of the United States joining us this evening?" Andy asked, nodding toward the device.

"Ain't ours," Maljeux said. "Your friend Mr. Cooper rented it for the evening. We're sure glad he had it installed, though. Considering."

"Considering what, Paul?"

"Considering we've got a U.S. Senator aboard, half the City Council, people from the mayor's office and the governor's office, about every socially prominent person you ever saw on the party page of *Louisiana* magazine, not to speak of distinguished visitors to our city like yourself, Miss Moran. Good evenin'."

"Good evening, Lieutenant." Paris was looking fidgety.

"Bleusette's back," Andy said. "Safe and sound."

"I know. She's on the boat."

"She's here?"

"Came with your actor friend, Dick Porter."

Paris took a step away.

"Anything on Katie Kollwitz?"

Maljeux shook his head. "Sorry. Nothing at all. She got family anywhere around here? Get a missing persons complaint and we can go into her apartment."

"Can I make out one of those?"

"Sure. Good idea. We'll take care of it first thing in the morning." His expression darkened. He pulled Andy aside. Paris, impatient, lighted a cigarette.

"We've got another homicide on our hands, Andy," Maljeux said, lowering his voice.

"Not Katie, you said . . ."

"Not her. A business girl of the Quarter. Rochelle Lewis. She of the interesting facial tattoos. Found her body in an alley back of Camp Street this afternoon."

"It's not over."

"Could be nothin' to do with nothin'. She sure ain't the first hooker to expire prematurely in this jurisdiction."

"Was her throat cut?"

"No. Someone blew her brains out. Heavy caliber round through the back of her head. Not much left of the front except for her tattoos."

"I want to go to Katie's apartment now, Paul. She could be lying in there looking the same way."

"If you want to go over to the station and make out a missing persons report, it's your right, Andy. But I'm in charge of the security detail here and I'm not going to abandon my post now. Not with all these mighties and worthies around."

Andy made a face.

"Let it wait until later—maybe morning," Maljeux said. "I think she'll probably turn up just like Bleusette did. If she doesn't, and there's something wrong, it doesn't necessarily mean she's dead or anything. And if, God forbid, she is, she ain't gonna get any deader."

"Thanks, Paul," Andy said, with some disgust. He started toward Paris, then stopped, turning back. "Which U.S. Senator?"

"Why, the honorable Henry Boone. Don't know what he's doing here on the River Styx." He grinned. "Andy?"

"What?"

"I'm sure glad you didn't set off that metal detector."

• • •

A jazz band was playing on the upper deck. Most of the guests were milling about on the main deck, with a few visible down on the lower. The boat was new, having just come into service on the river that spring, and larger than the other paddle wheelers working the New Orleans tourist trade. Andy wondered where Cooper was hiding the cost of this party in *Street of Desire*'s production budget.

Crewmen stepped forward to swing the gangplank back on the deck as soon as Andy and Paris stepped aboard.

"Well, ah do declare, Mr. Derain," Paris said. "There's a table with liquor bottles on it. Why don't you-all go fetch us some refreshment?"

" 'You-all' is supposed to be plural," Andy said.

"I plan to have more than one, honey bunch. Make it champagne. I'm feeling elegant."

The boat's deafening whistle sounded as Andy gave the bartender his order. He felt the deck shudder from the diesel engines' throbbing revolutions. The big red paddle wheel at the stern began to turn as the bow slowly swung out into the river.

Porter appeared at his elbow, asking the bartender for a beer.

"You don't mind I brought Bleusette? I came by looking for you and found her instead. She was as blue as her name. Really down. I thought this would cheer her up."

"When I asked her to come she stiffed me."

"Girl's got taste."

"Where is she?"

"Over there by the rail, with those two old guys."

She was standing with two City Council members, whom she appeared to know. When Andy caught her eye, she made a face at him. She was wearing the same black Junior League party dress she'd had on—and taken off—on their night of nights. Andy hoped there was a news photographer or two on board taking pictures for the feature section. Bleusette certainly looked like she belonged there.

He brought Paris her drink, with Porter following. She was eyeing the crowd unhappily.

"This sure isn't the fun bunch you associate with New Orleans," she said, sipping the champagne.

"Straight arrows," Andy said. "At least when they're in public."

"Well, I'd better get to work and mix and mingle. My cleavage on straight?"

"Spectacular."

"You go do your stuff, too. Both of you. Sell them on the magic of movies."

They watched as Paris stepped into the crowd, turning her incandescent smile on one of the city fathers. The man kissed her hand.

"I'd sure buy whatever she's selling," Porter said.

The boat was heading upriver, the spire of St. Louis Cathedral rising above the low buildings of the Quarter to the right. If the captain followed the pattern of most of the nighttime party charters, he'd continue upstream till he passed under the Mississippi River Bridge, head back downriver to the Inner Harbor Canal, then turn back and repeat the circuit until Cooper called an end to the festivities.

"Have you seen Ben Browley?" Andy said, looking aft, then up toward the bow.

"Not sure what he looks like."

"A very tall Texan, who looks as rich as he is. His wife is supposed to be with him, though she may not have wanted to risk seeing me again."

"I'd recognize her all right, but I haven't run into any woman that good-looking except for Paris and Bleusette."

"I'm sorry Emily couldn't be here."

"She doesn't like parties."

"Maljeux said Senator Boone's on the boat."

"Him I've seen. Last I looked he was standing down by the stern, not exactly happy. Made me feel good."

"Let's go see if we can make him even less happy."

"Hold on, man. He's got two of those giant economy-sized bozos with him, plus a dumpy lookin' woman I take for Mrs. Boone."

"You don't want to try throwing him in the river or something?"

"Come on, man. My face is worth big money."

"All right. I'll settle for an unfriendly chat."

• • •

As they went aft, the deck narrowed to some six feet between the main cabin wall and the rail. Boone's bodyguards came forward and planted themselves at the far end, blocking the way.

"You want to rush them?" Andy asked.

"I want to get another beer."

Andy pressed on.

"Would you excuse us, please?" he said to the biggest lout.

"You can't go back there."

"The hell we can't. This is a private party and we're invited guests. Are you?"

"Let them by, damn it!" said the senator. "I want to talk to them."

Brushing by the two lunks, Andy walked over, bowing with exaggerated courtliness to Mrs. Boone as they introduced himself and Porter. She stuck out her hand, looking dazed and uncertain.

The senator was in no mood for such civilities.

"Who are all these people, Derain?" he asked, gesturing toward the bow.

"Your fellow public servants, Senator. And the flower of our city."

"I don't mean them, damn it. Those others. They're movie people, aren't they?" He glared at Porter.

"What did you expect?"

"Expect? What kind of party is this?"

"It's a party thrown by the cast and crew of *Street of Desire* to thank the city of New Orleans for its hospitality and cooperation."

"It's supposed to be a Democratic fund-raiser!" Boone pulled a formal, engraved invitation from his breast pocket. "It says so right here."

Andy took it, reading "The Democratic Party of Louisiana Invites You to a Reception in Honor of the Candidates for Legislative Office . . ."

The name of the boat was right. The date and time were right, but something was terribly wrong.

Andy handed Boone his own invitation, which was tendered by Belle-Aire Films for a reception honoring "the City of New Orleans." Boone stared at it darkly.

"Someone's fooling with you, Senator. Sent you a phony. I'm surprised they let you aboard."

"Of course they let me aboard! But now I'm getting off. This is outrageous. Movie people."

"I'm afraid you're stuck, Senator. They're not going to put into shore just for you. So, unless you're convinced you actually can walk on water . . ."

"Just get away from me, Derain. I don't want to be seen with any of you."

"That's too bad, because here we are. And we have a few things to talk about, don't we? Mr. Porter and I are thinking about pressing charges against you for the assault and battery your 'campaign workers' entertained us with on Dauphine Street. I'm sure you have a lot of influence with the courts, but the newsies will be interested, especially since Mr. Porter was involved. And we have some fascinating things to tell them about, don't we? Miss Jones. Mr. Marengo. And the lovely Rochelle Lewis."

Boone grabbed him hard by his bad arm and thrust him back along the deck to the aft railing, away from Mrs. Boone.

"Are you threatening me, Derain?" he said, voice low.

"Am I threatening you?"

"Where's that goddamned picture?"

"Are you telling me you don't know?"

They stared at each other, unsure.

"You said you had a briefcase, Derain. And a picture. If you want to live a long, happy life when you get off this boat, you produce them. Understand?"

Andy pulled his arm free, wrenching his shoulder. "Where's Katie

Kollwitz?" he said, when he'd unclenched his teeth.

"You tell me. As far as I'm concerned, she is no longer in my employ. I don't tolerate absenteeism. My people are hard workers."

"Henry," Mrs. Boone called out. "Could you please get me some ginger ale?"

Andy stepped free, then he and Porter went back toward the boat's middle section.

"What did that accomplish?" Porter asked.

"Not a lot, but I feel better. Let's go find out what happened to Ben Browley. He must have come aboard."

"And Mrs. Browley."

"This is one time I could do without her."

D.J. Cosette was at the bar, helping himself to a large martini.

"Yeah, Browley's aboard," he said. "All those Texas guys are. Cooper's got a VIP suite for them belowdecks. I think he's making some kind of pitch. Word is they're not as happy with the progress of *Street of Desire* as Cooper thought."

"Where belowdecks?"

"A big cabin forward, by the bow."

• • •

They could hear earnest voices behind the door. It was closed, but unlocked. Andy went in first. Porter, holding a fresh beer, followed.

Candy's eyes were the first to alight upon them. Her face flushed. She seemed torn between fleeing the room and shooting Andy with the nearest gun.

She was standing near the center of the cabin, with two well-dressed men. They turned to follow her stricken gaze.

Cooper pounced on them.

"Beat it, Derain! This is VIPs only."

"Like Mr. Browley there?"

Cooper stepped in front of him. "Get outta here, goddamn it. Don't fuck things up."

Andy ignored him, moving by. "Mr. Browley!"

Candice's husband was in the center of things, doubtless where he always tried to be. A weird smile came onto his face as Andy approached. The others near him fell silent.

Browley was in his early fifties, but still a remarkably handsome man—dark, with brown, sun-hardened skin, and big arms and shoulders. Like James Dean in *Giant,* he'd started out as an oil-rig worker. Now it was country club tennis, but the result was the same. Ben Browley was not a man Andy would want to brawl with. He stood nearly six-foot four.

Browley looked at Andy evenly, unflinchingly. His dark eyes were marble-hard, but had a sad cast to them. In the process of acquiring a billion dollars, the man had been around.

"You're André Derain," Browley said, with feigned affability. "The photographer, right? Candice has told me all about you. Probably more than you'd like."

He stepped close. Andy was unused to anyone towering over him like this.

"Do you have business with me, Mr. Derain?" Browley said.

"For starters," Andy said, getting control of himself, "I'd like ninety-seven thousand, three hundred fifty dollars."

"For what, Mr. Derain?"

"For Bleusette Lescaut."

Browley's leathery face showed no reaction. He turned to Cooper.

"Is this something to do with our movie?" he asked. "Do you owe this man money?"

"Not a cent."

"Then why should I pay you ninety-seven thousand dollars, Mr. Derain?"

"Because it was with the briefcase."

"Which briefcase?" Browley looked truly puzzled.

Candy rushed forward, taking Andy by the arm—again, his bad one.

"I'll take care of this, Ben," she said. "Andy's made some mistake."

She shoved him out the door, and then along the deck until they were at the bow railing. It was fully night now, and the river was very black.

"Goddamn you, Andy!"

"You're not pleased to see me."

"Andy! Listen to me! He doesn't know you took the briefcase! You idiot! He doesn't know you were even in the house. Or in Texas."

"How could he not know?"

"I told him it was a burglary! That's why I set off all the alarms. I broke a fucking window. I don't know how much he believes me, but he hasn't said a word about you."

"But . . ."

"You come bursting in here. You almost blurted out everything! What are you trying to do to me? I wiped off your fingerprints. I got rid of the plates and wineglasses, everything. The cops bought it. We're in the clear. And you . . ."

"Candy, do you know what was in that briefcase? Your loving husband had a pack of thieves, spies, and murderers working for him. Most of them are dead. Somebody, maybe one of them, snatched the briefcase from me, along with my landlady's life savings."

She glanced back at the cabin door. Porter was standing there, looking troubled.

"Now is not the time to mess with him!" The words came out in a hiss. "Let him get his business done and get out of here. We'll work things out later."

"There may not be any later."

"Drop it, damn it! He's got other things besides us on his mind now. Something big. Just stay out of his way. If I was strong enough to throw you off this boat, I would. Just go get lost somewhere. I'll call you as soon as I can."

"Candy . . ."

She was walking away. "I'll tell him you're drunk. It's probably close to the truth."

The door slammed hard behind her.

"And now?" Porter said.

"Let's get drunk. Not much else left to do."

• • •

After getting another beer, Porter abandoned him for Bleusette. Andy took a scotch and water to the rail, and leaned over it, glumly observing the shoreline. The boat had made the turn under the big bridge, and was heading downriver past the Quarter again. The wharf and the building fronts beyond were brightly illuminated. The warehouses further along the river were dark. Cooper's blow-up boat, moored alongside the nearest warehouse, was a ghostly silhouette.

Andy caught a glimpse of a light in one of the craft's windows. It would likely be one of the security men Cooper had guarding the boat because of all the explosives on board.

Their own paddle wheeler churned relentlessly if pointlessly on, making a pretty sight for the tourists still strolling the quay. He'd taken so many pictures of riverboats he was sick of them, but their romance never failed to affect him, even now. In a moment, he'd go find Paris and pry her away from whatever honored guest she was lobbying. The jazz band had taken a break, and it would be quiet on the upper deck.

"You got too many women in your life," Bleusette had told him. He had only ever wanted one.

The boat began a slow turn to the right to follow the sharp bend in the river. They were passing the end of the quay, the last of the street lamps before the darkness of the warehouses. A lone figure was standing at river's edge, stark against the brightly lit pavement. It was a woman, and she was all in black, reminding Andy of a New England whaler's wife, watching the sea from a widow's walk.

All in black. A long black dress. My God.

There was no way of telling. The distance to shore was too great for her to hear him if he called out. She didn't move, but the riverboat swept on, and in a moment she was lost to view behind the craft Cooper had moored by the warehouse.

Andy gulped some of his drink, deciding he was indulging in wild imagining. He wanted the solitary figure to be Katie, wanted to know that she was still alive, so his battered, beleaguered senses had produced just such a vision. It could have been anyone.

An arm went around Andy's waist.

"You haven't mingled much, honey bunch," Paris said. "Don't let the home team down."

"I've mingled, but not to much effect. Anyway, I really don't think you guys have a big problem with the local pols. This town is on its ass. It has been for years, and I'm sure they appreciate your money.

Hell, they had the Republicans here for their 1988 convention, and that was the one that nominated Dan Quayle. What's a riverboat explosion compared to that? If they were really going to stiff you about that boat, most of them wouldn't have shown up tonight."

"Hope you're right, sport. I may be losing my mind, but I'm beginning to think Cooper's not just bullshitting about this picture. It's got some great moments, you know. The way everyone's been stressed out, it plays with the script. I may even let them put my name above the credits."

"Would you like to see the view from the upper deck? It doesn't have so many politicians in it."

"You got something adventurous in mind, rakehell gent?"

"No more than usual. Mainly I'd like to put some distance between me and some of our fellow passengers."

They refreshed their drinks and mounted the stairs, going forward to a place at the rail near the pilot house. They held hands at first, then Paris moved nearer.

"Andy, whatever else this night is, it's goddamn sensual. Don't you think it's time for my first riverboat kiss?"

"That's what we rakehell New Orleans gents are for."

It was a long one. When they finished, Paris let out a long happy breath, then lighted a cigarette.

"That one should be up on the screen," she said. "Almost as good as a fuck."

"My pleasure, mademoiselle. Two true words."

One of the jazz musicians came up, but only to fetch something from a chair. The band was apparently through for the night.

"Let's move to the other side," Andy said. "The boat's turning around again."

They watched the helmsman for a moment as he completed the maneuver, then found a vantage point at the opposite rail where they could continue their dreamy contemplation of the city. New Orleans still had some sweetness left.

"When we finish this picture, I want you to do me a favor," Paris said.

"Sure."

"I want you to come out and spend a few days with me in L.A."

"Come on, Paris. We've already talked about this."

"Just a few days, damn it. You can come right back. I'd like you to talk to some people. Take a look around. Hell, we've got everything you've got here. Good restaurants, even if you have to drive a hundred miles to get to them. Decadence up the ying-yang. L.A.'s on its ass, too. Last time I looked, you could fire a cannon up Rodeo Drive without hitting anyone with a current credit card. And up my way at the beach, we've got those glorious sunsets for you to take pictures of. All the sun does here is slide back into the muck."

"I'll think about it."

"Think hard. Anyway, Andy, you could do with a few days off from getting your head beaten in every five minutes."

"I'll think hard. Like my head."

What he was thinking about, though, was the woman in black who'd been standing on the wharf. The scene had reminded him of a painting he'd seen at the Museum of Modern Art in New York. One of the German modernists. Ernst Kirchner, or that mordant woman painter from Prussia that Hitler had put under house arrest because her works were so full of human suffering. Andy couldn't remember the woman's name. Then, suddenly, he could.

"Son of a bitch," he said.

"That's not a very endearing term. I hope you're not addressing me."

"Käthe Kollwitz."

"Oh boy, here you go up the nut tree again."

"There was a famous German woman artist named Käthe Kollwitz. College kids used to put her prints up in their dorms—poverty, death, suffering. The peasants' revolt, all very symbolic of social conscience."

"Yeah, I know her. The kids at Berkeley had a lot of her stuff."

"She did one of a naked old woman with a dead boy in her arms. *Woman with Dead Child*. I was looking at a print of it the other day but I couldn't remember the artist."

"This is a hell of a time for an art history lecture, Andy."

"She was using her name. 'Käthe Kollwitz.' She had a Kollwitz print in her room."

"Who was?"

"Katie Kollwitz. She's a phony. Maybe something worse. She's as phony as that George Graves we had around here. They even dressed in the same kind of clothes. All black."

"Andy, honey, I think I need another drink. And I think you need a few less than you've had."

He pressed out over the railing, his eyes searching upriver along the line of darkened warehouses. A tug pushing a long train of barges was coming toward them on the left, narrowing the space they had in which to pass by Cooper's movie boat.

He could see it not far ahead. There was something odd about it. The boat's entire length was visible. It was sticking out into the river perpendicular to the shore, the way riverboats had docked a century before, the way you saw them in the old pictures.

"Paris. That riverboat Cooper's going to use for the climax. He's got all the special effects explosives on it, right?"

"Yes. He wanted everything ready so he could go with the scene just as soon as the city gave him the green light. What's wrong?"

"That boat's coming loose from its mooring."

"Coming loose?"

"Coming loose. Cut loose. I don't know. Goddamn, it's moved away from the dock!"

He looked quickly to the pilot house of their own craft. The helmsman was standing steady at the wheel, though the captain had stepped up beside him.

"I've got to stop this thing," Andy said.

"Stop what? What's happening?"

Andy took Paris by the shoulders, leaning close to her face.

"Listen to me. I'm not drunk. And I'm not crazy. I want you to do exactly what I say. I think we're in for big trouble here. Can you swim?"

"I'm not going to swim across the goddamn Mississippi River!"

"Paris, please! Go down to the main deck. There are life jackets in overhead bins. Put one on and get in the water."

"I won't."

"All right. Put one on and stand by the rail then. But if that boat gets close, jump! Remember that prop gun with the real bullets in it?"

She was duly scared now. "Yes."

"Well, this could be a thousand times worse. Do it, Paris. Go. Hurry!"

She looked at him uncertainly, then pulled off her shoes, jammed them into her purse, and ran toward the stairs. Andy lunged for the door of the pilot house, flinging it open.

"Reverse your engines!" he shouted. "Stop the boat!"

"Sir," said the captain. "You can't come in here."

"That boat ahead, it's full of explosives!"

The helmsman, bewildered, looked to the captain.

"Sir. We see the other vessel. There's plenty of room to pass."

"There won't be if we get much closer! Please, stop the boat!"

He shoved past the captain and grabbed at the wheel, spinning it to port. The helmsman moved aside, but the captain clutched Andy and shoved him up against the bulkhead.

"Damn you! You want to run us into those barges? Get out of here! Are you drunk?"

Andy struggled, but the man had all the leverage. He pulled on Andy's arm and then spun him out the door onto the deck.

The door slammed shut. The helmsman moved quickly back to the wheel. The riverboat was proceeding on its dreadful course.

Andy stood with fists clenched, his bellows drowned out by a sudden, long blast of the boat's whistle.

He had to save his friends, all the innocents. He flung himself down the stairs so recklessly he twisted his ankle hitting the bottom. A few of the guests glanced at him but most just continued with their conversations. Andy looked at them helplessly. How was he going to get them all to jump into the river?

Porter appeared at his side, a curious smile on his face. "What the hell's happening, man? Paris just ran by pulling on a life jacket and . . ."

"Dick! We've got maybe three minutes to get everybody off this boat. It's about to get blown up. I'm serious, goddamn it. How am I going to get them to move?"

"How about yelling fire?"

Andy nodded quickly, slapping him on the shoulder. He looked frantically about. There was a bullhorn affixed to a rack on the outside wall of the forward cabin. He broke it free and shoved it into

Porter's hands. "Do it! Where's Bleusette?"

"Went to the ladies' room."

"Make sure she gets off this thing. Get her into a life jacket!"

He pushed through the crowd of partygoers by the bar, telling them to put on life jackets, but got no useful response. One man tried to shove him back.

Swinging to the side, he clattered down the steps to the lower deck. He heard Porter's amplified voice, announcing in disaster movie fashion: "This is not a drill! We have an emergency! Put on life jackets and go to the rail! This is not a drill! . . ."

Andy feared they'd take him for a drunk, too. Porter should have just started yelling "Fire!" If it caused a panic, at least they'd start moving. There was another blast of the boat's whistle.

The door to Cooper's VIP cabin was locked. Andy pounded on it till his hand began to sting. A man he didn't recognize opened it. Andy flung the door aside.

"Can't you people hear? We've got an emergency! There's a fire! You've got to get out of here!"

"You get out of here, you goddamn looneytune!" Cooper yelled. "Or I'll call the captain!"

The man who had opened the door put his hand on Andy's shoulder. Browley was looking at him with as much uncertainty as hatred. Candice's eyes were wide, staring. She came forward.

"Andy, for the love of . . ."

He grabbed her arm and pulled her outside. They could hear running feet on the deck above.

"This is the real thing, damn it," he said. "If you want those people to stay alive, make them understand!"

He looked ahead. The explosives boat had drifted well out into the river. It was terrifyingly close. He could feel the engines beneath the deck planking shift and thump and slow. There was another thunderous sound of the whistle. The captain was finally turning the craft to port.

"The hell with them, then," Andy said. "Get yourself a life jacket and get over the side."

A few people had begun to jump. It was a long drop from the main deck and they made big splashes.

"This is for real?" she said, pulling her wrist free.

"Yes! Come on, Candy, for God's sake!"

"All right, all right! Let me go back to Ben."

"Move, Candy! Hurry!"

They'd closed the door again. She stood before it. Andy couldn't wait for her. There was still Bleusette. He struggled back to the others.

More people were jumping. Porter had finally created his panic. One middle-aged woman, her life jacket in place, sat poised on the rail, terrified of moving further. Andy shoved her. One of the jazz musicians was trying to pack up his trombone in its case. "Forget it!" Andy screamed at him.

Up on the next deck, a politician was at the bar, taking a last drink from a bottle. There was always one. There were probably people like that on the *Titanic*.

The whistle blasts were now continuous. Andy got to the women's room just as Bleusette staggered out of it, a bottle of Pernod in her hand. She'd had entirely too much to drink.

"Andy, this is one loud fucking party."

The big paddle wheel had stopped. Their boat had swung broadside to the other, but its momentum was carrying it closer. The downstream current had full charge of the other vessel. Andy could see its windows clearly, the lettering on its side.

He flung his arm around Bleusette and pulled her to his chest, grateful that she was so small. She struggled. "Goddamn you, Andy! Let go of me!"

Taking a blow from her tiny fist in the ear, he dragged her to the rail, then lifted her and heaved her, arms flailing, into the black water below. He got himself up onto the top of the rail, then pushed away, kicking.

The explosives boat detonated just as he hit the water. A searing wave of heat and light swept over them, instantly followed by a horrendous roar. Debris sang and spattered overhead like hail in a driven rainstorm. There were screams. The two boats had not yet collided, but were coming inexorably together.

Bleusette was just a few feet distant, burbling and sputtering. As he tried to swim toward her, a shrieking pain shot down his left arm and back. He'd forgotten about his wounded shoulder. The agony was paralyzing. He could barely make the muscles work.

Her hand caught at his. He treaded water, pulling her to him. The riverbank that had looked so near from the top deck of the boat now seemed miles away.

She wrapped herself around him and they went under, into blackness. Somehow he fought his way back to the surface, but with the drag of her weight it was pointless. It was killing him just to keep his head above water.

There was splashing behind him. A strong hand took hold of him, lifting him.

"Hang onto me, man," said Porter. "We can make it."

Still alive. Had anyone ever written a song about that? It could be jazzy, rejoicing, a hot gospel tune, or better, a long, slow, cool blues lamentation, thoughtful, perhaps remorseful. The latter better fitted Andy's spirits. The exhilaration of rescue had drained away to a bone-cold numbness. Andy felt very, very old.

They sat safe but exhausted on some concrete steps at the rear of the wharf, Bleusette shivering in his arms, watching the burning boats in the river, a sparkling, macabre tableau that might have been an entertainment provided for some despot of antiquity. The first vessel had been so devastated by the explosion little was left of it above water but a few curls of flame licking at the night. The paddle wheeler they'd escaped from was blazing at the forward end and along one side, but two fireboats were cannonading it with jets of water, and seemed to be gaining in their contest with the fire.

A police boat busied itself nearby, and smaller craft buzzed and chugged about as well, looking for survivors. The guest list had been limited to fifty, but with the crew, the musicians, and the catering staff, there were probably two dozen more to be accounted for, a task which could take a very long time. Andy could still see many orange life jackets in the river. Happily, a large number of people were already standing or sitting huddled on the wharf around them, waiting for ambulances, or permission to leave. A few were drinking coffee a nearby restaurant had swiftly brought over. Porter had gone in search of something stronger.

A helicopter, its searchlight playing back and forth, chattered overhead, heading out toward the boats, the lettering on the side that of a local television station. The police had set up barricades to seal off the area, and news reporters were rapidly collecting behind it. Bashaw waved, but Andy declined to respond. He had no wish to be on the news again.

He'd leave that to Porter. A man who looked more like a tourist than a newsie had been recording the scene on a small video camera. He was standing on the quay with it when Porter had brought them ashore. The actor had played to the camcorder as if it were a studio movie camera. He would probably be able to double his asking price for film roles after the nationwide publicity he'd get from this.

Paris and D.J. Cosette had been among the first to get back to dry land. They'd waited until they'd seen that Andy was safe, then gone back to their hotel. Andy had told Paris he'd meet her at the hotel bar later.

A fireman brought a blanket and put it around them, but Bleusette's trembling wasn't from the cold. She was crying, the first time he'd ever seen her do that in all the years he'd known her, even when that long-ago abortion had gone bad. The tears and sobs eventually subsided. In a moment, the shaking did, too.

She turned her still-wet head, her dark eyes seeking his as though unsure he was there.

"God bless you, you goddamn Andy."

"God bless you and keep you, *ma chère* Bleusette."

She leaned back against his shoulder, her damp hair against his cheek, and snuggled close. "God bless Richard also." She sniffed, rubbing her nose with her hand. Both Andy's arms were largely without feeling, but he kept them around her.

Porter returned with a bottle of very expensive brandy. Bleusette accepted it gladly. Andy did, too.

"How many do you think got off?" Andy asked.

"Most everybody, I guess," said Porter. "The main deck was clear when I jumped in after you. I don't know how people made out in the river."

"Have you seen Mrs. Browley?"

"Nope. Not Cooper either. Boone made it, though."

"The Lord be praised."

"You making a joke?"

"Somebody is."

The flames disappeared from the hulk of the first boat, as it slipped beneath the surface. The other continued burning, then suddenly shuddered, as a huge writhing ball of yellow-white turned orange and burst forth amidships, knocking down both smokestacks. The echoing boom carried past them into the city. The fireboats began backing away as the stricken craft canted sideways and then pitched down, the motionless paddle wheel rising above the water.

"If that guy with the camcorder is getting this he's going to be a rich man," said Porter.

"Cooper's colossal climax."

"Worthy of Francis Ford Coppola."

Some people came up behind them. Andy looked around to see several men in suits, and with them, Paul Maljeux.

The lieutenant crouched down. "How you doin'?" he asked gently. He touched Andy's shoulder, and then stroked Bleusette's head.

"We're happy to be here, I guess," Andy said.

"So are a lot of people, and I guess that's mostly thanks to you guys. Andy, you know Captain Alpena here from the main station. And this is Special Agent Mulroney of the New Orleans FBI."

Two of the men in suits nodded a curt greeting. Maljeux didn't introduce the other men. They didn't look as though they wanted to be introduced.

"You did some good work out there, Mr. Derain," said Mulroney, "but we'd like to know how you knew this was going to happen."

"I saw the explosives boat swing out from the dock."

"But how did you know someone was going to detonate it?"

"There was a woman standing on the dock just before, watching us. I recognized her, or thought I did. She goes by the name of Katie Kollwitz. Works for Senator Boone. Or did. She's been mixed up in this from the beginning."

Mulroney stared at him skeptically. "You saw a woman on the dock and decided this was going to happen?"

"You had to be there."

"You know where this woman lives?"

Right. She'd be sitting there, calmly waiting for them, playing with her gargoyles.

Andy stood up, lifting Bleusette to her feet.

"I'll take you there."

• • •

Using one of the little picks and jimmies he always carried, Maljeux opened the door to Katie's apartment. Unholstering his revolver, he stepped inside. They all filed after him. Porter had come along and was the last one in. Andy clicked on the lights.

There were still pictures on the wall, covers on the bed, dishes in the kitchen, and the computer had been left in its place on the table in the smaller of the two rooms. But Katie's clothes were gone. Nothing personal of hers remained, except for a small, black furry creature lying feet up in a corner of the bathroom, just behind the toilet.

"What the hell's that?" said Porter. "A rat?"

"Not a rat," Maljeux said. He turned it over with his shoe. "It's a guinea pig. No, a gerbil."

"She let it run loose," Andy said.

"You've been here before?" Mulroney said.

"Social visit."

"Little thing must have tried to climb in the toilet," Maljeux said, pushing the creature aside. "Thirsty or something. Hot enough in here to get thirsty in a hurry."

They went back into the main room. In the smaller chamber, one of the plainclothesmen was standing by the computer, looking around the table.

"No diskettes here." He turned on the machine. When the screen glowed green, he punched a few buttons. "Nothing in the memory."

"Looks like she's gone for good," Maljeux said.

"We're entering the case," Mulroney said. "Assault on a U.S. Senator. You say this woman you observed at the scene worked for Senator Boone?"

"Yes sir."

"How long?"

"Not long. Boone can tell you about her."

"You got a picture of this lady, Andy?" Maljeux said.

"She wanted me to take one, but I never did. Senator Boone must have one. Photo ID or something."

"Senator Boone hasn't been very cooperative," Mulroney said. "He even questioned our jurisdiction. He ought to know better than that."

"He does," said Andy. "I think he's just worried about what's going to end up on the news."

"What do you mean?"

"Nothing." He didn't want to bring up the briefcase, and all the things he had done. He certainly didn't want to tell them about all the money Bleusette had kept secret from the IRS. "You never know what might turn up. The senator isn't big on this kind of screaming headline."

"This woman—she involved with any civil rights organizations, left-wing groups?"

"Civil rights organizations? She worked for Boone."

"I mean before that."

"Not that I know of."

"These recent murders, one of the victims was Afro-American. Did this woman of yours know her?"

"May have. I don't know."

"She always wore black, this woman you saw on the dock?"

"Yes."

"Underwear, too?" The man was taking notes.

"What?"

"Undergarments."

"I don't think she ever wore any."

Mulroney studied him a moment, then closed his notebook. Porter was staring at one of the pictures on the wall, the huge print of the artist Kollwitz's *Woman with Dead Child*.

"This is weird," Porter said. "It looks just like one of the pictures I saw in Graves's office in Houston."

"You're sure?" Andy said.

"Never forget it—that dead little kid."

"Who's Graves?" Mulroney asked.

"A private detective in Houston. The lieutenant will explain."

"I've got a file," Maljeux said.

Mulroney gave the apartment a few more cursory glances, then started for the door. "Let's go."

As they went downstairs, Maljeux hung back, pulling Andy aside on a landing.

"You were afraid she was dead, that Kollwitz woman," Maljeux said. "Bet you wish now that she was."

"I don't wish anybody dead."

"Too bad she didn't hang around to watch the rest of the show," said the lieutenant. "She must be halfway out of Louisiana by now, if what you say is true."

More sirens could be heard back by the river.

"I'm afraid Special Agent Mulroney is kinda mystified by your tale of the lady in black," Maljeux continued.

"Boone was tricked into going aboard that boat. He got a phony invitation saying the party was a political fund-raiser. I'm sure it came from her."

Maljeux took off his hat and rubbed his head. "That's just going to mystify him all the more. I think he wants to run her fingerprints through their computers in Quantico before he does anything more about her."

"By that time she'll be halfway to Florida, or wherever in the hell she's going."

"Their system works, Andy. These boys have put a lot of evil people out of circulation."

"You believe me, don't you?"

Maljeux stepped closer. "Remember when I told you I didn't recognize the voice of the person who made those calls to me—about Bobby, and that picture?"

"Yes."

"Well, that voice was a woman's."

"With the FBI in on this, Paul, are you going to be all right?"

Maljeux grinned. "I'm an artful dodger, Andy. It's the way of the Quarter."

"Before this is done, Loomis'll find out about you and Bobby."

"Oh, he knows. I told him. I figured he'd learn about it sooner or later, so I chose sooner. Clean out my mind, not to speak of heart and soul. I figured this case was a hell of a lot bigger than I originally supposed. Now it's about as big as they get."

"So are you and Loomis quits?"

"He was very forgiving. Had to be. Turns out he had a friendship with Bobby, too." Maljeux started down the remaining stairs. "Mulroney's in a hurry. He ain't from here, you know. You can tell."

• • •

They took Andy, Bleusette, and Porter down to the Vieux Carré station house to record statements about what they had witnessed aboard the boat and to take down everything Andy had to say about Katie Kollwitz. He told them most of what he could remember—her having been married to a man now dead, her needing periodic kidney dialysis and having lived in Texas and Los Angeles, her association with Graves and Marengo. He had to add he had no idea if she'd been telling him the truth about any of it.

Toward the end, Mulroney didn't seem very interested at all.

When they finally were released, Andy left Porter to take Bleusette home, and he went on to the Westin. In the bar, D.J. and Hub Cleveland told him Paris was up in her room.

He had to knock several times before she finally answered. She had changed into a robe, which was hanging open, and she had a drink in her hand. Her face was a mess of wretchedness.

"Sorry, sport," she said, letting him in. "I've been crying. Told you I did that every picture. This time I've got more reason than most."

They sat together on her couch. She had only one lamp on, and the lights of the Quarter were visible through the big windows.

Paris lighted a cigarette, retaking full control of herself.

"I called Sommer, the producer," she said. "We're going to have a meeting in the morning. Figure out what to do."

"About what?"

"The fucking picture. It doesn't look like Cooper made it off the boat."

Andy thought of the director as he'd looked in his trailer—well on the way to this kind of fate. "Was he married?"

"Several times. I think the starlet who's so good at blowjobs was about to become Mrs. Cooper number five. Now she's going to be a nobody again."

"She survived the boat. That makes being a nobody worthwhile."

Paris took a deep drag of her cigarette, then tilted back her head and exhaled, closing her eyes. "You want to spend the night again? Getting to be a nice habit."

"If you want. Dick Porter's taking care of Bleusette."

"No doubt vice versa. I had a shrink once who'd probably tell me that getting laid would be the best thing for me right now. But, honey bunch, I just couldn't swing it."

"Me, neither."

She opened her eyes, then leaned to put out her cigarette. "Andy, could you just hold me?"

"Sure."

"Hold me till I go to sleep."

"For as long as you want."

24

He left her near dawn. On the walk home, limping along the empty streets, he remembered something. In that stack of canceled checks he'd thrown onto the highway in Houston, there had been one from the real George Graves made out to a Marlene Krauser. Entries in the little paybook bore the initials M.K.

Marlene Krauser. Alias Katie Kollwitz?

Birds were singing when he reached Bleusette's house. The gate was open, as was her back door. He stepped inside the kitchen, softly calling Bleusette's name, then quietly made his way upstairs. She and Porter were lying naked in her bed.

Returning downstairs, he made some coffee, and sat at the kitchen table thinking. He didn't want to go into his own house.

Porter, wearing only jeans, stepped through the doorway.

"How long you been here?"

"Not long. I spent most of the night with Paris."

"I don't blame you," Porter said, pouring himself some coffee.

"How well do you get along with reporters?" Andy asked.

"Not all of them are fucking scum."

"My feelings exactly. You still want to help me find Miss Kollwitz?"

"Yeah, sure." Porter didn't sound enthusiastic.

"Come on, I've got an idea."

• • •

Andy's car, behaving like its old self, refused to start, so they took a cab over to the newspaper. Andy couldn't tell if Bashaw had worked all night or had come back after a few hours sleep, but he was at his desk, slumped in a chair in front of his computer. His wastebasket was full of empty cardboard coffee cups.

"Morning, Carl. I need a favor."

"I needed one last night, but you wouldn't talk to me. I had to get everything from the cops and witnesses who didn't know what the fuck was going on. Now you show up hours after my deadline. All you're good for is the second-day lead. I've been trying to think of one for an hour."

"You can make it a good one. Mr. Porter here, hero of the disaster, is willing to give you an exclusive interview."

Bashaw sat up straighter, rubbing his eyes. "It's a deal. What do you want?"

"You know anyone on the *L.A. Times?*"

"If I did, I'd ask them for a job."

"I'd like you to make a request for information from their files—paper to paper. I need to know anything they might have on a woman TV reporter who once worked out there named Marlene Krauser. She might have been in an accident or something. If they can fax a picture, that would help, too."

Bashaw bent over his console. "I think I can do this through the computer. Save time. Does this have anything to do with the boat disaster?

"No," Andy lied. "We'll be in the bar down the street."

• • •

Bashaw took long enough for Porter to knock off two beers and Andy to finish a coffee and bourbon and start another. When the reporter came into the saloon, he was carrying a manila envelope, which he handed to Andy before sitting down and ordering coffee.

"Computer printout," Bashaw said, as Andy opened the envelope. "There was nothing on a Marlene Krauser, but I think I got lucky with a Marlene Mason. The fax of the picture is on top. Is that her? Good-looking blonde?"

"Not a real blonde."

But it was unmistakably Katie. The fax was a stock publicity photo, but unlike most of its kind, she wasn't smiling. Her eyes were suspicious, wary. She didn't seem to trust the camera, or the photographer, or perhaps the world.

Andy turned to the computer printout.

"She worked for one of the UHF stations out there," Bashaw said. "Some place down in Orange County. Did general assignment, features, sometimes sat in on the anchor deck on weekends."

Andy's vision was blurry, and it was difficult to read the faint type of the printout. He contented himself with glancing over it while Bashaw continued.

"They canned her," he said, "because of some trouble she'd been in. Some TV writer dug up or got tipped to the fact that she'd been convicted on drug charges a few years before in Mississippi. Her husband was a dealer. He got killed in a police raid on their house. She was charged with possession and being an accessory, just for being in the house with him. Must have been a lightweight beef, because they gave her probation. When all this got into print, the TV station bounced her. Nothing in the *L.A. Times* files after that."

"Pascagoula, Mississippi," Andy said, reading. "The drug thing happened in Pascagoula, Mississippi."

"Her real name, or at least the one they arrested her under, is Maureen Halloran."

"Thanks, Carl. I'm much indebted."

"You're sure this has nothing to do with the boat blast last night?"

"Not really. She's just someone who worked for Boone."

"What about my interview?" Bashaw asked.

Porter set down his beer. "You want to know what I think about New Orleans?"

"Sure. For starters."

"It's a real nice place to visit, but I wouldn't want to die here."

• • •

The rain came out of nowhere. The hazy morning sky thickened to gray, then suddenly darkened. In a moment, they were walking into a wall of water. Andy started for a doorway, but Porter had seen a cab and dashed into the street to stop it.

The driver was a grizzled black man with an earring who smoked a cigarette while he drove. He had a slightly wrinkled magazine picture of Vanessa Williams taped to his dashboard and a chain of beads hanging from the rearview mirror. The radio was playing what sounded like voodoo music.

He'd make a good picture. Andy had to start carrying a camera again.

"So is this just about a wrap?" Porter asked. "Once they've got her?"

"Guess so. Hope so. If and when they find her."

"I'll come back for the trial."

"They'll probably make you."

"Will it come out about Senator Boone and Danielle Jones?"

"If they get their hands on that briefcase."

"Wouldn't mind seeing some kind of good shit come out of all this."

Andy could see in the rearview mirror that the driver was listening to them intently. The heavy rain had produced an almost opaque sheet of water over the windshield. The cabbie seemed to be steering from memory.

"Excuse me, sir," he said. "You want to go to the police station first, or the hospital?"

"The police station."

"No offense, man," Porter said, "but I'd like to get the hell out of this town now. I mean like tonight. I mean, it's been great, but I like this kind of shit a lot better when it's just stuff in a script."

"I don't blame you."

"I think I may charter a plane. If the doctors say it's okay, I'm putting Emily on it."

"You could be back in Venice Beach tonight."

"You want to come by the hospital and say good-bye?"

"I think I've already done that."

"She'd like to see you again."

"In L.A."

"Okay. In L.A. I'll count that as a promise."

The rain was lessening, splattering instead of thudding.

"I'm sure glad Paris made it," Porter said.

"If she hadn't, I'd have jumped right back in the river."

"And your Texas girl?"

Andy shrugged, holding back his sadness. "Don't know if she got ashore or not. I should have stayed with her."

"You had to get Bleusette."

"Yes."

"Hard choice?"

"I like you, Dick, but give it a rest."

By the time they pulled up at the Vieux Carré station, the rain had stopped. Andy opened the door. Porter reached to shake his hand.

"You look like shit," he said, grinning.

"So do you."

"I'll tell Emily you'll see her in L.A."

25

Maljeux had gone home at least long enough to change into a crisp clean uniform. Walking into his office, Andy noticed fresh beignets and hot coffee on the desk. The lieutenant moved his cup aside when Andy handed him Bashaw's envelope.

"It's her, Paul. Her real name's Maureen Halloran. Your first move ought to be to check with the cops in Pascagoula. In that printout you'll see she's got a rap sheet—a drug conviction."

"I'll get this over to the FBI right away," Maljeux said, "but, to tell you the truth, I don't know how interested they're going to be. They're treating this mainly as an assassination attempt on Boone, and they're really hot on the race angle. Like some black power group was responsible. I think Mulroney's string is being yanked from Washington."

He picked up a yellow legal pad with writing on it, and leaned back in his chair.

"Casualty report, Andy," he said somberly. "Pretty fucking grim. Only a few serious injuries. Burns mostly. But fifteen dead. Considering everything, that's an amazingly small number, but it's a hell of a lot of corpses for a happy town like this. We got ourselves a major historical event."

He ran a ballpoint pen down the list of names, tapping as he went along.

"I don't know if anybody told you, but your ladyfriend, Mrs. Browley?"

"Yes?"

"She's among the living. She was among the last they took out of the water. Headed straight for her hotel, checked out, and took off for the airport. Wouldn't even hang around long enough to identify her late husband's remains."

"Remains?"

"There was a bunch of them trapped in a lower-deck cabin. The boat took a bad hit in the bow when the other went kaboom. Started taking water. A couple of them got out by breaking a window but the rest never made it. Poor bastards drowned. At least it wasn't smoke inhalation or fire. We sent divers down this morning at first light. Recovered them all."

"Ben Browley's dead."

"Yes sir. And your director friend, too. The rest of the movie folk got ashore, including Hub Cleveland. I don't know how this black-power thing would have worked if they'd blown him up. But maybe there is a racial angle after all." He leaned forward again, setting down the pad, tapping his pen against his fingers. "The security guards assigned to that explosives boat turned up in a warehouse—all tied up and worked over. They said a couple of black guys took them by surprise. We found the body of what must have been one of them bobbing around on the Algiers shore. Real mess, he was. I expect both of them were on that boat when it blew up. Cut it loose and took it out into the channel without knowing it wasn't going anywhere but sky high."

His tapping became more insistent, then ceased.

"Your Mrs. Browley is now one of the wealthiest widows in the country, wouldn't you say?"

"I don't know what legal agreement they had, but yes. The surviving spouse share alone would make her that, no matter what the will says."

"That's mighty interesting."

"Paul, she had nothing to do with this. She was in the cabin with them. I went down there and tried to get them to leave, but they treated me like I was crazy. Candy was the only one to take me seriously."

"I don't mean the lady tried to blow herself up, but what's really interesting is what the divers found when they tried to get through that cabin door. It wasn't only locked. Someone had stuck a table knife in the keyhole and broke it off. The lock was so fucked up the knob wouldn't even turn."

Their eyes stayed fixed on each other for a long moment, then the lieutenant set down his pen.

"Well," he said. "Accidents happen."

• • •

Andy went back to his studio and flopped onto his old couch, falling instantly asleep and staying that way until late in the afternoon, when he was awakened by someone at the door. He thought it would be police or the FBI, but was pleased to find it was Paris, looking much happier than when he had left her.

"Sleep helps," she said, stepping inside.

"Helps some. I had to stop by the police station, then I just came home and crashed. We're looking for a woman named Maureen Halloran."

"So Richard told me this afternoon. If she ever shows up for a casting call, I'll break her arms."

"Cooper drowned. Positive identification."

"I know. He was a no-good slimeball, but he didn't deserve this."

She sat down on his couch, stretching out her legs. She was all dressed up again, this time wearing a trim, lime green designer suit.

"Funny thing is," she said, after lighting a cigarette, "what killed poor old Alan ended up making his picture. We got our climax. Some guy caught the whole thing on videotape. I offered him twenty-five thousand for it on the spot before he could start thinking greedy and he snapped it up, signed a release and everything. I told him I was with a network, which occasionally I am, if you count miniseries. If he'd known it was for a movie, he might have held us up for a lot more."

Andy seated himself wearily beside her. "A tourist videotape will work?"

"Sure. Make a transfer print on film. Fool around in the lab and the editing room a little. The script calls for daylight, but we can change that easy enough. Our beloved producer thinks we're sitting pretty. Trouble is, Cooper was way over budget. All our backers went down with Cooper. You know anyone with a couple of million to spare so we can finish this masterpiece?"

"Maybe I do. When you get back to L.A., call Mrs. Candice Browley in Houston, Texas. Tell her I said anything she puts into your picture would be a very wise investment."

"That lady's not going to want to have anything to do with us. We killed her husband, so to speak."

"Yes she will. Just tell her for me that a key works better in a lock than a broken-off table knife."

"What the hell's that supposed to mean?"

"She'll know."

Paris knocked her cigarette ash off into a glass he had left on the table.

"I guess I mostly came by to say good-bye, honey bunch. I'm getting out of here tonight. Richard's rented a business jet. There'll be him, his sister, Emily, a nurse, D.J., and me. That leaves a free seat for you, if you want it. Tomorrow morning you could be curing all that ails you catching some rays on my little stretch of beach."

"Can't leave just now, Paris."

"You're sure?"

"Afraid so."

"Talked to my agent. He said he's been getting all sorts of calls today, ever since the papers hit the stands this morning with headlines about Richard and me. Things are looking up."

"Silver lining."

She stretched, the effort pulling her silk blouse tight across her breasts.

"I may even do a movie with Richard. Wouldn't that be something."

"You'll be back to a million a picture before you know it."

She smiled. "Sure you won't change your mind?"

"Oh, I'll come out and see you, by and by. Sooner, if you need me."

"I'm going to take you up on that, sport. You know that I am." She squeezed his hand, then stood up, looking at the photographs on the wall. "That picture of me is a real doozy. I'd forgotten I used to look that good."

"You still look that good."

"Yeah, well, don't share this particular view with too many of your nefarious friends."

"I'll keep it in my private collection."

"Got to go, hon'."

He walked her out into the courtyard. Bleusette saw them, and came out through her screen door. She handed Andy an envelope.

"This just came for you," she said. "Some stupid messenger. Couldn't find your address. I was going to send him over, but I didn't know what you were doing in there."

She gave Paris a quick smile.

The envelope bore only his name. He stuck it in his back pocket.

"Richard and I are going to have dinner at Brennan's before we go," Paris said. "You two want to join us?"

"No, thanks. I've got some work to do. But Bleusette might."

"Brennan's? Who'd say no?" said Bleusette. She was again wearing only a slip. "I'll go get dressed."

"Meet me out front," Paris said. "I've got a car."

Bleusette gave Andy a curious look, then disappeared inside her house. Paris came close to him.

"Well, honey bunch, I guess this one will have to last a while." They kissed, tenderly, then hugged. Andy held her tight, kissed her neck, and stepped back.

"Take care of yourself, rakehell gent."

He watched her saunter out of the courtyard. She turned only once, giving him a slight wave, then was gone. He returned wearily to his studio, which now seemed depressingly empty. Pouring himself a drink, he sat down on his couch and finally pulled out the envelope.

There was an airline ticket inside, but nothing else. No letter or note. One wasn't needed. The ticket was one-way, destination Houston.

Candice the resolute.

He dropped the ticket onto his table, then leaned back against the couch, stretching out his legs. He could drink a while, and go back to sleep. He could sit and think and brood. He could do something useful. He hadn't worked in days.

All the negatives from the many and varied stills he had taken during the movie shoot were in his dark room. Some of them probably belonged in his New Orleans book—the pretty ones of Emily and Paris, the darker ones of Cooper in his rages and of the man in the black suit, as he'd been caught by Andy standing on the sidewalk, smoking his small cigar. Mr. Menace. Andy had been thinking of using a picture of a woman for the cover, but one of the mystery man might be more appropriate and compelling. He'd need to jigger around with the shots, make some enlargements, do some cropping.

After finishing his gin, he went into his darkroom, comforted by its familiarity. He turned on the radio he kept in there, tuning it to his favorite jazz station. It was playing a rare piece of music, something from the 1940s by guitarist Django Reinhardt.

Engrossed by his work and the music, he didn't hear the darkroom door open, but he sensed a movement of the thick, black curtain that hung just inside the door. He turned, slowly, and stared at it, though little was discernible in the dim, pale red work light. He was about to turn on the switch for the overhead fixture when the curtain parted.

"Hello, sailor."

26

Katie Kollwitz had resorted to a dismaying number of aliases, but no disguises. She was once again dressed in black, her pale face tinted a macabre rose by the darkroom light. She seemed to him more apparition than real, an ephemeral, wraithlike figure who belonged in one of Clarence John Laughlin's *Ghosts of the Mississippi* photographs; someone who might have haunted Edgar Allan Poe in the worst of his whiskey dreams.

Now she was haunting him. He was grateful Bleusette had gone off to dinner with the others.

"You're out of your mind to come here," he said. "Or should I say simply that you're out of your mind?"

Flippancy might at least provoke words. He needed some from her if he was going to control his fear. If this was happening out on the street instead of in his darkroom, he'd be running all the way to Houston, begging to be put back in the nice, safe cell.

"I've been in your house a long time, Andy—since last night. I came down once and watched you sleeping this afternoon, but I didn't want to wake you."

The thought of her leaning over him made him shudder. He hoped she didn't notice. He didn't want to start acting like a victim. It might impel her to make him one all the quicker.

"I thought you'd be at least to Mississippi by now," he said.

"I don't like Mississippi."

"The FBI is looking for you now. So are a lot of police, including Lieutenant Maljeux."

"They won't look here. They're not going to find me. They're not that good. Nobody is. Black is very hard to see at night, isn't it? I followed you quite a bit without you ever noticing. Night after night. You learn how to do that. It's one of the first things you learn."

"Learn how?"

"Dopers." It was a simple statement of fact.

"Are you a doper?"

"Not really. It has nothing to do with why I'm here."

"Is that a gun you're holding?"

"Yes it is, Andy."

"You don't need that."

"Yes I do. Have for a long time. Had it with me every minute we've been together."

"What do you want, Katie?"

"I want you to take my picture. Like you promised."

"Just like that, as though nothing's happened."

"You take pictures all the time—no matter what's happening. You take pictures of anyone."

"Fifteen people died from that explosion."

"I don't want to talk about that. Come out into your studio, Andy. Bring a camera."

"You really think I'll do this."

"Yes I do, Andy, because you don't want to die. That's my edge, sailor. People never want to die."

"I'll have to set up lights."

"Take your time. Your friends won't be back any time soon."

"After I take your picture, what then?"

He could see a slight smile. "Then I'll be on my way."

Andy draped a paper backdrop against one wall, set a wooden chair in front of it, but she didn't like that. She asked to be posed lying on his couch.

"It's kind of ratty-looking," he said.

"All the better."

He put two reflector screens and his strobe light into position, then measured the exposure before affixing his Nikon to a tripod. He worked quickly. There was no point in trying to stall for time.

She reclined on the couch, perfectly relaxed, crossing her legs at the ankles, holding her pistol loosely in her right hand. It was a small automatic—a pistol for a purse. Her gray eyes stayed on him constantly.

"I'm almost ready," he said.

"Good."

He thought of turning the strobe so it would flash in her eyes, but she'd likely notice him doing that. Even if she didn't, her first reaction would no doubt be to start firing the pistol.

"Why don't you tell me your story?"

"My story."

"You were born in St. Louis? How did you get from there to here."

"The hard way, Andy. That's all you have to know."

"Somewhere along the line, you got an education. You learned about art."

"What kind of story do you want? Once upon a time there was this beautiful little girl? Crap like that?"

"If that's the way it was."

"My parents were schoolteachers. My mother taught art. My father taught sixth grade. He lost his job because of drinking. I had the bad luck to be born a beautiful child. He started doing to me what he always wanted to do to the girls in his class." She paused, studying his reaction. "When my mother tried to stop him, he beat her up. She killed him one night—with a gun. She's still in prison. I moved in with my aunt. I took off on my own when I was fifteen. I looked eighteen, maybe older. I survived. I had some good jobs, and some bad jobs. And some very bad jobs. But I made out. Nice story, right?"

"Not so nice."

"Do you believe it?"

"I don't know. Should I?"

"It's bullshit. Not the part about my parents being teachers, or my father's drinking, or what he did to me. But my mother never killed him, and he never lost his job. I got all the way through college. I became a teacher, too, but I hated it. The piss-poor money. The nobodies I had to work with. Not all beautiful women get into the movies or into your magazine pictures, Andy. Not all of us marry handsome, successful men and live happily ever after. For some of us, it's a real bitch. Some of us get stuck in god-awful lives in god-awful towns full of god-awful people. My second year teaching third grade, in this horseshit suburb of Kansas City, I went a little crazy. I got into trouble. Being as good-looking as I was can get you into a lot of trouble in places like that. I took off. That's when I started taking some funny jobs, started moving around."

He set his camera for a wide shot, encompassing the full length of her body, adjusted the focus, and then the light. Returning to the viewfinder, he snapped off two shots.

Her expression was too impassive. She revealed nothing of herself. He moved the camera closer.

"You really were a fashion model?"

"And I really was on TV. Those were good jobs. You don't want to hear about the others."

"You married a man named Halloran."

"How do you know that?"

"Newspaper files."

"You're a clever man, aren't you?"

"Not clever enough."

"I was nuts about him. He was an unbelievably handsome man—better looking than you, than any other man I ever saw. I don't mean pretty, like a male model. I mean handsome. But he was incredibly self-centered, and essentially a bastard, used to having his way all the goddamn time. He wanted me to marry him, so I did. He wanted me to smoke dope and snort coke, so I did. If he had asked me to turn tricks or climb Mount Everest or shave off all my hair, I would have done it. Maybe not my hair, but everything else. I loved him, Andy. I must have fucked a hundred men, one place or another, in my time—but all my life, he's the only one I ever loved. He was crazy about me, too, in his way. Jealous, but not a pain in the ass about it. The only thing wrong was that he didn't tell me he was dealing. I found that out the hard way."

As she talked, he kept shooting, watching for changes in her eyes and the set of her mouth. His lens had a zoom. He moved in for some tight close-ups. Her face seen like that was electrifying. He'd set the lighting just right, her high-boned cheeks defined by dramatic shadows. She'd talked about her beauty. His camera had found it.

"How many is that?" she asked.

"About half the roll."

"Wait," she said. "I'm going to take off my clothes. I want you to take my picture naked, just like all those girls on the wall."

"If that's what you want." He stepped back, folding his arms, waiting.

He faced the fact, as calmly and dispassionately as he could manage, that he might have just a few minutes to live. Was he ready to die? Was any man or woman ever—even those ancient people in Nicholas Nixon's geriatric-ward pictures? He'd thought he'd been ready those last months in New York, when he'd stopped working, when he'd been drinking a quart of gin a day and had been advised by friends to see a psychiatrist before it was too late. He'd relished the dead end he'd been rushing toward because it would mean an end to the emptiness—and the pain. But he hadn't been ready. He'd come back to New Orleans, back to life.

And now Katie Kollwitz, dressed like death, had come and found him. It was as though he owed an enormous debt finally come due.

For all her menace—perhaps because of it—he was fascinated by his subject as he could not remember being with any other.

She stood up, keeping a wary distance. She had difficulty with the zipper, but then the dress quickly slipped off. As before, she had nothing on beneath. She stepped out of her shoes, then lowered herself to the couch again, still holding the gun. It was an extraordinary image. Incredibly bizarre, but in no way artificially posed. Here was a beautiful murderess, naked to his lens.

"Your scars will show."

"I want them to."

He began shooting again.

"What happened to your husband?"

"He never had any trouble from the local cops," she said, "but some narcotics agents decided to shut him down. They hit us in the middle of the night. I didn't know what was happening—what it was about. They killed him before he could roll out of bed. He had a gun. I guess they had cause. But they almost killed me. They tried to. I'm sure of that."

The shadows made her breasts seems those of Grecian sculpture.

The scars on her abdomen stood out sharply, like marble cracked and pitted.

"I was six months pregnant," she said.

"Didn't they know that?"

"Who knows what they knew—or if they cared. The baby never had a chance. The bullets tore me up all over. I lost a kidney, had a hysterectomy. Had a lot of operations. There was a bad infection and I almost lost a leg. I never had to do any jail time. The doctors didn't think I would live. I've got one now who thinks I still won't. But I keep going. Maybe because I don't care. I haven't cared whether I lived or died since I buried what was supposed to be my baby."

He stood there, staring at her. "I'm sorry."

"The compassionate man. I don't want your pity. I don't want that from anyone."

"All right."

"It doesn't do a damn bit of good. It's like prayers at funerals."

"I'm done."

"Give me the roll."

Andy hit the rewind motor button. He snapped the film out of the back of the camera housing.

"Give it to me. Toss it. Carefully."

He did so, waiting.

"This one's for me," she said, dropping the film in her purse. "Put another in the camera."

He went about this. "What for?"

"For more pictures. For your book."

"Will there be a book?"

She smiled, spreading her legs slightly and lifting the knee of one in a more provocative pose. She cocked back her head. Her eyes were fantastic.

"I want there to be a book, Andy, and I want to be in it. That's all I ask."

"Then will you leave us alone?"

She said nothing, enjoying the look on his face.

"Sure," she said, finally.

"I'm supposed to believe you."

"You don't have any choice. Let me put it this way. If there isn't a book, if my picture isn't in it, you won't sleep very well at night. You haven't been sleeping too well as it is, have you, Andy?"

"No."

He advanced the film to the first frame, then removed the camera from the tripod, moving to other angles.

"Not too close," she said.

"Don't worry."

He kept moving and shooting. She responded to him, to his lens, like the fashion model she had once been. If she'd been incapable of sexual pleasure before, she was enjoying something of the sort now, just being looked at, wantonly projecting herself onto his film, completely uninhibited, caring nothing about what those who would see these pictures might think—just like the whores who had posed for Ernest Bellocq.

"Were you George Graves's secretary? The real George Graves?"

"I don't want to talk about that."

"I know you were called Marlene Krauser. The police know it. They'll find out more. Maybe everything. It doesn't matter what you tell me. I'm not going to help them, Katie. They haven't helped me."

"What difference does it make what I did for George Graves?"

"I want to know if Albert Ferrier was coming to kill me, and why. I want to know who cut Emily Shaw's throat."

"I wasn't Graves's secretary. I was his assistant. I didn't have a private investigator's license, but I was smart, a lot smarter than Graves, and got to be as good at his kind of work as he was. Better at some things. Benjamin Browley hired Graves. He was the biggest client he ever had. George had a reputation for doing things nobody else would do. But he wouldn't do everything Browley wanted."

"And just what did Browley want?"

"He wanted evidence against you and his wife, and then he wanted you dead. He wanted to find out what was going wrong with that movie, and then he wanted it shut down, so he wouldn't look like a fool for backing it. He wanted to get enough on the senator to keep him from running for president and stirring up all the blacks and liberals. He wanted a lot of things. He thought all it would take was money. And he was right, once he found the right person to do it all for him."

"Not Graves."

"No. Me. Even in his prime, Graves was nothing but a two-bit sleaze. He bent the law a lot but hardly ever broke it. Hadn't a lot of guts, you know? Browley made him really nervous, and he had that ulcer. Tried to fire Browley as a client. Tried to fire me when I kept on doing stuff for Browley. Threatened to tell one of his friends who was a cop."

"So you killed him?"

"Not me. Someone I hired."

"The same one you hired to take Graves's place? The late Mr. Meeker?"

"I hired a lot of people. Browley provided me with a pretty big bankroll. It's interesting how much alike people look when they're wearing black suits and sunglasses—kind of like John Belushi and Dan Akroyd as The Blues Brothers. One tall, the other small and fat, but they looked alike."

"You had Meeker mess around here in New Orleans as George Graves so they'd blame Graves for it all."

"Think what you like."

"And Graves would turn up conveniently dead."

"He did."

"Before you wanted him to, though—right? Screwed things up for you."

"I'm doing all right. Keep taking pictures."

Why was he asking her these things? Why was he letting her tell him so much that he couldn't afford to know? Every word she uttered was another brick in his burial vault.

But talking like this was keeping him alive. So was his camera.

He had only three exposures left. He bent down to the viewfinder, and sacrificed one of them. What was that? A third of the rest of his life? Or should he cling to the hope proferred by her threat and promise about his book?

"I'd like to shoot another roll," he said. "Slightly different exposure."

"Take your time, Andy. I'll give you time. But don't go back into your dark room. You've got film in a drawer of that table. I checked it out."

"It's color."

"I don't mind color."

"All right." He fetched two rolls and reloaded his camera with one of them.

"You sent Albert Ferrier to kill Candy and me," he said.

"Just you, on Browley's orders. He was big on the idea of it being done by a homosexual. He wanted the queer done afterward, so you'd be found together. I did what he wanted, hired those two guys, but I fucked it up for Browley—deliberately. I picked a night when you'd be with his wife, and I made sure Marengo got to Ferrier before he got to you."

"Ferrier's last word was 'Boone.' Why was that?"

"He knew Marengo was doing work for us—for the senator. I guess he thought Boone had sent him."

"And Browley didn't like the way that turned out."

"No, he sure as hell didn't. But like I told him. Shit happens."

Andy came as close as he dared, wanting her face to fill the next shot. He was working—framing—as a movie director would now. He wondered how those insanely beautiful gray eyes would look staring out from a gigantic movie screen.

"I did everything Browley asked me to," she said, "but it never turned out quite how he expected. I saw to that. You know the short story 'The Monkey's Paw?' About the three wishes?"

"A man wishes for money, and he gets it in the form of an insurance payment when his son is killed," Andy said.

"Then he wishes for his son to come back to life, and he does, a monster corpse crawling out of the grave and pounding on his parents' door. Then the father uses his last wish to send the boy back to his coffin. I was Ben Browley's monkey's paw. I granted all his wishes. My way."

She paused. "He was a very bad man, Andy. I've known a lot of them, but none as bad as him. Not just mean. Beyond cruel. He believed he could do absolutely any fucking thing he wanted. He was paying me enormous amounts of money. At first I wanted to see how much I could take him for. It was a lot. Unbelievable. He didn't know when to stop. He became addicted to what we were doing. So did I. It's like being God, Andy. Or the Devil. Or both at once. All it takes is money, and not worrying if you're going to die. He ended up so frustrated he wanted to kill me, but by then, there wasn't a damn thing he could do. I had him by the balls, Andy. All of a sudden, he was fresh out of power. I enjoyed that a lot. In a way it's a fucking shame the bastard's not with us still. I could have put him in jail. That's where he belongs, rotting in a cell, busting sod on Parchmant Farm. Having every lowlife in the world pissing all over him. Now he's no worse off than my poor chump of a husband. Than any of us are going to be."

"Turn over."

Her expression went cold.

"I want some shots from the rear, the curve of your back, of your body. It's all right. You can look over your shoulder. I want you to. It's the shot."

She hesitated, then turned onto her side and stomach, her head held awkwardly, her eyes wary, the hand with the gun resting on her thigh.

"What other wishes did you grant him?" he said.

"Browley had kinda weird taste in sex. He wanted everything, everything there was. That's why he didn't like sleeping with his straight lady wife. He wanted me to get him a really exotic fuck. He wanted me at first, but I'm not so good at that stuff. So I fixed him up with this mondo bizarro creature I knew from Pascagoula. He never had anything like her. Like him."

"Danielle Jones."

"He became addicted to her, too. Gave her piles of money."

"You fixed Boone up with her, too."

"Browley wanted Boone set up, with a black woman if possible. He got his wish."

"But in the end, you killed him. He didn't wish that."

"I'm not comfortable in this position."

"It shows. It makes a good picture. Trust me."

She rolled over onto her back again. He didn't like the look in her eyes now, and she gave him reason. She raised her knees as she might for a gynecological examination, then aimed her pistol at him between her legs.

"Does this make a good picture?" she asked.

"Yes. It does." He snapped it.

"If I shot you now, it would be called André Derain's last picture."

"Nobody would care."

"I would care. It would please me."

"Why did you blow up the boat when Browley was on it? Did he run out of wishes?"

"He never did that. But he got mad as hell because I had such trouble shutting down the movie. You goddamn people never gave up. Browley came here for that boat party to try to do it himself. Bad timing. It's not my fault he was on that boat. But he got his wish. The movie's kaput."

Andy held back an impulse to tell her that the film was probably going to be finished anyway. He didn't know how much that would bother her. Controlling things seemed to be as big a kick to her as it had been to Browley.

She could find out about the movie when it hit the screens. A small piece of revenge, though she might not care. She might even enjoy seeing it. He could imagine her, a dark shadow in the back of a theater, watching it over and over, waiting for that bloody spectacular of a last scene.

"I was on that boat. So were a lot of people who meant nothing to you."

"Most people mean nothing to me. As for you, I gave you a little warning, didn't I?"

"Standing there in the lamplight on the dock? That's kind of subtle, don't you think?"

"No more subtle than Käthe Kollwitz. I thought you'd get that, too. Took you a while."

"I'd be more amused by all this cleverness if it weren't for what happened to Emily Shaw."

She stretched out her legs, folding her arms, keeping the pistol at the ready.

"I don't know how much of all this you believe. I don't know why I've told you so much. But believe me when I tell you this, Andy. I had nothing to with your pretty little Emily. Miss Danielle took it upon herself to cut the two of you up that night. She knew you were shacking up with Mrs. Browley. That's who she was after. It took her quite by surprise to learn later that you'd changed partners."

"Why would she want to hurt Candice?"

"Money, honey. And she didn't just want to 'hurt' her. She wanted to off her. Danielle—née Daniel—she was fucking good at that. She and Albert worked as a team, rolling and carving up gays and sick johns. Pascagoula. All over the South. I didn't appreciate what she did to you. Had Frank Marengo take care of that, too."

"And then you arranged some quick, convenient justice for him courtesy of Lieutenant Maljeux."

"Cop's job."

"What about Charles Meeker—the other Graves. Were you going to put him out of his misery, too?"

"You took care of him, Andy. You've got some blood on your hands. Watch where you point your finger."

"And Rochelle Lewis?"

"Who is Rochelle Lewis?"

"A prostitute, with an extra set of eyes in her face. The one in the picture there."

"I don't know her."

"You don't? Someone blew her brains out. I was told your senator friend might have been one of her clients."

She shrugged. "Then ask him. He knows a lot of prostitutes." She made a face. "I'm getting tired. I think we're through."

"One more roll."

"No. I've got one. You've got two. That's enough. You could do a book just with those." She got to her feet, stretched, and then, with her free hand, reached down to pick up her dress.

The instant she did, a single gunshot boomed and rattled through the studio. A curling cloud of smoke appeared between the partially opened shutters of one of his windows.

Katie, uninjured, swiftly moved behind him. The bullet had missed her, striking one of the pictures on his wall, the one of Candice, shattering the glass.

He should have flung himself to the floor, and let Katie and the mysterious shooter conclude this episode on their own, but he just stood there, stupidly, his mind concerned only with a dumb curiosity about what was going to happen next.

The front door to his house swung open violently and Bleusette stepped in, holding Browley's big .357 Magnum in both hands.

"Get out of the way, Andy. I'm going to blow her fucking brains out!"

"She's got a gun, too, Bleusette," he said, as calmly—as calmingly—as possible. The wild, hateful look in Bleusette's eyes seemed as deadly as the cold, dark circle of the Magnum's barrel. "You'll only get us both killed. It's no good."

"She took my fucking money, Andy!"

Katie could start firing now. A couple into his back, and, when he dropped, the rest into Bleusette. Why didn't she?

He took a step forward, keeping between the two women—and their weapons.

"Give me that damned pistol, Bleusette. Let me handle this."

"That witch gotta die, Andy! Get out of the way."

He came closer. The Magnum wavered, as did the look in her eyes. For all her raging talk, Bleusette had never knowingly injured anyone in her life.

"Andy . . ."

Another step, and he had the Magnum in his hand. He took a deep breath, then turned to face Katie, keeping Bleusette behind him.

Katie had her pistol pointed straight at his head. Her face was perfectly expressionless again, the catlike gray eyes simply watching.

"You want it to end like this, Andy?" she said. "I don't."

"I want it to end."

"You know I don't care if you kill me. In fact, I'd like it to be you. I don't want to die in some hospital—full of tubes. Go ahead, Andy. But it's going to be all three of us. I'm quick. You'll find out."

Still alive. If he survived this, he'd get someone in the Quarter to write such a song.

He stepped back, shielding Bleusette, but moving her toward the wall.

"Put your clothes on, Katie. Then go. Far. Let us be. We'll let you be."

"Just like that."

"The whole neighborhood heard the gunshot, Katie."

The gray eyes darted to the side, then back at him.

"Go! Please!"

"Will you keep your promise? About the book?"

"The hell with the book! Just go while you can!"

She smiled. He didn't like the look of it. Slowly, she lowered the automatic, then stepped into her dress.

He could fire now, and that would be that. But it wouldn't, would it? And he couldn't, could he? The violent image would stay fixed and frozen in his mind for the rest of his days. A camera was not like a gun.

Katie didn't bother with the zipper. Still holding the pistol on him, she took up her purse.

"I don't trust you," she said.

"Trust me? I'm letting you go! Hurry!"

"You'll call the cops, won't you?"

"No. I won't. I just want you to disappear. For good."

She walked slowly toward him, halting as her face came even with his, gray eyes wide.

"But I won't, Andy."

A moment later, she had vanished through the door.

"Goddamn you, Andy!" said Bleusette, exploding. "You should have killed her! She's a fucking murdering goddamn thief of a witch!"

He put his arm around her shoulders, keeping her from going to the door.

"Give her a few minutes. Then we'll call the police, if they're not on the way already."

"They'll just take statements, jerk us around. What's all this shit about a book? You going to put her in one of your books?"

"She thinks I am. She came here to make me take her picture."

"Fuck this." Bleusette moved out of his grasp, and went for the door.

"Where are you going?"

"Into my house. And then to the Razzy Dazzy. If you're smart, you go there, too. You stay in there all night. That crazy hoodoo woman just gonna come back."

• • •

He remained in his studio only a few minutes more. The fear he'd held back for so long now took complete possession of him. He couldn't stop his hands and knees from shaking.

He needed a drink, the refuge of friends. He didn't want Bleusette out there alone. Reaching the door, he looked back. He'd set his camera down on his table. He had a peculiar but perhaps not unwarranted fear that it might not be there when he returned—whenever that might be.

Snatching it up by the neck strap, he headed out into the night.

• • •

Bleusette was down at the far end of the bar, talking excitedly to Long Tom. Andy went to his usual stool, glad to leave the chore of explanation to Bleusette.

"Double Jack Black," he said to Freddy. "Then I'd appreciate it if you'd just let me be."

"Sure thing, Andy. Sure thing."

When he brought Andy's drink, he set a glass of Pernod down beside it. Bleusette joined him a moment later, knocking back a stiff belt of the liqueur, then stretching out her arms, arching her fingers like cat's claws.

"Fucking hoodoo witch," she said.

"She's gone now."

"You bet your ass she is."

"Did you call the cops?"

"I called Maljeux."

"Why did you come back so early? Didn't you like your dinner?"

"I had this creepy feeling. I was worried for you, Andy. With goddamn good reason, *bien sûr.*"

"Maybe you saved my life."

"You sure fucking well saved hers."

They sat and drank. Long Tom had disappeared into his back room. Roybal put on some music. The mournful saxophone soon got caught up in another sound. Sirens, coming near and fast. From the volume of them, Andy presumed Maljeux had for once pulled out all stops.

A young black man burst through the door.

"Hey, Freddy!" he shouted. "There's a fire! Over on Burgundy!"

Bleusette's head snapped up, then turned to fix Andy with cold yet burning eyes.

• • •

There were fire engines all over the intersection of Burgundy and Conti, but the flames weren't coming from Bleusette's house. The blaze, billowing fiercely up into the night, was in back. They wouldn't let Andy through the passageway, but he could see enough. Both floors of his little place were burning. All he possessed in the world now was his camera, his old car, and the clothes on his back.

And his friends.

27

For five days and nights, Andy stayed mostly on the old horsehair couch in Bleusette's seldom-used front parlor. He also stayed drunk—never uncivil, but happy to awake in the morning because it meant he could go back to drinking, and happy in the stupors of late evening because he'd soon be unconscious again.

In between times, he wasn't happy at all.

Bleusette had tried talking him out of it, pleading him out of it, arguing him out of it—had tried going to him nude and offering sex to get him out of it, had even gotten drunk a couple of nights with him to help hasten whatever process was at work. But when he wouldn't let himself be reached, she gave up and went coldly about her business, leaving him alone except to bring him food.

Andy's only other distraction was the parlor windows that opened onto Burgundy Street. He sat at the end of the sofa, staring out the nearest of them every morning and afternoon, watching the traffic and pedestrians as might a caged creature in a zoo. How many faces in windows like his had he seen and idly wondered about while walking through the Quarter? Drunks sitting by windows, keeping their secrets, wishing no closer contact with life than bleary visions of it glimpsed through a screen.

He realized that he'd at last put himself into one of his pictures.

Finally, Bleusette began to get itchy and edgy—and bitchy, doubtless remembering her experience with the saxophone player who had failed so miserably with her and with life. After serving Andy a meal one night, she just stood in the middle of the room and began swearing at him, telling him every sorry thing about himself he knew to be true.

The next day, he tried to stop drinking, and mostly succeeded. The seventh, he cleaned himself up and asked her if she could find him some decent clothes and drive him to the airport. She was happy to oblige—happy for anything that would effect a change in the situation.

As they drove out of the city, the old Cadillac coughed and rattled every time she accelerated.

"All the things I do for you, Andy, and all you leave me is this shitty car."

"A small down payment. I'm going to get you back everything you lost because of me."

"I'm not worried about that. No big deal right now. You just straighten up yourself, okay?"

"Okay."

"Maybe you're gonna get some money from your cousin Vincent. You know the film you had in your camera, the pictures of the witch? I had it developed. Paul Maljeux asked for one of the prints but the rest I give to Vincent. He likes them a lot, Andy. He said finally you take pictures that say something to him. Maybe he can get some good money for them."

"He can keep it. I owe him."

They were wheezing along the freeway in the slow lane, the highrises of downtown and the monstrous football stadium well behind them. They passed billboards and neighborhoods of modest, hot-looking little houses, broken up by junky business sections that seemed mostly garages and fast-food outlets. The sign for the airport turnoff came much sooner than he expected, than perhaps he wanted.

She pulled up in front of the terminal in a no-parking zone, leaving on the engine.

"So you think you got to do this," she said.

"No place else to go."

"It's goddamn hot in Houston."

He looked up at the hazy sky. "Right."

"She's a bad woman, that Candice Browley."

"You all are." He smiled, then patted her knee. "Who knows? I could be back in a few days."

"And maybe never." She looked at him. He was wearing one of Tom Calhoun's suits, which ill-fitted him. "All you got is that airplane ticket, right?"

"It'll get me there."

Her purse was next to her on the seat. She opened it, taking out a thick fold of currency. She pulled several bills from it, and pushed them into his hand.

"This is five hundred dollars," he said.

"I don't want you begging that woman for walkaround money."

The bills were crisp. "Bleusette, you haven't . . ."

"Gone back to the life? No fucking way. I work something out with Long Tom. I'm okay, Andy. You don't have to worry about me."

"But you're out . . ."

"Just put it on the tab. Anyway, you'll have insurance coming for all that photography equipment that burned up. We can talk about it later."

"Thank you." He slipped the money into his pocket. He smiled again, then leaned to kiss her. Afterward, she took his hand.

"Someday maybe we fuck for love."

"What about you and Dick Porter?"

"He's a nice boy, but he's a boy. You know what I mean?"

"He might surprise you."

"I don't want no more surprises. Go on, Andy. You're going to miss your goddamn plane."

"I'll call."

"No, don't call. You just come back to me sometime."

"Okay."

"I don't forget."

"I know."

The terminal was uncrowded, most of the people in it tourists wearing their ubiquitous shorts and T-shirts, or poor travelers in cheap clothes. Cajun music was blaring from one of the souvenir shops. Two men in dark, expensive business suits were standing just inside, looking like aliens from another planet.

Andy went to a flight schedule board. He had only a few minutes if he was going to take that plane. His eyes traveled over the menu of destinations. It hurt him to think how much a one-way ticket to Candice free of Ben Browley would have meant to him just a month before.

Things change. Shit happens.

He got into the "Purchase Ticket" line. By the time he stepped in front of the agent, his flight was boarding.

"I'd like to trade this in on another ticket," he said.

28

When he'd thought about Bleusette—as he'd often found himself doing while staring out of airplane windows, eating alone in restaurants, ending his nights in strange bars—there was always music playing in his mind. As he stood before her back door again, there it was, a jazz tune, gladdening him, though the recording was one of Miles Davis's more mournful trumpet solos.

She wasn't in the kitchen. He found her in the parlor, naked on the horsehair couch, sipping coffee by the open window, a newspaper on the carpet in front of her.

He'd already read it—in the cab coming in from the airport. The principal story on page one announced that the FBI had arrested some black radical students from Tulane and charged them with conspiracy in the attempted assassination of Senator Boone. The agency had released only that simple statement, but the article quoted police sources as saying the students were part of a group that had made death threats to the senator in the past and had been circulating inflammatory leaflets. An eyewitness had seen the two on the waterfront the night of the riverboat explosion. Lieutenant Maljeux had been quoted as saying the NOPD was bringing no local charges—that it was strictly a federal matter and up to the U.S. Attorney's office to prove the case. He'd added that he knew of no other suspects.

There'd been a sidebar story: Senator Boone had held a press conference in Washington to proclaim that the country was under siege from black terrorists.

"I saw you through the window when you get out of the cab," Bleusette said. "I am happy to see you, Andy. I was having a blue day."

"I said I'd come back."

"I believed you, and then I didn't. You didn't go to Houston."

"How do you know that?"

"Friend of mine saw you in the airport. You were in a bar there, long time after I left you."

Andy sat down beside her, noticing that her tan was fading some.

"I forgot how pretty I made this room," she said. "I don't like to sit in the kitchen now, with that burned-up house across the courtyard staring at me through the window. So I come in here now. You drinking?"

"Not like before."

"I bring you something."

He watched her go out of the room, the natural, sensual motion of her extraordinary walk enhanced by her nudity. She returned with a bottle and two glasses.

"All I got today is Pernod. Okay?"

"Okay."

"Where'd you go, Andy? Not L.A. I know because Richard called. He said his sister wants to see you, that Paris wants to see you, but no Andy. Not even a call from you."

"I'll call." He had come within a few seconds of boarding a plane that would have taken him to Paris's beach house. He supposed he might think a lot about those few seconds in the rest of his life. "Did he say anything about Emily?"

"She's getting better. Talks a lot now. Richard asked me if I wanted to go out there and be in movies. What do you think of that?"

She sat down beside him and poured. She'd just bathed, and smelled good.

"I think you'd be wonderful."

"Bullshit. All I'd be out there is his girlfriend. Even if he put me in his movies, doing God knows what, I'd still just be his girlfriend, his number-one fuck. No better than the life, *n'est ce pas*?"

"*Peut être*. I've heard that said."

"So where'd you go?"

He took a sip of the Pernod, swallowing fast to get past the licorice taste.

"I went to Charleston."

"Charleston? What business you got in Charleston?"

"Katie Kollwitz said she hoped she'd end up in Charleston. She's not hard to figure out, really. She always does what she wants."

"What business you got now with Katie Kollwitz?"

"I don't know. The end of her story."

"Did you find her?"

"I went to all the hotels and motels. There aren't that many. I went to nice restaurants like Carolina's, and dives that make the Razzy Dazzy seem like Maxim's. I went to cemeteries and funeral homes and old mansions, every place I could think of she might like. Nothing. All a waste of time.

"Then, yesterday afternoon, I took a walk down Meeting Street to the Battery, where they fired the cannons at Fort Sumter? There's a park there, and a beautiful old inn. It has a wide veranda, with chairs and swings. A woman was sitting there in a wicker chair, reading a book. She was thin, dark-haired—a kind of dark auburn, but the cut was just like Katie's. She was wearing a red dress, not black, but even though she was turned away from me, she looked just like Katie Kollwitz. I was sure it was her. It seemed such a perfect place for her to be, that it was fated I'd find her there."

Bleusette lifted her own glass, staring at it. "Yeah? Then what?"

"I called out her name. She didn't move. I went right up to her, almost to the steps of the veranda . . ."

"And she pulled out a big fucking gun."

"No. I just stood there, and then I turned around and walked the other way. She never looked at me."

"What would you have done, Andy? Killed her? Told her you loved her? Asked to take her picture? Asked her how's tricks?"

"I didn't know what I would do. I don't now. That's why I walked away."

"It wasn't her, Andy."

She lighted a cigarette. He watched her exhale. She smoked differently than Paris and Katie Kollwitz. More like a man.

"She's dead," Bleusette said.

He'd expected that one day he would hear those words. He'd caught himself several times hoping that he'd hear them soon, so that there would at last be peace, conclusion, release. But now that he'd finally heard them said, he wished he hadn't. He wished that she'd been sitting in that swing in Charleston, and that he'd gone on up the steps and stood in front of her. He could almost hear her say something like, "Took you a while, sailor."

"How do you know that?"

"She never got out of the Quarter. Long Tom and me take care of it."

Andy drank, not caring how it tasted. "That night."

"That night, *bien sûr*. Before she go anywhere else. Before she do anything else—like set more fires. Long Tom knew about her car—where she was keeping it. Hard to hide a goddamn car."

Bleusette looked at him, as though expecting anger, but finding only sadness.

"Who did it?" he asked.

"Friends. Don't matter. Just business to them. I won't say she didn't suffer, but she didn't complain. Her body'll turn up in the river. Maljeux knows. There are no worries. *L'histoire est complet,* Andy."

"Saying it in French makes it sounds almost poetic."

"Or like a song."

"Like a song."

"We got rid of her car out of town. It was the same fucking black car she chase me in all over the bayous. She had everything in the trunk. I got my money back, Andy. Shit, was there a lot of fucking money. Long Tom took some, for his troubles, but there's a lot left, more than enough to set you up again, to set us both up."

"No thanks." He refilled his glass.

"I'm going to open my restaurant. That Richard, he make L.A. sound very, very nice, but I can't leave here. This is me, yes? I can't change me."

"Wouldn't want you to." He tried to keep the melancholy out of his voice. Bleusette seemed no different to him than before. He couldn't understand why.

"That briefcase was there, too. This woman, she not very cautious.

All those pictures and shit are in there. I got it upstairs. What should I do with it? Maljeux say burn it all, but I want to ask you."

Katie hadn't finished her work. He could say that much for her.

"You know Carl Bashaw, the reporter?"

"Yes. I think I fucked him once."

"Get them to him, no questions asked. Maybe he'll get his paper to put a different kind of story on page one."

She turned toward him, sitting up cross-legged on the sofa.

"So, you back to stay, Andy, or maybe just passing through on your way west?"

"I'm back to stay. I might go out of town to work once in a while, but I'm back. Like you say, this is me. We can't change ourselves."

"Your cousin Vincent sold one of your pictures—of that woman. It was to some guy from an art museum in Cleveland, no less. Vincent say you're going to be famous again."

He looked down at the cheap but clean carpet.

"Cheer up, Andy. Don't you want to be famous again?"

"I guess it's okay to be famous in Cleveland."

"You want to move in with me? I don't mind—if you're going to start working again. I would like that. You and I know each other a real long time, Andy."

"Sure. I'd like that, too."

Her dark eyes sought his.

"But I think maybe I get married someday, become a respectable lady. What do you think of that?"

"You've always been respectable to me."

"I think I would like to be a married woman. I think maybe it's time."

He looked up at the framed picture he had taken of her that was on the mantel. It wasn't a new idea to him, though he'd never given it voice. He'd always been terribly fond of Bleusette. Years before, when she'd been only a teenager and he'd sat holding her hand in a cheap room sweating out her near pass at death after that bungled abortion, he'd loved her with all the mad passion of every artist who'd ever loved a whore—Van Gogh, Modigliani, Man Ray. Leaving her had been one of the many hard things about moving to New York.

But there would be penance in this, too. He had to admit that to himself. Marrying Bleusette would be the next thing to marrying Katie Kollwitz.

"Why don't you marry me, Bleusette?"

"Are you being crazy? Like before you left?"

"Probably, but I'm asking you to overlook that."

"You mean it, Andy? You would do this?"

"Of course I would. But would you?"

"I think so, Andy. I think so."

"You could do a lot better."

"What, some fucking movie star?"

"He's a nice guy. He could change your life."

"I don't want to change my life. Just make it more happy, you understand? But I think maybe I won't stay in this house. I think I will move out of the Quarter. I will have a restaurant here. Hang around. Have some fun. Be with friends. But I don't want to live here no more, Andy. Too many weird characters comin' into the Quarter these days, don't you think?"

Andy said nothing.

"So what you say if we move into that big house you got in the Garden District? What do you think of that?"

"It's a very nice house."

His Auntie Claire wouldn't mind. She'd never figure it out. His mother, were she alive, would of course be outraged—would scream and yell and tear her hair out and rave about the "disgrace."

"I'd be proud to have you in my house, Bleusette."

"You love to ride the streetcars."

"I love to ride the streetcars."

"You think we can be happy? That maybe real life don't have to suck?"

In the end, there was no one to blame, because everyone was to blame, because everyone lived first for his or her own self, or learned to, wherever that might lead them. In the end, the sinner and the saint are doing exactly what they want.

But you tried to be kind.

Take what you want, said God, but pay for it. The hard part wasn't the paying, but the choosing.

"Sure. Why not?"

"Come and kiss me, Andy. I don't want to think about why not."

About the Author

Rex Dancer is a veteran newspaper reporter, columnist, and photographer who has ranged widely through the American South during his career, covering such stories as the assassination and funeral of Dr. Martin Luther King, Jr. in Memphis and Atlanta, the New Orleans role in the alleged John F. Kennedy assassination conspiracy, the "Canal Girl" killings in south Florida, the crime scene in Savannah, Georgia, and the recent CIA terrorist murders at Langley, Virginia, as well as happier events as the Cattle Baron's Ball in Dallas and the Kentucky Derby in Louisville. For several years, he also followed the New York social and fashion scene, and the motion picture community in Los Angeles.

Though he now resides in Virginia and West Virginia, he counts New Orleans and Charleston, South Carolina, as his favorite cities. He is married and has two children.